About the aut

Born in Derbyshire, England, Christopher Bolsover joined the Derbyshire Constabulary at sixteen, then the Royal Military Police, serving in Germany and Northern Ireland, the latter as an investigator with the Special Investigation Branch during the major Troubles there. He emigrated to Australia in 1974 and was a private detective before starting his business career, which took him to the heights of Corporate America with multi-billion-dollar companies.

After being shot in the back three times in a house invasion in South Africa — a wake-up call — he started writing the novels he had always wanted to, calling upon his abundance of experiences.

He has lived on five continents, visited nearly every country in the world and currently resides in the UK with his wife and two children. Christopher also has four grown-up children and five grandchildren who reside in Australia.

The use of the word 'Indian' when referring to Native Americans is no longer an accepted term, but was commonly used in the 1970s, when this story is set. It is not the author's intention to offend, rather to portray authentically the world as it was at that time.

THE HELLFIRE CLUB PART 2
THE CLEANSING LIST

CHRISTOPHER BOLSOVER

THE HELLFIRE CLUB PART 2
THE CLEANSING LIST

30 JUNE 2022

Vanguard Press

VANGUARD PAPERBACK

© Copyright 2022
Christopher Bolsover

The right of Christopher Bolsover to be identified as author of
this work has been asserted by him in accordance with the
Copyright, Designs and Patents Act 1988.

All Rights Reserved

No reproduction, copy or transmission of this publication
may be made without written permission.
No paragraph of this publication may be reproduced,
copied or transmitted save with the written permission of the publisher, or in
accordance with the provisions
of the Copyright Act 1956 (as amended).

Any person who commits any unauthorised act in relation to
this publication may be liable to criminal
prosecution and civil claims for damages.

A CIP catalogue record for this title is
available from the British Library.

ISBN 978 1 80016 282 2

Vanguard Press is an imprint of
Pegasus Elliot MacKenzie Publishers Ltd.
www.pegasuspublishers.com

First Published in 2022

Vanguard Press
Sheraton House Castle Park
Cambridge England

Printed & Bound in Great Britain

Dedication

To my wife, Monica, for her inspiration and dedicated support, without which I would never have completed my novels.

Acknowledgements

To the many characters I have met in my life, the good and the bad, who have inspired me.

Chapter 1
1978 The Pyre

He scratched his balding head and then his buttocks. The fire was still blazing brightly and the stink of burning human flesh filled his nostrils. Nothing smelt as bad as a human burning. There were three corpses on the pyre badly burnt, one without a head. The headless one was a woman, the faces of the two others were not as badly burnt, so he assumed one was a white Caucasian and the other — the smaller one — Hispanic.

The lone fire engine had done its best.

"Stop that!" she said sharply, looking at his hand movements. FBI Special Agent Sonia Turner was standing behind him with a scarf across her mouth and nose. Her first murder scene.

"Oh, just me thinking," Senior Special Agent Steve Stanley replied.

"You're always scratching yourself. It's rude, crude and annoying. What FBI agent does that?"

Well, yes, he thought sarcastically, *you tick all the boxes: law degree from Harvard, black, female and gay, and will probably be my boss in a year or so. Transferred in yesterday and on immediate active duty. My partner put on a desk job — you must have some clout at head office. Pity you have no field experience.* He allowed his bitterness to influence his thoughts.

"Are you taking over?" the young keen LAPD detective Jake Brody asked.

"Not today, son, you keep on it and keep me informed," Steve said, handing over his business card. The detective showed him a plastic bag containing a partially burnt Amex card.

"One of the account digits is impossible to discern, but we should be able to get a list using all the possible combinations."

"Good thinking. Please let me have the list when you get it so I can see if we can help. Thanks."

"Is it hard to get into the FBI?"

"Solve this one and you will be a shoo-in."

The young LAPD detective left and went back to the scene-of-crime experts who had sealed off the area. There was a spring in his walk.

Special Agent Sonia Turner had just been transferred from the FBI head office in Washington for field experience. It was dislike at first sight between her and Senior Special Agent Steve Stanley. Not her ideal of a senior field agent. It was mutual: there was no love lost between them.

"What? This is obviously our serial killer; we need to take over the investigation!" Sonia was surprised he had not taken jurisdiction.

"Not so quick, my dear."

She shrugged as he patronised her. *White Male Chauvinist Pig.*

She couldn't understand that Steve would not take on this case as it was common knowledge that a serial killer with a similar method was on the loose. The FBI had even named the case 'Chief Longbow'.

She wiped her eyes and nose with a tissue as she turned her back on him. He walked off to look around the surrounding areas.

The Gods are not smiling on me, hooking me up with this partner, he mused.

Back in LA, the station chief had them both in the boardroom.

"So, Sonia has laid a complaint." The chief stopped and thought about teamwork and bonding. "Well, let's say an *observation,* that you walked away from this case which could be our killer 'Chief Longbow', or as the media calls him, 'Geronimo'," the chief asked, knowing there was more to Steve's explanation.

"Well, I am not sure if this is just a copycat. I drove to the old spa down the road and looked around. I found an old bedroom at the back of one of the blocks. They were busy with moonshine, growing cannabis and making some kind of white stuff — not sure for certain yet what it is. I just looked in. I sent the SOCs there when they had completed work at the scene. That was these hippies' business; probably selling the stuff in Vegas."

The chief knew Steve was an expert on drugs, so for him to not be sure meant it was some made-up shit for unknowing sorry punters that were buying crap.

"That doesn't mean it was not our serial killer. Ten people in three states all shot with arrows," Sonia butted in.

"Well, yes, so let me enlighten you a little. This is what we think we know so far: one, he has only so far killed white people who, we think, he believes in his twisted mind have taken Indian land, or so he says in his notes to us; two, he uses Apache home-made arrows and then slits their throats and burns them. So, here there was one Hispanic and two white people killed. The arrows were hunting-bow arrows from a sports shop and no throats were slit. The two men looked like they were also shot, so mostly not consistent with his *modus operandi*. The throat-slitting and using real Indian arrows has never been made public, so could be a copycat," Steve explained unemotionally and without lording it over her in front of the chief.

"So, he adapted somewhat, it happens — any profiler will tell you. They change and develop and can grow in confidence. The Apaches were also badly treated by the Mexicans before the whites took their turn." She emphasised *whites*. "Just how did you know all this anyway?" Sonia stated, grasping for a reason to counter his insights she had missed.

"I checked with a colleague leading the case on what was kept back from the media and the rest of us." Steve touched his nose as he did this to let her know that time in the FBI gave you contacts and info not available to novices. This would do nothing to enhance their relationship, the chief was sure.

An agent came into the room. "An urgent call for you, Steve. Excuse me, sir" — nodding to the chief — "but the LAPD detective said it was very urgent."

Steve took the call. After, he turned to Sonia and the station chief and said, "I think we need the jurisdiction."

Chapter 2
Two Weeks Earlier

Liberty had landed at New York JFK airport. Despite flying first class with guaranteed luggage out first, hers came a good twenty minutes after the carousel was cleared of all the luggage. Searched by somebody, she was sure. This made her very nervous. They were looking for the videos; dumb fucks, as if she would carry them with her, knowing the whole goddam world seems to be looking for them; from the UK Government, US rogue murder squad, Russian mafia and KGB and UK gangsters, Met Police, and who knows who else! As she waited, looking around her regularly, she knew her best bet was to disappear and write her big story, sell it and bring it out in the public domain as soon as possible, and then maybe disappear for good.

As she exited the airport, the media was there in big numbers. They were shouting questions, video recording, and the camera flashlights burned her eyes, asking about her time in the UK.

"Was it true what you claimed?" "Do you have proof?" "You have been branded a fantasist by the media and UK government. How do you respond to that?"

Lights from the live broadcast cameras blinded her altogether, adding to the flashing of the many other photographers.

Here she was on national TV and probably in every paper tomorrow, when all she wanted was anonymity and to disappear. She pushed through the crowded media and got into a yellow cab. They pressed forward and called into the taxi. She wound down the window and out of temper said, "We will see who the fantasist is!" Not the right thing to say at this time, she reflected later. A thin, bald man in a shiny blue suit stepped forward and offered his business card. "I can help. Call me."

She stuck the card in her jacket pocket and the taxi took off. "Queens," was all she would say. The cabbie nodded; he didn't know exactly where in Queens, but thought that she would tell him when she was ready. She was obviously a celebrity and it didn't seem like she wanted small talk. So, after several attempts to give her his thoughts on the world and ask questions, he gave up.

Liberty had a plan. Go to her mother's. Change out of the designer suit and shoes. Dye and cut her hair. Get some very casual clothes too big for her. Lay low for a few days and make her way to California, being careful not to be followed, then get the videos off an old school boyfriend she had not contacted in many years so no one would be able to find the connection. Assuming John Eager, her UK detective friend, had sent them as promised. Hide away and write the full story. A book, magazine articles, maybe a screenplay. Then sell them and get the videos and her story in the public domain. A simple and exciting plan, if no one interfered. Her one regret was cutting her hair and the disguise she would dress in — she knew in her gut this was necessary and not an over-reaction.

She prayed John Eager, her Brit policeman special friend, had lived up to his word and forwarded the video copies as promised, otherwise it was all for nothing.

The traffic, as usual, was awful and the taxi was constantly blocked for what seemed ages. She had time to think about her spell in the UK with the tabloid newspaper the *Daily Crier*, how it ended badly with a government cover-up and her work visa being revoked. The weak men on the board of the newspaper who sold out; Sir Richard Carlton, the chairman, who gave in to pressure and promises of government advertising revenues; Gavin, the editor, who was a good guy, given he was not strong enough to save her; Logan McAllistar, the centre of the drama, who was now recovering from his gunshot wounds; the Harker brothers, Brit gangsters; Nick, the youngest, also in hospital, shot by the SAS and awaiting, she guessed, an attempted murder trial. Then there were the two young boys she rescued who were both brutally sexually assaulted by that dirty creep of a government minister at the 'Hellfire Club'. She had saved them only to find they had been taken away by social services and the whole thing covered up. There were many more under-age children, including very young children. Their lives would never be the same ever again: sex slaves, paedophiles, drug runners, human trafficking at its worst. Investigating had been her big story,

15

which created a lot of danger for her and anyone who helped her. She knew taking on the super-powerful establishment was the most dangerous and she had experienced this with the American hit team, who were probably still looking for her.

Then there was McClements, the Prime Minister's communications guru and fixer. Known as 'The Bulldog', he had certainly set her up and led the government cover-up. Let them see if they get re-elected next year when all the dirt they had supressed and which she was going to spill, comes out. Would they let her? Would they try and stop her by any means? They had already named her as a 'fantasist', destroying her credibility and career for their own ends. They deserved what was coming their way. Also, what about Travis Preston, the presidential hopeful? Does he know there is a second video of him beating Karlien to a pulp? Having had Karlien killed would not stop his fate. This was his turf and he was the most powerful and dangerous contender of them all.

Changing her thoughts, she reflected on John Eager, who she had teamed up with in the UK. A decent older guy, then detective inspector on the way out of the force; now, to keep him quiet about the society perverts they had discovered, promoted to detective chief inspector with a promise of being Superintendent. Would he risk his career and pension by sending the videos, especially since she couldn't bring herself to say she loved him at Heathrow Airport when she left? Would he play safe, or was he genuinely sick to the stomach with the government covering up for so many high-profile perverts? It was important he also sent the handwritten detailed list of the high-value, high-society perverts on the videos. But would he? One was a list given to the UK PM, and no other version was supposed to exist; that is why it was handwritten and not on a computer or typed file that could be found later and used against them. His boss, Detective Chief Superintendent Charlie Allcock, the only policeman allowed to watch all the videos, had made the second handwritten list as he, too, was disappointed in the cover-up. He did not know why he did it, maybe a show of defiance, but he had indicated to Eager where to find it in his desk.

She had promised Eager at the airport she would get payback for what they did to her in the UK and all those vulnerable abused kids they had used, and she meant it. She was angry during the five-hour flight and drank heavily, falling asleep and dreaming of the red carpet when her film of all this comes out. Just a dream, but it took her mind off the anger for a little while.

Now she had landed, she was apprehensive and had a sense of urgency to keep moving and get this all done. She gave a false address to stop at, paid the cabbie and when he had gone walked two blocks to her mother's apartment. She didn't know what was worse: wondering who might be following her, or facing her mother's lectures that were sure to follow.

Chapter 3
Forgiven

"Forgive me, Father, for I have sinned," a sad, plaintive voice came out of the big guy in the confessional cubicle.

Through the small wooden lattice-crossed window, the priest answered, "What do you want to confess, my son?"

"Father, when in London I went with a prostitute."

"All men have needs, my son," remembering his own that still haunted him day and night.

"Not just that; I have had to order some deaths to protect me."

"You were born to lead this country, to protect it, to enhance the lives of its people. You have been groomed to take the world into a better place. Sometimes there are casualties for the cause. Christ was crucified so we all can have eternal life. It is the way of things we often do not understand."

"More will have to come, Father, as I cleanse those that can stop me and destroy my lifetime's work, my destiny and my family."

"I see," pondering for a moment. "Is this absolutely necessary?"

"Yes, Father, I see no other way."

Silence for a minute as both men breathed heavily.

"In the name of the Father, Son and Holy Ghost, you are forgiven, my son. Your sins are absolved. Say ten Our Fathers and five Hail Marys as your penance."

"Thank you, Father."

"Your generous donation is gratefully accepted. Go in Peace." He folded the cheque the penitent had pushed through the wooden lattice window into the side pocket of his cassock.

Chapter 4
Crossroads

Eager had gone to the local pub, as he told Liberty he would after her flight had left. George, the publican, was an old police friend and a good ear to listen with common-sense advice. Together with his wife, they ran the pub near Eager's home called 'The George and The Dragon'. His wife, Doris, was often referred to as the dragon.

It was eight at night. The public bar was busy, however, so Eager went into the Snug bar that just had an over-friendly young couple snuggling up together. He rolled his eyes as they kept kissing and cuddling. He reflected that Liberty had asked at the airport if he would have married her if she had been able to stay. He told her the age difference was a problem and that if he was twenty years younger, he would. When he asked her the same in return, she had responded by laughing and saying 'no'. Was it a reaction to his comments or her true feelings? He would probably never know.

George did not ask what he wanted, he just brought his best bottle of pub chardonnay with two glasses to his table and sat down opposite him.

"The big cheese is here. She's gone, then?" said George, pouring two big glasses of wine. The dragon must be out, Eager thought.

"Just got back from Heathrow. May not see her again," Eager said dolefully.

"You will, my boy." Touching Eager's knee. "You were great together; I have never seen you so happy."

"Wrong age, wrong time, wrong country."

"That is all in your mind. You only live once — make the best of it."

"Oh. I was hoping for another one, cos I've wasted this one."

"Aren't we all," George said sadly.

Eager lifted his glass. "Cheers to that."

"Any chance of action from the government?"

"The bastards say they stand for law and order and protect the perverts for their own ends." Eager was very bitter.

George finished his glass with a gulp and nodded. "That's politics. Drink up, you're staring at your glass."

"George, it is just not right, and losing her feels like fun has left my life."

"Well, it would. It was an exciting time — danger, love, living on the edge, instead of being that straight policeman who worked within the rules and the system all his life. You drank excitement and tasted freedom for a while."

"I guess so. Where's the dragon?"

"Bingo night. Young lasses holding the public bar down. We are always busy when they are on duty. Shows you what low-cut blouses and mini-skirts can do for business. Will you send the video copies?"

"Yes, I will tomorrow, every one of them. I debated whether to send the American one. Safer, as they could kill her if they know it exists, but I guessed it might be an ace card if she has it. Not sure I am signing her death warrant. I can't imagine facing her again if I didn't; she has quite a temper, my girl."

Eager thought about the notes of the names on the videos that Chief Superintendent Charlie Allcock had handwritten for the Prime Minister, but kept a copy. Video number seven just had 'verbally only' written against it. He figured that despite the rest being very high-level individuals, this one must be super-special, maybe the reason for the cover-up — not that the rest on the list would not rock British society. He had watched some of the videos, but not this one.

"I know the feeling! The CIA have the original video of the high-ranking US politician, so it may get out anyway," George said, and then poured two more glasses and the bottle was empty. He turned it upside down in the ice bucket and took it back to the bar.

Hiding the evidence from the dragon, Eager thought.

George returned with another bottle.

"I doubt it. They will use it for sure if it benefits them, but my guess is they were involved with the hit team for him and are complicit in it all. So it will disappear." Eager reflected on the way the CIA would operate with such a powerful piece of blackmail material on a man with the potential to be the next president of the US.

"Hey, she will smell it on your breath," Eager warned.

George just shook his head. "No, bingo night she takes her mother out and stays with her."

"Oh, well, I'll finish this and better walk home and get some rest. Quite a stressful day." Eager looked and felt tired.

"How about we ask the lasses for a drink when we close the pub?" George had obviously been drinking before Eager got there.

"George, you wish! They are far too young for you." Eager was preaching.

"Now look who's talking, the baby-snatcher himself. What was she, twenty-five and you twice her age?"

Eager stood up and grabbed his overcoat. George's words were true, and they hit him hard; real life was the hard truth, the reason his affair had ended.

"Good night, George. Thanks for the drinks and the reminder of my age." He swallowed the rest of his drink, jumped up and left.

George just shook his head. *Sensitive old fart.*

Chapter 5
The Maybe List

His office was the biggest on Capitol Hill. Overlooking Washington with a panoramic view. Outside his office entrance stood a stuffed big brown bear with its mouth open, baring its fierce teeth and claws up in the air to greet visitors. The taxidermist had been extremely good at his job: it looked so real, new visitors were often shocked for a moment. This was the impact he wanted and a statement that he was the big guy on campus.

"Gerald, welcome, please sit down." The big man behind the large wooden carved desk that resembled a boat shape gestured towards a chair opposite. He never offered to shake hands. The visitor was a dapper man around fifty-five years, dressed in a blue suit that fitted him like a glove. Not an ounce of fat on him, just solid muscle. He was six foot tall with short-cropped grey hair. Even though he was in civvies, he looked every bit a soldier by the way he carried himself: straight back and shoulders with a very confident air about him — you could tell he was a senior army man.

"Travis," Gerald said as he sat down and made himself comfortable in the large laid back cushioned seat. Not his style at all.

Travis got up and as he closed the office door, he told his assistant that no one at all, not even the president, can bother him during this meeting.

"A bit of a cluster-fuck, general," he said calmly once the door was closed.

"Can we talk openly here, sir?" The general realised that the tone and mood had changed and was now more formal, so he reverted to his formal army talk to a superior. The big man nodded. Gerald understood this man really well after serving under him in Vietnam and other theatres of war. Travis ended up a five-star general and mentored him, leaving him a colonel when he went back to civilian and political life. He owed him a lot for his own success.

"I lost a good man, sir, in this process. The tape has been destroyed, and the girl put on ice, so to speak. There is no evidence that can find its way to you. No witnesses that have proof. A bit messy due to all the players involved; however, I consider it a positive result under very challenging circumstances."

"What about that reporter, Liberty whatever? I saw her on TV arriving back. She probably saw the video, knows who I am. What in God's name about her?"

"I won't worry about her, sir. She was compromised in the UK when the Brit government got back all the Hellfire Club videos, so she was called a fantasist by the PM's communications guy and kicked out. The press here and there bought it and her credibility is zero. No matter what she says, she will not be believed."

Travis got up and walked around. The situation was stressing him and he needed space to move and breathe; fortunately, his office was a little short of a basketball pitch, or it seemed that way. He lifted his big hands in the air. To the general, when he stopped and looked at him, it seemed he was at a dangerous point and ready to attack him, like the bear outside his office.

"What about the Brit police? Did they see the video?"

"They say no one watched it, and MI5 handed it over to Gina, CIA head at the London Station. She brought it to me directly."

"Do you believe them?"

"No. They had the videos, all with red backings, no names or markings on, just numbers. So, to hand the video over they had to know which one, so I'm guessing this Eager and probably his boss watched it."

"This Gina, do you think she also watched it then, before bringing it in?"

"Not to my knowledge. She was told it was of high value to us and not to watch it, just bring it to Langley and personally hand it to me. I destroyed it in the furnace within minutes of her arrival."

"You cannot be sure. It's her job to know what's going on. Curiosity alone would have made her view it."

"She is very ambitious and I am sure a suggestion of promotion after you become president would swing it; she would be part of the team, no issues."

"Mmm, so I live with it?"

"I think she is safe," the general said, but with no real confidence in his voice.

"Did you watch it?"

"Well, I had to be sure it was the right one," he said quickly.

"But she could have watched and even copied it?"

"Yes, possible." He hid the fact that the CIA technicians in London had said it could be a dupe, not the original, although they could not be sure. It didn't make sense to him, as it is the dupe that shows degrading, not the original. Either way, he was not going to mention it and risking the big man exploding with fear.

"MI5?" He trampled up and down, slapping his right hand into his left palm with each word he uttered.

"Our guys literally dropped the agent on the case on his head from their chopper. The head of MI5 may have looked, said he didn't, but odd for a spy not to, brought the video direct to us. They are our close allies."

That did it. The big guy was now going red and his hand slapping got quicker and louder. He sat back down. The general poured him a Jim Beam on ice from his bar. It was quiet then for a while. Travis leaned back in his chair and sipped slowly. He closed his eyes and the general could hear him whisper, "Sweet Jesus".

"Other Brits?" Travis asked quietly, a danger sign.

"I would assume that these Harkers may have seen it. Certainly, the lawyer Javelin, who set you up, would have. The detective Eager and his boss Allcock, and this Liberty girl."

"So, what you are telling me is just about all of London has seen the video and you are suggesting I do not worry? Any other contenders?" He seemed calmer, but dangerously sarcastic. The general thought for a while, remembering the debriefing from his team and the London CIA head.

"The guy who took them from the club, McAllistar, maybe the MI5 boss, but I doubt he would say anything too sensitive. That's it."

"You think that's it? You think that's it? Half of fucking London!" He got up and poured himself another Jim Beam and swallowed it in one go. He didn't offer to get one for the general. The booze seemed to calm him down slightly. He looked the general straight in the eyes, holding his stare.

"Gerald, I have worked hard for the opportunity to lead this incredible country and the world. God only knows the world needs strong leadership as it is going to wrack and ruin. The 'Moses Rose'[1] democrats have ruined this country — it is almost as left as the communists. My great grandfather came here from Ireland without a cent in his pocket. He sweated and struggled to make a living, he did not ask for hand-outs, free this and free that…" He stopped and sipped his drink and took a breath.

Good, now I am Gerald again, but where is he going with all this? The general was worried.

"My grandfathers and father built an empire because of the freedom and opportunity this country offered. My father trained me from birth to lead this nation. I will not let this situation stop me." He looked at the general, who showed no emotion on his face. He could not read him; was he sympathetic? He continued, "She drugged me, for God's sake, taunted me, I was set up. I did not know what I was doing. Surely you see I am in the right here and should not be punished by having my destiny taken away. You know when the elections come all the dirt the Democrats will try and dig up and throw at me? They will only find a clean-living, Christian, family man, unless they find this. Evidence or not, just people saying they saw the video is enough to destroy me. Rumours have destroyed many presidential hopefuls."

The general now had his head dipped slightly towards the floor. He knew what was coming and could not find an argument to stop it. When Travis was President, he would maybe be secretary of state, his right-hand man. An incredible role for a back-street boy from poor beginnings, made good in the Army and now on the brink of greatness. Hell, maybe even get to president one day.

"What do you want me to do, sir?"

"I want you to make me a 'Maybe List'."

---

[1] Moses Rose was believed to be the only man who fled the Alamo before it was over-run by the Mexican Army in 1836.

"A maybe list?"

"Yes, a list including all those that maybe have seen it, people for the cleansing."

Chapter 6
The Escape

She stayed at her mother's a few days in Queens. Liberty felt that she was being watched day and night. Maybe she thought she was paranoid, but remembered an old saying, 'If you think they are out to get you, they probably are'. Her mother was concerned. The media had tracked her down regardless of the fact she had a different surname and were asking for interviews with her daughter. They were annoying, although at least they had not camped outside her front door. She guessed the story was not big enough in the US or maybe getting old, yesterday's news perhaps, she hoped.

Liberty would dress up in her finest sexiest designer clothes and when the coast looked clear would strut down the street to local shops and restaurants, always staying where many people were. She wanted them to get a good look at her as she was now. Meanwhile, she bought some old baggy clothes from a second hand store, an army back pack, blonde hair dye, and a big dusty knitted fold-over beanie and a skateboard.

She could not tell her mother much as she knew it would frighten her. Their discussions she edited carefully and just gave her the gist of what happened and that she was not a fantasist, liar or all the other names she had been called. She did tell her she had to go to California, but did not want the paparazzi to follow her. Her mother agreed to send on her clothes and typewriter by FedEx to the address in LA she had given Eager to send the video tapes.

"Mum, only send from your office, use another name, not mine. Do not send from home, otherwise they will track it, and tell no one, please; this is important."

Her mother got the message and she knew she was the kind that would not deviate from the directions; that's the way she was.

27

So, at dusk one night when the street was filled with groups of kids playing basketball, some skating and others sitting around on the steps smoking, talking and romancing, she came out of the side of the apartment block and skated down the street with the back pack, cut blonde hair mainly covered by the beanie, and looking a cross between a homeless person and a poor kid on the street. She made the Greyhound bus station in Queens Village, bought a ticket for Los Angeles and sucked up the long journey and many stops. She arrived in the downtown LA bus station at ten twenty-five p.m. the next night. She was certain no one had followed her, so got a cab to the corner of the street where her dad lived in Beverly Hills.

Her dad was an advisor to a major film studio on police procedures. He had been a New York detective for many years; however, he had left quickly under a cloud of suspicion. He was thought to be too close to and co-operating with a mafia family. They were known to have ownership connections with the studio he now worked for, so it rang true for her. When she became an investigative reporter in New York, his underworld contacts were of help to her; however, many police contacts treated her like a pariah. So, she changed her surname to Bell from McGill.

She thought there was a chance that whomever 'they' were knew about him. If, though, they believed she was still in New York, she had a chance to get his help and move quickly away and drop off the radar. She was definitely paranoid, although, she rationalised, for good reason.

She rang the bell at his big house on Kings Road, up the hill overlooking Beverly Hills, off Sunset Strip. It took some time for him to come to the door. He had cameras watching her, she knew. The door was opened slightly and the security chain was still on. There he was, looking at her, trying to check who it was for certain.

"Liberty?"

"Dad."

"What the hell? Is that really you?"

She was sure he was holding the door with one hand and had a gun behind the door in another. *I'm not the only paranoid person in this family*, she thought.

"My new style, do you like it?"

He laughed and opened the door. A big blonde lady, his latest, was in the background near the stairway, watching her closely.

"What happened to…?"

"Long story," he cut her off. "Liberty, this is Cynthia. Cynthia, my daughter Liberty."

"Nice to meet you. I have heard so much about you," said with the true LA sincerity, like let's do lunch some time. Cynthia came across and tried to hug her, but due to her old clothes and down and out dirty look, gave her the widest air kiss she had ever had. Liberty immediately took a disliking to her; however, she could see the attraction to her dad. Blonde, voluptuous figure, made up even in her dressing gown going to bed.

They went in and whilst Cynthia made drinks, they sat in the big lounge room. Her dad was different from her mum: she could share her true story whilst he would listen, not judge or lecture. He was pragmatic and any advice from him would be good and helpful. He had kept up with her situation from the TV news and read all her negative press stories.

Liberty was tired from the trip, but had to get out her adventures and needed her dad's help badly. Cynthia gracefully retired and left them to it, which saved her from asking her to leave, as she could not have her true story being discussed in a Beverly Hills beauty parlour or gym.

"Don't be long, honey," she said as she left, in a voice that tried to be sexy to entice him to bed. She obviously needed some of the attention Liberty was getting.

Her dad drank whiskey sour and she stayed with a combination of beer and white wine. Liberty told her story in a logical sequence like a true reporter, and her dad just listened, whistling a few times.

"So, dad, I need your help to disappear until I can get the story out in the public domain."

He sat back, absorbing all she had told him. He was a clinical thinker and took time to weigh everything up. Thinking of the angles and dangers, how best to proceed.

"So?" Liberty asked, trying to get him to stop thinking and comment.

"So, you are in deep shit, young lady. That's what I think."

"You're telling me! So will you help me?"

"Goes without saying; we McGill's stick together." He never understood why she changed her surname, and that had hurt him. He went quiet again.

"So, yes, I can help you disappear; my advice, though, is to destroy the videos and go somewhere until it all blows over."

"My big story, dad!"

"Look what all your efforts so far have got you. Yeah? You are virtually on the run, looking like a tramp. Your name and reputation have been destroyed. So hide out until after next year's elections; if he wins and you do or say nothing, you should be safe. Well, maybe."

"Well, maybe? What about those perverts? The rich and famous screwing kids? They will just go on as if nothing has happened. More and more kids will be traded and hurt by these bastards."

"Liberty, not time for you to moralise. Time to stay safe. Those Brits will not come after you like they will here."

The discussion went on until the early hours. Their problem was they both were too much alike. Eventually, her dad held up his hands. "Okay, time for bed. I am on set at five a.m. and it's past two now. I will make a plan and we can talk when I get back tomorrow."

"Thanks, dad."

"Oh, Liberty, for God's sake take a bath. There are some of your old clothes in the room to the left." Pointing upstairs.

Chapter 7
The Funeral

Logan McAllistar had recovered quickly from his gunshot wounds. He was called 'Lucky' by the surgeon who operated. The bullets missed all vital organs, one going clean through the top of his leg, another lodging in his hip bone. He just needed regular visits to the outpatients for wound cleaning. Apart from walking slower and being slightly bent over from his normal six-foot four inches height, he felt okay.

He was out of ICU within a week and a few days later back at his home, to what was called by his adopted parents as 'McAllistar's Cottage'. Whilst he was recovering on the physical level, he was emotionally distraught. The doctors wanted him to take trauma counselling, which, in his hard-headed way, he refused. He often entered into violent rages for little reason and had no patience left. The guilt he carried for getting the only mother he had known, Aunt Bessie, hurt so badly she had died. He had promised her that he would not bring any danger to her door when he came out of prison and stayed in the cottage she and her late husband had given him. She was not his real mother, but the family he stayed with for holidays as a poor kid, getting out of the dirty steel city of Sheffield and away from his alcoholic natural mother.

The Russians searching for the compromising videos he had taken from the Blue Haven Club had beaten her senseless. If only he had come back on time. If only she had not gone to the cottage, probably to help him. If only. His promise to her was broken, for what? He, as the security chief at the club, had stuck his nose into things that should not have concerned him. Just for a girl that he thought loved him. She was a lady of the night and, he found out later, part of the conspiracy to blackmail an American billionaire and politician. To top it all, she was in love with her girlfriend. So he had set the wheels in motion for nothing but hurt.

My life is a bad joke.

He was set-up with a drugs bust, to get him out of the way. A year of his life wasted in jail and all he could think about was revenge on the Harkers, crime lords, for his missing girlfriend and setting him up. Good job he had taken the videos before he was put away. They blamed their lawyer, Tazewell Javelin, a guy he never trusted anyway. Someone hard to figure, and he got a bad feeling every time they talked. He couldn't put his finger on exactly why, but he did feel this guy was not genuine. The Harkers put the blame on him for McAllistar being set up. True or false, he was their lawyer, so no difference really, all should pay.

She did take the bullets for him from the American hit team guy, and part of his quick recovery was down to the bullets' momentum slowing down through her body before they hit him. Her girlfriend, who looked like her sister, had taken Karein's place after her beating by the American on what she thought was a dream vacation to South Africa. There she had been murdered as the hit man assumed she was his target. So, five women dead, assuming the girl from the club who talked too much and was killed at home was another of their victims. The Russian KGB agent, Olga, and her support guy, plus two other Russian mafia thugs, Nick, his one-time friend and now his enemy as one of the crime lords seriously injured in a shooting with the SAS, plus five of his henchmen dead. A man dropped from the American hit team's helicopter, who he thought was MI5. Scotty's police dog, Rex. The bodies kept adding up — all because of him. He also knew, deep down, it was not over. It was hard to sleep and everything felt so unreal.

He would receive a handsome pay-out for wrongful imprisonment. His record had been expunged and the press now played him as a hero again for his Army exploits, and apologies all round. Even some of his old Army mates had visited him in hospital. The same guys who shunned him when he was sent to prison for drug dealing. Aunt Bessie had left him her farmhouse and all her worldly belongings. Even so, it was hard, though, to see the silver lining in any of this.

He had thought about it all nearly every waking minute since his shooting.

There were only a handful of people at the funeral. Aunt Bessie had few relatives left. His re-found friend, the policeman John Eager, was sitting beside him. Phil the Nosey Postie was in a back pew. Phil had interrupted the shooter, which probably saved his life. In the same pew was Ned, the old farmer, and his faithful sheepdog, Rebel. Ned had put up Eager, McAllistar and that American woman, Liberty, in his old farmhouse B&B during their troubles.

She be the devil, Ned had thought, thinking of Liberty and her sexy way of dressing.

He had been part of the action with the Russians, sticking a pitchfork (he called Pete) into the big woman when she was not looking and who was about to kill Eager and Scotty, the retired police dog handler. So they both felt part of the drama that had unfolded in Derbyshire. Ned was dressed in a black suit, white shirt and tie. The suit was too big for him and made his head look small, peeping out of the white shirt neck two sizes too big. Phil had his postie's uniform on, as Logan assumed he would be doing his rounds after. He always boasted that the post always got through, as he had worked forty years without a day off.

On the other side of the chapel sat the immaculate Detective Chief Inspector Fenwick from the Derbyshire Constabulary. He had interviewed them all after the shooting incidents. He was shocked at the happenings and particularly DCI Eager from the Met, who he felt had brought all the troubles to an otherwise reasonably quiet county of Derbyshire. He was not here to pay respects for sure, but to see who was who. He also wanted to keep his twitching eyes on McAllistar and Eager to ensure no more trouble. He had not given up on finding something to charge them with, even though his chief had told him what happened was classified, need to know, and he didn't need to know, much to his chagrin.

The rest were a few old lady friends and Scotty the retired police dog handler and his wife. Romeo, his retired police dog, waited patiently outside. She had got her revenge for the Russians killing her lifelong partner Rex, so was also part of the story. Scotty had given her a male dog's name as when she was a pup, she always wanted to be the alpha dog and proved this to be true in her police work. The service was pleasant: the vicar had been an old friend and said all the right things. Logan gave the eulogy and broke down a few times. He talked long about her kindness when he was a boy. Soon, it was over and back to the farmhouse for sandwiches and tea, which Aunt Bessie's lady friends had arranged. To his surprise, Fenwick also came. He was extremely polite and mixed with the locals well.

He did ask DCI Eager for a quick chat outside the house.

"It's been quiet around here for the last few weeks," he started addressing Eager, who had found a bottle of beer from the fridge.

"Yes, I think it will stay that way," Eager responded.

"You think or you know?"

"I believe that to be the case."

"I was told to keep out of everything by my chief. Strange, with so many murders, I thought. Need to know, I was told." He twitched and one eyebrow went up as he was speaking. He was fishing. Eager just supped his beer out of the bottle and did not respond.

"I'd better get back inside. Logan is still hurting and needs support."

"Oh, by the way, I ran across something strange. The video shop owner in Matlock was charged with duplicating videos and breaching copyright."

"I guess it happens all the time." Eager shrugged and tried to turn away. Fenwick touched him on the shoulder to stop him.

"No, the funny thing was, he said two policemen who insisted on duplicating videos in his shop told him he would never be prosecuted — police protection."

"Interesting. Look, I have got to go."

"Yes, interesting, as his description and that of his sales girl fit you and McAllistar."

Eager shuddered inside. *If this gets out, they will all know that they did not get the only copies. The shit will come downhill to me in bucket loads.*

"Look, no one offered him police protection. We had to copy a few videos for my boss as a safeguard on the case I was on."

"And McAllistar impersonating a police officer?"

"No, he never said anything of the sort. The guy assumed he was, being with me."

This guy is a total prick, but dangerous!

Eager turned away and went back into the farmhouse, hoping Fenwick would just let go of this and move on.

Chapter 8
Partnership of Devils

Jimmy Harker sat in the small café in Soho thinking hard. Tazewell Javelin, his one-time lawyer for the Blue Haven Adult Entertainment chain and procurer of drugs and other activities, was late for their meeting. Was this his way of demonstrating he had the upper hand. *Arrogant fat little bastard.*

This was the man who had suggested 'The Hellfire Club' concept be added to their portfolio. A club based on debauchery clubs in the seventeen and eighteen hundreds. Where very rich people could go to perform lewd acts in the safety and security of a secret club. Highly profitable and good for protection for his business, having the top echelon of British society under their thumbs. It was though the beginning of the Harkers' downfall. It was clear to him now that Tazewell, like Dickens's Uriah Heep, had played the 'ever so umble' loyal lawyer whilst plotting against them big time. They had trusted him to handle the senior police they paid for protection. Deal with the Russian mafia for drugs that had then disappeared. He had obviously set up Logan McAllistar he blamed for the missing drugs and had him imprisoned. This was the start of the whole mess they were in now.

The twisted, fat bloody yank lawyer who was trying to take over our empire.

He had obviously got McAllistar out of the way as he was too nosey as the security chief for the club and too close to this Karein call girl who he was working with to set up a big score on the American politician. He had set up the meeting for Karein with his US friends and had all along planned to blackmail the guy. He was a billionaire politician tipped to be the next president, someone who could pay hundreds of millions to keep this quiet. He did not count on the response from the politician, an ex-five star general, to be violent. Tazewell had then even worked with the rogue US hit team to track down the videos Logan McAllistar had taken, one with this politician beating Karein badly, then raping her. He had set it up and was playing both sides and even all three sides. No doubt he had Karein's friend killed in South Africa as it was supposed to be her, but they had switched places.

The double-crossing turd, does he ever have time to sleep?

It was him that brought this hit team to Hellfire Club in the old disused abbey in Kent to kill both brothers, that pest of an American lady reporter, McAllistar and Karein. He had somehow got the message he was not trusted any more and would be the next one on the chopping block as the truth started to unfold. Nick, his brother, had barely got away with his life and team, but the whole abbey containing the Hellfire Club was burnt down. Nick did it to get away and cover up what was going on there as much as he could.

Jimmy knew he needed to be less obvious with Tazewell in this meeting. He needed to let him win some and feel he was in charge, or at least an equal partner, and he would then plot the trickery and eventually neutralise him for good. So be cool and his usual smooth self. Not react like Nick's bad temper that always got him into trouble. Like the deep trouble Nick was now in.

Nick was shot by the SAS when he was chasing after Eager and that reporter, trying to kill them. Bad luck, very bad luck. He was in a prison hospital recovering and awaiting trial for two attempted murders and carrying a weapon. He would go down for a long time. He needed to think a way of getting him out of his problems. Killing or intimidating all the witnesses might be one way. Not very subtle he knew, but what else?

Just then, the door opened and in walked Tazewell. He was overweight, balding and with a bad hip which made him walk a little sideways. A John Wayne-style walk. His big black glasses stuck skew on his face, trilby hat looking small on his large head, long black trench coat and with that cheesy smile on his face. Jimmy could see through the window several 'Yardies' outside. The 'Yardies' were taking London by storm in the poor black areas, selling drugs, prostitution and protection — any crime was their forte. The police had yet to come to terms with these very violent well-armed gangs who had no compunction in maiming and killing anyone. Especially if they felt they had been disrespected in any way. They originally came from Trenchtown in Jamaica, where they were used to clean people's gardens and yards, hence 'Yardies'. They dressed in designer clothes with lots of bling jewellery on display, from gold watches and big thick necklaces and wrist chains, plus diamond studs.

They were not only a police problem, but stiff competition for the Harkers, and it seemed the only way to stop them growing and taking more territory of their market was meeting violence with violence. Jimmy, not one to do violence himself, always found people who would, for a price. Taking them on would, though, create a Chicago, Al Capone street war-type situation, and no one would be winners. Police would come down on them all like a big hammer. No, he had to work with them at an arm's distance and then trust that he can set them up with his police helpers and bring them down with their new friend Tazewell, the poison creep.

Tazewell opened the conversation as if they were friends. "Hi, Jimmy. How is Nick doing?" Then he sat down at the small four-chair coffee table opposite.

As if you care.

"I thought it was a one-on-one meeting; come alone was the message." Jimmy pointed outside at the 'Yardies'.

"Oh, they are just my transport. I am sure you have some yourself. I wanted to be sure this business meeting — where we could get on with making ourselves richer than we had ever dreamed of — went well. No threat, Jimmy, I assure you."

Lying little scrotum.

Jimmy composed himself, shifting positions slightly to face Tazewell dead on. He was a handsome fifty-year-old, long blond hair, slight, good looks, he was like a male model. He wore a light blue suit with a yellow tie and pocket hanky. He made Tazewell look fat, dirty and ugly.

"If you are interested in Nick, he is recovering, but in deep shit, as you well know."

"Jimmy, no matter what you think of me, I do care and I have a proposal that will pull him out of the latrine, so to speak." Tazewell looked pleased with himself, taking his glasses off and cleaning them with a blow of hot air from his mouth and using a glass cloth from inside his trenchcoat pocket.

"Tell me more."

"First, what about my proposal?" Tazewell was asking about his written proposal which Jimmy saw more as a greedy set of demands.

"I can say that in principle I can agree. I mean, give you a third of our clubs and other business if you can deliver a bigger market at arm's length for us by using these 'Yardies' to expand. They are very aggressive and will eventually bring the police down on them. Neither you or I want to be caught when that happens." Jimmy spread his fingers across the table, the scar of the ring finger the American hit team cut was red and obvious. Tazewell wondered what he was doing.

"They can be good friends or terrible enemies." Tazewell was threatening in a subtle way.

"I have been busy recruiting." Jimmy kept spreading his hands wide as he made sure that Tazewell knew he had replaced the team Nick had lost in the shootout. Tazewell began to think it was nerves showing, even though Jimmy looked his calm, assured self.

"Yes, I heard: heavies from Glasgow, Northern Ireland and Newcastle. Do you think they are any match for these crazy Yardies?"

"All ex-military or other not-so-legal violent organisations. Probably just as nuts," Jimmy said coolly.

"Word on the street is you have employed Mad Mike from the Ulster Volunteer Force. You do not really want to start a war; we can create a win-win situation for all of us, and no one need get hurt."

"So, tell me how all this will work from your side, our role and how the hell we can get Nick out of the shit."

"My pleasure."

Chapter 9
Arturo

Liberty was headed up the old Route 66 to Las Vegas from LA the very next day. Her dad had brought her a car from the studio that no one could trace or expect her to be driving. It was a loan car; however, to her it looked more like an old petrol-guzzling Chevy. It was very bright white, very noticeable, and not really a car that wouldn't get attention. A Chevelle Laguna which she figured had been used in some of the car chase movies. Still, it was transport and she needed to move quickly.

Her dad had wished her luck and said he had put an emergency kit under the bonnet. She had no idea what he was talking about.

She had firstly taken the 5 highway to Glendale suburb, where Arturo, her boyfriend at school in New York, had moved to. She had lost touch; however, every Valentine's Day until she was twenty a card arrived at her mum's for her. The last one was sweet, with a note saying he would love her forever. Big sop, she thought, but it was good for her ego anyway. For some reason she remembered the address on the card: 14 Glen Dale Boulevard Road, Glen Dale. She thought it was the fourteen Valentine's Day and easy street to remember. A call to her dad, which was a small risk at this time, and he had checked out that his family still lived there. She had given Eager this address as the relationship was at school so long ago no one would ever make the connection. She told him to put a big sign on it: 'ARTURO, HOLD FOR LIBERTY MCGILL — PRIVATE. DO NOT OPEN'.

His mother answered when she knocked on the door. She looked so much older than Liberty remembered. She looked at her strangely and then when she told her who she was, let her in. Yes, a parcel had arrived and Arturo had taken it with him. Was she supplying him drugs? Why, after all these years? Arturo did not live here any more: he had dropped out of college and done nothing but drugs for years. He was a damn hippie now. His father would turn in his grave. She had cried and cried because she couldn't help him. Liberty had a way with people and had made coffee. She assured her that it was not drugs but part of her secret work as an investigative reporter. She would help him if she could.

As luck would have it, Arturo had called in for some of his things and another loan a week before and had taken the parcel. He seemed happy with Liberty contacting him after all these years, but the druggie girlfriend was very jealous. It took time to find out where he lived. He had previously taken his father's Airstream Clipper vintage trailer and said he was camping off a sleepy road on the way to Vegas, or was it a ghost town or both? The mother was a little confused and seemed to have mixed up the message he had left for Liberty. That was as much as she could remember. Not too helpful, Liberty muttered to herself. I am an investigative reporter, so finding him cannot be that hard.

"Oh, Liberty, another parcel arrived for you. I feel like a post office."
Good, mum was true to her word.

She left in a hurry — she needed to get to him as soon as possible or this hippie may sell the videos for drugs or something as dumb as that.

A map of the Interstate 15 road from LA to Vegas she got at the local mall book shop with some tourist brochures of activities en route. She got herself a good strong black coffee and sat at a small café. There was the Calico Ghost Town off the old Route 66 in the Mojave Desert. It seemed like a big tourist place, maybe not where you would camp; then again, he was a hippie, according to his mum. Then there was road Zzyzx off the Interstate 15, a deserted mineral spring and health resort. Someone had named it so it would be the last word in the English dictionary. Crazy people are all around. Sounded like sleeping to her, getting your Z's. God, she wished Eager was here to help. If nothing else, he had the logic of a detective — no, Sherlock Holmes maybe — but together they worked things out.

After the second refill, she got it put into a takeaway paper cup and headed off to Z-land, as she called it. It was a hundred and thirty-six miles from LA and a hundred miles then on to Vegas. So at, say, an average of sixty miles an hour, traffic permitting, she could be there in just over two hours. The I15 was often a busy road as people left LA for a Vegas weekend. This was Wednesday, so she hoped it would be lighter traffic. If she drew a blank, then Calico would be the next visit. Her stomach churned; her big story now depended on this hippie, school boy love, softie, actually holding onto the videos for her. The 'what ifs' came again — what if the jealous girlfriend destroyed them out of spite? What if they viewed them and realised their value? What if she couldn't find them? Her fears started to get a hold on her and she was well over the seventy miles speed limit. She knew she had better slow down; no need to attract the police — that would be a big mistake.

She was not a worrier by nature; however, she had endured so much for her big story. She had gone undercover as a striptease artist, been used to please a fat old woman, been cheated and belittled, called a fantasist by the Brit government, career in tatters, almost killed, and pretty sure that she was being hunted by some nasty faceless people.

It was now approaching noon and she was getting closer, looking at her odometer to the distance she had covered on the hundred miles for the Zzyzx Road turn-off. Soon it came up on the left and she followed it down a dirt road for about five miles. Sure enough, in the middle of the Mojave Desert was a beautiful spring lake and the old health spa buildings that were empty and unused. With little road signs in the spa area like 'Blvd of Dreams', it had once been a thriving sixty-room spa, she had read in the tourist brochure. The creator had used Government land under false pretences and was kicked out. He was a radio preacher and self-proclaimed healer with no qualifications and he was not even ordained. The area was now used for university desert research studies.

She drove around, but it was ridiculously hot. The air conditioner in her car struggled and she wound down the windows. Not a person or trailer in sight; yes, a ghost town. Yet she found nothing — a totally blank search. She stopped to check the spring water. Taking off her shoes, she stood knee high: it was cool and refreshing for her legs. She would have bought water at the diner just down the road or even lunch if her search wasn't so urgent. As she was about to give up, she saw some smoke at the other side of the spring lake. Holding her hands above her eyes, she could make out a really small dirt road and, yes, smoke rising. Back in the car, she drove around, trying to find the road. Eventually, she went down a very narrow and uneven, bumpy dirt road.

Her heart began to beat faster as she was sure this would be them and the end of her searching. The beginning of her writing. Not paying a lot of attention to her driving whilst she was deep in thought, suddenly from her left came a group of Big Horn, mountain sheep jumping across in front of her. She braked hard to miss them and since she was not wearing her seatbelt, she banged her head hard on the window. Her body hit the car's horn in the process and she passed out.

Chapter 10
The Investigation

"So now you get it," Sonia sneered.

"Yes, I get it, but not for your serial killer concept," Steve shot back.

"Okay, Steve, out with it — why did you change your mind so quickly?" the chief, tired of the bickering, said loudly.

"Liberty Bell's was one of the Amex card's missing digit possibilities."

"The reporter kicked out of the UK?" Sonia seemed confused but very interested.

"She claimed that she was being hunted in the UK for the videos she had showing top Brit paedophiles. She also claimed it was a government cover-up." The bureau chief was up to date with all news channels and papers.

"Yes, she made a statement on TV, something like 'we'll see who the fantasist is'. Like a challenge that she was going to prove what she had claimed," Sonia added.

She's getting it now, Steve thought so strongly and he almost believed he said it out loud.

"She could have been hiding out in the desert and been in the wrong place at the wrong time," Sonia added, still keeping her serial killer theory alive, although the change of mind was a break to pursue both angles.

"True, this does have international possibilities. Someone in the UK wanted to shut her up. Or yes, maybe wrong place, or wrong digit person. I guess we need to check it out," Steve said in a rather conciliatory manner.

"So let's get the investigation going and don't get too excited both of you, we are nowhere near a junket to London," the chief laughed.

"We are on it, chief," Steve said. "Either London, or we go after Geronimo — wasn't his home near Mexico?" They all laughed, even the serious Sonia.

"Oh, by the way, guys, a happy team is a good team. No more fighting; learn to work together as we do in the FBI culture, got it?" The chief's message was clear and firm.

"Got it," they both said together.

Chapter 11
Dead

The call came to Eager from his boss, now Commander Allcock: he needed to see him right away.

Shit, that Fenwick has stirred things up, Eager surmised.

Eager was on his way to Met HQ anyway and the call had come through his new DCI car radio phone. He approached the commander's office with a little bit of trepidation. Making up a believable story to cover for the dupes. Who has them and where are they now would be his first questions, he thought? Although Charlie was retiring soon and was also sickened by the cover-up that had happened from the PM's office. He and Eager did get promoted, which they both knew was a pay-off to shut up and move on. Charlie had actually tipped Eager off as to where his handwritten list of the people on the tapes was. An unknown copy of the one given to the commissioner to take to the PM's office. They did not want anything typed into computers. So Eager knew he was on his side, although he retires now on a commander's pension and wouldn't want to do anything to risk that.

As he entered his office, Charlie said in a quiet tone, "John, please sit down."

Charlie was calm, and this made Eager even more worried.

"I am not certain what is happening, so I will tell you what we know."

Shit, bad news.

"Well, let me get straight to the point, John." Charlie was known for his wild gesticulations with his big arms waving about. He would go red in the face with anger at times. Nothing today; he was still, big arms folded by his sides and talking in a very soft way.

"We have had an enquiry by the FBI regarding Liberty Bell. They think that they have her body."

"Her body?" Eager jumped up from his seat and interrupted.

"John, please sit down and hear me out. Nothing is certain and there are some big missing pieces."

"Like?" Eager was breathing very heavy.

"They had a mass murder in the Mojave Desert in California, that's on the way to Las Vegas. They have a body of a woman, similar age and size to Miss Bell, without a head."

Charlie was talking too slow for Eager. *Spit it out — get the fuck on with it!*

"Well?" Impatient.

"The only real connection is a burnt-out Amex card found at the scene that had eight of her account numbers, except two were not clear. All the other possibilities are being checked out, although six have already been cleared, leaving two people's cards plus hers."

Eager knew the parcel he couriered had gone to LA, so not out of the question that it was her in California. *My God, NO!*

"They killed her!" Eager shouted. "They bloody well killed her!"

"The Americans?" Charlie asked, half-knowing that was the best bet.

Eager, head in hands, tried to speak. "Yes, I think they probably did. The Harkers are in disarray and it is too quick for them. The Russians wanted the tapes which they believe she now doesn't have, so no point. Yes, probably the hit team that came here."

"The local FBI office want to interview you and anyone else involved with her here to see where it leads. I am not telling you what to do. It is difficult for you to comment totally truthfully as it is classified and has massive implications."

"I would like to take leave, sir, right now, and go there to see the body, and they can talk to me in LA."

"Her father and mother are there trying to identify the body — it has been badly burnt. Sorry."

"I am off, sir. Can I have the details of the FBI investigators?"

"It's all here," handing him a brown file. "It's Charlie, John, leave granted. I didn't realise you were so close. I will inform them, so let me know your flight details. Be careful."

Chapter 12
The Finder's Fee — a few days earlier

She woke up inside a trailer on a single bed. She was covered in a dirty blanket. The whole trailer smelt bad with a sour smoke stench and probably unwashed, very dirty clothes.

"Jesus! Liberty, are you okay?"

It took a few seconds for her vision to clear. Her head hurt and she could feel the blood dripping down her forehead. She felt it and found a loose dirty bandage wrapped around her head and pulled it off. The blood was slowing — better than getting an infection, she thought.

"Arturo, is that you?"

He was thin and looked emaciated, face wrinkled and old. He wore a red bandana around his bald head. "Yes, Liberty, it's me. You don't look good."

"You don't look so good yourself," she shot back.

What happened to that handsome boy and his beautiful full head of black hair the girls at school loved?

She sat up. She needed to get out into the open air. It was too hot and smelly in the trailer.

"The parcel — do you have it?"

"Yes, I kept it for you. It's here."

"Show me now," she demanded. He rustled in one of the cupboards filled with junk and brought out the parcel. It had been opened. She counted them — all twelve were present.

"Arturo, it's been opened! I wrote a note not to open, just save it for me."

"It is lonely out here. Javier has a generator and a video player in his trailer; sorry, we watched some of them. I didn't know you were into heavy porn, Liberty?"

"How many people watched them? Tell me?" Her worry and anger were bursting through her voice.

"Just Sheila, myself and Javier. They are sick — after the first two, I couldn't watch any more."

"Where is Javier now? Did you recognise anyone?"

"Easy. I didn't, nor did Sheila. No idea. Javier watched a lot of them and then stopped. All he said was that he was bored with this shit."

"You idiot, idiot! Where is he now?" Her head hurt even more now — a big headache. Arturo was taken aback by her insults; not what he had expected when he met her.

"Oh, he is in Vegas, selling some of our stuff."

"What stuff?"

"We are trying to survive; this country doesn't care for us."

"What stuff?"

"Some dope and pills we make up for the tourists — mostly powder, nothing too heavy."

She rolled her eyes. "I've got to go, Arturo." She got up and made for the door.

"Since I kept the tapes, can you see your way to lending me a few hundred dollars for supplies? Things have been tough."

You mean drugs are expensive.

She could still see those puppy dog eyes when they were younger. Making her way to her car, she searched her purse and all her money was missing except some change.

"Who did this?" She looked at the thin, drug-abused Sheila. Putting her fingers together, she told her to hand back her money. Reluctantly, she did — all five hundred dollars. Liberty gave him one hundred as she needed the rest for petrol, food and accommodation, as the credit card could be traced. She started to drive off, keen to get out of this place and away from them both. Winding down her window, she called out loud.

"Arturo, get out of here as quick as you can, go home." She hoped he got it; just in case, she skidded around and came right back up to him.

"Arturo, get out now. If Javier is talking, there are some dangerous dudes looking for these videos. Just get out of here; you have been warned!" Then off she went carefully down the dirt road, watching for the sheep this time.

"Just stupid advice; no thanks, then. Bitch only gave me a hundred," Arturo complained.

"I got her Amex card." Sheila waved it in front of him and they both laughed.

Javier was in Vegas. He had sold their dope on the streets to a lot of half-drunk Mexicans having a good time. He stopped for a beer at the Jimmy Buffett's Magaritaville bar on Las Vegas Boulevard, watching all the activity and people partying and passing by. There were thousands of them, like ants going in all kinds of directions, some in a conga-type chain dance, forcing their way through the thronging crowds, knocking people over as they went. He slowly counted the earnings under the table. It added up to one and a half thousand dollars.

Two weeks getting the ingredients and making the stuff and a day selling. One third for me, one third for Arturo and Sheila and the rest to buy more stuff. Hard work for so little. If only I had more cash to buy more quality shit.

The news came on and headlining was the announcement that Travis Preston was leading in the polls to be the next US president in just over a month's time. Javier supped his bottle of Corona slowly and watched. There was something familiar about the man talking. He shouted to the barman, "Hey, bro, turn the sound up." Which the barman did.

The man was talking. "It's time we got back to good old family values in this country. I have been married to my beautiful wife, Betsy, for thirty-five years, we have five kids that have grown up into solid citizens. Too many kids today grow up without fathers; our morals and standards have dropped to an all-time low. When I am president, we will set about…"

The penny dropped and Javier's mouth was wide open. This was the guy he had watched on the video beat the girl, then fucked her stupid.

Family values, my little Mexican ass!

The anchors on the news were now talking. "Well, Kathy, does he have a chance?" the smarmy man asked.

"Phillip, he is a billionaire who could afford his campaign himself if needed, a decorated five-star general, majority leader of the House, experienced successful businessman and a dedicated family man with the values this country needs so desperately. I think he will walk right into the White House."

Someone changed the channel to football. Javier sighed and ordered another beer — he needed to think. He'd been living in a very hot, dusty desert in a trailer, scratching a living for too long. He felt a tingle in his left hand — money coming to him. Here was an opportunity to get rich quick, very rich. He was not the brightest of men, but he had cunning. He soon realised the video was worth a fortune. This dude was a billionaire. He couldn't work out how many millions that was, so he asked the barman.

"I think a thousand million or something like that. Don't tell me you won that amount of money." The barman was laughing and shaking his head as he walked away.

The plan came to him. He needed to cash in on this as soon as possible, as Arturo had said he was holding the videos for his ex-girlfriend to pick up. When will she come? Could he get back and get the video or maybe all of them? Who knew who else might be on the rest? He'd never heard of this Travis Preston, although his reception in the desert was not good and he preferred Mexican films and soap operas. Maybe he didn't have time. He'd seen it on old movies: a swap in the desert — the video for big bucks cash — but how much? Could he ask for a few million, or would it be quicker and safer to ask for a million dollars and make it easy to pay, no questions asked? Was this blackmail? No, he decided, this was a finder's fee; he wanted to save this Travis so he could be president. He would say he was a loyal supporter wanting to do a good deed. That is how he would position it. A quick exchange, peanuts to this guy, and he moves back to Mexico and lives like a king, happily ever after.

Arturo and Sheila he would give enough money, so they could fry their brains over the next weeks. He was sure they had been using his precious raw materials, so they would get what they deserved.

"Hey, bro, how do I contact this Travis Preston?"

"Who?"

"The guy just on the TV."

The barman thought about it; was this guy drunk? "You'll never get through to him on Capitol Hill. No, he wouldn't take your call. Why?"

"Just wanted to help him." Javier was a little deflated.

"Tell you what. You go straight down this boulevard and look on your left and you will see his posters. They are setting up his campaign office for him."

The barman watched as Javier jumped up, threw a five on the bar and walked away. Shaking his head, the barman thought only in Vegas could a small Mexican in a crappy rhinestone cowboy outfit think he could talk to the next president. He shook his head again, picked up the dirty five dollars with his fingertips and went about his business.

Javier found the office and saw it was closed. There were people inside and he kept knocking on the glass doors. They were just moving in furniture and computers. Eventually, a tall, thin guy dressed in jeans and tee-shirt opened up.

"Can I help you?"

"I'd like to call Travis Preston."

"A lot of people would, but he is too busy to take all the calls." The man was amused at the audacity.

"He will take mine, bro."

The man was getting annoyed; however, everyone was a potential voter and the Hispanic market was huge.

"Just ring and tell him that I have seen the video with his girl. I can get it for him for a finder's fee."

"That all, video, girl?" The man was the campaign manager in the area, newly appointed. He was smart enough to pass on the message. Something was amiss.

He couldn't go directly to Travis; he would ring his boss in the capital. The word was passed on with an immediate response. Hold him there, ask him what he wants, tell him he will get it, take him and buy him lunch, whatever, just keep him there. Do not get involved in any of his claims or details — he is a liability. Keep him there; the Feds will sort him out.

The campaign manager was surprised when he asked for a one-million-dollar finder's fee. He nodded agreement slowly, saying Travis is okay with that, not knowing what it was all about.

"Gerald, this needs sorting with no links back at all. It might be a hoax or a shakedown by this reporter using this guy. Too close to home."

"Understood."

Chapter 13
One More Favour

He was uneasy and shuffled in the passenger seat.

"What do you want, Mr Javelin? I have to get back to work."

"Inspector Samuels, we are old friends. I just want a favour. Besides, the old dead bodies are not that urgent." Telling him he knew what was happening inside the Met force by other informers.

"Yes, I have been demoted and put on cold cases. I am out of the hustle and bustle of police work. I can't help anyone. Aren't they looking for you?"

"Cleared up; no real evidence connecting me. I cut their case to pieces, had it thrown out. It's not true, you can help us more in your current position. We paid you and the ACC a lot of money and you are still our man."

Samuels turned to face Javelin in the back seat.

"Did you not hear me? I am out of it all. I nearly lost my job and could have gone to prison." He was frustrated; this was a ghost of the recent past now haunting him. He wanted it all to go away.

"You are out, Samuels, when we say you are. We have records of our payments and recordings of your calls to me. The ACC conveniently committed suicide rather than face it all, and he was the only link inside the police that could have caused you trouble."

"What do you want of me? I helped you and the Harkers a lot; surely that is enough?"

"One more favour, that's all, and unless you contact us, we will go away." A lie, and Samuels could see how Tazewell's eyes went to the left as he spoke. A sure sign of a lie.

Samuels was quiet, his head twisting around, not knowing what to say. His ambition and greed had brought him to this place. The ACC had groomed him, promoted him and used him. Yes, he had made money, and yes, he started out as a good cop, not a bent one, but was seduced by the close proximity to the top echelon and power. The ACC had killed himself not because of the money he made providing protection for the Harkers' empire, but because he was a dirty paedophile caught on their Hellfire Club videos. If he had known, he would not have had anything to do with him. Yet they covered it up and even gave the bastard a Queen's Medal and a police funeral. 'Overworked stressed cop tops himself'.

Javelin was impatient. "One last job, one big payment. Audio tapes back and we all move on." His eyes still went to the left as he took off his glasses to clean them, as he often did.

Silence. Eventually, Samuels had to ask. "What do you want me to do?"

"You are in cold cases with access to the evidence room, right? You can choose your cases and sign them out, right? So we want you to find the case box on Nick Harker and bring out any salient original evidence and give it to us."

"There is video surveillance in there. I could be seen."

"Come now, you are very smart. Get a case close to this one and fumble, change boxes or whatever; you will find a way."

"Like what? His gun will be in the armoury."

"Anything that may cause a mistrial. Like swabs taken from him to prove he fired a weapon, his clothing, original reports, just anything they cannot replace."

"How long have I got?"

"Probably two months. He is still recovering and we can play that he is not fit for trial."

"How much?"

"Five thousand," Tazewell said proudly.

"Not a lot to save him a life sentence. This happened in Derbyshire — surely they are prosecuting up there?"

"Not the only string on our bow. The case attempting to kill a police officer goes to the Old Bailey; plus, he tried to shoot one of your guys."

"I can't promise, but I will see what I can do." The car had been circulating around London.

"You do that." It was a threat, he knew.

"Let me out here." He couldn't wait to get away, so jumped out on Baker Street. The limo was blacked-out and he hoped crime intelligence didn't have Javelin under surveillance.

Chapter 14
LA Bound

Eager briefed Denise Williams, who was once his sergeant and now a Detective Inspector and still his trusted second-in-charge. She would take over the Harker case and cover for him.

He seems more distraught than he should; maybe he was closer to her than I thought. Denise knew Eager and Liberty were close, but had no idea how close.

She was extremely loyal to Eager and had a bit of a crush on him. She was a beautiful black lady who was an excellent boxer. She dressed in business clothes and heavy shoes that made her look rather butch. Her black hair, ebony skin and piercing blue eyes made her stand out as a real beauty. She was not just a dedicated lady detective in a man's world, but a lady who was going to smash through the glass ceiling they talked about. Eager treated her as an equal and never noticed her respect for him was also affection. She kept him honest and never let him off the hook if he was, in her opinion, headed in the wrong direction on any case. He could leave with confidence and an easy conscience; she would look after the team and current cases. They would bring down the Harkers' empire together eventually.

He made two phone calls. The first one to Gavin, the now ex-editor of the *Daily Crier*, to inform him of what may have happened to Liberty. Gavin had brought Liberty into the UK from New York to add some spice into their investigation stories and he was right — she was different, sexy and aggressive. She could handle anyone at any level.

Together with Logan McAllistar, they had formed a team during the Hellfire Club saga. Gavin told him he had been sacked due to falling circulation. This was because the board of the *Daily Crier* made him apologise to Minister Stephens about the story of his child abuse at the club. Front-page retraction and embarrassing for Liberty and himself. They were seduced by offers of big government and party advertising and some were, he believed, blackmailed by McClements, the PM's communications guru, who had the videos and probably used them to get his way. He was a tough and uncompromising fixer they called The Bulldog. The video evidence had been taken from the newspaper's safe and handed over to the government, he assumed. He also believed Sir Richard, the chairman, had done this after he lost the fight with the board. The apology and retraction had created a lack of confidence in the *Daily Crier*, and no matter how many tits and bums he spread across the pages, circulation plummeted.

"I'm coming with you," he demanded.

"Why? It may be a waste of time and expensive."

"One, she was my friend and I want to know what happened to her; two, I was screwed over like her; three, they paid me off big time, making me sign a confidential agreement, plus, can you believe, this is an official secrets doc; and four, I have nothing to do — my reputation is also in tatters and no one will employ me."

"They can't prosecute if you expose wrongdoing."

"Exactly. I will help expose the story in the US and write the book she was going to do. I can also help you. I have media contacts there."

Eager agreed and gave him details of his flight and where he was staying at the Beverly Hills Hilton, courtesy of the FBI he had contacted earlier.

The second call was to Logan, who was now living in the farmhouse. He had spent time securing the property and adding outside lights and beams and a steel fence on the wall surrounding the house. He was a little paranoid as they talked, and Eager understood he was still 'gun shocked'. He had been in Northern Ireland during the big Troubles, risked his life to save the general commanding and his army mates. Even Nick Harker, who was in Northern Ireland with him, he saved and they became great friends, hence the offer when he left to be the security chief at the Blue Haven Club. Medals and mentions in dispatches for bravery, he had survived without a scratch from shootings and bomb blasts and was then shot in his cottage in England. He needed to heal physically and, most importantly, mentally.

He wanted to go with Eager, but was talked out of it. He needed to heal, get fit, as otherwise he would be a liability, and Eager promised to call him regularly with any update.

"If you need help, I will be there." McAllistar was serious. A first-class weapons expert, ex-army regimental boxing champion, and a calm and calculating dangerous foe.

He packed the following morning as his American Airlines jet was leaving on an evening flight to Chicago's O'Hare airport, their hub, and then change to a domestic flight five hours on to LA. UK was eight hours in front of LA and the flight around twelve hours, meaning he would get there just after midday LA time.

He made time to go to the George and Dragon and have a pint with his friend George and update him. He had hosted Eager's Hellfire team in his pub when things got tough. His wife, the dragon, would not let him get involved other than working on communications co-ordination with the team, helping Gavin. George was shocked about Liberty and the dragon, his wife Doris, played the sad lady; however, there was no love lost between her and this out-going, over-sexed hussy. She had seen George ogling her when Liberty had dropped her raincoat to show the guys her striptease outfit, if you could call what she had on an outfit. Liberty was going undercover at the club, playing the dancing entertainment girl part. Doris feared he would never get over seeing up front and personal such a body wiggling in front of him. She also thought that Eager was too old for such a young woman. In her mind it was all disgusting and maybe her death was the best for all.

As Eager was leaving, after four pints and a glass of chardonnay, George asked him to wait and went upstairs. He brought down an old-fashioned London Bobby helmet known as a tit helmet.

"Take this, the American cops will love it. Might help to take them a present."

Eager was not sure about this, but thanked George, who was trying in his way to help. He was surprised that in the morning he did put it in his carry-on bag.

Denise turned up at three p.m. in the afternoon and drove him to Heathrow. She seemed sad for him and squeezed his hand when she said goodbye and good luck.

"Look after the farm," was all Eager could manage.

Heathrow was a zoo as usual, and he queued up at the American Airlines desk for what seemed like an hour. Extra security did not help due to the ongoing terrorist threat.

Suck it up, John, go into remote control. It's a long way in cattle class.

When he eventually got to the booking-in desk, readying himself for the long journey, the clerk surprised him.

"Mr Eager, you have been upgraded to business class."

"Why?"

"Does not say on the system, but you are." She issued his ticket; he had wanted an aisle seat, and that was available as well. He would have thought it his lucky day if he wasn't on such a sad trip. Well, maybe Liberty is okay? He tried to think positively, but still his heart ached.

The trip was okay except for the model-looking lady in the window seat. Business class had big leather seats, folding back a decent way, plenty of space and a good foot rest. The model lady with flowing ginger hair and heavy make-up was wearing a complete leather suit. She was attractive; however, every time she moved her leather suit creaked, rubbing against the seat leather. She tried to make conversation which he was not into, so she left him alone after several false starts. Still, the food was good and the wine even better. The oldest air hostesses on international flights got the cream routes as they had tenure. One seemed eighty and was struggling with the coffee pot after serving dinner. He felt he should help, but then had second thoughts she might get upset.

The wine, food, a movie and, to his surprise, a good sleep. When he got to O'Hare and the plane parked, the captain made an announcement for everybody to remain in their seats until told differently. There was a group moan coming from the passengers. Two hefty plainclothes men got on and went straight to Eager's seat.

"Sir, FBI, can you please follow us. Luggage will be looked after."

They were dressed immaculately in blue suits and red ties. Eager, in his old comfortable tracksuit after a long flight, felt dirty at the side of them.

"Oooh, are you being arrested? Have I been sitting next to a major criminal?" The model seemed turned on by the events.

Eager just got his bag from the overhead apartment, looked down at her and said, "Yes, I murder young ladies in creaky leather suits." He then left before he could see her face.

When he got inside the airport, the agents introduced themselves to him.

"You are going FBI class from here on, Chief Inspector Eager."

Sure enough, he was walked through Customs and immigration and put on a Learjet to LA. This really gobsmacked him: the treatment, the plane and courtesy shown a fellow officer.

I think I am in the wrong force.

Chapter 15
The Curse of the Videos

The campaign manager told Javier it would take time for the right people to get there from Washington — around four hours — so maybe he would like to have dinner on them and wait. Javier was excited and nervous. The manager gave him a hundred dollars for dinner and told him to come back at seven p.m.

It's working; this is my lucky day!

He went to Nacho Daddy, a Mexican restaurant on the Strip. This time he ordered more beer and a lot of food. The excitement and nervousness made him very hungry. The time passed so slowly; after the meal he found a public phone and called his drug dealer supplier in LA.

"I'm going to buy a lot off you soon, Holmes."

"How so?" The guy knew that Javier was just a small-time pusher. Javier could not contain himself and blasted out the full story, except for the name of the politician. He was wise enough after all the beer to hold that back. It was his Ace.

"Where is the tape, bro?"

"I will have them soon if this Liberty reporter doesn't get it first."

"Tell me more," said Holmes.

He told him about a friend getting the tapes from this Liberty girl. That's all he knew, except for the name of the politician. He gave no more information and after putting the phone down immediately regretted making the call. They only knew he lived in the desert somewhere. Through the fog of beer, he feared they might come for the tape and take his fortune away.

He walked back to the office at seven as requested. It was getting dark and the whole of the Strip was lit up with flashing lights and big video screens working hard promoting all the stars and events. He knocked on the door and it was opened straightaway. There was a petite, pretty blonde lady dressed in a designer suit.

"I'm sorry, mamacita, I was asked to come back by the guy."

"Yes, Mr...? I am the personal assistant to Travis Preston. I have come here to find out what this is all about. What video? Is this a hoax? You know you can go to prison for blackmail."

"Then he can kiss his big ass goodbye to being president."

She then looked serious and ordered him to sit down. She was aggressive for such a small lady, about his size though. He told her his story, what was on the tape and how he had seen it. It said it was urgent as this Liberty someone was coming to pick them up. She got the sense of urgency and asked him where it was.

"No, no, mamicita, show me my finder's fee first." Wagging his finger in her face.

She turned around and opened a large briefcase. He gasped — it was stacked with hundred-dollar notes.

"So, Mr X. Let's go get the tape." He had ignored her attempts to get his name. She was small and on her own, why not go? They went by her helicopter as she explained that time was of the essence and he got nothing if the tape was gone when they got there. It was located at the airport just down the street, and she promised to bring him back for his car. No, he didn't care, he would get his friends to drop him back the next day. As they were flying, she found out that there was only three of them at the camp near the derelict spa. He was not sure if they had watched the video. Her microphone on her suit jacket sleeve was broadcasting to her team right behind her flight in another black chopper.

They landed a short distance from the trailers. Arturo came out to see what was happening. His druggie girlfriend had climbed onto the roof of his trailer as she did at night to look at the beautiful heavens full of stars. She had taken quite a bit of LSD from their stash and had a headphone on her portable audio tape player. Listening to *Lucy in The Sky with Diamonds* by the Beatles, her favourite track, unaware of the chopper landing.

"Arturo, she is the police; they want the videos," Javier spat out; he did not want Arturo to know about the big money coming to him. Arturo seemed puzzled and now scared, hearing Liberty's strong warnings coming back to him, alarm bells in his head.

"She picked them up two hours ago, so they are gone," he stuttered out.

"Who picked them up?" the blonde demanded.

"Aah, man!" Javier was distraught. The worst had happened… end of his lucky day.

"Liberty McGill, old school girlfriend; they were hers, I was just holding them for her. Not sure what was on them," he lied.

"What was she driving?"

"A big white car, not sure what it was; maybe a Chevy. Very white."

"Mind if we search everything?"

"Sure, they are not here, I promise. We…" Just then, three shadows came out of the dark, armed men in combat kit.

"Javier, what the fuck have you done?"

"No, man, the tapes are worth a lot of money; we can share it. Tell them where she went."

He hasn't understood what is happening, the blonde thought.

She turned to the dark figures. "Clean up here. Get what you can out of them in case they are lying, and then leave no trace — only confusion for the cops. There should be another girl; she is missing, probably not far. I am going after the one who is driving the white Chevy. She has not gone far." She picked up her money briefcase.

Arturo started shaking. "What the hell!"

"Hey, man, that's my money!" Javier shouted as they laid him on his back on the floor.

Total dick brain, this one just doesn't get it, the blonde thought as she hurried away.

Chapter 16
Warrior Chief

He was a quiet man of twenty-eight years. Born in the San Carlos Apache Nation to Eskiminzin (meaning warrior chief) and Dahteste (meaning warrior woman). He was proud to be Apache, which meant 'enemy'; the real name for the tribe was Ndee, meaning 'The people', although they mainly used Apache.

He often sat in his grandfather's teepee and listened to the stories about the history of the Apache nation. His grandfather was a relative of the famous Geronimo, warrior and fighter who operated in both Sonoma, Mexico, and Southern Arizona. Geronimo's wife and three children were killed by Mexican soldiers, so he hated them intensely. When Mexico ceded a large part of their land to the US, the white Americans were no better. The Apaches were rounded up and moved from their lands to a reservation called San Carlos Apache Nation. Geronimo and his followers hated this and saw it as imprisonment. He continuously escaped and caused the US soldiers and government much embarrassment.

The area was called 'Hell's Forty Acres'. It was wracked by disease and the money meant to feed the Apache Nation most often never got to them. The Army used and killed them for sport. It was a captivity Geronimo and the nation could not understand.

His name was Diablo, and he was born in 1950. His grandfather and father taught him his tribal ways and traditions. His father was very hard on the boy as he wanted to make him a great warrior of the past. This involved all kinds of trials and tests. Leaving him in the cold desert lands for days with nothing but a bow and a knife to survive. He wanted him to be able to run long distances without stopping, like they did before horses became their way of life.

His father was unhappy with his life and he became a very heavy drinker of whisky, and if he couldn't afford that, the cheap gut-rot wine.

After his many bouts of liquor, he often beat the boy badly for no more than the wrong look or word, and being sorry afterwards did not help, as Diablo was scarred. When sober, his father blamed the whites for the reservation life which was not healthy and not natural to the Apaches, who were born to live on the plains. It was captivity, a prison; that is why he told him Geronimo and others always escaped to be free in a country that cherishes and promotes freedom. The Indians, though, were doomed to an unnatural existence.

He did, though, become a great hunter and tracker. He spent his evenings learning about all the other indigenous tribes and their terrible treatment by the whites. He also developed into a Shaman or medicine man to his tribe, following in the footsteps of Geronimo, who was never a chief but also a shaman to the Chihahua Apache tribe.

He loved the ways of his ancestors, from worshipping, hunting, medicine men and treating the land with respect and dignity. He disliked the way the white people were destroying the environment with mines, industry and a total couldn't-care-less attitude about mother earth and the future. Just sheer greed for money and power now.

In 1968 he was going off to college when he was conscripted by the US Government to the out-of-control Vietnam War. He had no choice, being a pacifist did not help him, as a lot of the recruits claimed to be the same. His skills as a tracker and hunter, plus his interest in medicine, sent him to the Green Berets as a Medic. He had six months' training before being shipped out. He thought it interesting that the paratroopers shouted 'Geronimo' when they jumped — a respect to a great warrior, he believed.

He kept himself to himself and put up with a lot of the racism directed at him continuously. He was often the butt of their jokes and often beaten as they took their fears and frustrations out on 'The Indian'. That was until they were caught in an ambush. The patrol was being cut to pieces on three sides by hundreds of Viet Cong. Many were dying and others crying for help. The radio operator had been killed with the patrol commander. The rest fired at will in every direction. He charged to the radio operator's location under fire and called in the situation and location. The fighting continued until a fleet of helicopters arrived and rocketed and machine-gunned the Viet Cong all around them. He stood up with his shirt off, waving it in the air to show them their position at great personal risk. The rockets distracted the VC and he took the opportunity to lead the men out of the area, all carrying their comrades that were wounded. There were ten left, four badly wounded and one who died on the way out.

He was later on his second tour, used to help clear the tunnels that the VC had built to get close to forts and surprise the US soldiers. There were thousands of these. He, with others called tunnel rats, went down searching for ways of clearing and closing. This involved killing the VC in the tunnels as quietly as possible. Many he killed by slitting their throats with his knife. He was good at it; however, the brutal killings took their toll on him mentally. Added to this, the second most difficult situation was when hundreds of VC had been killed by the AC30 'Spectre' gunship and other air support craft. The bodies were piled up and burnt in a huge heap, hundreds of them together. The US soldiers either stood silent or laughed out of relief that this fight was over. He stood silent — these were human beings that had been slaughtered, and the stench was awful.

He was treated differently after his battle worthiness was evident and received the Medal of Honor later. He was also used by the government for a public relations campaign for the war. This he hated and tried to stop them, but was rolled over by the army machine. Like all Vets, he suffered this war for three years and was eventually badly wounded in the back and, with his Purple Cross, sent back home. He would never be the same. Introverted and bitter, with now an inbuilt ability and callous nature to kill and kill.

Diablo lived in a teepee by choice. Today at San Carlos Indian Nation there was normal housing and the place was developing fast, even talk of building a casino. He went back to being a Shaman and a social worker. He didn't talk much at all. His people saw him as a loving soul and sought him out to be in his company. He would tell the children the history of the Indian nations and was employed at schools to do this and teach them Indian culture, singing, praying and dancing. It was a peaceful and modest existence. After Vietnam, he did begin to drink strong liquor and often fell down comatose in local bars.

When he read about any kind of abuse of his brother Indians by white people, his blood would boil and he raged, his anger out of control. One day, he started his journey as a serial killer, hearing about a white farmer who had whipped a young Indian caught stealing, to a point where the boy could have died. A big urge came over him he could not control. With warpaint, bow, arrows and his knife, he went out to seek retribution. After bringing down the farmer and his wife with arrows, he slit their throats to finish them. He then burnt them like they did in Vietnam. When he got back to the reservation in his truck, he cried and cried and prayed that the urge would never come again.

It did a few months later. Arizona cowboys drunk at a rodeo. Lassoing an old Indian man and dragging him around with their horses. When taken to court, they said the man was drunk and picking a fight. The old man died a few weeks later and they got off with a fine. Only one witness — an Indian not taken seriously. Their names were in the papers, so Diablo was able to find them and kill them one by one using his style and what now would become his trademark method — warning all white people. The urge was too strong, and the sorrow and vow not to do it again followed; it was now a pattern. He did go farther afield to Utah and New Mexico. His body count was now ten white people. The press called him 'Geronimo', which he was proud of, and he was sure that this was putting fear into those who abused native Indians and was payback for stealing their land.

He had sent two messages to the FBI telling them he would continue unless the white man relented and stopped abusing Indian people, gave their land back and looked after mother earth. He had driven several hundred miles to post the letters that were made up of words from newspapers, careful not to have fingerprints. He had dressed at the post office like the white man with a big jacket and hood to hide his features.

He read the newspaper on the Mojave Desert murders and was angry, and that urge started to come over him and his whole body shook. He was getting the blame for killing innocent people. Hippies and a Hispanic guy minding their own business in a hot, dry desert. Someone was copying him and giving him the blame, not to mention taking credit for genuine killings he had done for good reasons.

He needed to find them and his urge was to punish them.

Chapter 17
Situation in LA

He was met by Steve and Sonia at LAX. They had a car waiting by the plane as he stepped off. "Don't worry about your luggage, it will get to the hotel," the man in charge of the aeroplane cabin stated.

They introduced themselves and Eager was asked if he wanted to go and freshen at his hotel. He did, as he wanted to change and shower and look almost as pristine as these agents. He told them he would be quick. The journey was about thirty-five minutes on the busy LA highway 405. They didn't seem to want to talk business in the car, just how was his trip and pleasantries. He needed to know if the body had been identified for certain. Liberty's dad had said it could be her. As delicately as they could, they told him the head was missing, being searched for in the lake, and most of the body was burnt badly — just an ankle and foot were found almost intact. Eager visibly cringed and looked down.

"If you need to get some rest, we can do this tomorrow after a good night's sleep?" Sonia suggested.

"No, I have come a long way to find out what happened and I cannot wait to get going. Besides, I had a good sleep on the flight. Did you guys upgrade me?"

"We heard you were coming on your own dime, so thought it was fair. Courtesy of the US government."

"Thanks."

"I am not thanking you," Sonia said, laughing. "I have never been to London; no junket for us, then."

Eager half-smiled to be polite. He was being treated very well, but still wasn't sure how much he would or could tell them. His gut was 'fuck it', if she's dead all bets are off with the Met and UK government.

He was true to his word. His bags arrived at the same time, and within thirty minutes of checking in he was shaved and showered and in his best suit and favourite silk tie. At reception he saw Gavin checking in and introduced him. They were reluctant for him to come to the first meeting, however, and agreed to meet the next day. Gavin looked relieved — he had flown cattle class and was physically knackered.

The FBI LA offices were on Wilshire Boulevard, a small drive from the Beverly Hills Hilton. They went straight to a private meeting room and the Bureau chief was called down to attend. He was a very serious guy, Eager thought, but polite and obviously experienced. No bullshit here. His name was Leslie De Silva.

Also in the meeting were two LAPD Homicide detectives: Sergeant Jerry Hill and Detective Jake Brody. They were introduced as working together with the FBI until what really happened could be established. Coffees all round.

"Well," the chief started, "let's see where we are. Thanks for coming all this way, DCI Eager. Where do you want to start?"

"Please call me John. I'd rather be caught up on the situation here first. I am almost — excuse the pun — eager, keen to know the full situation." They smiled and Sonia thought what a great accent and a good-looking guy.

The chief looked at Steve and Sonia. They looked at the LA detectives. Sergeant Hill looked at Detective Brody.

"Oh, me? Well, yes, the deceased first." He handed out a single piece of paper with names and backgrounds of Arturo and Javier.

He then gave a verbal report, starting with Arturo Kohler, who had had police arrests for drug use. "His mother once reported him for stealing from her and then withdrew the charges. He was of Italian descent, twenty-six years old, father died when he was eighteen at college and he dropped out at that stage. Mother's address and telephone number are on the report. Post-mortem revealed he was tortured, with cigarette wounds, some teeth missing, a broken arm and then shot in the chest by a hand gun, type not yet known but suspected to be a Sig Saur P220; no bullet case was found on the scene. A hunting arrow was in his chest from close range. Cause of death: the bullet right through his heart. Mother identified the body.

"Javier Gonzalez, small-time crook and drug peddler. Several convictions and over twelve months in prison. Mexican immigrant. No fixed abode. Went off the police radar a year ago. No relatives known in

US. We sent Mexican police a request for more information and background and as usual still waiting. It was almost identical killing to Arturo, except no torture. Strange — looks like they didn't need any info out of him, just this Arturo.

"Third victim was either Liberty Bell or Arturo's girlfriend, Sheila Hollis, who lived with him and has not been found yet. Bell was an old high school friend of Arturo, according to his mother. It appears that the deceased was on the roof of the trailer when it was set fire and the big gas cylinder exploded. Head is currently missing, probably in the lake. A foot and ankle were fairly intact, and Liberty's father could only say it could be her but he could not be certain. Dental records therefore cannot be used at this stage until the head is found, although Liberty's mother said she had perfect teeth and had no dental treatment, just cleaning. We are searching for Arturo's girlfriend, who could be the victim, or maybe she wasn't there at the time or has run away in fear of what she saw. If she is alive, then she could be our best witness.

"The Amex card results for the one found with the missing digit comes down to Miss Bell's and another that was stolen a year ago from a Katie Smith, Arkansas address." He stopped at this point. Eager was visibly shaken and the rest must have heard it all before.

"Steve, Sonia?"

"Sonia interviewed the mother." Steve handed over to Sonia. She seemed pleased.

Sonia outlined the interview. "Broken woman. She had received a parcel from the UK which had 'Hold for Liberty McGill', her real name, marked 'DO NOT OPEN'. Arturo had taken it with him into the Mojave Desert, where he said he lived. Liberty had turned up asking for the parcel and Arturo. She had told her he was at a ghost town in the desert. A second parcel had arrived for Liberty which she took with her. She had promised to help her son and left in a hurry."

Sonia surmised that whatever was in the first parcel was the reason for the murders. Drugs? Information on her claims in the UK? Implicating someone who had the wherewithal to have her silenced and get the evidence back.

Eager tried to look nonchalant and swallowed hard as he knew what was in the first parcel and had decided not to tell them at this stage.

"When Liberty arrived back in New York she was called by the press a fantasist and made a threatening statement on national TV saying that they would see who the fantasist was." Sonia continued. Eager thought this was typical Liberty.

"The murders seem to be a copy of our current serial murderer," said Sonia. She went on to describe the crimes of 'Geronimo', as he was known by the media, explaining that these murders were a deviation from his method of operation. Steve was impressed that she was now open on the chances of it not being the serial killer.

"Over to you, John. Can you spread some light on her activities in the UK and who might be responsible?"

Sonia could see that Eager was emotional after listening and she raised her eyebrow in surprise.

Must have been something between them.

Eager had to be careful; his gut feeling was to tell all, but his cautious police mind won the battle. He detailed the investigation into the UK drug lords the Harkers' activities following the release of Logan McAllistar. He explained their major adult entertainment chain across the UK and the creation of a Hellfire Club for perverted rich people. She worked for the *Daily Crier*, a tabloid newspaper, and was exposing their activities for what she called her big story. Logan McAllistar had taken from the club eleven videos of UK high society influential people doing lewd acts. He avoided talking about the twelfth, the American politician, as it was too early and his trust level in this team was not there yet.

The videos were handed over to the police eventually with his help. He explained that the KGB, Russian mafia, some dodgy UK policeman, the Harkers were all involved in chasing down the videos and Logan McAllistar. Again, he did not talk about the hit team from the US and possible CIA involvement — that would come later when he was ready and knew what had happened to Liberty. He went on to tell them that eleven of these videos were handed over to the UK government, the PM's office no less, where they were told it would be handled at that level, thus no further action by the Met. Her newspaper article on a junior minister backed up by a video of him with two young boys was retracted after the tape apparently went missing. Her visa was cancelled and she came home.

The story is bigger, with quite a few killings along the way. He said he was tired now but would hand over a detailed summary for them the next day. It was a complex situation.

"Whew! You can certainly say that again," Steve added, scratching his butt, as was his habit. He was trying to get his mind around it all and thought better that way. Sonia just turned her head and rolled her eyes in disgust.

Sonia offered to take Eager to the Beverly Hilton. When she parked outside, she turned to him. She had a full figure and her business suit skirt had lifted quite high above her knees whilst she was driving.

"John, can I buy you a drink or dinner?"

Was she coming onto me or working me for more information?

"Sorry, normally I would, but I am cream crackered."

"Cream crackered?"

"Sorry, rhyming slang: it means knackered."

"Knackered?"

"Very tired, I mean."

She said, "I understand. We appreciate very much you coming all the way here to shed some light and assist us. I can't help feeling, though, that you were holding something back. My intuition was screaming at me in there."

Eager shrugged. "Maybe jet lag. I'll come at it fresh in the morning. What time?"

"Why don't you sleep in, then have time to write or add to the summary you mentioned? They have a business office in the hotel. We will come over in the morning with the LAPD guys and pictures of what is left of the body, if that is not too painful. Outside chance you might be able to identify. Say ten o'clock in the restaurant?"

Does she know we were close?

"John, if you think of anything, please call me, no matter what time." She handed him her business card again. "Oh, if I can help you in any way, let me know." She seemed to emphasise 'any way'. Then she just stared at him, which made him a little uncomfortable.

He was not used to American women, and this did seem like a come on or at least extremely friendly.

Eager nodded and got out of the car and disappeared into the hotel. He thought about how quick his luggage had arrived and how it had been put into his room for him. They may have done this as a courtesy or had time to check out what he had brought in. Yes, his trust level was low and maybe he was just his old self — a suspicious cop.

Chapter 18
Hideout

Liberty drove as fast as she could out of the Zzyzx Road onto the highway. She had seen a sign for Peggy Sue's 50s Diner just up the road. She was starving hungry by this time. She'd only had a coffee today, so against her better judgement she stopped for food. A good old-fashioned American burger and Coke would go down well.

After pulling into the car park, she first checked the video box and found in an envelope in the bottom the list of high-profile people on them as Eager had promised. Number seven on the list was odd: 'verbally only'. She couldn't wait to watch it, as it must be a big name to keep this secret, even off a handwritten list. She had the urge to call Eager and talk to him. A strong urge; she missed him a lot — was that crazy? He must love her to put his job on the line or was it his anger at the cover-up or both? She shrugged her shoulders as she had a feeling that someone had just walked over her grave, as her grandmother used to say. A premonition of something bad, very bad, was going to happen.

She took the box of videos into Peggy Sue's. She sat in a retro red leather booth and after looking around, taking in the nineteen fifties décor, she ordered her meal. The old waitress dressed to complement the diner must have been here when it opened, she guessed. She was alone and even missed Logan and also Gavin, her former editor. This was the odd-bod team she had worked together with on the Harkers' Hellfire Club saga, helping with her big story. She felt very lonely and excited at the same time. She could not contact her dad again, nor her mother, as 'they' might be listening in. She was paranoid; maybe 'they', whoever they were, did not have a clue about her and the dupes of the videos, or maybe not?

No sooner had she had the first bite of her burger when there was a big explosion down the road. Huge flames had shot up, reaching into the sky, followed by a torrent of smoke. The diners and staff got up and went to the windows. Not much could be seen other than the flames and smoke.

Someone said it was like the fourth of July. Others laughed. Liberty went outside, clutching her purse, video parcel and Coke. These videos were never going to be out of her sight ever again. The smoke was definitely coming from the direction where she had just been.

Oh, shit, Arturo, she thought. *What have I done to him?*

"Miss, Miss..." The old waitress lady was following her. This got her attention, as she had made her mind up to just go. If this explosion was what she thought, 'they' were nearby. She shuddered again and turned to face her.

"Your check."

"Oh, I wasn't leaving, just seeing where the smoke was coming from."

"That would be the Zzyzx Road, I'm guessing."

Liberty decided she must go right away and gave the waitress a fifty dollar note and then ran to her car.

"Miss, your change." It was too late. Liberty was speeding out of the car park and back on the I15 highway as fast as she could and headed south for Palm Springs. Her dad had given her the keys to a friend's holiday home even his latest lady did not know about. She could only guess the relationship he had with his 'friend'. Still, it was in a quiet back street and no one could trace it. A perfect place for her to hide out and write her book and articles.

She was driving for several hours and kept the radio on, switching from station to station, but there was no news about the explosion.

Chapter 19
Meeting of the Chiefs

The commissioner was entertaining the chief constables from most forces in Britain. It was an annual conference and update meeting which the Met, being the biggest and most important police force, always hosted.

This was the welcome cocktails evening prior to the weekend's conference. It was also the opportunity for his colleagues to congratulate him on his forthcoming Lordship and retirement at the end of the year, as the word about it was all over the grapevine.

Sir Michael circulated, welcoming new and old colleagues. He was in a great mood: everything felt good and he was looking forward to retirement, a good pension and all the benefits being in the House of Lords would bring him. Yes, he had earned his time on the 'gravy train'.

He eventually bumped into the chief constable of the Derbyshire force. Harold was an ex-colonel in the military, having jumped into France in the war to get his medals and after he got his police role. He liked his whisky and had already had a few. Sir Michael did not want to stay with him long; however, courtesy dictated he do the right thing. After a few pleasantries, he was about to move on when the chief constable said, "All that nonsense sorted now with the Russians and your London mobsters?"

"Yes, mostly squared away. Still, though, following up on some loose ends."

"Yes, quite a lot of excitement on my patch. I have a chief inspector that still wants to follow-up, even though I have told him it's being handled by the Met and is hush-hush."

"Thanks, Harold, I have to go and meet Janet over there." Excusing himself to get away from him to people he was close to and enjoyed their company. As he turned, Harold made a last comment.

"Even your guy duping videos and supposedly giving a local video shop operator police protection was getting under his skin."

"What?" He now had his full attention.

"Nothing. They were duping some videos he said for his boss. The guy probably lied about protection and they did pay him."

Sir Michael was confused and a little scared. He could see his Lordship disappearing from the New Year honours list, floating down the Thames like the garbage in it. The PM and her cronies were tough, unforgiving cookies.

"Yes, I am sure it was okay." He turned and almost ran to the hotel lobby.

He called Commander Allcock urgently. What did he know about Eager copying the video tapes? Was that possible? If so, where are they now, who has them? Why wasn't he told? Who was working with him?

Charlie Allcock, feeling the heat coming down the phone line, tried to be calm and said he knew nothing about it. Was he sure? Who told him? There was a lot of bad feeling in the team about the cover-up from the PM, not sure if these extra tapes existed. The commissioner was irate when he discovered Eager was in the US on leave due to the alleged murder of this reporter Bell. Did she have them? Get him back now. Interview whomever was with him. Was it this McAllistar guy? Does he have the tapes, do you think? Go to Derbyshire quickest way possible and get a search warrant. Meet this DCI there; he would get his name and contact details and call him back. Find out everything he knows.

"It's twenty-one hundred hours, sir. I'll set off very early tomorrow for the five-hour drive."

"No! Get a chopper and a team together and go now!"

Fuck, he is raving mad; not even interested in the cost. Glad I have only a month to go to my retirement. Not involved, not much they can do to me. Eager, though, is in for it big time.

Chapter 20
Gavin

Eager had rested enough on the flights. Lots of leg room in his cabin and good reclining chairs over the Atlantic, plus the speed and comfort of the Learjet. His mind was in a flurry over the details the FBI had shared; emotional and upset, he wanted a drink or a few drinks. He was not ready for bed and knew he would not sleep well unless his friend Mr Chardonnay helped him.

They had four bars, or lounges as they called them, and he chose the one by the poolside. It was a nice warm evening in LA and the area was comfortable and relaxing. His mind was racing as he sat down at a little table by the pool. He ordered a Kendall Jackson Chardonnay he had heard was a good wine from an American friend and looked around while he waited.

He recognised the back of a man sitting at the bar. Well, he was almost sitting; he seemed to be slumped over it. He walked over, tapped the man on the shoulder, and sure enough it was Liberty's old editor of the *Daily Crier*, Gavin Hastings.

"Eager! My man." He turned around and greeted him, slightly slurred, but did not seem surprised to see him in the bar. Eager got Gavin to join him at the table.

"Here to help. Shit, it's bad news about Liberty. All over the TV." Pointing around, looking for a TV, but there were none at the pool bar. "Sorry, my old pal." He was definitely worse for wear and Eager guessed he had a combination of jet lag, too many drinks on the plane followed by a long nightcap of drinks at the bar.

"I wanted to come and help her write the book and negotiate with the media. I have a lot of experience paying for goddamn crap, and she, I mean we, will get a big bundle of cash. Lost my job through it, you know." He repeated what Eager already knew and with that he swayed and almost fell off his chair.

"Gavin, you are jet-lagged and a little tipsy. You need to go to bed and I will meet you for breakfast and we can talk."

"You know they keep playing the news of when she arrived in New York, her saying she was not a fantasist and she would prove it. Always had big balls did our Liberty."

"She said what?" Eager made Gavin repeat what she said. He couldn't word for word, even though he had sat in one of the other bars most of the afternoon watching the news and, of course, drinking. Eager recalled the FBI mentioning her arrival interview and her comments, but it had not struck him as really important until now. The waiter had brought two glasses and the wine bottle in the bucket full of ice. He poured a bit in Eager's glass for tasting, and when he nodded okay, he filled his glass. The waiter was about to pour Gavin some when Eager waved him not to. Not deterred, Gavin just grabbed the bottle and poured himself a glass.

"No, no, tell me what you know? Where is her body?"

"Hold it! The police are not one hundred percent certain it is her, so let's not give up just yet," he said with the certainty he did not feel.

"What, not sure? So she could still be alive?" Gavin was hopeful. He told him about the Amex card and her ex-boyfriend who had been murdered, his girlfriend missing and how Liberty's father could not say for certain it was her, although she might have been in the wrong place at the wrong time.

Gavin whistled. "This is like a movie! I expect Clint Eastwood will be in it. Two books and two movies — one in the UK and one in the US." He stumbled off his chair.

Eager eventually got Gavin to go to bed and slowly sipped his wine whilst he thought. He took his police notepad out of his jacket pocket and got one of his pens; he always carried four. Yes, he needed to think. So he wrote a checklist of what he needed to do the next day. He already listed an information report for the local police, so no need for an early morning editing and writing session of the document he had already brought with him. He would edit out the information he wasn't prepared to share just yet. He wrote:

1. See the body or the pictures of what is left.
2. See her father, get contact details.

3. Mother if around from New York or call her.

4. Visit the site of the killings. Talk with LAPD. Were any videos recovered or what was left of them?

5. See the mother of her ex-school boyfriend.

6. Learn about this Geronimo serial killer. The FBI may help him — they seemed good guys.

He then threw around in his head: if she was killed, then who might have done it?

The Harkers — no, Nick was in hospital and Jimmy had his hands full with members of his gang dead and rumours of the Yardies moving in on him. A long way to go for vengeance. They would go for Logan and himself first. No, not them.

The Russians — unlikely. They think the videos are no longer with her. Their sources would have told them.

The UK Government — no, this was not a James Bond, licensed to kill, movie. Also, they think they have the only copies of the videos.

Some of the high-worth individuals on the tapes maybe paid for a hit? Probable, but a long-shot. They may be perverts, but having the contacts and ability to arrange a hit here so soon after her arrival takes organised and specialist resources. He shook his head and swallowed the remainder of his glass and refilled it.

He had been cautious all his police career not to jump to conclusions but to think every aspect out clearly. He did believe there was no such thing in police work as a coincidence, although he also knew every now and again some people went down who were innocent due to this belief being followed blindly and zero other scenarios considered. Nothing in police work was simple or perfect. So he came to three options. One, she was in the wrong place at the wrong time. Fetching her videos from small-time drug peddlers who may have stood on Mr Big's toes. Two, was Geronimo for real? It was in the Mojave Desert — was that Indian Territory?

Or three, what he had thought when he had heard what she said on the news: Travis Preston wanting her out of the way of his presidential campaign. She was still a witness and even though compromised, his opposition would use her for sure to damage him. What did she say on the TV interview when she arrived in New York? He needed to know exactly. He moved inside as his wine was finished. When he thought and was nervous, he drank quickly; well, he always drank quickly when he was stressed. He went to an inside bar with TVs everywhere, ordered another bottle and watched and waited. The barman was kind enough to tune it to a local Californian news channel.

He was about to leave when eventually the news came on. Yesterday's news often gets bumped as old news. He waited patiently until almost the end of the broadcast when the newsreader talked about no news on the identity of the woman killed in the Mojave Desert mass murder. It was generally believed to be Liberty Bell, who had just arrived back in the US after being kicked out of the UK under a cloud of false reporting. They then played the arrival clip. Sure enough, she said, "We will see who the fantasist is." A challenge she made out of temper. She signalled she was going to be trouble and he guessed you could read into it that she could prove what she claimed.

Definitely the Americans' doing.

Chapter 21
Safe

The phone was ringing off the hook; she could hear from outside the house. She was fumbling in her pockets and bag to find the house keys. That damn phone stopped and started again. This was not the discreet slip-in arrival without neighbours noticing she had hoped for. Being such a quiet place, the neighbours not recognising her and seeing her street rags may think it was a break-in and ring the police. Not what she needed right now. The phone stopped again as she dragged her belongings inside. Then it started again and she grabbed it — only her dad knew where she was.

"Hello."

"Liberty, is that you? Hell and damnation, why did you not answer the phone?"

"Just got here via the hippie's camp on the Zzyzx Road on the way to Vegas. I got the videos!"

"There was an explosion there on the news, a few people killed they think, got to be connected."

"Yeah, gotta be, one of the guys staying with them had viewed the videos and was in Vegas, probably told someone. Do they know for sure people were killed?"

"Pretty sure, by what I saw on the news; a lot of tents covering up I assume the bodies and packed with scenes-of-crime people. Local police and I'm sure FBI."

The phone went quiet as Liberty was processing what she had heard, and the dangers she was now facing were her worst nightmare. Nothing is more real and a slap in the face than callous murders.

"Liberty?"

'I'm okay, dad. Got what I wanted. Just going to put my head down and finish the job."

"Fucking hell! These people are not messing around. You need to give this all up and get out of town for a long time. TV news say three dead, all unconfirmed, maybe they are guessing broadcasting from the scene this makes dramatic news. I doubt if the police have told them anything yet. The media think it is Geronimo, as they were tortured and shot by arrows and burnt, same MO as this serial killer. There is a girl without a head and they cannot confirm her identity. The trailers were burnt down. If it is not the serial killer but people after those damn videos, this is like a scorched-earth policy, making sure that no evidence and most importantly incriminating videos were found. Just in case they were hidden or copies made. Stop this, for Jesus's sake! Does your mother know you have been in contact with this Arturo?"

"Yes, she sent some of my gear to his mother by FedEx."

"I need to tell your mother you're okay before she sees the news mention your friend's name; she will make the connection and have a heart attack."

"No, don't, dad; they may be listening in on her phone! Let them think it's me."

"Consider how they found out where you were? The bad asses probably know it was not you. Arturo would have told them, begging for his life, that you picked the videos up. Description of the car and all, I bet."

"Well, true, though I don't want the police to know now. I don't need them on my tail."

"If it's money you want, I know a way I can help you."

"No, dad, it's my reputation, career I want back, and some payback I want. Money will follow."

"I should have put you across my knee more when you were a kid."

"You were hardly ever there, remember?" she said in a sad tone.

He went quiet for a moment.

"Didn't mean that I didn't miss you and love you." Her words had hit him hard right in his heart.

"Yeah, and you gave me your bloody Irish stubbornness." Liberty tried to lift the mood.

"I guess so. I cannot come there as I may be followed. I am using this phone at work; no one has a clue which of the many office phones I can access. I have to tell your mum somehow. She will probably fly here anyway."

Cynthia will love that. Poor dad.

"Okay, promise me that you will not tell her where I am or the number. I do not need her lecturing me at this time. Also, Cynthia; she might be okay, but she does not need to know I'm alive — too risky. Promise?"

He agreed and asked her to think about her predicament and see sense and that he would call her the next day from work: he would ring three times and then hang up and call again. She sat down on the big comfy sofa, found the remote and put on the TV with the sound low. She thought about what she had done to Arturo and began to cry uncontrollably. When her sobbing had stopped, she got angry with everyone. He was told not to open the parcel, for god's sake; why didn't he follow instructions? They are pigs, what they did to him. The videos are cursed for sure, she reflected. Then she cried again and before she fell asleep on the sofa, she wished Eager was with her.

McGill went home with the revolver he always carried at his ankle half-cocked. He was super-aware as he drove home. Continually checking his mirrors, watching carefully when cars overtook him. On red alert for any approach or action that might take place. They wanted Liberty and the videos, so they would try and take him alive and kick the info out of him. He would not let that happen. He had to talk with Cynthia to make her aware of the possible security threat and prep her that his ex may come to town. This was not going to be a fun evening.

As soon as he got home and secured the doors and closed the blinds on the windows he opened his armoury cupboard, found his automatic hunting rifle. Both guns now locked and loaded, the revolver he kept on him and the rifle behind the bar in the living room, just in case. If they could do what they did to those hippies, they might start interviewing relatives who they assume could tell them where she was. He put the alarms on around the house. Beverly Hills cops had a great record of less than two minutes for a response. He wrote down their direct telephone number — 911 would take too much time in an emergency.

We are all at risk from these guys.

Meanwhile, he was formulating a plan in his head to end this and make a lot of cash for Liberty and himself.

Chapter 22
A Secret is Never a Secret

The Met Police HQ was always full of gossip. A secret is never a secret if people made you promise not to tell anyone, which, of course, was always the message passed on with the secret. It started with Commander Allcock's private secretary, who had put through a very angry commissioner. The commissioner was normally so polite and friendly, something was amiss, and so she listened in. The commander was red-faced and came out with a lot of instructions. Call the team off duty in, call the chopper people to be ready in thirty minutes. Get DI Williams in here pronto. Get DCI Fenwick at Derbyshire Constabulary on the line; yes, if not available leave a message, he needs to call back immediately on or off duty.

She was due to go home and had stayed late due to workload. A cup of tea in the canteen was what she needed when her tasks were complete. During which she had a secret chat with the other staff on duty having their break.

"But keep it a secret."

They all agreed that DCI Eager was in big trouble and he should stay in LA.

Of course, it wouldn't be long before this information reached the ears of DI Samuels and other informants. It would be early next day when Jimmy Harker and Tazewell Javelin got the information. Copies of the videos existed and Eager had gone to the States to get them, it was assumed. This was an unexpected turn of events and a lot of new 'food for thought' for them and the gossip mill.

Chapter 23
Finding Liberty

"So, these are the pictures we have of the deceased and the scene of the crime." Brody, the LAPD detective, handed Eager a file. He went straight to the picture of the foot and ankle. Not a pretty sight, and it made him wince thinking it might belong to Liberty. He looked closely; yes, he had massaged her feet on occasions, but could he recognise this as hers for certain? Size looked right, but it seemed very thin, or was he imagining it?

"What's this on the ankle?" Eager asked.

"We believe it is a start of a tattoo of some kind; well, according to the ME. The bottom of a small heart, we can only guess. Would you know if she had a tattoo?" Sonia asked, searching his eyes, as they all watched closely for his reaction.

Eager almost smiled as he knew Liberty did not have one; she had told him on several occasions, "Smalls, my body is a work of art on its own, why would I change anything that would scar it and make me look cheap?" She could be arrogant when she wanted to be; well, always, he reflected.

So she is alive! Now he had to think fast. Why would they think he would know about a small tattoo on her ankle? Did this Sonia have an inkling about their relationship? He pretended to re-look carefully at the picture to give him time. Her father had said he could not be certain. Wouldn't he know her views on tattoos? Did he not want them to be sure it wasn't her, to protect her, or had he been so remote from his girl he did not know? He decided to play it safe. Shaking his head and looking as sad as he could, he just copied her father's comments. "No, nothing stands out, not that I looked at her feet, but I cannot be certain it is Liberty's... er, parts. Sorry."

"The tattoo?" Sonia pushed.

"She could have, I am not sure. Like I said, I wasn't in the habit of staring at her feet and ankles."

Liar. Sonia knew she had seen pictures of Liberty in short dresses with long legs, high heels — and that sort of woman wears this body art to show it off. Men would ogle at these women and her gut feel was that Eager and Liberty were more than just good friends. If so, he would know about a tattoo on her body no matter how small. She looked at Steve, who just exchanged a knowing glance.

The rest of the morning Eager was able to see all the files and get information on her mother, father and Arturo's mother. They seemed open with him and not afraid he would start his own investigation. Sure, he had been her friend and had every right to talk to the relatives.

Eager had handed over an edited file on the Hellfire Club investigation. Details on the players involved. The Harker brothers, Tazewell Javelin, the Russians and other possible suspects for the FBI. The videos he had handed over to the Government he had not seen and did not have the details of the participants, he claimed. They would have to ask the Met officially, and good luck. This would get him in hot water back home, but what the hell; maybe this would shake things up. He could not lie in a statement to the FBI would be his defence. He had not lied but omitted key information and felt bad about it. Although he did not know and trust these guys yet and maybe the tentacles of this American reached into the FBI? Wasn't the CIA somehow involved with the US rogue hit team in the UK?

They took turns in asking a lot of questions. He fielded them as honestly as he could. Steve and Sonia regularly looked at each other in between, as if not believing all that he had said. They thanked him and asked him how long he was staying. He told them he would see the parents and hang around a week to see if more news comes to hand. Since he was on leave, he would look around, maybe even go to Disneyland he'd heard so much about. After he left, Steve said to Sonia, "Maybe we will get a junket to London after all."

It was early afternoon when he met Gavin for a late lunch at Chipotle Mexican fast-food restaurant down the street from the hotel. Eager was not on expenses and most restaurants in this part of LA were really expensive. Gavin needed a good feed; he had slept in to lunchtime and

Eager had to call his room to get him moving, otherwise he seemed in good shape. He was dressed in blue jeans, white tee-shirt and black pumps, the best Eager had ever seen him. Normally in a crumpled suit and tie askew with bits of a hurried 'got to meet the deadline' carry-out lunch pieces down the front of his shirts and jackets. Eager guessed Gavin was used to late nights and he probably got over hangovers quickly, body conditioned to drink. The food was great and now they knew Liberty was alive they had big appetites, devouring several big dishes each. Apart from maybe Mexico, LA was the best place to eat Mexican, they now believed.

"What is your plan?" Gavin asked with a mouth full of tacos.

"First, we need to move from the hotel; it's far too expensive. Let's find a small motel and share a room. Then we need a cheap hire car and a good map to get around. After which, we visit her father and call her mother and see what they know; after that, this Arturo's mother and pay our respects. If nothing comes up, then we go and check the scene of the crime."

"If they don't know anything, how the hell are we going to find her?" Gavin was worried; he was banking on working with her and sharing the profits and the kudos.

"She had to have help, and my guess would be the parents. I could be wrong; if not, we are stuck."

"Why don't I write a press release and send it to my contacts here? 'Met Police Inspector here to help FBI with potential killing of Liberty Bell.' She may read it and try to find you?"

"It might put me in the firing line as well. If over the next two days we draw blanks, though, then I am game for anything."

They checked out of the hotel. The concierge gave them the address and telephone number of a Holiday Inn hotel in West Los Angeles. He sniffed in a condescending pitying way when handing the piece of paper over. The tip they gave him was also an irritation, as Brits are not used to tipping. He resisted the desire to throw the five dollar note in the rubbish bin in front of them. Using a taxi, they went to the LAX and got a deal from Avis car rental for a small car. Avis provided a map and Gavin drove whilst Eager map-read. Neither had been to LA before and this was an experience negotiating the five-lane highways and driving on the right. After some wrong turns and Gavin nearly killing them turning into the oncoming traffic at a light, Eager leant over.

"Here," he said, "tie my hanky to a finger on your right hand to remind you we are driving on the right."

They eventually arrived and checked into a clean, decent room with two single beds, bathroom and shower and a small fridge with some goodies in. Eager called Pat McGill first; it was late afternoon. It was his home number and Cynthia answered. Eager explained he was a friend from the UK that had worked with Liberty there and wanted to pay his respects. Pat was expected home any time soon as he started at five a.m. with the filming. Eager had difficulty getting her off the phone as she loved his accent. He gave her his hotel room and telephone number and asked if Pat could call him back as soon as possible. It was four o'clock in the afternoon; nothing to do but wait.

Eager checked some messages given to him by the concierge at the Hilton before he left. One was from the FBI guy, asking him to contact him urgently, and one was from Charlie Allcock. again urgent: he must call as soon as possible. He called Steve at the FBI office.

"Apparently, your boss wants you back in the UK. He seemed rather flustered and asked me to call around at the hotel and get you to contact him urgently. You were out, so I left the message."

"Do you know why?"

"No idea; seemed very urgent. Hey, keep in touch, we may need to talk again. Is the motel okay?"

"Cheaper as a base for some tourist stuff. Pound versus dollar not good. Nice and clean, though." Eager knew Steve just wanted him to know he knew where they were. Concierge I bet, he thought.

He rang off. Eager's first thought was to say, 'Fuck them, I am on leave.' His curiosity got the better of him and he called Charlie's home number as he was eight hours ahead, meaning it would be midnight in the UK. His wife answered after being woken up. Not pleased, she said that Charlie had had to fly to Derbyshire; she was not sure why the commissioner had directed him to do so immediately. Shame he works such long hours and retirement just a month away; you'd think he'd send a junior there — but no, he had to go. Eager thanked her and rang off.

He guessed it was something to do with the previous happenings and called the farmhouse where Logan was staying. He was surprised when it was answered after the first call.

"Logan, it's Eager. Are you okay?"

Logan stood up and walked around the phone table and faced the wall, and in a low voice muttered into the phone. The connection was good.

"I have a lot of visitors tearing the farmhouse and my cottage apart. Looking for, they claim, duped tapes."

"Shit! What did you say?"

"Can't say much, being watched. I told them I lost them in the bogs on the moors when I was being chased by the American hit team. Not sure where, the bog hoppers and I were running for our lives."

"Did they know I was with you when we copied them?"

"Yep. I covered for you again, told them it was my insurance and I wouldn't hand over the originals unless you helped me."

"Thanks. The commander is there, right?"

"Charlie and I are old friends now," he laughed. "Threatened to arrest me and fly me to HQ. I told him I was saying nowt more and needed a lawyer. Already got one pay out for false imprisonment."

"Tell him, I will call him first thing in his morning. Not coming back. Be careful. Liberty is alive, keep it secret. These guys do not mess around. Stay safe."

Tell me about it. Logan didn't need to be told how dangerous they are.

"Mmm, risky. His face is already bright red. Good news, though, about Liberty. Gotta go, he's coming towards me."

Chapter 24
Pat McGill

Pat McGill called the hotel from a payphone at his regular bar on Sunset where he ended most days before going home. He seemed very wary at first. Eager introduced himself and his rank and the background of working with Liberty. Pat relaxed a little; however, he asked a lot of questions, checking Eager out as best he could. Liberty had talked a lot about him during their evening together. He was obviously a close and trusted friend, if not her sugar daddy.

"What did she call you, I mean the nickname?"

"Oh, yes, it was always 'Smalls' — no idea why." Eager could feel Pat relax as he breathed better over the phone. He asked where he was and said he would pick him up in thirty minutes. Not going home, too dangerous; he would take them to a bar. Eager explained that Gavin, her old editor, was with him.

Too dangerous? Eager pondered that remark.

True to his word, Pat was outside the Holiday Inn on time. Eager and Gavin were waiting there, ready. He opened the front passenger door and shook hands while still sitting in the driver's seat. He was dressed in a tight yellow polo shirt, brown chinos and brown leather boots and was driving a red Ford Mustang, top down; seemed very flash to the Brits. He was muscular from his neck down. Maybe even a six-pack under that shirt, thought Eager. He had short cropped brown hair, a long nose and a square, strong chin. He looked very handy in a fight and every bit Eager's idea of a tough Irish New York cop.

Gavin squeezed in the back seat of his two-door sports car. He took off fast. The Mustang made a lot of low throbbing noises and Eager assumed this was a mid-life crisis vehicle. He took them to Carney's Yellow Train Car restaurant on Sunset Strip.

Sitting in a dining car on Sunset Strip was interesting, different and unusual, Eager thought. Gavin was more interested in a beer and a burger. After some pleasantries, where Pat thanked them for coming, Eager thought he would test him.

"We are very sorry for your loss, sir. Liberty was such a special lady."

Eager and Gavin watched him closely. Pat was struggling with what to say; in the end, he said, "Yes, it has been devastating for her mother, and I couldn't identify her... well, what was left of her for certain, so there is still hope."

Eager watched and was silent, letting him talk. This was not a devastated father but a cautious ex-policeman scared of something.

"Yes, there is still hope. Could be the missing girlfriend."

Eager decided that he knew Liberty was alive, not just hoped. Gavin was ordering his second beer.

"I did."

"You did what?" Pat sat up.

"I saw from the foot and ankle that it was not Liberty. She has never had a tattoo. Hated them, thought they were cheap and nasty," Eager said slowly and watched.

"You have to be careful. John, isn't it?"

"Careful?"

"Yes, you know better than me, having been through the UK drama with Liberty. If, say, she was alive, she would need to be hidden away until everything is public and then maybe protected for years after. Are we playing games?"

"I think so. You know she is alive and where she is, right?"

"If I did, why would I tell you?"

"Because we can help her get through this."

"How?"

"We know all the players, the background. I can assist as a senior police officer in the UK and, if needed, liaise with the FBI, when I can trust the guys on the case."

"I have worked in the media all my life. I have the contacts around the world to get the story out quickly. Once in the public domain, not much can happen to her. She was hard done by in the UK; we can make it up to her," Gavin cut in.

Pat didn't look convinced this was his only motive.

"She is my daughter. I have to do everything I can to protect her."

"Understood."

"Say I did? I would need you both to keep it secret that I know she is still alive. Did you tell the FBI it was not her?"

"No, thought I would play it safe as well. Said what you said, that I couldn't be sure."

Pat was constantly looking around nervously and wanted to move away fast. The constant looking around gave Eager the heebie-jeebies. Gavin just drank.

"Good. I will get back to you tonight. Stay at the hotel. Does anyone know where you are? Do not phone my home. The bad dudes know she is alive."

"No, we moved due to cost and told no one," Eager lied, not wanting to scare him off helping. "I know they probably know she is alive and are searching for her and not messing around. I agree we all need to be super-careful."

"The FBI can find you if they want, so be careful." He walked away and then suddenly turned and came close to the table, leaning over. "Are you guys armed?"

"No, we don't carry guns."

"It might be wise to do so if you don't want a bullet in your heads. I left Liberty a gift under the bonnet of the car I got her."

Pat threw a twenty note on the table and said farewell; he didn't have time for any more pleasantries. He also needed to get back to his bar and phone her from there. Gavin looked at Eager whilst sipping the dregs of his second beer.

"Well, that was easier than I thought. The service is good here."

You mean the beer is good here, Eager knew.

Chapter 25
Not a Good Meeting

"So, is Eager on his way back?" the commissioner demanded.

Commander Charlie Allcock had come through the force with the commissioner since they were probationers. Normally on first-name terms in private, this was not, though, one of those occasions.

"No."

"No, no! He will do as he is bloody well told or he will be suspended and drummed out of the force! Did you tell him that, Charlie?" The commissioner's hand was trembling with anger.

"Sir, the situation is as I reported. No dupes found. McAllistar says he forced Eager to dupe them as his insurance before handing over the originals. Lost his backpack with the dupes, he says, when he was chased through the bogs. SAS leader says when they picked him up he didn't have a backpack on him. Eager had the same story."

"So you believe them?"

Charlie thought about it. "I can't be certain, but it makes sense. Eager is on leave to see if the potential murder of this Liberty Bell is true; they became close friends."

"Why the hell didn't he tell us about the dupes?" The commissioner was a little calmer.

"There is a lot of bad feeling in the team about the government cover up, protecting these scum, for political reasons. I don't think he wanted us to know in case these were found and handed over as well."

The commissioner walked around the room and stopped at his window with a good view of London. He looked towards Buckingham Palace, where he would get his Lordship, but if this all goes south it would float away down the Thames as per his recurring nightmare. He was also sick in the stomach with the cover-up, as it was hard for him to justify it. Still, he was in sight of his deserved Lordship and needed to play the game one more time and not create waves that could come back like a tsunami and drown him.

"Action is being taken, Charlie, just not public."

"Sir, one bishop paedophile now retired early and sent to the Vatican to live a life of luxury and continue his disgusting habit. That is not action. The rest are still operating as normal; maybe got a smack on the hand, 'do not embarrass us again, be more discreet' — not what they deserve."

The commissioner knew Charlie was the only one entrusted with viewing the videos and handwriting the names and activities of those involved. The handwritten note was handed to the PM's communications guru, McClements. He was the one advising her, in his opinion badly; however, the elections were close. He had been bought off by the PM saying he would be made a lord in the New Year's Honours list. He deserved it, but it was definitely a strong message to 'go along with this strategy and keep quiet, that's a good boy'.

"Charlie, ours is not to reason why, eh? The PM thought the very fabric of British society would crumble if this was made public in a heavy-handed police way."

"The PM has made law and order and justice her main platform for next year's elections; we both know why this happened."

The commissioner was stumped, not knowing what to say, because this was the truth, and he quickly changed tack.

"If Eager won't come back, then get the FBI to pick him up and send him home."

"I would not do that, sir. He is travelling with Gavin Hastings, ex-editor of the *Daily Crier*, according to McAllistar. Imagine the press that would receive? Open a whole new can of worms." Charlie's arms were flailing around as he gesticulated. He did this when demonstrating a point to the team and sometimes in restaurants he would hit waiters by mistake. Today he was working up to a new anger at his boss.

"Damn the press. When he comes back, he will regret his disobedience."

"If he doesn't call a press conference after he has arrested the PM's McClements guy for perverting the course of justice."

"What the bloody well are you talking about?"

Charlie stood up as the commissioner turned quickly from his window towards him. Charlie said nothing.

"Well?"

"Time to pick sides, Sir Michael."

"What?"

Charlie just nodded and walked out.

Chapter 26
The Fix

"So, Ronald. It is Ronald, isn't it?"

"What are you doing here? These are my private chambers!"

"You prefer Judge, then?" Jimmy Harker was at his coolest. He was dressed immaculately as usual, wearing his clothes like a model. All his suits were made by Huntsman from Savile Row, one hundred and seventy years of sartorial elegance serving royalty, style icons and film stars. He looked the part of an aristocrat or a film star.

"I asked you a question. Look, I am going to send for security, so get out."

"Tish, tish, sensitive, aren't you? Were you that sensitive when you were giving this girl" — he pulled a photograph out of his jacket inside pocket showing an underage girl looking very young and scared — "a good sorting out at the Hellfire Club?"

"Get out! Or I will get the police. Now!" He stood up, waving his fat arms about aggressively.

"Ronald, you don't want to do that unless you want your wife, kids, neighbours, friends and the rest of the judiciary seeing the pictures and the statement she has made, identifying you and what you did to her. The media would go crazy — goodbye career, wife and family, not to mention reputation, and maybe hello to a long stint in a cell."

He sank back in his seat. "This is blackmail. I came to your club for privacy, and this is how you treat me. How was I to know she was underage?"

Jimmy sat opposite him, raising his eyebrows at that statement. She didn't look a day over thirteen. "Let's not call it blackmail; it is more me doing you a favour and asking for one in return, and then we all move on."

"Your... your," trying to find the right words in anger, "type will never leave me alone," Ronald said quietly.

"My type? No, you are wrong; this is not about money, but a one-off favour, and I will never bother you again. That's my word."

"Your word with your reputation is worth zilch!"

"I am a legitimate businessman who knows that this world revolves around people scratching each other's backs. I do not want to hurt you, but I will if you do not listen." He said it all calmly but with a force of conviction that made the judge listen carefully.

"Speak," was all Ronald could say.

"My brother's case is coming up here in a month or so when he recovers enough to stand trial. I just need a mis-trial, that's all."

"What? How can I as a judge declare a mis-trial without it being an obvious miscarriage of justice situation? The Crown prosecution would appeal and then you would have another court and another judge, so the exercise is pointless. Plus, I am not listed to try his case."

"Well, get on the list. You are the senior judge around here and probably schedule the trials. Leave the reason for the mis-trial up to me."

Ronald sat silently, his Scottish blood boiling inside him and his heart beating fast in his fat body. He wiped his tufty ginger hair and forehead several times with a cloth he kept close by. The judge's wig always made him sweat when wearing it in court. His big red lips and red hair had given him the nickname, Ronald McDonald, the beefburger judge.

"If you are so sure you have enough facts to create a mis-trial, why do you need me?"

"Just insurance in case a judge misses the point."

"Just leave me alone. I will do my best, that's all I can promise."

"I am sure you will, or I will do my best to expose you if my brother goes to prison."

Jimmy walked out as if he owned the place and slammed the judge's chamber's big wood-panelled door behind him.

Chapter 27
Getting Closer

The *LA Times* was delivered to their hotel door during the early morning. Gavin slept soundly as he had continued drinking in the bar well after Eager had gone to bed. Gavin snored badly; this, and the fact that Pat McGill had not got back to them the evening before, had kept Eager restless. He assumed he knew where Liberty was and would talk to her to get the all-clear for them to meet up.

Time was passing slowly. He decided, after making a coffee, to read the *Times*. He was half way through the front section when he saw a headline. 'UK TOP COP FLIES IN TO HELP FBI WITH LIBERTY BELL INVESTIGATION.' It was a short article that named him and talked about his knowledge of her investigative reporter activities in the UK. It made him out to be a Brit Sherlock Holmes re-incarnated. Who would have done this? The FBI? Leaks at the LAPD? Just then, Gavin snored.

Gavin!

Others were reading the *Times*, and it wasn't long before a phone call to Washington was made. Amanda, the cute, small blonde, was in a local gym. She was working out, fighting two big guys freestyle. As Travis Preston's private assistant, she had time each day to hone her skills. The men had laughed when she challenged them both at the same time and they still thought it was a bit of a joke. They had pumped their muscles that morning and were skilled in self- defence. If they had checked her out with the other gym guys, they might have learned better.

"Come on, boys," she beckoned with her left hand. "Don't be shy. I won't hurt you too much."

"Come on, let's not do this, lady," one said, feeling this was stupid.

"Are you afraid of this little lady, then? Cowards!"

They came towards her, to teach her a lesson. Her speed was incredible: one foot hit the closest man straight on the chin and he sagged and fell to the canvas. The other looked over at him in surprise, which was enough for her to jump up on his shoulders and put her thighs around his neck. It was like she was riding a bucking bronco. He tried to throw her off, thumping at her legs. She just exerted more pressure on his neck and slowly he also fell to the floor. She jumped up; however, he did not move. Stone cold knocked out, or nicely sleeping, as she preferred to think.

The other was just getting up and went towards her. Mistake. He expected a kick and was surprised when she just stood there and let him get close. He swung a big haymaker punch and she ducked, and with amazing speed again hit him six times in his solar plexus. He bent over in pain and she just pushed his forehead and he fell to the canvas.

"Hey, Jimmy," she called to the gym owner, "can't you find some decent competition around here? A girl needs a good work-out?"

He laughed, as he had seen this so many times before. "All right, next time, Amanda, I will take you on."

"Promise?" she said, and he just laughed again.

Tough guy, ex-boxing champion; I think I could take him.

Her male assistant came in as she was showering. He was gay and she did not mind him being in the bathroom with her.

"Got a lead, Amanda dear. Will you please not keep beating the guys up; there will be none left for me," he joked.

She came out nude and started drying herself off.

"Like what?" She read the article.

Interesting. We need to pay this Brit cop a visit.

Eager shook Gavin, who woke with a start.

"What the…?"

Eager held the *LA Times* to his face. "Did you do this?"

He looked sheepish. "Oh, they printed it. Sorry, I thought it would help us find her or her to find us."

"I told you not to unless we run out of steam."

"Sorry, I had already done it."

"Oh, well, if people are looking for Liberty, then they will definitely be looking for this brilliant tracker detective who's bound to know where she is!"

"Sorry," was all Gavin could say.

Eager calmed down as, with any luck, they would be on their way to meet her if Pat McGill came through. They waited for four hours after breakfast and were almost ready for lunch when a call came through to the room. Pat's voice told them to come down to reception. Relieved, they met in a discrete corner of the reception area at a small table with three chairs. He had the *Times* with him.

"What's this?" He held up the article.

"I think that young LAPD detective or the FBI planted the article," Eager jumped in, before Gavin could say he was sorry and admit liability.

"Well, you are in the spotlight now. Not sure you should try and meet Liberty now — you might lead them right to her."

It went quiet and a gloom set in with them.

"What name are you booked in here with?"

"Mine, Gavin Hastings," Gavin spoke out quickly.

"Nobody knows you moved?"

"Not yet, I assume," Eager lied, hoping that they could still get going to meet her.

Pat leaned forward. "You have to move quickly then, real quick." He handed them two driving licences as false IDs. He told them to go get a ticket cash to Vegas, a thirty-minute flight from LA, from the Burbank Airport, and they leave every hour or so. "Upon arrival, take a hire a car with the IDs," and he handed them a credit card matching Eager's 'John Houston' false ID.

"The hire companies will only take credit cards. Do not get excited, there's only one thousand on the card. When you see Liberty, give it to her, as she is probably running low." He told them the pin code.

"Then drive to Palm Springs, dump the car back at the hire company at Palm Springs International airport, two miles from the city centre, and then go by cab to the city centre. No loose talk with the cabbie; stop on the high street, but not close to where you are going to meet her. You need to walk to the Desert Fox Bar and wait outside. If you move quickly, you can be there early evening."

"Convoluted way to get there?" Eager questioned.

"Yes, and get some tourist stuff on. The IDs are from Arizona cowboy land. Try dressing up, as they are looking for stiff upper lip Brits."

"Thanks," Eager said, not liking the description but appreciating the help.

"How do we find her?" Gavin asked.

"You don't. She will find you if she thinks it is okay, no one following you."

Convoluted okay.

They went to the Beverley shopping centre, exchanged some traveller's cheques for cash and found a Western-style shop. Jeans, boots, shirts and cowboy hats seemed to do the trick. Gavin's hat was an enormous white Stetson, and Eager could not help laughing as it fell over his head and Gavin had to keep pushing it back up.

"No one will recognise these uptight and tight-lipped Brits. Especially not you, pardner," Eager teased. They then caught a cab to Burbank Airport and followed instructions to the letter. In the small plane, Gavin's hat kept getting in the way of the other passengers. There was no room for it in the overhead carry-on holding compartments and the hostess came to talk to him.

"Apologies, mam, not used to riding these big horses," Gavin tried his very bad American accent. Eager cringed. The hostess looked at them both, shook her head slightly; she had seen it all before on the many flights to Vegas, and walked away.

"Just do not speak," Eager told him.

It was going to be a long day.

Chapter 28
To Tell or Not to Tell

"Sit down!" The PM was curt and pointed to the chair opposite her desk to the right. It was known as the 'uncomfortable' chair by those that had been there for her wrath and tirades. The Bulldog McClements sensed this was not going to be a good meeting.

"Yes, PM, is there a problem?"

"In our job there is always a problem." She seemed exhausted; it was past eight p.m. after a stressful afternoon at PM's Question Time in the Commons and then, as usual, meetings after meetings.

"I had a visit from Sir Michael. A very difficult meeting for him and myself. He had to tell me about the possibility — he stressed possibility — that the tapes were copied."

"Fuck! How?"

"Seems this McAllistar would not let go of the originals until he had insurance, so dupes were made. Says he lost them on the moors in a bog when he was under attack."

"Why did you not call me into the meeting?"

"This is a very sensitive issue and you and Sir Michael do not get on very well. No need to inflame the situation. His team are upset that these perverts have not been brought to book, using his terminology. He is worried that if no action is taken, perverting the course of justice could be a case for us to answer. A PR nightmare with an election coming soon enough."

"So, on a scale of one to ten, how sure was he that they have been lost? I mean, the bog will degrade them quickly if they were, so no issues."

"I never asked him that straight, but reading him I would say it was fifty/fifty."

"Not good at all. I have been following this Liberty Bell in the US and it seems she is either dead or hiding. She made comments that she would prove she wasn't a fantasist upon arrival with confidence. Now the *LA Times* has our DCI Eager in town helping the FBI, which I was told was an unofficial trip. Add these two together and two and two make more than four."

It went quiet as the PM was thinking hard for, it seemed, a long time. The Bulldog just waited, hoping he had analysed this wrong. Not likely, though; he got to be Number Ten's communications guru due to his intuitive thinking.

"Which means?" The PM was getting a little frustrated and tapping her Montblanc pen on her desk harder and harder. If he could make out the beat properly, he thought it was to the tune *Anything Goes.*

"In my opinion, she has the dupes, possibly helped by Eager."

The tapping on the desk continued for almost five minutes, as no one spoke. Both were weighing up the situation. The Bulldog's neck veins bulged.

Her private secretary barged into the conference room. She just held up her hand.

"Not now, Sir Jeffrey!"

"I thought I could be..."

"Not now!" He scurried away. "Advice?" She stopped tapping the pen and looked him straight in the eyes.

"Options are limited. The safest way is to move into some sort of defensive action where we can say that this is a high-level investigation and action is in progress. Then when — excuse my English — the shit hits the fan, we can say that investigations are ongoing and at a sensitive stage."

"A real investigation? You know the names on this list! I may as well resign and hand the keys to Number Ten to that other party." He was always amused that she never said the 'other' party's name.

"Well, the only way out, it would seem, believing she has the tapes, is to pre-empt her announcement that the Met Police have broken a major paedophile ring, with our support, of course. I mean, the headlines would read, 'PM SETS UP SPECIAL TASK FORCE TO STOP A MAJOR PAEDOPHILE RING AT THE VERY TOP OF BRITISH SOCIETY'. The PM says no one is above the law and so on and so forth."

"You have the list; these are major supporters, key people in society and at least one government minister — and what about number seven?"

"Acceptable losses, collateral damage, if this government is to survive. God, your ratings will jump up."

"You want me to tell that to Her Majesty? Do you?"

Chapter 29
Jigsaw Puzzle Progress

They sat in the big conference room. Steve, Sonia and the chief, De Silva. It was mid-morning, and they all hugged coffees as if their lives depended on the caffeine hits.

"So, what have we got?" The chief was straight to business.

Steve and Sonia looked at each other to see who was going to go first. Steve decided it should be her in the hot seat, as he was the senior.

"Not a lot; however, some of the pieces are coming together. Let me bullet point them and Steve can update you on the Las Vegas end," she started, using the whiteboard with key points and talking through them.

"DCI Eager and his media friend have managed to go off our map. No idea where they are at present. They left no contact details; last seen leaving the motel, luggage en tow.

"The Met have not answered any requests for more information and I have asked for our local team to visit Commander Allcock and the commissioner, if possible, to get answers. Certainly to check Eager's story.

"The head has been found, and it is more than likely this was the girlfriend, not Bell. Awaiting confirmation from the ME. Steve?"

He stood up and avoided the whiteboard — he didn't need props that slowed him down. The chief was busy and had little patience, he knew. His impatient heavy breathing said, 'Get on with it.'

"Las Vegas office has confirmed that our 'midnight cowboy' Gonzalez was there in full rhinestone cowboy regalia that day. He was a well-known character on the Strip and stood out like a sore thumb, so it was easy for them working the Strip to follow his movements. Barman at the Margarita Bar says he was there around seventeen hundred hours that night, had a few Coronas and watched TV News. He says he asked him how much a billion dollars were and seemed interested in the news on Travis Preston's announcement about his presidential run."

Sonia looked a little shocked and annoyed he had not shared this information with her prior to the meeting and he was bringing Travis Preston into the picture. She stared daggers at him and if looks could kill, Steve would be lying on the floor in a body bag, stiff as a board, awaiting the undertaker's box.

"And?" The chief wanted him to keep moving.

"Well, this is where it gets a little strange. He told the barman he wanted to ring Preston and was virtually told to dream on, and he replied that he would take his call. The barman thought he was on something, but he did direct him to Preston's new campaign office further down the Strip. The campaign manager was interviewed and just said he remembered this strange cowboy Mex... sorry, Mexican," Steve corrected himself as De Silva's heritage was Mexican, "knocking on the window, wanting to come in. The office was just setting up and was closed. He asked him what he wanted and he told him to join up to support Preston. Considering him maybe drunk, he sent him away. The manager was young and seemed a bit nervous when being interviewed."

"That it?" the impatient chief asked.

"Not quite. He was then seen at the Nacho Daddy restaurant on the Strip later, around seventeen hundred and thirty. Drinking more, eating a lot and he told the waiter he tipped a twenty to that this was, and I quote, 'My lucky day'. He was upbeat and left around eighteen forty-five. Not seen again after that."

"What do you think he meant by his lucky day?"

"Probably made a lot of cash with his drugs and had been drinking a lot. Preston is popular in the Hispanic community, so maybe he was keen to help," Sonia cut in.

"Not sure a potential Republican president is for illegal immigrants, so how could he be popular with Mexicans?"

"That's what I hear, that's all," Sonia muttered.

The chief considered this. "So, Steve, what do you make of all this?"

"I don't think we should make too much of it," Sonia cut in again. "A Mexican drug pusher had a good day. Drank too much or maybe also smoked some of his own stuff, saw the news and in his state decided he would get involved in politics. It's funny, really. He probably sold more dope than usual, which was why it was his lucky day."

"Mmmm," the chief said, not totally convinced. "Steve?"

"That's all plausible and possible. They found an old car on a back street in Vegas today with some papers with his name on. He left the Nacho Daddy and paid in cash, according to their till receipts, at eighteen fifty. He was killed at approximately nineteen thirty-eight in the Mojave, according to the ME. So how did he get approximately one hundred miles in forty minutes? Even if he got a lift, this beggars belief; the traffic is always very busy at night on the I15."

Sonia was breathing heavily. She did want to kill him. Talk about being blindsided.

"A lift is possible," she came up with. "Fast driver, it is possible, averaging over one hundred; maybe he felt too drunk to drive, or his drug lord's henchmen or Geronimo got him."

What else was this bastard holding back? she thought.

"One scenario I agree. Connecting the dots and making some assumptions…"

Steve waited for the most impact. He had them held tightly in his hand, totally absorbed, awaiting his conclusions. This is where his experience served him well.

"Yes?" The chief brought him back.

"Yes, well, as I said, connecting the dots. DCI Eager we both agree was holding something back. He didn't trust us for some reason, so I feel we didn't get the whole story. I know Sonia felt the same way. So, if these videos left with this Arturo guy in the lonely desert were looked at, did he see someone he recognised? That set in motion his demise?"

"Travis Preston, you think? Wait a minute, Steve…" The chief caught on to the thread of his conclusion.

"Really? Travis Preston. Steve, you are jumping to conclusions. Do you really think Travis came and killed this guy? You are not only jumping to conclusions, I think you are jumping wider than the Grand Canyon! Really!" Sonia decided it was time to stick it to the old timer.

Steve scratched his crotch so she could see, when the chief stood up and turned around to get another coffee. He knew he could drive her crazy. The chief did not offer anyone else a mug. They could get it themselves. He was thinking hard. If Preston was involved, this was way above his pay grade. If he let Steve go off half-assed, then both of them would be lucky to be cleaning the FBI toilets in Alaska. If an iota of this was true, this could be the biggest case in recent history, the making of the new Director of the FBI. Risk and reward. That awful balance. He wasn't like the British SAS, whose slogan was 'Who Dares Wins'. He was a senior FBI officer. Things were thought out, facts found, then conclusions made and political implications considered. He could not afford to jump to conclusions like Steve. Even if a rumour got out — and, as with all agencies, rumours do — then the higher-ups would fall on him.

He also had in Sonia a new member of the team to consider. Teams drop to a low level when a new member is introduced. It takes time and trust until the efficiency of the team gets back to a reasonable level. She obviously has clout at HQ. Steve and she seem to hate each other, and she always takes the opposite view. If she leaks this as even an avenue we might be pursuing it could cause chaos, especially if he was not going to report this at this point. He had to be seen to cut this option off at the knees right now. Steve would just have to take it on the chin.

"Steve, top marks for creative thinking, but this is too way out there for us even to consider. No, you have to look at alternatives. Get off this horse. Preston is a great guy, a war hero and probably will make the best president we have had since Roosevelt. You need to find Eager and Bell as soon as possible."

Steve was dejected. Sonia was enjoying the rebuke and smiling at him. A 'told you so' look.

"Mr McGill, Sonia?" The chief saw what was happening and he needed to break up this dysfunctional team soon.

'Well, yes. I think it is pretty certain he helped Liberty and knew she was okay. So he lied to the FBI, although I can't prove that at the moment. Checking at the studio where he works, he took out an old white Chevelle car from the props department; however, he is not using it himself, nor is his girlfriend. He has a Mustang and she has a Merc, this year's model. It coincides with Bell being here and Arturo's mother says she was driving a white car when she visited. I would like to have an all-points bulletin put out in California?"

"Get it done. We need to find them. I can only guess that Eager and this Hastings guy have connected with her."

"That all?"

"Yes." They both answered.

"Well, this is what we do next. Sonia I am authorising your trip to London. The local staff do not have the insight we have, never interviewed Eager and, of course, are not up to date with recent events. Work with the Bureau chief; I will call her tonight to expect you. We need to know everything, especially if there are any videos with our people on them."

Steve looked deflated. Sonia beamed, giving Steve a sly look.

"Steve, get onto finding them — and I also have a guest for you to look after."

Chapter 30
The Cleansing Lists

He sat near the big window in his den at his ranch, 'The Plum Creek Bar' in Texas, watching a Learjet land on his runway. The ranch was named after the victory over the Comanches in 1845 and it used to be the name of Lockhart town. Bar denotes that the ranch has registered blood lines tracing back to the legendary quarter horse racing stallion Three Bars were resident there.

He was dressed in blue jeans, cowboy boots and a checked Western shirt. He held a cold beer in his hand, his fourth this morning. The room's two side walls were filled with all his hunting trophies, heads of anything that can be shot on plaques with name, date and place inscribed below. The walls had beautiful wooden mahogany panels matching the big desk — a few trees had to be slaughtered to make these. The floors did not escape dead animals: all types of skins — lions, leopards, bucks, bear — simply spread out all around. People mostly walked around them in some sort of homage to the hunter and the hunted. The wall behind his desk was full of memories: Army pictures from various theatres of operation, pictures of him with several presidents, medals, campaign rallies, music and movie stars he mixed with. A big dramatic picture of a major oil well blowout was front and centre. His family's start to riches.

To the side of his desk was a secret metal door hidden under the mahogany panels that went into his personal armoury. With these and the weapons he kept in and around his desk, there was enough of all types to start a small war and win.

The wooden bar was something else; it could have come out of the biggest pub in Ireland. He loved entertaining and serving guests from behind it. Every major beer you could think of was on tap and other specialist beers in the fridges. He reckoned he had a beer from every country in the world. The walls held an amazing number of liquors and other fridges were especially designed for wines from all over the world.

His red wines kept at room temperature in the dark and he got them re-corked in Italy every five years.

Beautiful and comfortable loungers were spread around the room, and in the centre was the biggest electrical bucking bull on the planet. He loved to test the skill and nerve of his guests.

Travis went back to his double-sized lounge chair. The big man's chair. It was a leather Chesterfield specially designed for him to his requirements. He called it his love chair.

Amanda burst in looking incredible; although in casual clothes, they looked straight out of a fashion magazine. Low-cut white blouse, tight-fitting leather jeans and white pumps. She ran and jumped onto his lap, to his delight.

"How's my big boy?" Sticking her hand down his jeans front. "How we doing down there?" She played with him a little until he saw the helicopter land.

"Up, young lady, we have company," he said. She seemed reluctant to get off him. He was never sure one hundred percent about her. She was ambitious, very ambitious, and had tied her future to his wagon. He was her chance of fame and fortune which she would do anything for. So it was maybe not love, but he could trust her and the sexual intervals were a lot of relief and fun. Wife and kids at their Hawaii home at present and he was often away in Washington and other trips, so plenty of opportunity to play.

The general walked straight to the back of the building and into the den via a small entrance door hidden in the back wall and covered by the mahogany panels inside. He had been here many times before and was trusted with the code for the automatic door. He was sure, though, to press the bell and look at the entry camera first, just in case Travis had been partying and then playing with his guns. He knew that Travis had bad flashbacks to Vietnam as, despite his rank, he always led from the front and was in many dangerous situations. The general knew he got a kick out of the action adrenaline, especially the killing. It was here, he believed, that Travis had become immune to murder, and it was carrying over to the new battlefield of civilian life and politics.

"Gerald, welcome. Drink?"

"No, thanks." He nodded to Amanda. He carried a small black attaché case handcuffed to his wrist. He was in a dark suit with an open white shirt, highly polished brown shoes, immaculate as usual. Travis pointed to a lounge seat opposite his. Amanda was behind the bar mixing a cocktail and putting on some coffee, as she knew they would need it sooner or later.

"If you are making coffee, Amanda, I will have one; just black, thanks," the general said without even looking in her direction.

"Me, too. Gerald, where do you want to start?" Travis asked, swilling the rest of his beer down. Gerald unlocked his briefcase first at the wrist and then the front lock. Out came three pieces of paper.

"First, what we know so far is the Bell girl, the detective from the Met and the newspaper editor are here and probably together. We have the car number, colour and make and have the police in CA on the lookout. Her dad probably knows where she is and we need to move on him as soon as possible."

"Why has this not been done already?" Travis asked in a now frustrated voice that came after alcohol.

"We are watching him to see where he leads us. Listening in even now at his work. There are at least fifty phones he might use there, so a big operation. If we take him he will probably not talk, as his rep is that he is a really tough customer. Plus, this is his daughter: get one, the other goes crazy. We need to clean up both at the same time."

"Fair enough," Travis conceded.

"We have someone in the UK checking out the rest and helping us plan where they are, so when ready we can move with speed in one sweep."

"Won't that make a big stir? Not many murders in the UK." Amanda, handing out the coffees, sat down.

"That's why I am here to discuss strategies, agents, methods and timing." Gerald coughed. He was not enjoying what he was doing.

"The cleansing list?" Travis was getting impatient.

"I have two; the first is a 'must do now' list and the second one is for consideration. I mean, do they present a threat in the future?" He handed the first list to Travis. Amanda walked around and sat on his chair arm to look over his shoulder. Gerald read out each name and highlighted who and what they were, in case Travis did not know or had forgotten.

Travis read out loud list one. Liberty Bell (recover and destroy the tapes), DCI Eager, Gavin Hastings (ex-editor, the *Daily Crier*), Logan McAllistar, Tazewell Javelin, Gina Jones, CIA, Phil Worthington-Brown, MI5.

The second list was handed to him. "This is a debatable list."

"Debatable? Nothing's debatable," Travis jumped in.

"This list has Jimmy and Nick Harker on it. They said they had never seen the video but knew of your visit, saw the girl afterwards and found out what the shakedown was that Javelin had organised. Nick's in prison hospital, Jimmy's well protected.

"Commander Allcock of the Met. He is known to have watched all the videos except yours, but we cannot be sure. DCI Eager may have told him — again, not sure."

There was a silence for five minutes. Eventually, Travis just said, "Do them all as soon as possible in any order. We must avoid any connection between the hits and, most of all, nothing to come back to me. Get the videos and Amanda must personally destroy mine as soon as it is picked up." He looked at her enough to say, 'You must be at the front of this; I cannot trust anyone but you.' Gerald caught and understood the inference of this statement, which did nothing to make him happy. "Then keep the rest; we might be able to use them later against the Brits. If needed in future when I am president."

"It must be done with some subtlety this time; no heavy-handed soldiers running around like they are on the beaches of Normandy," Amanda butted in. Gerald disliked her. He knew she had been a CIA agent and was good at that type of work — the black arts. She, though, had too much influence over Travis and he could imagine her putting his name on list three.

"I have the supplier list of people and skills we might use. They are not cheap, but it can be done without a trace leading back to us. I also have a strategy that I think will work of getting some of the dirty work done by others on the list, spreading confusion and stopping the police connecting the disposals."

"We can work together on the details," Amanda put in. Travis did not want the details; nor should he be lumbered with the how. He knew the why, and that was enough. He just needed it cleaned up, pronto.

"Good idea." Travis was comfortable with Amanda and the general involved together, a good balance to get the cleansing done. Turning to Gerald, whose face betrayed his thoughts. "I see what's left of your hit team from the UK are not on any of the lists?"

Gerald simply shrugged.

Chapter 31
McAllistar

Logan did as many sit-ups as he could. His daily exercise routine was nothing like it was when he was fit in the Army, nor when he worked out in prison. He was impatient with himself and disregarded a lot of his doctor's advice on how he should recover. He tired easily and took regular breaks, determined to get fit. Gone were his Army regimental boxing champion days, when he could run for miles and work out for hours. The anger inside him had kept him going. It was now hard for him to sleep as he felt so responsible for what had happened, especially to Aunt Bessie.

The nightmares usually had him trying to exact revenge, but never being able to hurt anyone. A punch would just bounce off his dark opponent like he had no strength, which he felt was partially true. He would see faces in exact detail taunting him, coming and going with no real time to hit them, except his unknown dark opponent; either way, it made no difference. Nick and Jimmy Harker, Tazewell Javelin, the Americans, Karein, even the dead Dirk Ryder — faces bopping in and out of his mind, tormenting him. Karein, he had foolishly loved and she had led him on, taken him down the wrong path; she had used him. How could he move emotionally from deep love to such anger and rejecting her? Or was it his lifelong feeling of being rejected?

She had saved him by putting her body in front of him when the shooter struck. So maybe she loved him at some level, even though she had told him she loved her girlfriend. A lie? A ruse to get rid of him?

He guessed he always wanted a home, a wife he loved and a family. Not having that as a child, he only glimpsed happiness and love with his adopted aunt and uncle on his short visits for holidays to their farm. They really loved each other and when he was in their company it was sheer happiness. They just did the simple things and could talk for hours together, despite their long marriage. He wanted all that, so he easily succumbed to a woman he thought he could change and give a home to. The happy ending that was fated never to happen for him and most people. He was down and morose.

He had made himself busy building defences around the main farmhouse and cottage. He strengthened the windows with wrought-iron bars. He got extra metal security doors to ensure what the Russians did breaking in would never happen again. No surprises were needed. He slept mainly in the farmhouse; however, he knew he needed to vary his routine, so sometimes he would bunk-up in the cottage and leave the lights on at the farmhouse as a distraction.

He believed in Attila the Hun's philosophy being that you can't protect everything, so protect what's important.

The farmhouse had an alarm, but he added more lights and beams around the place. Trip wires in the garden to set off flares. The feral animals could set these off at night, which was a problem he was prepared to live with. The farm was so big, with barns and outhouses that people could sneak up and hide behind. The back of the house faced fields going up the hill. Little cover for anyone approaching; just the stone walls and a few small copses. To come that way would be difficult, as you had to walk over three fields uphill back to a road, so the escape route would be a problem for a quick exit. The farm had two shotguns and a few cartridges, which was good enough for him. He made small spears as stakes with his Army knife. On top of this he kept boxes of flares his Army friends had brought him, plus some fireworks. They used to be penny bangers for Guy Fawkes's night, not too harmful; however, tie three together and they would give people a big fright. Not the best explosives around, but safe and enough to help him to distract and defend and maybe then attack the intruders.

He did not discount a sniper who could shoot accurately for miles, so his movements outside were always quick. In Northern Ireland during the Troubles the soldiers who were shot were the ones standing around on corners, smoking or moving slowly, which was very sloppy. The Marines, paras, guards and other elite forces never stopped moving on patrol. Hard targets to hit, and if you missed, the retaliation would be deadly.

It pays to be super-sensitive as I've already been shot and the drama has not yet ended.

Scotty had called in once or twice with Romeo to see he was okay. He always rang first to ensure he did not surprise Logan. That could be bad news for both of them. He had offered Romeo for security and company, but McAllistar couldn't accept. Scotty and his wife were still at risk if the Russians decided to get revenge for him killing their agents. Plus, he knew the emotional trauma the dog had suffered losing its mate. Again, something else on his conscience.

Phil the Nosy Postie came at eleven a.m., his regular time each morning, if he had mail. He wanted to talk about anything and everything; this was not, though, Logan's style. Logan said little as a rule — he believed if everyone in the world were given just so many words at birth and would die when used up, they would use them wisely. Less gossip, less abuse, less politicians. Phil always mentioned that it was good he kept a routine and that he had saved Logan's life by ensuring the mail got through on time.

If I hear that one more time.

Still, Logan put up with it as it was true, and he moved Phil on as quickly as possible. The mail was mainly for Aunt Bessie: bills, flyers and the odd letter he guessed from old friends who had not heard the bad news. *They must live in Outer Mongolia*, he thought. Never opening anything in the mail without his name on. He just piled the rest up in the fire basket. He was waiting on his notification that his compensation for false imprisonment had come through and an update from Denise, Eager's sidekick and friend. She used mail and a false name to keep him informed. Telephoning was risky. Not that there was much news from the US.

He knew he needed to get into a better frame of mind. He had let his hair grow and now had a scruffy beard clinging to his face. It tickled and annoyed him and he thought of shaving it off, but somehow never got around to doing it. He wore the same Army desert combat trousers, green vest and boots day in, day out. Not the smart soldier McAllistar he was used to.

At lunch he would drink beer and later in the afternoon a few bottles of wine. Never getting to a point of being out of control, drunk or even tipsy, as he had to have his wits about him. He worried, though, that he was drinking more and more. Boredom, loneliness, anticipation of what was to come, he was not sure; maybe all of them. So he spent his afternoons thinking about where he was in life, what had happened; and then, after a couple of glasses, tried to plan a future. Meditation used to be one of his main types of relaxation. He would just hand over his issues to the universe to find the answers. Letting go was his mantra. Now he found this hard to do when he knew that the current situation was not over; his mind would take him back to the now and what could happen. Of course, people worry about hundreds of things in their life that never ever happen. It's called stress and he totally believed that is where cancer comes from. Normally calm and cool and worry-free, he was now becoming a basket case.

He looked straight into his own eyes, staring into the old mirror in the bathroom. *Logan, you have got to get yourself together. Together. Together.*

He reviewed the police raid. Commander Allcock had screamed at him, where were the tapes? Who has them? Have you spoken to Eager? Water off a duck's back to Logan. If the Army did one thing for him, that was to understand the screaming and shouting, most of which was not real. Like on parade, the sergeant-major walking behind him. "Am I hurting you, son?" "No, sir." "Well, I bloody well should be — I'm standing on your hair!" Allcock was all right, he believed, as once the search team had done its job and he went up to the cottage, he sat down with him. A totally different tone and demeanour.

"Look, son, if you talk to Eager, tell him to contact me on the QT. He knows which side I am on. Right?"

Logan was his usual self, not commenting like, 'Why the bloody hell have you flown in and ripped my house apart then?' This guy was tired and only doing his job, probably pushed by the higher-ups. There are always higher-ups. Then there was that creep DCI Fenwick. He saw regular police patrols drive by after stopping and looking down the drive for a minute. If he wasn't mistaken, he had seen Fenwick do the same several times. Protection or just prying, awaiting an opportunity?

It was happy hour again and first he locked up securely. Alarm and lights on and shotgun loaded. Curtains were always drawn for the mythical potential sniper. He laughed to himself about that. He heard a bicycle and a knock came to the door. "It's me, Phil the Postie," came the shout. This was not Phil's time to come and he was so regular. Logan's heart started beating heavily. Logan peered out carefully and only saw Phil. He had a letter in his hand, waving it.

"I missed this in my bag this morning," he said dolefully, feeling he had let himself and the post office down.

Logan took the letter. Phil started to say, "I think this is your girlfriend, by the sweet smell of it. Being a postie all my..."

"Thanks," was all Logan would say, and he closed the door and bolted it.

"I always get the post through," Phil said to himself and jumped on his bike, a bit sad that his extra effort in his own time had not been more welcomed.

It was unsigned and undated, but he knew it was from Denise. Good news and bad. Eager had said Liberty was still alive and kicking. Gavin was with him on the way to find her. The situation still volatile and dangerous there and a warning to Logan that they might try to clean up anyone who had seen the US tape. Stay safe. Burn this, please. He had to admit that he missed the little team he had reluctantly joined.

He mused over it, read it several times, and reviewed his current situation in the UK. After two cigarettes and a bottle of Chardonnay, suddenly his plan moving forward became clear.

Chapter 32
The Start

"Jesus fucking Christ, how the hell did you get in here?" Jimmy was startled.

The man sat in the dark on the chair at the side of Jimmy's bed. Jimmy's mind raced. *He's going to kill me.* Tazewell's guy, McAllistar? He needed to jump up and at least try and protect himself; not really his forte, though. As he tried to make him out in the darkness, the guy seemed small and thin, all dressed in black. If he wasn't mistaken, he had a priest's white collar around his neck.

"I am not here, Mr Harker, to kill you. If I was, it would already be done. Quieter that way, and better that targets go off in their sleep. Gives me a warm feeling. So calm down, I have an offer — like they say in the movies — you simply cannot refuse."

It made sense to Jimmy, who sat up slowly. Where the bleeding hell was his security guys? How did he get around the alarms? Obviously, this guy was a professional killer. Stay calm, see what the deal is and talk yourself out of this situation.

"Can I put the bedside light on?"

"No, definitely not, Mr Harker. If you did you would recognise me and I would be forced to terminate this meeting." The emphasis was on terminate, and Jimmy had no doubt what he meant.

"Okay, please tell me, what is this deal I cannot refuse?"

"Actually, from what I have been told, this is a good deal for you, so I am sure your current concerns will just dissipate once you have heard what I have to say."

He sounds Asian-American, cultured voice, calm, cool, polite and expert for certain, definitely a paid hit man. The way he talks and his voice is higher than a man's should be; could it be a woman? Jimmy's mind was racing and he wanted to gather as much info on this intruder as possible.

"That's good; please continue." Jimmy was getting back some of his cool.

"It's simple. My people would like you to help clean up a mess that was created at your club under your watch. If you comply, then we will leave you and your brother alone."

"And?"

He put forward the deal quietly and succinctly. He did not ask for an answer, he simply produced a pistol and fired into Jimmy's neck.

Mad Mike and Jordy found him at eleven a.m. in his bedroom. He was fast asleep. Mike shook him hard. Slowly, he started to come around and then tried to go back to sleep.

"Get water!" Mike shouted at Jordy.

"Propa? Where?"

"From the bathroom, buck eejit." Good job Jordy did not understand half of what Mike said, and vice versa. Mike was an ex-terrorist with brains but no morals or scruples, whilst Jordy was pure muscle, who enjoyed hurting people badly and always thought he was even-handed, as in each case he convinced himself they deserved it. Bald, with tattoos down his neck and all over his body. MOMMA tattooed across his left-hand fingers and JOLEN across his right-hand fingers. *Jolen* was supposed to be the song *Jolene* by Dolly Parton, which his mother liked so much. He was drunk and fell asleep as the tattoo artist worked. Counting was not one of his big skills and spelling was the tattoo artist's failing. "This one's from momma and this one is from Jolen," he would say as he punched his poor prey stupid.

Mike was a scruffy-looking boy from Belfast. Average size, long black hair, overweight and always wore his lucky black duffle coat, which went down to his knees. He grew up on the streets burning buses and throwing rocks at the police and Army. Recruited into the IRA and then the Provos when fully tested and trusted. The Provisional Irish Republican Army, which is the right-wing military organisation, a branch of the political IRA. They found he had an interest and talent for explosives and long-range rifle shooting: a born sniper. They invested in him by sending him overseas to other terrorist organisations to learn more and practice. He had no fear at all and was responsible for many

122

deaths, not only of police and Army personnel but also innocent civilians. His last bomb was in a Protestant town's marketplace, which killed twelve civilians, including four young children, and maiming thirty more. This was an unauthorised action. Which meant no warning had been given, as was the practice for public-place bombings. It brought down bad PR for the IRA and a loss of public donation income from overseas, notably the US. He got out of NI before he was knee-capped or worse and became a freelancer.

"Give me the water." Mad Mike then threw it in Jimmy's face. He came around again this time with a start. He sat up and wiped his face on his silk pyjama sleeve.

"Towel!" he shouted. Jordy ran off back to the bathroom to get one. Jimmy then wiped his face and neck. When he did, he found the hole where the dart had gone in — he had been tranquillised. Breathing deeply, trying to stay calm. The big headache was like someone was hitting him over the head with a club. They waited for him to speak. It took time, as he seemed to be completely groggy. More water was brought, and headache tablets.

"'Bout ye?" Mike asked.

"About me? Just dandy — what do you think?" The sarcasm went over their heads.

"Propa?" Jordy asked.

"Really! You idiot, I was almost killed, shot with a tranquilliser that was probably meant for an elephant. Hole in the neck, head feels like it's about to come off. Propa!" Jimmy understood a bit of Jordy slang.

"How the fuck did he get in? This is three storeys up; no alarm, and no security bloody awake?" Mike was angry.

"Bathroom window is open, boss. I thought you'd opened it for fresh air. I do that." Jordy was not doing himself any favours.

"So, we are dealing with Spiderman," Mike added.

"More like a priest." Jimmy explained he thought the guy or woman had a priest's collar on.

"Dead on. If not Spiderman, then it's those bloody prod vicars." Jimmy was sure Mike must be joking with a straight face. He held his tongue; he needed these guys now more than ever.

They checked everything around the house. The bathroom window must have been the way he got in. Then they interviewed, with a few punches, the two, night guards. They probably went to sleep after the boss lay down, Jordy thought, so they deserved a good slap. Also, he was now to stay every night to watch them. That alone deserved a few punches in their balls.

The deal was simple on the surface. The Harkers had to clear up the mess they or their staff created — that being terminating (a word the intruder loved) Tazewell Javelin and Logan McAllistar. Done in a manner that no one suspected would be in any way connected with or anything to do with the claims the reporter Bell had made. It was a good deal, Jimmy thought, as both were enemies and were down in his book for the same treatment when the time was right. In exchange, the Harkers were left to live, provided they gave proof of their involvement in the murders to ensure they would move on and did not become an issue further down the track.

McAllistar had been shot by what they had claimed to be a US hit team. It was made clear to him that this time it needed to be clearly different, where the blame goes nowhere near the US. Tazewell was with the Yardies, a violent gang. The police must be onto this, so not a stretch of the imagination that they could be blamed. How was the question?

"Get me Sammy the Squirrel and let me get up."

Sammy had been wounded in the burning down of the Hellfire Club at the abbey, known as the 'Gunfight at the OK Abbey' by the press. He had recovered and as no weapon had his prints on and he just claimed to be there and innocent, he had got off any charges. Sammy's skill was that he was a whizz at finding people. Small, scruffy and wearing his trademark raincoat, he arrived within thirty minutes. Jimmy was in the kitchen, drinking water and taking more painkillers. Jordy had just called him and gave no reason, nor did Sammy need one.

"Boss, you called?"

"Sit, Sammy, I have the most important job you have ever done for me."

Here it comes. It's been too quiet. Sammy anticipated an important mission.

Jimmy explained the deal and what happened. Sammy looked like someone off the street or down on his luck; however, he was intuitive and very street smart. His brain was as good as anyone's at the subjects he excelled in, that being tracking, finding and recruiting talent for the team. He had his ears fixed to the ground and his eyes wandered everywhere. He knew what was going on in the city of London's underworld. He earned well off the Harkers; most he spent on his big weakness, gambling on the horses.

Jimmy gave him a run-down of the night's events. Sammy whistled, surprised that his boss could be so easily compromised.

"Your tasks are to find this assassin dressed, I think, as a priest. Someone will know, or has he or she just flown in from the US maybe, or Hong Kong? Not sure he has to be staying somewhere in London. At the same time, find me a way of getting at Taz. Can we set him up somehow?"

"Received and understood, boss. On my way."

"Oh, Sammy, I have a tight deadline, a very tight deadline."

"Got it, boss."

Jimmy liked this about Sammy. He needed only a quick brief and asked few questions, unless they were pertinent to his task. He was like a squirrel, always running around, storing away information, and hiding his nuggets of information like a squirrel hides its nuts for winter. Always reliable and loyal to the last.

"Mike, McAllistar was in the Troubles in NI, a soldier, a Marine, and at some stage, according to Nick, on the streets in plainclothes with this group called Hush Puppies. Surveillance or assassins, no one is sure."

"Troubles? A war, so it was. Heard of them — yes, they were taking out our guys for sure. A mingin' lot. So?"

"It is not beyond the realms of belief that your old lot would seek him out and kill him, is it? I mean, payback for some, let me say, crime against them."

"So it has to look like the IRA. Bomb would be the best. Then a call saying he was a murderer and claim the killing for them."

"You got it. In one."

"They will be miffed and may come looking to find who blamed them."

"A risk we need to be willing to take, eh?"

"Me?" Jordy asked.

"You keep me safe. Even if you have to sleep at my door. Check everywhere I go. Be my shadow. Get a gun you can conceal. And for God's sake check the windows and every door every night personally."

He needed now to ring the Guv in Nick's prison, the prisoner boss who runs the place, to tell him what happened and the need for extra security to keep Nick safe, and then call Glaswegian Fergus and get him to earn his keep.

There is no one who knows the higher criminal world in London as well as I do. Jimmy loved quoting Sherlock Holmes.

Chapter 33
Reunited

Liberty had tucked her skateboard under her arm and was wearing a simple summer dress from the wardrobe at her dad's house. Big flower patterns all over it, which she hated. Still, it fitted in with this sleepy area with mainly old retirees living there, and she wasn't risking wearing her scruffy street disguise as it would scare these people. She looked back and could easily see the trunk of the white Chevelle sticking out of the car port leaning to the side of the bungalow. A dead giveaway — she needed to cover the car.

She carried a bag with her cap and scruffy clothes she had arrived in LA with. After a couple of blocks, she stood at the back of a big tree and quickly whipped off the dress and put on her disguise. If her neighbours had seen her new gear, they would have called the police. If the local sheriff had been around while she did this she would have been arrested for indecent exposure. Only an old guy with a tiny dog passed by, and he must have looked when her dress was coming off as she heard him cough. She hoped he didn't report seeing a stripper in the street, or worse still, his pacemaker giving up. She laughed, the first time for a long time.

Dress in the bag over her shoulder, she skated several blocks down and crossed the main road. Her eyes darted everywhere, not taking any chances. Everything seemed normal. She was excited to see them again. Her life was lonely and full of danger she could not share. They had become a kind of family, people she was more than comfortable with and trusted.

They were not hard to spot, sitting on the sidewalk chairs and table outside the bar. She had to stop herself giggling at their disguises and white English faces.

Those damn Brits. Disguised as cowboys and still looking like English tourists.

She skated by them several times. Gavin was into the biggest glass of beer he'd ever had. Eager had a glass of wine and a bottle of water. He was looking around, trying not to be obvious. Right, she thought. She almost hit the table and was amazed they did not cotton on it was her. Well, Gavin was busy and he had the enormous silly cowboy hat at his feet. Again, she felt like giggling. Best she had felt since she arrived back.

She stopped twenty yards past the bar and sat on her skateboard on the sidewalk. She asked people passing by, begging for money, while she watched around. Lots of people; nothing out of the ordinary, it seemed. John Wayne and Gary Cooper, she thought, were oblivious to her. So much for Eager saying he was an expert in surveillance. Huh!

After an hour of observing in all directions and receiving a fair bit of abuse — 'Get a job!' 'Get off drugs and drink.' And the worst being, 'Come with me, I can save your soul,' the old creep — she decided it was all clear and was ready to make her move.

She noticed Eager looking in her direction. Knowing him, he was probably feeling pity for the beggar on the street in such a beautiful city. Big softie, it was a wonder he hadn't got up and come to donate some cash. Lots of begging in London, and at least it was warm here. She was willing him to come look see. No chance. So she stood up and walked slowly by, stopping in front of them and holding out her hand. In it she had a small piece of paper hidden from view. Gavin looked up and said, "We don't need your money, luv." He then laughed. Dick! Eager looked at him, annoyed, and dug into his pockets for some change. Her hand was still extended almost into his face. He didn't look at her and proffered a dollar bill.

"Cheap Brit," she said. He looked up, a little taken aback, still not recognising her until she said, 'Right, Smalls?" He looked into her eyes and the penny dropped. "Read the note and follow me in fifteen minutes," she whispered.

"Cheap ass!" she shouted and skated off. He was left with his mouth open.

"Another?" Gavin asked, not aware of the beggar being Liberty, too busy enjoying his beer.

"Yeah, but pay the bill when you order. You have fifteen minutes to drink up."

"I don't think she is coming soon." Gavin was probably hopeful. He was having the coldest and best beer he had drunk since being in the US. *Jesus!*

She waited several blocks away, where she could watch them and anyone following them. It seemed a long fifteen minutes. Eager had read the note under the table, just a scruffy map pointing across the street and up two blocks straight. Then they started moving casually, pulling a case each and bags over their shoulders, and walking as if they were just looking around for their rental.

Take the fucking hat off, Gavin; you look like an undersized Hoss Cartwright. Liberty shook her head as she thought this.

When they got close and clocked her, she started to skate to her changing tree. Quickly changing, giving them too much of a view, she then walked on quickly. She stopped on her street and let them catch up, so it looked like a normal situation: a small group of people walking home. She told Gavin about her hat suggestion, who had just realised from the striptease that it was her. He quickly took it off and struggled to hold it under his arm.

Eager had told him to leave it on the airplane. The hostess had caught them up waving it as they were exiting the plane. Then at the hire car company in Vegas he told him to leave it in the toilets. Again, the sales assistant found it and stopped them leaving. Same thing dropping off the car and in the taxi. That damn hat would not stay lost, Eager murmured to himself. Was it good luck or a jinx? He was not sure.

Eager moved close to hold her. He wanted so much to hug her and kiss her after days of not knowing if she was alive and knowing how much he had missed her.

"Steady, cowboy, when we get out of home." She sensed his need to be near her, but needed to caution him whilst they were in the street.

"Right."

They got inside the house through the side door under the car port, only stopping to lock it securely. She ran and jumped into Eager's arms, legs as usual wrapped around his waist.

"Smalls. You came! You came!" She started to laugh with relief and cry at the same time.

Gavin had to run to the toilet. Eager was amazed at her short-cut blonde hair as she had removed her cap; it made her even sexier in his eyes.

The living room in this small bungalow was covered in papers. A lot of screwed-up papers on the floor where she had been starting her story and press releases and changed her mind. The small roller desk had her portable typewriter with pen, papers and her reporter's notebook. She had kept notes whilst in the UK and filled in the blanks on the trip over. The videos were not in sight. The dining table was in the same room and it had empty wine glasses and bottles and unwashed cutlery, plates and coffee cups all over it. The window blinds and curtains were all drawn so no daylight could get in and no one could view inside and see not even a shadow.

She sat on Eager's lap until Gavin came back into the room. She then jumped up and hugged Gavin around the neck, kissing his cheeks several times.

"You came, too, Gavin, my hero! How I have missed you both." He went red in the face; it was the most emotion she had ever shown towards him.

"Coffee? Tea maybe, or a glass of wine? Sorry, Gavin, I ran out of beer last night."

"I can see." He perused the empty Budweiser cans on the table and in the rubbish basket.

Everyone was then okay with wine. Gavin chose a Screaming Eagle Californian Sauvignon, Eager and Liberty a Kendall Jackson Chardonnay from the wine fridge. Gavin had no idea the price of his drink, which was one of the most expensive wines in California. The owner would not be pleased when she returned, then neither were Liberty or Eager.

"You have plenty of wine, though," Gavin commented.

"Well, not mine. The owner has a big supply here on the rack and in the back room. I am going to try and replace the many I have had since arrival or dad will be mad," she laughed.

There was a lot to catch up on. Eager and Liberty sat on the little couch and Gavin in a comfortable armchair. She held his hand and kept patting it.

"I can't believe you guys came. How is Logan?"

"Doing well. He wanted to come when I said you may be dead. What a scare that was. Anyway, he is recovering fine. Hard to kill is our Logan."

"When I was dead?"

"I guess he wanted to kill the perpetrators."

She leaned into Eager. Gavin rolled his eyes and secured the wine bottle next to him on the small lamp table.

"He must be angry, though, about Karlein?"

"Especially when Aunt Bessie died," Gavin put in.

"Shit! No. Karlein and Aunt Bessie!"

"So, young lady, apart from giving me the scare of my life. Look, I lost a lot of weight." Eager patted his middle. "Tell us what happened here; catch us up from the moment you landed."

She did just that, leaving nothing out. Even the guy who handed her his business card at the airport. Gavin wanted to look at it and then shook his head, not recognising the name as anyone in the media he knew buying or selling stories. This took several bottles of Chardonnay and one bottle of red. Gavin was sipping slowly for a change, which was a good job as he was running up a three thousand tab without knowing. But at least he was listening intently.

"That's me. Now your turn. I want every last detail from when you left Heathrow. By the way, you have lost some of that belly; looking good, Smalls."

"I went back to the George and Dragon and celebrated."

"Because I left?"

"No, because of your rejection." He then laughed.

"Really?" She reflected on telling him that she would never have married him when he asked if she would at the airport. She was chewing her bottom lip.

"Well, it was a relief."

"Really." She tickled him under his arms until he couldn't stop laughing.

"Enough!"

"Enough all right. You guys need to get a room." Gavin rolled his eyes again.

Eager told the story on a timeline as a detective would, missing no detail out, with Gavin interrupting at times to get his situation updated for her.

"So, you are both in deep shit back home," Liberty summarised.

"Food. Food," Gavin spurted out — drink made him hungry. Nothing in the house, so they ordered pizzas and salad from Rocky's Pizza restaurant. When it came, Gavin paid cash at the door. It was devoured in minutes.

"What next? We should develop our plan, the next steps," Eager put forward.

"Nope, it's late. Gavin, there is a single bed in the back room." She grabbed Eager's hand and virtually dragged him into the master bedroom.

Chapter 34
Buzzards Circling

"Why me?" Sonia complained to the chief. "Steve is senior and is the more experienced person to send. He deserves this trip."

Steve and the chief were both surprised at her statement. She was packed and booked to leave in the evening on a commercial flight. The director of the FBI had spoken to the Met commissioner and their chief to his counterpart in London, plus he had got through to Commander Allcock.

"You wanted a trip to London. This is a big deal and I make the calls who is best to go." The chief was emphatic — no debate.

He turned to Steve, who seemed keen to talk.

"Well, don't say you want to go."

"No, we have had a sighting of the car like the one Bell was driving. A bit of a breakthrough. A deputy sheriff who is a bit of a vintage car fan spotted a white Chevelle coming into the Palm Springs city limits the night of the incident. Took notice as he'd seen it in a film."

"And?"

"It was driven by a blonde with short hair. He was miffed that he had no reason to stop it as she was driving well under the limit."

"Blonde? She has dark hair," Sonia added. "Maybe not her; lots of expensive vintage cars in Palm Springs, all those rich retirees."

Steve tipped his head to one side. He could not understand why she seemed to fight and debunk everything he brought to the table. This was possibly a major breakthrough.

"The waitress at the Peggy Sue's said she headed south on the I15. Could be her, and she has probably changed to avoid the media attention. A pretty well-known face now," Steve pushed home.

"Okay, Steve, get up there now. Take some support and work with the locals to make sure this is a priority. Bring her in kicking and screaming if need be, even if you have to arrest her. You also need everything she has. I expect Eager is with her. Him, too."

"Got it." Steve grabbed his coat and almost ran out of the room, taking time to make a show of scratching his backside as he passed Sonia.

"Young lady, on your way. Commercial flights don't wait for us," the chief ordered. She left reluctantly.

"We have a lead to the whereabouts of our person of interest."

"Yes?" Amanda started to breathe heavily with excitement: could this be closer to the kill.

"Palm Springs," the general stated in a flat tone. No excitement at the find at all.

"Exactly where in Palm Springs?"

"That's all I got from our source. Her car was seen driving there on the night of the incident by a local deputy sheriff. You probably missed it from the chopper that night."

"How do you want to handle it?" She let his jibe go.

"I have sent a six-man surveillance team there in three separate vehicles. The FBI are on the way as well, so we need to move fast."

"They just need to find the location and then back off. I will handle the take-down."

"Understood. Our two visitors may be there. What about the FBI and locals?"

"Collateral damage if they get in the way."

"On your own?"

"Yes. A young woman and two unarmed guys? No problem."

"Understood. Stay on the secure communications. I will pull our guys out as soon as they have the location."

He thought this would be three off the list, videos secured if this works. Moves were on the way for others. The nightmare will be at the beginning of the end.

Chapter 35
Sleepless Nights

As usual, Logan couldn't sleep. He paced the cottage floor. Coffee at four a.m. was not a good idea — the caffeine would make his sleep even more impossible — still, he had a mug. He had changed locations, as he did on a regular basis. He walked up the narrow stairs and could see out of the small porthole window the farmhouse behind. Well lit, quiet, maybe too quiet. He learnt it paid to be a little paranoid, especially at this time. As he watched there was a boom like a gunshot and a big flash of light. He jumped and his coffee spilt down his tee-shirt.

"Bloody hell!" He stepped back up and scanned the farmhouse. A fox, maybe? Nothing moving. No shadows. He watched and watched, still nothing. Should he black-up and go out? Stay put and check in the morning? What was he scared of? Everything and nothing, a voice in his head said. No time to be the hero, you've done that — too old and wounded now, it added.

"Fuck you!" He was talking to himself, or was it the coward in him? No, he wasn't a coward and he knew from wisdom that being afraid does not mean that. Being afraid and still facing up to things, being careful yet bold when necessary was the way to go and conquer fear. He made his mind up to sneak out and have a look. He could not face not knowing for the rest of the night.

It took him a few minutes to black-up, put his Marines knife down the side of his boot, add a lighter and several firework bangers in his front trouser leg pockets and potholing torch on head, to be used when needed and not taking up a hand. The shotgun was clumsy and big but necessary; just to be sure, he checked that it was loaded and pocketed four more cartridges. The cottage he kept dark and it was easy to slip out the back door and slide into the field at the side of the small lane leading down to the farmhouse. He gradually crawled down the side of the field by the road, stopping every minute to listen and look. His arms were scratched just wearing the tee-shirt and not a combat jacket, but this type of pain never bothered him. It was one hundred yards to the farmhouse. The outside lights lit up thirty yards around it.

He rolled over further into the field and darkness. Was that a shadow moving away? Yes, he could barely make it out, but it was moving up to the top of the hill. Should he shoot? No, too far away for a shotgun. There could be others around.

He blasted the shotgun both barrels anyway. Relieved his tenseness and some frustration. The shadow disappeared. Seconds later, he heard the sound of a motor-bike start up and drive off.

"Best I check in the daylight and get back to Fort Knox," he said out loud. He stood up and started walking back carefully when the thought hit him that it could have been a diversion. Could others be coming from the main road down the front past his cottage? He quickly reloaded the shotgun and held it ready, pointed forward. Heart racing, senses at a very high level, as is usual in these situations, creating a super-awareness. He believed he could hear a spider move in this state. Nothing. He lowered the shotgun at the back door he had come out from, which was still open. He took out his knife as the shotgun was of little use in a close-quarter situation. Once inside he was prepared to drop it. So, knife in left hand and shotgun leaning on his right arm, he jumped inside and immediately switched on his torch to blind anyone in the dark. It was empty, but he still searched it after locking the door behind him. No point being taken from the rear.

The blue police light and siren of the Ford Granada police car was coming quickly up the road. He hid the shotgun in the priest's cubby hole under the stairs. He knew that the police did not carry guns normally; however, the highway patrol cars had weapons locked in boxes in their boots. Permission had to be granted by the chief constable to open the boxes and use the weapons. He put on the lights in the cottage and awaited the knock on the door. It was a thump with a truncheon and a shout. They were being careful.

"Anyone inside? Identify yourself!"

"Logan McAllistar."

"Are you okay?"

"Yes. I am opening the door."

"Mr McAllistar, come out slowly."

He did not actually do it with his arms up, but held them in front to show he was not carrying anything. If he was, he figured he was safe as they had nothing to harm him with. There were two of them with torches, no weapons. They looked confused and not relaxed, even after they recognised him. He guessed Fenwick had briefed them, and as with the regular patrols past, they knew who he was and that maybe some mischief could be afoot. Another car came fast up the road from Matlock. It was Scotty and Romeo.

"You okay?" he said, jumping out of his car, followed by Romeo. "I heard the bangs from Matlock."

"Come in, gents. Cup of char?"

They did not have time. He then explained that he had flares in the field around the house meant to stop the foxes and one went off. Nothing to worry about, no further action required.

"Oh, aye," said the sergeant. "I suppose you like looking like a black man early in the morning with your own headlight?" He had not had time to take off his head light nor his black camouflage face paint. Hence the stares and looks of confusion.

"Old Army habit; sorry if I scared you. When I heard the flares go off, I went to look and put this on; old habits die slowly."

All eyebrows lifted, even Scotty's. The policemen had heard of him and were in a bit of awe of this army hero, although Fenwick had warned them that dead bodies seem to follow him.

"Let's have a look, sir."

"No need to waste your time, officers."

"All part of the service, sir." Not being put off.

They drove the patrol car with big light beams out of each side of the front windows down the lane towards the farmhouse. Searching the areas not lit up.

"Do you have weapons out anywhere, Logan?" Scotty asked.

"Just the shotgun I hid, and my knife is still in the house."

"I would hide that, too. Fenwick has probably asked them to find anything at all on you and I am sure the knife is so big it is illegal and you probably have no licence for the shotgun, so deny having one."

He ran inside and hid the knife with the shotgun and then took off the paint and light. They walked down the lane, Romeo alongside. Should he let the dog go, Scotty had asked. Logan said no, maybe when light comes; he was worried about the other flares going off whilst the cops were there.

The police patrol were now out of their vehicle with torches, searching around the back of the farmhouse. They came back after a while and shook their heads. Meanwhile, their radio had been calling them. Logan told them and it seemed urgent. It was a sitrep request on the status. There was nothing to report. It was agreed that it was probably a fox.

"Do you have any weapons, Mr McAllistar?"

"No, just these." He took some firework bangers out of his pockets.

"This is what you used?" said the sergeant.

"Just to scare foxes."

"Tom, that accounts for the three bangs." The sergeant had turned to the constable. They had found one flare only, and this seemed to satisfy them.

"Get your hens, then?" the young constable asked.

"Aye."

"I didn't see any?"

"Yes, all gone, lad, that's why I hate these bloody foxes. Little bastards they are."

The sergeant's faced screwed up as he considered the response, not totally believing him.

"Sir, I think the flares might be too disruptive just for foxes. If they keep going off, we will be out every night. Unless you need them for something else?" the sergeant probed. He had noticed other trip wires in the fields.

"My shooting has made me nervous. I will see if I can make other arrangements," Logan said to move them on. They obviously knew the whole history of events and his explanation was not adding up for them.

Back in the patrol car, driving away, the constable asked, "Did you believe him, Sarge, about no weapons?"

The sergeant pulled out two cartridges that smelt like they had been recently fired.

"We need to report these and ask him about the shotgun. Fenwick will ask," the constable stated.

"Fuck Fenwick," the sergeant said, as he threw them out of the window into the hedgerow.

Scotty turned to Logan. "They were definitely looking around for more than an intruder."

"Yep."

They had coffee together and discussed the past, when Scotty would take the young Logan out on night patrol with Rex and Romeo. He took the risk of having him with him; the young boy was good company and a lost soul trying to find himself. He loved the dogs and the dogs returned that love.

It was soon coming up to six a.m. and the morning sunlight was upon them. They decided to look around. The flare had gone off half way up the hill to the right-hand side of the farmhouse. They let Romeo go sniff around. She picked up a scent and led them right up the hill. It was a bit of a hike. Logan started to get tired from his wounds. He had not noticed during the excitement as the adrenaline had kicked in. Scotty told him to go back and get something stiff to drink. When Scotty and Romeo returned, they had found a farm gate open way over the top of the hill — not normal for farmers to do with animals — there was some oil just outside on the dirt road on the way back and two human turds behind the stone wall where the intruder had been hiding. Logan had told him he had heard a motor-bike.

"They must have sussed this place out on previous nights; only locals use and know that old lane. It would not be on any map, for sure," Scotty noted.

'The human shit was an IRA sign they left when bombers or snipers were waiting for the kill, like a police or army patrol. Nerves. Someone is not leaving me alone; not sure it would be the IRA. The Yanks coming back to complete the job?"

"Too many to think about." Scotty made a nervous laugh. He had his own nightmares to contend with. The loss of Rex, killed by a Russian, and the complete madness that came over him for revenge. Romeo got hers with the shooter who killed her lifelong partner, Rex. Scotty finished the job when he was threatened that they would never give up until he and his family were dead. Two shots, two dead to ensure they never did. Killing anyone, no matter how bad they were, never leaves you; you are never the same again.

Scotty took a hip flask out of his inside jacket pocket and took a pull, then handed it to Logan. They stood in the courtyard of the farmhouse. Romeo was wandering around Aunt Bessie's old car complaining, looking underneath.

"Did you run over any animals?"

"Nope," was Logan's short reply.

"Well, something is under there."

"I can guess what," Logan said with a knowing nod.

Liberty couldn't sleep. Eager was flat out on his back. It had been a long day; evening and bed exercise had been too much for him. Still, he had a smile on his face. She could hear Gavin snoring loudly through the walls. She thought of going in and putting his big cowboy hat over his face and holding it there until he was unconscious.

Something was irritating her and she was trying to think of what? She got coffee and looked around. Yes, she would have to clean up in the morning; she would organise the guys to help. It was a pig sty. She saw car lights going down the road. That was it — the car. She ran outside and looked at the Chevelle, its trunk and distinctive rear sticking out of the car port, visible to the street. Why hadn't she fixed this before? Too busy writing and feeling safe? She ran inside and found an old bedspread and put it over the trunk and back window. It still looked distinctive. So she found old cardboard boxes and loaded them on the trunk under the bedspread. It almost looked like the back end of an old truck. Not perfect, but enough to disguise it. Job well done.

She was still bothered, which worried her, as other nights there she had not had a nagging concern like this. Were the guys followed?

You never know, she thought. Was it time to move on — but where?

Fenwick arrived clearly irritated, as his twitching was ravaging his face today. The police cars were at the top of the drive. Bomb squad's black truck was closer to the farmhouse. The bomb experts in full protective gear. One half under the car and the other holding a big shield in front of him. The one under the car came out and they talked. The one with the shield came across to Logan, Scotty and now a twitching DCI Fenwick. He took off his mask and spoke directly to Logan.

"It's a bomb all right. Plastic. Hooked onto your exhaust. If you had moved... boom, goodbye." He thought it was funny. His way, Logan believed, of dealing with the danger of his work. Classic IRA job. It would not get Logan, as he always looked under his car before leaving since his time in NI.

"Talk to me," Fenwick almost shouted. "I'm in charge here."

"And you are?"

"DCI Fenwick."

The bomb disposal guy had taken an instant disliking to him.

"Well, be my guest, sir. If you are careful, it won't go off when you are under there. Pull it out real slow." He pointed to where the car was.

Fenwick was lost for words, just twitching.

"Thought so," the bomb man grinned, and then turned to Logan. "We can take it out with risk or blow it under your car." Aunt Bessie's car blown up? Logan was horrified, but prepared to let it go. It happened, he guessed, in NI — a car blown to bits was better than losing a life.

"Just joking, sir. We've disconnected it and now need to move it very slowly. You all need to stand back further just in case Bob's parts fly around."

Yes, definitely a joker.

Chapter 36
Mr Green

Detective David Brody of the LAPD brought Mr Green into the FBI conference room. He was excited since the call from the Bureau Chief De Silva. Could he help out on the Mojave Zzyzx case (as it was now known) in the absence of Steve and Sonia as he had the most knowledge on the murders and the scene of the crime? Could he! Maybe this was his chance to shine and get an opportunity to get into the FBI. The cream of the world's crime-fighting agencies.

De Silva had not arrived yet, so he got Mr Green some coffee and offered some of the cookies that were lying around the room. Lots of them. This showed how national budgets worked — he had to buy his own doughnuts at LAPD.

He looked Mr Green over. Dressed in blue denim jeans, brown cowboy boots and a white Western cowboy shirt. Leather bolo necklace with a turquoise stone at the top and ends that ran down the shirt with beads on them. Slim and muscular, about five foot ten, Brody guessed. Leather bands on both wrists, some with brown beads on them. Good looking and tanned. His hair was long and greying, tied in a plait that hung down his back. He carried a small leather sports bag and to his surprise a golf club bag, which was well worn. His face had several scars around the right cheek and on the forehead. They looked like knife wounds.

Brody was chatting pleasantries when the chief entered the room. They shook hands and the chief nodded for them all to sit down around the conference table. He took the leader's seat at the top of the table after pouring himself a coffee.

"Mr Green," the chief started.

"Call me David," was the response. Brody kept quiet, as he was making sure when he did say anything it was worthwhile, so he stayed quiet and let the chief lead.

"Not really an Indian name," the chief stated.

"No. A kind of nickname I picked up in the Army. My Apache name was too hard for the guys to say. So it stuck." He spoke perfect English in a deep baritone voice.

The chief looked through his file and some papers before speaking again.

"We are honoured to have such a war hero helping us. It is much appreciated. Diablo Herrero Eskiminzen. Diablo the Devil." The chief pronounced his Indian name in Spanish perfectly and the meaning of his first name, also in Spanish, in a light-hearted way.

"That's me. I'm impressed," David Green said as he almost looked like he was blushing.

"Well, the Washington guys thought it worthwhile for you to come and look-see since you are assisting in the Geronimo — sorry, Chief Longbow — serial killer case. We have several alternative leads we are following; however, there are some similarities to the Longbow case and some confusing evidence on changes to the MO. I'd rather you look at it with a fresh eye, though, and not influence your opinion before you are caught up on all the details." He stared at Detective Brody to be sure he got the message. Show him everything, but don't throw in your opinion or anyone else's for that matter.

"Agreed." David Green was not big on talking, mainly dreaming and chanting.

The chief looked at the golf bag.

"Thinking of getting a game in whilst you are here?"

Mr Green laughed. "No, tools of the trade. Real Apache weapons to match anything you may have."

"John," turning to Detective Brody. It was Jake, but he wasn't about to embarrass the chief. "I have organised a chopper to take you to the scene. I would appreciate it being a quick trip, cost and use is high and can blow budgets out. Can you give Mr Green all the background information without assumptions, please. Show him the weapons and bodies and so forth. I think, though, a look at the scene would be the best place to start. Thanks also for helping; Sonia is in London and Steve in Palm Springs, following up some leads." He handed Jake the file he had.

Brody was keen as mustard and kept asking question after question over the headsets in the chopper to Mr Green. He wanted to know about Vietnam, Apache Indians, and the Chief Longbow case. This passed the time as they flew to the scene. Diablo warmed to him. Although he would not speak about Vietnam and his role or the serial killer case, he did get enthusiastic to educate him on the Apache race.

The Apaches had many tribes and many names. Yes, they lived in the Southern plains which included Arizona, Oklahoma, Texas and New Mexico. They were hunters and fishermen and good with herbs and roots. They were the first indigenous people to ride horses and were very fierce warriors. Buffalo, elk, turkey, foxes and other animals they hunted. Their teepees, or Wickiups, were made with buffalo hide, as were much of their clothes. The name comes from the Spanish word Apachu.

He talked about the murder of Indians in California. The abuse of them, Geronimo and other Apache wars. He was proud of his heritage. They were spiritual, believing in animism, which says all objects have souls: animals, rocks, forests, rivers and so forth. They burnt their dead on pyres. Dancing, praying, meditating and singing were all part of their culture. They say that a warrior could run one hundred miles in a day and climb a mountain without getting out of breath. Well before they adopted horses as their main form of movement.

The time passed quickly and they landed to the north of the crime scene. Mr Green wanted them to land a fair distance from the scene. He changed into some leather moccasins and jumped out just as the helicopter landed. Jake was amazed at his speed and agility. He did not go directly to the crime scene — they had told him that to get there so quickly from Vegas it must have been via helicopter, and they did not find any indentations due to the hard surfaces. He went in smaller circles until he came across some hard ground with sand laid on top. Underneath were two ruts, probably from the helicopter's landing skis. He looked up further afield. He shook his head and went towards the scene of the crime, which still had police crime scene tape around. He wandered, looking into every nook and cranny he could find. The burnt caravans, marks on the ground, the lake; footprints were few and he knew that the police would have taken casts. The ones he saw were boot marks, probably Army type, and scuffed ground made by the covers the SOC people wore on their feet.

He asked Jake Brody to describe the scene when he arrived. The bodies had been thrown on the caravan fire. SOC officers had pegged places where they believed, from blood and ground marks, the bodies had been tortured and murdered.

It was lunchtime and not much more to see. The real information was in the file: pictures, SOC reports and the ME's examination reports. Brody suggested they go back, conscious of the chief's 'make it quick' remark. Back in the conference room, Diablo was left to read the file and look at the arrows that were found. He read carefully and slowly, ensuring he did not miss a thing, including some pen comments Steve had written as side notes for his own information. Jake got a burger and Coke for himself and a salad and water for Mr Green from the café.

The chief returned when Brody had called him.

"Well, any thoughts?"

Diablo took his time to think about it. He wanted more involvement to find the impersonators, so he had to balance his thoughts up somewhat.

"The throats were not slit as per his MO. The arrows are not Apache; you know this, though." He opened his golf bag and pulled out five knives, a bow and several arrows as a show-and-tell.

"So, not Chief Longbow then?" the chief said, believing all the time this was not the case, but not wanting to let him feel his trip had been a waste of time.

"Does not seem like it, although he could have changed his methods, run out of Apache arrows. It is certainly a copy or looks that way. Although without the details that were held back from the media."

"If it was him, for argument's sake, why in the Mojave Desert? What beef could he possibly have had with these victims?"

"Well, the Navajo lived there by the lakes at one time. The Silver Lake was the most popular, although the different tribes lived all the way up to Utah by the lakes. California was the scene of Indian massacres hundreds of years ago. The Navajo were an offshoot of the Apache. The victims lived by a lake and created a pretty messy environment, from what I saw. Not sure why he would choose these people, though."

"One was not white but Mexican."

"The Mexicans did as much harm to the Apache as the Anglos. So not out of the question that the killer would consider him as a target."

"He found helicopter ski ruts hidden near the scene," Brody cut in.

"We thought as much, but no one found anything to prove it. So that explains how he got to there from Vegas in such short order. Only one other car track, apart from his car he left in Vegas, and we assume that was Bell's."

"Had to be another vehicle or another helicopter. Who covered up the ski marks?" Diablo added.

"A helicopter further away which we did not look that far?"

"Possible."

"Washington says he has not sent a letter claiming these murders yet."

"Maybe he feels we are getting close and changed what he does to throw us off, or he is still travelling?" Diablo added.

"What other involvement have you had with this case?" the chief asked, looking sceptical at Diablo's assumptions.

"I am a medicine man, teacher and a part-time policeman on our, let me say, on the reservations." The word 'reservation' seemed to stick in his throat, but he knew the white man understood this better. Mr Green, or Diablo, had been co-opted onto the serial killer task force. They needed someone on the inside of the Apache nation, especially in San Carlos. His Army record and his honoured position in the tribe made him a perfect choice, someone they could trust. He could move around not only in San Carlos but also other reservations with ease. He had advised them on all aspects of the weaponry and the mindset and culture of the Apaches. The killer was giving the Apaches a bad name and the fear had created a lot of verbal and physical attacks on them, so his position was that he needed to help clear this up.

The profiler at FBI HQ had said this was an Apache with a big grudge. Someone shunned by society outside his Indian nation. Someone who was immersed in Apache history and culture. A warrior or hunter the traditional ways, who could shoot an arrow straight into a person's heart area from a distance. He could make his own weapons. A spiritual person who burnt his victims like they did with pyres to honour their dead and send them on their way to new hunting grounds. It was a ritual he didn't have to do for his victims. Male, between twenty-five and forty. He could have been a chief, shaman or teacher. Possibly, like Geronimo, he would think he has supernatural powers, being able to see the future, walk without footprints and hold back the dawn if he wanted to. The Apache warriors were very crafty and often changed tactics if needed, much to the chagrin and embarrassment of the US Cavalry tasked with bringing them in or down.

Not far from my profile? Diablo had noted.

The chief was tapping the desk with his fingers with a small amount of impatience, thinking this was going nowhere.

"So it is highly unlikely that these murders are part of your serial killer case?"

"It seems that way. It was certainly a copycat murder, or could be a change in tactics for a lot of reasons, like he ran out of Apache arrows when he needed them, as an example."

"Anything else you could add?"

"I am interested in your other avenues of investigations. Jake told me about this Bell woman and the victims selling drugs."

The chief did not look pleased and glanced at Brody a 'loose lips sink ships' look. He thought about it for a while.

"We do not like throwing around too much about the investigation."

Brody looked down — he had broken an FBI rule.

"I understand. I am, though, trusted by your colleagues, who will be sure to ask me in detail about this case and how I feel about it."

The chief gave him a thumbnail sketch of the possible involvement of Liberty Bell and that maybe someone was after her to stop her publishing what she knows. Her background in the UK and the fact she was missing, currently presumed alive and kicking in hiding.

"Seems a good alternative to the serial killer. Always a chance, though, that she was not connected — just passed by." Diablo wanted to stay involved and get more information on the copycats. He also had another way to do this.

"I would like to go back to the site and perform a 'vision quest'. This is a way that I can connect with the spirits of the dead and maybe learn more about what happened and who did these murders."

"You what?" The chief was surprised and confused. He didn't believe in new age bunkum or ancient Indian rites. Diablo knew he was sceptical: it was written all over his face and body language as he folded his arms tightly across his chest.

"We need to stop this killer. Not sure what I will come up with, and even if it's not connected, I may get a vision that might help your investigation."

The arms tightened. Brody tried not to look, as he believed in what Diablo was saying, but was still smarting from the chief's rebuke.

Diablo explained that this was a meditation at the scene. He needed anything recovered from the murders they could loan him, even a body. This was not going to be the case, and he could see it on the chief's face.

"Your time. John, can you take Diablo back by car. You will be responsible for whatever evidence you sign out for him."

Jake Brody knew this was his punishment.

Chapter 37
London

Sammy the Squirrel was working the streets. He had put the word out that they were looking for a slim man or woman, maybe American or Chinese, maybe with a priest's collar, very fit, cat-like, new in town possibly. A big reward for anyone finding this guy or girl. He understood from the screwed-up faces of the people he briefed that this was a long shot.

London is a big place and it is easy to drop out of sight. He got some coffee at a small café in the heart of London opposite the US Embassy. This was situated on Nine Elms Lane in Battersea. This was as good a place as any to start, he mused. Sammy had a touch of arithmomania, an obsessive-compulsive disorder which made him continuously count objects around him. He credited his ability at finding people to this disease; he was sure it helped pay attention to all kinds of odd details. He counted seven elm trees on the street, not nine. That always annoyed him and he took a note to research how that was. He had his little notepad out that he carried everywhere. He wrote in his own code that he had developed in case he was picked up or lost the book. The word had been spread, but really the boss did not have a good description of this hit person. He had told the people to check out gyms, martial arts studios, tourist areas, hotels, churches, restaurants, gay bars and clubs.

His very logical brain told him that this was all related to the American team that his boss had met previously. They were then after McAllistar and Karlein. So it made sense, with the little info he had, that this was another American. So could he be official, working for the CIA or FBI? Maybe not, but the last time these guys were supported and connected. So he and several of his contacts were watching there, the CIA and FBI offices, for anyone coming and going that was anything like the description. It was again a long shot, he knew. If only he had the police resources to check flights in and such. Jimmy would be working his police contacts to get what he could.

If he gave the boss a short deadline: what, one week? Then it was logical that he would stay around waiting on a result. If he was a top pro, why then did he need the Harkers to do the dirty work? Why? Then there was Mr Javelin. Jimmy had told him to find a way to get him sorted. He understood this was payback, but why did the hit man want him gone as well? He knew he was missing some pieces of the puzzle. McAllistar and Javelin would lead the police directly back to the Harkers, so they needed to be extra careful. He found he was recounting the sugar sachets and dividing them between real sugar and the alternatives. This helped him think. He looked around — the staff weren't watching. He liked to blend in; however, he knew his habits and the way he dressed made him stand out in upmarket venues.

He walked in, looking around left to right. He spotted Sammy in the corner. He thought he was not easily spotted, but also, he could probably smell him. He was immaculately dressed in grey suit, white shirt, yellow tie and brown shoes that shone. His tanned Indian skin, white teeth and wavy black hair made him look like a Bollywood movie star. He sat down opposite Sammy.

"What do you want, Sammy?" He spoke sharply and was obviously irritated. DI Teddy Samuels needed to distance himself from the Harkers and Javelin. He wanted to move on. He just wanted it all to go away and build his career — the right way this time. He already had Javelin making him steal evidence on Nick Harker, which in itself could send him to prison. He imagined being thrown in the Scrubs full of hard men he had put away. It gave him nightmares.

"Coffee, Inspector?"

"Just get on with it." Samuels waved his hand in the air as if swatting a fly.

"Do you know why they call this Nine Elms Lane when there are only seven?" Sammy was trying to annoy him for sure.

"I don't have a fucking clue. What, I say again, do you want?"

"Be calm, Inspector; just a little help."

"So?"

"There is a man in town, possibly American, maybe Chinese, probably arrived over the last three days or so. We need to know where he is staying."

"Oh yeah, bloody funny. How the hell can I possibly find that out on such skimpy information?"

Sammy started counting the sachets again, looking down.

"This man is possibly a paid assassin. Professional. Maybe came in by an American airline or British Airways. Most likely business class or first. Thin, could have an Asian look, able to climb well like a burglar, could be gay or even a woman."

"Oh, bloody great! Bound to find him, easy peasy!"

"No need for that attitude, Mr Samuels, we are all friends here."

"I am not your friend." Samuels grabbed Sammy's hands to stop him counting and to get his attention, knocking the sugar sachets out of them.

"Mr Harker would be very grateful for any help you could render, and your services would be well rewarded." Sammy handed him a piece of paper with the club telephone number, which he knew anyway.

"What has this guy done to Harker?"

"Let's just say he is not a friend."

"I will see if he is on anyone's radar and look around. There is little to go on and if this guy is what you think he is, he will be well under the radar. Tell Mr Harker I will try, that is all I can promise. Good luck, you are after a needle in a haystack." He stood up, nodded and left the door banging behind him.

Horse's ass!

Sammy had another coffee and stared towards the embassy gates. He was stumped as what to do next. Get back to the club; one of his lookers may have rung in with a lucky break? You never know. He just needed to tidy up the sachets first.

"So, Sonia... you don't mind if I call you Sonia?"

"My pleasure, Commissioner."

Sir Michael sat behind his large polished oak desk which was covered with pictures of his family. Commander Allcock sat in front, with Sonia facing him. DI Williams stood at the back of the room, arms folded across her chest. Sonia had spent the morning with them, getting just as much as Eager had told her, and now was being given the big boss treatment as a matter of PR for the FBI.

"I am sorry we can't be of more help. I can assure you that Ms Bell's allegations were proved to be false. I cannot comment on what she is doing now, and DCI Eager went to the US once he heard she had been murdered, to see if he could help in any way."

"There were rumours that one tape had an American on it?" Sonia pried.

"Not heard about that. Charlie?" Turning to DCS Allcock.

Charlie Allcock was not impressed, and his body language showed it. In the morning when he spoke, he was gesticulating, waving his arms about, and Sonia could read him. Now he sat quietly, arms by his side; clearly his answer would be under protest.

"No, sir," was his curt reply.

"DI Williams?"

She unfolded her arms and moved to the side of Sonia. Again, Sonia could feel the tenseness in the air.

"No, sir, not to my knowledge." She then refolded her arms and stepped back.

"These Harkers, could they have tried to get her in the US? I mean, she worked on them pretty hard, causing a lot of damage," Sonia persisted.

"Charlie?" The commissioner handed the question over.

"I doubt it. One is in a prison hospital and the brother is fighting for his turf against these Yardies. He lost most of his henchmen in a shoot-out. His main US contact has changed sides and they are enemies, so I doubt he would help him."

"They could be suspects, though. I mean, paid someone in the US or other contacts where they sourced drugs?"

"Possible. Javelin, their US lawyer, was the main contact with international, shall I say, rogues. I doubt they got involved too much as they always kept their hands pretty clean; others always do their dirty work. We have them under surveillance and nothing out of the ordinary to suggest this has come to our notice," Charlie responded.

"Can we interview them? I mean put it to them and see how they respond?"

"You would get sweet nothing," DCI Williams cut in.

"Worth a try, though?"

"No. Believe us, it would be like getting blood out of a stone. If we saw them murder someone on the street in front of us, they would deny it so convincingly we would start to think we got it wrong. We are watching and waiting twenty-four-seven. Now is not the time, I assure you," Charlie said firmly.

"Do I put that in my report? No assistance from the Met Police?"

"That is a little unfair, Sonia. We have sensitive investigations underway that can be compromised. We have already been accused by Badluck — sorry, our nickname for their sleazy lawyer — that we are persecuting them for no proven reason. We cannot at this stage approach them on this incident on foreign grounds unless we have some direct evidence." The commissioner was firm.

"Interview over, then?" Sonia sounded miffed.

"If we get anything at all, a whiff of a connection from our surveillance, you will be the first to know, I assure you." He completed the sentence and stood up, offering his hand. Sonia asked for a photo with him and he obliged, shaking her hand, smiling in his full commissioner regalia.

Charlie took her to the entrance with DI Williams.

"We will keep in touch," he said, shaking her hand. "Sorry, I have a meeting to go to. Denise will assist you back to your hotel." With that, he strode off.

"Lunch?" Sonia suggested.

"Oh, I don't know." Denise was hesitant.

"On the FBI. Somewhere nice. No expense spared."

Denise knew she wanted to work her and she so wanted to spill the beans, the cover-up, but she was too loyal and knew for certain she wouldn't. 'Careless chatter changes things that matter.' Her mentor and boss Eager, who was known to keep a lot to himself, often told her.

When the taxi got them outside the Slug & Lettuce restaurant at Tower Bridge, Sonia couldn't help but laugh.

"The Slug & Lettuce?"

"You wanted British cuisine, this is the place. Tower Bridge with a backdrop of the Tower of London."

"The name is not what's on the menu, right?"

This time Denise laughed and escorted her inside. Once seated, Denise ordered her Toad in the Hole and Spotted Dick for dessert. Sonia seemed to loosen up and laughed again at the names. They talked about Eager and what was happening on the case. Sonia said the jury was still out on the incident in the Mojave Desert. A case of being in the wrong place at the wrong time; coincidence probably, she believed. They had even brought in an American Indian expert to assist. Sonia pried about Eager. Was he married? Did he have a girlfriend? Was Ms Bell involved with him? How old was he? More than a passing interest, Denise thought, answering the questions she could, that she didn't really know much about his personal life.

"It's a pity the commander couldn't join us. All his experience, and he looks like the type to tell interesting stories. He was, though, not too communicative today." Sonia fishing.

"It's not a snub, Sonia. He is retiring soon and has a lot on his mind. So he goes to his muse and eats meat pies several times a week that he doesn't tell his wife about."

"Muse? Meat pies? Where?"

"A very small café in a back street near the Met. Called Sally's. He is her best customer for sure. Says she is an ex-con he put away who now helps him with the street gossip."

"Every day?"

"Two or three times a week. He always goes on Fridays, as he loves the fish pies."

"The pies must be good."

"Sure, if he doesn't have a heart attack with them before he retires to the countryside."

After a lunch full of questions, Denise dropped Sonia off at the FBI offices and went back to the Met HQ.

Fergus entered the Blue Heaven Club via the back door. He was a bulky six-foot man, dressed in jeans and a denim shirt with a black vest showing underneath. He wore big black boots with steel caps. His ginger hair was in a short crewcut topping a face that had been battered and scarred. His mouth had what they called a 'Glasgow smile', the scars down both sides where his mouth had once been widened, a big scar across his cheeks from the cut-throat razor blades many of the Glasgow gangs carried. He was a fearsome-looking man, a man of violence, and people would be scared of looking at him in case he noticed and took offence. One glance from him in their direction was enough and then people quickly looked or ran away. His voice made a deep gruff sound. The smile now written across his face was deceptive, as he had no sense of humour at all unless he had drunk too much. Even then, his humour could disappear into a violent rage at a moment's notice.

He was an ardent Scottish Nationalist who hated the English for domination of his country and the battles they lost hundreds of years ago. He would sing 'Flower of Scotland' in his gruff voice and talk about Scottish victories such as Bannockburn and English atrocities. There were many wars, though, and few victories for the Scots. You did not mention these or argue with him.

He was a hard man from the hard man city of Glasgow. Now he was a 'gun for hire' — as much as he hated the English, he would take their money. Jimmy Harker, in his panic after the shooting of his brother and most of what he called his 'team', needed some muscle to combat Tazewell Javelin's use of the crazy Yardies. He had bought time to rebuild his empire by giving Javelin a partnership. A partnership he intended terminating as soon as he was strong enough. Nick normally looked after these necessary violent activities, but he was laid up in a prison hospital and he was sorely missed. He had offered Fergus, Mad Mike and Jordy more than they could possibly have earned elsewhere so that they would form the backbone of a new, stronger team helping him get back his turf and street respect.

Jordy was sitting on a chair outside Jimmy's office with a revolver on his knee and a machete by his side. Fergus nodded to him and then knocked the office door and just walked in. Jimmy looked up with a smile.

"Fergus."

"Gaffer." He sat down opposite and stretched his legs out, arms behind his head.

"I've got an important job for you."

"Aye?"

"I need to find out where Tazewell is located."

"Aye?" A man of few words who listened well, which was one of his good traits.

Jimmy just looked at him, expecting questions.

"Drink, Fergus?" He pulled a whisky bottle out of the cabinet behind him.

"No, too early for me."

"MacCallan Fine Oak, twenty-one years old; are you sure?" Jimmy knew he would know the best whisky from a cheap blend.

"I've no' had a wee drop of that for a long time. Past midday, so why not?"

"Ice?"

The look was enough, he didn't have to say 'no'. No self-respecting Scot would add ice.

He poured and watched Fergus swirl the drink around, before sipping it slowly.

"I need you to get a hold of one of these Yardies, take him to the docks tank and make him tell us where Tazewell is and how we can get at him."

"Aye. Who will come to my funeral, then?"

"I'm asking too much?" Jimmy was careful with his words, as anything could shoot Fergus into violent anger. So asking him if he was scared would be a mistake.

"They are crazy, nearly always together, heavily armed, they are all bam pots."

Jimmy tapped his desk top with his pen again, as he did when thinking.

"I have asked Sammy to try and locate him. He has another task and I need to find Tazewell urgently. So I need extra insurance so we can find him as soon as possible."

"When we do?"

Jimmy just crossed his throat with his finger.

"I will need some honey."

"Money?"

"No, a bonnie lassie who doesn't mind what she does. I have one in mind, but she is not cheap. A big risk the way I see it for her."

"Money is no problem."

"A driver as well."

"I will call Willy the Wanker. Best driver we have."

"The old guy?"

"Yes, he is good and discreet. Non-threatening. Knows London like the back of his hand."

Fergus did want more money as well as the honey trap cash. Jimmy impressed again the urgency on him. He then told him about his intruder which, to his surprise, he already knew the details. Gossip travels fast in the underworld.

Chapter 38
The Deal

"So, Pat, long time, nice to see you, pal." He was good looking, slim build with long dark hair, big brown eyes and a tanned complexion women would die for. Theodore Siegel was known as 'The Pope' in Mafia circles. It was a comment on his immaculate good-guy image and many contacts of politicians and celebrities. He was also known as 'Teflon Teddy', as nothing ever sticks to him, including law enforcement attempts to link him to many crimes in California and Las Vegas. Pat knew he works as an 'Associate' for the LA Mafia running various legitimate businesses for them. Some were just a cover and others used for money laundering. An associate is a person who works for the Mafia but is not of Italian descent, therefore could not be a 'made man', their term for a protected member.

His office had a grand view of Century City in Los Angeles. He preferred soft furnishing and all his business was done on comfortable couches. The room had several televisions which were always switched on to the news.

"How's business?" Pat ventured.

"You know, Pat, lots of competition in LA. All those ethnic gangs moving in on us and surrounding us." He laughed.

"Not a big Italian population here to recruit soldiers from, I guess."

"Yep. How's our movie business? Treating you okay, Pat?"

"Always lots of police films going on. They need technical advice and mostly basics in police work — easy and well paid. So I am doing great, thanks to you."

"It was a favour for your friends in New York. They ask and who dare refuse." He laughed again and waited until Pat came out with the reason for his visit.

"How you getting on with them?" Pat watched as Teddy gulped a little bit and he could see a slight twitching on the side of his temple. A normal person would not notice these things, but Pat was an expert at reading people.

"Could be better. Is that the reason you are here, to deliver a message?"

"Oh, no. I have a proposal to make on how you can assist the Banannos family; could help you a lot."

"You have my undivided attention." Teddy leaned forward. Pat could see that he was a little relieved.

These guys make millions, but live on the edge all the time.

"Their Don went to prison last year. I hear a twenty-eight-year sentence, and he is seventy-five." Pat waited and watched for a few moments to let the direction he set sink in.

"Yes, he will never get out. All those murders and crimes and they only get him on tax evasion and laundering charges. So?"

"What if there was a way to get him out? How would they feel?"

"Seriously, have you been in Hollywood too long? Do you want to bust him out with Arnie and Sylvester?" He laughed again.

"President's pardon."

"What?" Teddy's head went backwards as he asked.

"A pardon, or otherwise he will die in prison. Got to be worth some goodwill, right?"

"Goodwill and a lot of money. Have you been drinking, Pat?"

It was Pat's turn to laugh. "Not yet. Are you interested?"

"Not only interested, but fascinated." Teddy knew Pat was a serious ex-New York cop, so this proposal was not out there in space.

"What if we could get him a pardon for a way for this dick to get re-elected this year?"

"Really? Is Jesus coming back to help? Because the way I read it, he is a one-act President? Still fascinated."

"So what if in late October his Republican opponent, which will be Preston, gets blown out the water?"

"Go on." Leaning forward towards Pat, almost in his face.

"There is a video of Preston that he would not want anyone to see. It is, I am told, dynamite, and he would just have to withdraw and run away when it goes public."

"You've seen it?"

"No, but my daughter has, and she has it."

"Where?"

"First things first. I need protection for her until it goes public, some cash — say one million to hold it to the right time and four more when it does its work."

"Can I see it? If I go to the Don and take their money and it doesn't exist, my life would not be worth a shit."

"Yes, but we need to move fast and get her into a safe location with lots of muscle, as we believe Preston has hit men out looking for the tape and to clean up anyone who has seen it."

"Seriously, are you taking something? It sounds like a James Bond movie." He did not laugh, but looked Pat straight into his eyes. Big eyes staring right through him.

Those big eyes, they should have called him Bugsy.

Pat explained the situation. Teddy listened carefully and Pat could see his mind ticking over. He knew he would ask for more money for himself, but did not care. He would have gone direct to them; however, the situation was immediate. He and Liberty needed help and protection right now; plus, if things went south, having Teddy as a go-between would be better — he had seen how they treat failures.

Chapter 39
Meditation and Mystical

Brody watched from a distance as Diablo sat cross-legged in front of the wood fire on the ground. He had bits of clothing that were left from all three bodies and the leftover part of the Amex card plus one arrow that was used. He wanted to have parts of the bodies, but that was a non-starter. He was close to the burnt-out Airstream Clipper. He had built a tent with branches and some cloth on top. A very crude type of tent with enough room for him to sit beneath.

He seemed to be smoking a small pipe and sweating profusely. He had herbs of sweet grass and sage around him. He was singing, chanting and swaying, holding the arrow. Brody heard him shout out 'Waka Tanka' a few times. Later, Diablo told him this meant Great Spirit or great mystery. All very strange and absurd to a white Anglo detective with no real religious beliefs. This ceremony lasted for several hours. He was thinking, does the FBI believe in this type of shit? It will be fairies and Father Christmas next. He could understand why they were using an Indian insider to help inside the reservations, but this mystic rubbish?

Diablo then fell over onto his side and looked like he was sleeping. Brody didn't want to go near him or wake him in case he got the blame for spoiling his dream-time. Eventually, Diablo got up, put out the fire and picked up his herbs and the materials he had used.

He had got a clear picture of two helicopters and armed soldiers and a blonde woman. The pain of the tortured and murdered. He was faced with a dilemma. Should he say it was Chief Longbow and obscure the search for him, or tell them the truth? It was, though, hard to believe he would have a helicopter at his disposal. He also now believed the deceased were just in the way and the murderers were after something else. He had seen a box and another woman in his dream-time.

When Eager and Gavin got up, the place had been tidied and cleaned. Liberty was packed and dressed, ready to go. She had coffee in the kitchen in the percolator for them.

"Are we going somewhere?" Gavin asked, surprised.

"We? I am not sure it would be better for you guys to go back to that cold, wet little island you call home." She sipped at the coffee, her third since getting up early. She was agitated, helped by the volume of coffee already consumed.

Eager poured two cups, passed one to Gavin and then turned towards her.

"We only just got here, no way we are leaving. What's wrong?"

She sipped more coffee and was quietly thinking. Gavin was searching the pizza boxes for some leftover food.

"Hello." Eager tried to get her to focus after waiting a few minutes for her to answer.

"Just women's intuition. I don't feel we are safe here any more. Not sure why my stomach is turning around and around. A voice inside my head says get out, get out!"

Eager leaned back on the edge of the sofa, facing her. "Something happened?"

"No, just this goddam awful fear and feeling they are watching and waiting."

"Why?"

"Oh, for fuck's sake, Smalls, stop asking me questions and help me make a plan to get out of here."

"Okay, but we are coming with."

She nodded in agreement. Gone was her cockiness, arrogance and fearless behaviour. Eager saw her for the first time as a young woman at the end of her wits. Her eyes were swollen, and she looked tired. Eager got the car keys and went to it. Finally finding the way to open the bonnet, he looked inside at the engine. Taped to the inside of the bonnet at the back was a cloth, inside which was an automatic pistol and some extra ammo. He didn't recognise the type and noticed the serial number had been erased.

"What the…?" Gavin was shocked when he brought it in.

"John, where did you get that?" Liberty asked.

"A present from your father, under the bonnet. A least we have some protection if your intuition is correct."

"My, you are becoming quite the cowboy, Mr English Copper," Liberty quipped.

Just then, they heard a car sound. Moving to the front room and looking carefully out of a small crack in the blind, Eager saw a black Mercedes van was cruising slowly down the road. It was not driving to the low back street limit, but far slower. The occupants were checking out the street.

"I think your intuition may be right," Eager spoke quietly.

Gavin went towards the window and Eager grabbed his wrist to stop him looking out. Liberty explained she had got up in the night to disguise the boot that was protruding out of the car port as the car was such a distinctive vehicle and colour. Eager checked all the doors to ensure they were now locked. He then checked the pistol to make sure it was loaded and he knew how to use it. The safety he left on.

I hope we didn't bring them here, Eager thought.

They discussed the situation over yet more coffee, stopping and staying very quiet every few minutes. What if the guys had been followed? What if the car had been compromised? What if they had checked her dad's friends and found the house? Where to go that was safe? Go to the FBI? No, they would take the tapes and here we go again, more cover-up, and how do we know we can trust them?

When the phone rang, they all spilt a bit of coffee.

"Jesus!" Gavin said, spitting out more of his coffee he had swallowed badly.

It rang three times and then rang off. It started again and Liberty picked it up, mouthing to them, "It's my dad."

They listened and waited. She was only on for around thirty seconds, limiting the ability to trace her number. She only seemed to say yes, yes, yes.

"Well?" they both asked together.

"Well, I think we are fucked!" Liberty started to raise her voice in a high-pitched nervous giggle.

Chapter 40
One Down

It was Friday. Commander Charlie Allcock had been summoned back to the commissioner's office at midday. Sir Michael was friendly, offered tea or coffee, which he politely refused. Sat down on the couch, with him trying to make it all informal.

"Charles, I gave some deep thought to our last meeting — it left a nasty taste in my mouth. We have been lifelong friends and I have always enjoyed your confidence and support. I want you to know that I truly believed that the PM's office would do something about these... people. I also believe that exposure of the wrong kind in the wrong way could damage the very fabric of our society. I have spoken with the PM in no uncertain terms and I believe she will review the position and a real investigation by us will begin. I want you to lead that investigation and am willing to extend your retirement date to accommodate."

Charlie just listened; sometimes it was best to let them speak, and by leaving a quiet gap they fill it and the truth sometimes comes out. This nearly always works.

"What we have to do is get Eager back here. Stop any early media release if they have dupes, until the task force is in place and actually working. You have the most influence over him. So, let's start pulling this big jigsaw in order."

"When?"

"I am awaiting another meeting with the PM. She said she would think about it and let me know," he lied.

"Then let me also think about it. I have promised her indoors to take a decent holiday and she has planned one right after I retire next month. She is always complaining that every one we have, always gets interrupted. I would have to talk with her about how important this investigation is," he also lied.

"Lunch, Charles?"

"Let me take a rain check, sir; you know, get my head around this properly."

"Pies and peas at Sally's, then?"

"What. How did you know?"

"Charles, it is common knowledge after the meeting there with Eager."

Commander Allcock went to his office, picked up some messages and told his assistant he would not be contactable for an hour, so pass anything urgent to DI Williams.

"If needed, can she get you at Sally's?"

He rolled his eyes. *Are there no secrets any more in this world?*

It was Friday, time to go to what was once his secret café and get away from the office. This was fish pie day and, being almost a good, practising Catholic, he would take fish instead of meat pie. His wife, Doris, did not know he ate so many pies, nor about Sally. She would be happy that as a devoted Catholic he was eating fish on Friday, but bloody angry about his diet deceit and suspicious about Sally, although there was nothing romantic between them. He had put her away twenty years ago, and when she came out supported her efforts to go straight. She would be angrier about the effect on his heart. He was overweight, drank too much, exercised little and had one of the most stressful jobs around.

'Back room, Charlie, your table is waiting. Fish pie today, then?"

"Big mug of the strongest tea you have, Sally. Thanks."

He had a pad with him, noting some of his thoughts down while he waited. The back room only had one table. It did have a view of the front of the café and the street. Only one other customer sat drinking a Coke by the window. An oriental-looking, well-dressed man focussed on his newspaper.

"Fish pie, chips and peas and a strong cuppa." Sally delivered his food with a big smile. Her café was a one-woman band. She cooked, served and cleaned.

"Need any help?" she asked, seeing he looked disturbed. Next to his wife, she thought she knew him and influenced him more than anyone. He was distracted, so she left him alone, scribbling on his pad.

He jumped up and went to the toilet out the back to wash his hands without saying a word, deep in thought. She went back to the kitchen.

Not chatty catty today, then.

Five minutes later, Sally heard a loud thud from the back room. He was on the floor, shaking and finding it hard to breathe. His face was contorted, and it seemed his tongue was just sticking out. He was trying to vomit and was wetting himself.

"Oh, my God!" She ran and dialled 999.

"It's the commander — he is dying!" she screamed. The operator got her to calm down, give the address and some details and despatched paramedics immediately. Keeping her on the phone and trying to get more information out of her.

"I've got to go to him and help."

"You said commander? Who?"

"Charlie Allcock, of course." She hung up and ran back to him.

He was frozen like he could not move a muscle. She held him and tried to talk to him, all the time thinking, 'Oh, my God, was it my fish? It's only a few days old.' Food poisoning would kill her business, she knew.

DI Williams and several uniform officers arrived before the paramedics as they were within walking distance. One officer knew first aid, but was at a loss how to treat this stiff man who was hardly breathing but still alive. The paramedics arrived minutes later, and he was made as comfortable as possible, oxygen mask on and whisked off to hospital.

His pie was only a quarter eaten; he had gone for the chips and tea first. DI Williams secured his notepad and pen from the table. She also ensured that the scenes of crime were called: the food would be taken and tested. It appeared like food poisoning, so all the ingredients in the kitchen needed testing as well.

Sally was a mess, sobbing and wringing her hands on her apron.

"Sit down and tell me what happened."

"Nothing. It is Friday, so he had fish pie, chips, mushy peas and a cuppa."

"Did he say anything at all?"

"No, not very talkative today. Will he be all right? I mean, the fish was fresh."

"Not sure. Look, I want to make a quick call. Lock the door; no more customers today."

"Do you want a cuppa?"

Denise just lifted her eyebrows and shook her head from side to side.

Denise rang the commissioner's office. He was at lunch, so she got his assistant to inform him immediately. Then Charlie's home. Doris picked up and she explained as best she could without panic. They said they were taking him to St Bartholomew's. She would send a police car for her, which she did next.

It took thirty minutes for the scenes of crime officers to arrive. The senior one, Mary, was grumbling.

"Just because he is a police officer, we are called out to a food poisoning. I have murder scenes to complete."

Denise lost it and backed her up to a wall and put her face directly in hers.

"Look, you. Do your job. He is a senior officer with a very serious condition. It may be poisoning, and we need to know exactly what happened. Understand? Or do I have to call the commissioner to get your head right?"

Sally came back. "He left without paying."

"What, Charlie? Are you serious?" Denise was still in fighting mode and shouted as she misunderstood what Sally meant.

"No, the other customer who was in here." Pointing at his table. "Bastard took his chance and left whilst I was busy with Charlie."

"Mary, when you've done here, check out the window table and any dishes the other customer used for prints. Sally, for God's sake do not wash or move anything. Right?" She nodded.

"We chasing non-paying customers now, are we? Waste of our valuable time, if you ask me." Mary hissed. Denise bit her lip.

She left two uniform officers to secure the scene and the SOC team to do its work. "Get a good description of the other customer from Sally. A good one, right?"

"Right," the young constable with the 'tit' helmet answered.

"And, guys, do not touch, drink or eat anything here, understand?" They nodded in unison.

167

When she got to the hospital, Denise flashed her warrant card and was directed to the emergency ward. Ten of the detective team were already there waiting, anxious. Doris Allcock was seated outside the operating theatre. Several doctors came out, heads down.

"Sorry, we did our best. He was gone just after he arrived. We tried everything, with no response. Please accept our condolences," the tall senior doctor stated with a long face he reserved for giving bad news to friends and relatives, which was a constant in his life.

Doris fell apart. Several of the women detectives tried to comfort her.

Denise took the doctors aside. "Can you tell me what happened? I mean, what did he have?"

"Not really, until the autopsy."

"Your best guess, then?" she pushed.

They were uncomfortable at guessing and hesitated.

"I need to know how to handle this?" She saw the commissioner and other top brass in uniform arriving, so moved the doctors into a waiting room.

"He was numb, had muscular paralysis, and couldn't breathe."

"Food poisoning? He had been eating a fish pie."

"We pumped his stomach. Helped him vomit; symptoms of very serious poisoning, but not sure I would say it was food. If it was a fish, then it was probably a month old and a whale he ate." His observations were not appreciated.

She took their names just as Sir Michael came in with an entourage of top brass.

"DI Williams, Denise, can you spread some light on what happened?"

She gave them a run-down on what she knew. The other detectives from the team were crowding around the back of the chiefs to hear.

"So, a very serious case of food poisoning?"

"No, sir, I'd say it seems more serious than normal food poisoning, which we will not know for sure until the post-mortem results." Mouths dropped.

They could hear Doris screaming and crying as they let her in to say goodbye to Charlie.

Chapter 41
Bad News

"You wanted to see me, boss?" Mad Mike Hegarty walked into Jimmy's office and sat down in front of him. Jimmy looked up from his paperwork, stone-faced.

"Well, tell me how you fucked this up?" Throwing the *Daily Crier* newspaper across the table.

"Fucked what up?"

"Read — no, the other side headline."

"Mmm. 'IRA Bomb Northern Ireland Hero.' Funny."

"What the hell is funny? You screwed up." Some of Jimmy's normal cool and calm demeanour had been lost during the last few months.

Mad Mike read with interest. Jimmy was tapping the table with his pen in a show of frustration and impatience.

Mike folded it in half. "It is funny, so it is, as I couldn't find a source for the explosives, so I have opted to snipe him. The rifle is in my car boot; took me some time to get the right one. I was seeing you and setting off up north. Not me, as he would be dead now for sure if it was."

Jimmy stared at him for several minutes.

"Then who?" They were both mystified. It was on the street that Mad Mike, ex-IRA, was working for the Harkers. This attempted bombing had all the hallmarks of the IRA. So, someone was either trying to kill McAllistar and set them up, or worse still, get him to come after them for revenge.

"We still have to terminate him," Jimmy eventually said.

"You're kidding, right? He will be on high alert. Police are probably giving him protection. It would be more than madness to try now. Better set up some protection around here."

"And the intruder?"

"Don't let this wee baby put the frighteners on you. We need to set a trap. Any word from Sammy?"

"Nothing so far. He normally comes through, but this guy is like a ghost."

"Could be him that bombed McAllistar?"

"What?"

"He may be under the same pressure time. Get this done quick for a big bonus; and he didn't trust us to get the job done."

"Or he wants McAllistar to come for me."

"Or it was the IRA."

"Do not confuse this any more than it is — and get rid of the rifle. You will be a police target, now."

The phone rang. Jimmy was saying yes and nodding. His face screwed up tight.

"Yeah, you bloody do that!" were his last words before he hung up, slamming the phone down.

"Boss?"

"Nick was attacked last night in the prison hospital, for God's sake!"

"He okay?"

"No thanks to the prison staff. Yes, an inmate tried to smother him in the night. Unfortunately for them, Nick being Nick had found and kept a needle, you know, a syringe with some shit in it. He managed to stick it in the guy's neck."

"How did he get that?"

"Part of the protection I am paying for, I guess."

"So, they are in action prior to us doing what they wanted?"

"My best guess, maybe a message to me. The prison authorities haven't bothered yet to tell me as next of kin, typical."

"Who was that?"

"Our new lawyer — he is connected to the big prisoner guv in prison."

The biggest conference room in the building was filled with the top brass to a point where the rest of the junior officers were standing around spilling out into the corridor. Charlie Allcock was a legend and a highly popular officer. DI Williams and her new boss, Detective Chief Superintendent Bill Sutherland, who had just been appointed in the absence of Eager and now Commander Allcock, were sitting at the end

170

of the conference table. The commissioner was at the top and the rest in order of seniority.

"Thanks for your support and attendance today. We will cover what we know so far. DI Williams?" Sutherland, being new to fine detail on the case, handed over. This was sensitive and he did not want to be tripped up in front of all the top brass and his new team. Using Denise Williams was safe and made him look like he did not grab all the limelight.

"Charlie, I mean Commander Allcock, often frequented Sally's Café close to HQ. He was acquainted with the owner, Molly Pollack, since he put her away over killing her husband twenty years ago. She was a continually abused woman, who eventually used a flat metal iron to the back of his head after her husband beat her stupid. She got three years for manslaughter. Commander Allcock was helpful in her rehabilitation and was known to love her pies."

Someone in the corridor said, "And the rest." Heads were turned in anger from the table, but the culprit could not be identified.

"We were able to fast forward the post-mortem. I attended with DCS Sutherland. They were only able to give us a verbal report and a theory at this stage, awaiting further test results. It is therefore thought that Commander Allcock died of a very serious poisoning. A substance called Tetrodotoxin, much more poisonous than cyanide. They based this, as I said, on prelim tests and his symptoms."

There was a mutter around the room. Someone said, "The bastards." It was quiet when the commissioner held up his hand and looked around with his more serious face of annoyance.

"Continue." He was inpatient for the full report and needed to hear the next steps.

"SOC are still testing the food. They did find in a dustbin at the rear of the premises, parts of several fish, one being a pufferfish. The proprietor, Ms Pollack, goes to the Billingsgate market every Friday at five a.m. to get the fish fresh. The pufferfish carries in some of its parts a poison called Tetrodotoxin. This fish, as you all probably know, is what the Japanese eat as a delicacy. Chefs are specially trained to cut out the dangerous parts; even so, around thirteen or so Japanese people die every year eating it."

"Are you sure it was a pufferfish from Billingsgate market? They are experts, would know a fish like that on sight," the commissioner cut in.

DCS Sutherland took over on this point, being an avid fisherman. "If I may, sir, the pufferfish — also known as the blowfish — is found in the Atlantic, Pacific and Indian Oceans, some in freshwater in Australia and the Amazon. It is possible one did get caught and got through the screening process at Billingsgate, although I doubt it. Could have been a special order. We have sent a team to interview and check out the market."

"It was used in the James Bond film *From Russia with Love*. If I remember right, the assassin's shoes with metal knife points were tipped in it. Said to be twelve seconds before a person dies. Bond, didn't he get an antidote," Bernie, a new DS, spoke up, which he regretted immediately.

"There is no antidote — that was the movies," Sutherland responded rather brashly. Bernie was glad he had not continued to say that Ian Fleming wanted to kill Bond off, but was talked out of it, hence the antidote coming into play. He didn't — he just slipped backwards into the corridor out of visibility from the senior officers.

"Witnesses other than Ms Pollack?"

"One who disappeared without paying during the time Commander Allcock was suffering on the floor. His glass and table were checked, with no prints. Ms Pollack thought he was wearing gloves. He was of slight build, with a pencil-thin moustache and a goatee. He was wearing black jeans and a zip jacket with a white turtle-neck shirt, black-rimmed glasses and a black beanie-style head covering. He spoke English with an American accent, she believes, but he only spoke a few words, ordering a Coke, so she is not one hundred percent certain."

Standing at the back, DI Samuels' ears pricked up. This could be the guy they are looking for. He made a note to call it in and get them off his back.

"That's a pretty thorough description; I mean for a casual customer," Samuels stated.

"She said he looked a bit odd to her, so she, in her terms, checked him out," Denise answered.

"What has she to say for herself?" the commissioner asked rather angrily.

Sutherland spoke up, "She denies any wrongdoing; says they have been firm friends for over twenty years. He helped her go straight. Vehemently denies buying a pufferfish and has no idea how the remains got into the dustbin. The pufferfish was not on her receipt from the market, although she paid cash and could have had a second receipt."

"Cautioned?"

"Yes, sir," DI Williams responded.

"Ladies and gentlemen, everyone under chief supers please clear the room." The commissioner wanted to ask questions, but he didn't want to be the centre of the Met gossip machine. There was a rumbling of discontent as they filed out. He nodded to DI Williams to stay put. When they had left, he continued.

"Charlie was a life-long friend of mine and the best copper on this force. It hurts me to ask this, but was there anything between them romantically? I mean, he was retiring, probably moving away. Could she have felt jilted in some way?"

DI Williams grimaced. Sutherland looked at her to answer. She responded immediately, trying not to let her loyalty to the commander show it was impacting her objectivity.

"Sir, I doubt that very much. Anyone who knew Commander Allcock well knows he is not the type. Last thing on his mind, loyal to his wife — only the job got priority over her."

It was the commissioner's turn to grimace as he considered himself a close friend and wasn't sure she was having a pot shot at him. He let it go. "Well, maybe, but Ms Pollack could have had other ideas? The evidence is pretty compelling in her direction."

"I have only seen them together on one occasion, and I didn't pick anything up of that nature, although I could be wrong," Williams retorted.

"Other scenarios?"

"We have the task force looking at all the villains he put away. Including the most recently released. We will track them all down. If I may speculate, though?" Sutherland was a master diplomat; that is how he came up from the ranks so quickly. "If this wasn't Ms Pollack, it would seem too sophisticated for our ex-cons. They would more than likely use extreme violence in a quiet non-public place. Unless this was a paid hit by a professional."

"I agree," the commissioner nodded.

Possible, but there are other avenues to check out, thought Denise Williams. She decided to hold her tongue until she put some more thoughts together.

"Others?" the chief pushed.

"The Harkers possibly, as his team were hot on them since the Hellfire Club incident. Again, a little sophisticated for them," Sutherland added.

Or someone on the tapes he saw that the government has held wanting to keep him quiet after his retirement. Did he have a book deal or anything? Denise decided this would infuriate the commissioner without some supporting evidence and took a mental note to check it out further.

The commissioner closed his folder and put his pen in his jacket pocket.

"So, we need to charge Ms Pollack with manslaughter." It was a command, not a question.

"If I may, sir?" Sutherland intervened. "I would like to check out every avenue possible first. Further interviews with her will, I believe, be fruitless at this stage, but we will still try. She has been cautioned and had the means and opportunity, but I am not sure after twenty years of friendship a concrete motive has been established. I would not like to lose any prosecution that eventuates."

"Bill, do what you have to do. I will make everything you need available and run interference if anyone slows you down. Turn over anyone with the slightest suspicion, bring them in whatever. DI Williams, you take Pollack and continue to push her. I will see Charlie's widow — she may know or felt something was wrong. I will, of course, be very sensitive. We need someone locked up for this... words fail me."

"Sir," they both stood up and said at the same time. As he was leaving the room, he turned, looked then both up and down and fixed his stare on DI Williams.

"And get bloody Eager back here now!"

Chapter 42
Stardust

Liberty said her dad was coming to pick them up, which would take a good two hours from LA, depending on the traffic. They were all now packed and ready to go, waiting anxiously, peeping through gaps in the window blinds, when they heard a car go by. They heard a bang outside and Eager actually dropped the pistol on the floor. It was the postman at the outside box delivering some mail. Liberty picked up the gun.

"Give me that," Eager demanded.

"No, Smalls, you are too dangerous with weapons — you could have shot one of us." He walked towards her, hand out. She put the gun behind her back and slapped his hand down with the other.

"Children, stop it! Aren't we in enough trouble?" Gavin was stressed and annoyed.

"He started it, and he is not having this back as Brit cops are not trained with firearms." She used her little girl voice.

"I did a course and came out fifth in the class," Eager said indignantly.

"Well, I bet that was so long ago, before I was born, eh? You probably learned on a musket or blunderbuss, and if you were fifth then there was probably only five in the class."

She started to laugh and so did Eager. She always seemed to get the best of him.

"Okay, keep it. I'm going out." He put on his jacket and looked towards the door.

"Oh, little baby, stay here, it's not safe out there."

"It's not safe in here with you and that weapon. No, I need to check-in from a public phone. I saw some on the main drag. I will be quick."

She stood blocking the door, gun pointed downwards to the floor. Gavin just shook his head in disbelief.

"Seriously? Out of the way."

"No. Remember the last time we had a fight? Who won?"

"I still have pain there, and you cheated. Look, I need to see what is happening at home or I will be out of work when I get back."

"You might not need work if they get you." She stepped aside and kissed his cheek as he left. "Be careful."

He found a few public machines and tried to work out how to use them. He would have to use his credit card. Still, they were leaving in two hours, so what harm could it do? He was amazed that he got straight through to Met HQ: DI Williams was in the canteen and would be called. He held on. Denise must have run, as she was panting when she answered.

"I can't talk long. I have so much to tell you about," he said.

"So have I," she said.

"Fire away and be quick; no small talk — they will find me if I hang around here too much."

"They? Find you? What is happening?"

"You first."

She told him about Charlie Allcock, the bomb attack on Logan and the attempted murder of Nick Harker. He was shocked and distraught and dumb struck. Charlie had been his mentor, boss and friend.

"Are you there, John?" Denise was concerned. What was he involved in there?

"Yeah," after a few moments. "Send something for me to the funeral, usual stuff. I will pay you when I come back."

"Commissioner wants you back now. Gave us an order to get you back." He didn't answer.

He then related quickly what had happened since he landed there, without giving away his location.

"When will she be able to go public?" Denise asked, concerned.

"She has typed up her articles and now needs to sell them carefully. Gavin is here and is checking, editing. They are leaving the book until the end of this saga."

"Or their end."

"Yes, quite. Get to Logan — there is a pattern here. I think they are cleaning up anyone who saw the tapes, so he needs to be careful."

"I think he knows that. When are you coming back?"

"As soon as she is safe."

"My new boss, DCS Sutherland, wants to talk with you."

"Tell him I will call when I am at our next stop."

"Where?"

"You know, seriously, I do not have a bleeding clue."

Pat McGill arrived at lunchtime in an old white Ford delivery truck. Two seats in the front and just old boxes in the back and no windows. It must have been used on movie sets to carry props around, they assumed. No one was allowed in the front, so they all hunkered down with their luggage in the back.

Pat could see blinds moving as neighbours peered out to see what was going on. Oh well, he thought, his special friend would not be pleased at the state of the place and the big Chevelle sitting in the drive. He would square it with her when she gets back from filming in Australia.

"That damn hat!" Eager noticed Gavin's outsized cowboy hat that they couldn't lose was in the truck.

"Not me," Gavin said.

"Dad threw it in, didn't want it staying there when his friend gets back," Liberty explained.

Just as they were backing out of the drive, a black Mercedes truck stopped right behind them, blocking the way. Pat had to put the brakes on hard and they tumbled around in the back.

"Get out slowly!" a voice shouted.

"They have balaclavas on and automatic weapons. Two of them, one on each side," Pat whispered. "Two of you get out and move to the front of the van. Use the gun, John, I will distract them?"

"Yes, we have found them. Talk to Tiger," one said on a radio.

Eager was shaking, not used to firearm situations; he hoped Pat was an expert, coming from New York City. He would follow instructions and realised this was now life or death for them.

"We are unarmed and law-abiding citizens. No need for guns. What do you want?" Pat stated calmly as he stepped out of the driver's side with his hands up and turned to face the assailant on his side.

177

Liberty slid the side door open on the other side and started to talk in her little girl voice.

"Help me, mama, these men are going to hurt me, mama." She dragged Gavin with her and they fell onto the next door's lawn.

"What the fuck! Get up." They had been told that 'Tiger' would tidy up and so were hesitating.

"Mama, help us." She rolled around on the grass, keeping Gavin rolling over as well.

The guy on the other side tried to see what was happening, distracted.

The voice on the radio said, "Waste them now."

Pat used the seconds Liberty had distracted them and pulled the revolver that was tucked into his trouser leg and fired two quick shots, hitting the man in the head. Eager, who was on the other side, threw the big Stetson hat out first high in the air and then jumped out and rolled over. He fired two shots, hitting the other in his foot. He sat up quickly and pointed his automatic weapon at them, when there was another crack. Pat finished the job.

"Move the fucking truck!" Pat shouted, and Liberty was the first to respond, jumping in and reversing across the street into a neighbour's drive. They then all jumped in the white van and Pat drove away quickly. Police for sure would be alerted by now. Soon they were out of town and they started to recover their wits.

"Mama, help me. What was that about?" Eager imitated and took the mickey out of Liberty, which would distract her from his uncontrollable shaking, he hoped.

"Oh, if I hadn't distracted them, we would all be dead by now, mister."

"I took a course."

"What, in making him not be able to wear shoes ever again?" They all laughed, as you do when you are nervous. Pat, though, did not laugh or speak; he just drove, keeping to the speed limits, continually checking all the mirrors to see if any back-up to the hit team or police were following.

Steve called the Bureau chief from the local Palm Springs police station.

178

"Talk about confusing. The neighbours said it was a shoot-out. Black Mercedes van with two hooded men with auto weapons and they think four people from the house in a white van. They were sure someone was shot. One saw a second black Mercedes arrive; however, when the sheriffs got there, no black vans and no injured or dead, just a big cowboy hat on the driveway. The neighbours got down on the ground just after the first shot was fired; they said five, others said four. The Chevelle was there at the house and inside it had been lived in for sure. No registration plate was noted, just an old white van, maybe a Ford, they were not sure; as usual, they said it happened so fast."

"There is more to this than we imagined."

"Yes, did Sonia get anything in London?"

"Nothing more than we knew. They were holding back Official Secrets Act cover. She has opted to stay over for a few days' R&R."

"We need to rethink this as we are definitely missing something big." Steve was sure. He also thought, *What the hell is she doing going on vacation mid-investigation?*

"Yes, and by the way, Eager's commander just died of suspected poisoning."

"Bad time to die."

"It always is. Get back here. I will ensure we send out an all-points for the van. I will send a team to pick up Mr McGill — he must know something and it's time to cough up."

"So, where are we going?" Eager asked Pat.

"I have a plan and a safe place," Pat answered. He was calm, considering he had just killed two men. If he was worried, you wouldn't know it, Eager thought. He felt bad enough just shooting the guy's feet. Gavin had made himself comfortable on two cases and was drinking from a water bottle. "The book just gets better," was all he would mutter. Eager was sure that the water bottle had vodka in it.

"Where we going, dad?" Liberty asked.

"The Stardust Hotel and Resort," he said proudly.

"We are going to Vegas? They will find us there."

"No, not with what I have set up; plus, we will have some heavy dude protection."

179

Gavin was smiling; he could see the bright lights, gambling and, most importantly, decent cold beer. Eager just sat back and listened. One thing he knew for sure was that Pat was a pro, and whatever he had set up would protect his daughter and them.

He reflected on Charlie and his untimely death; he was sure it was murder and connected. Just before he retired. He reasoned that if those government bastards had done the right thing, this would all be public, and he would still be alive. Total and utter political animals, only after power and more power, no matter the cost. He was sure he was on the right side of this and would give DCS Sutherland a piece of his mind when he got him on the phone. No more kid gloves — time to call it as it is. He was angry, very angry, and didn't give a damn for the first time in his life about losing his job.

The rest of the journey everyone was quite deep in their own thoughts. When the bright lights of Las Vegas appeared, they relaxed a little. The place was crowded with vehicles and people on the streets. They pulled into the Stardust and immediately four big men, security guards, took them with their luggage to a High Roller room in a tower designated for them. The van was driven away and lost in the lower ground car park and covered.

Eager and Gavin were amazed at the sheer luxury of the suite. It had three bedrooms and three bathrooms. The lounge and kitchen were bigger than the bungalow they had just stayed in. Flowers and chocolates decorated nearly every surface of the room. The fridge was full-sized and loaded with all types of alcohol, with some bottled water and juices. The kitchen was fully equipped, although Eager doubted whether a high roller would ever use any of the facilities. Gavin was into the beer almost before their cases hit the ground.

"A room each," Pat said. "I am going back tonight." He handed his Colt to Eager. He couldn't take it on the plane.

Eager, don't say anything; dad doesn't know we are together. Liberty was trying to tell him with her eyes.

"Telephones you can use, and you will not be traced. The room will be guarded twenty-four-seven. Downstairs, armed guards will stop anybody from using the elevator. All have been briefed on potential problems, although I doubt anyone will find you. Your names have not been used, nor credit cards. Do not go out, though. Room service is great, so no need."

"Thanks," was all they could say.

"Liberty, can we talk privately? I need to explain the deal I have made."

Chapter 43
Hit and Misses

"Tazewell?" Jimmy picked up the phone at his house.

"Stupid move, Jimmy."

"Stupid? What are you talking about?"

"Picking up one of the Yardies' boys."

"Come again?" Jimmy was thinking fast. Fergus must have got one; however, the trail must lead back to him somehow. How? "Are you crazy? We have a deal and it's working and can only get better."

"He is the brother of the leader, Jumaane, and he is called Crazytennisfan. Hand him back!"

"Not us, believe me. Is that name a joke or what?"

"No, not a joke. Would I be calling if it were? They are going crazy and if they think it's you, a world war will ensue. That's not what anyone wants, right?"

"They operate on the streets and have used violence to push other gangs out of their areas, so they have many enemies. We have a partnership — why would they think it was me?"

"The description of the girl: I think I have seen her at the club. He met her at a bar and she got him to go with her yesterday. Not seen since."

"Tazewell, we have hundreds of girls through our club. I am not responsible for all of them. Description?"

"Dyed long blonde hair, rings through her nose and ears, big boobs, long legs, very tall, has a scar on her upper cheek, dresses like a cheap slut."

"Could fit a lot of girls. I think I know who you mean, though, I've seen her around. She is on the game and probably operates in a lot of pubs and clubs. In fact, I think we have tossed her out and banned her. I can check and see if anyone knows her and where she lives and get back to you."

Bloody Fergus: all muscle and little up top. Why would he use someone so distinctive? Why not one of the girls with a wig and not body art jewellery in her face. Someone who could change and not be recognisable. Jimmy knew it was his fault for not giving clear instructions. He didn't fancy her chances when she hit the streets looking for punters or a fix. It would lead right back to Fergus and then to him.

If brains were dynamite, he wouldn't have enough to blow his hat off.

"You'd better not be playing with me! I haven't mentioned you to them yet." Tazewell was threatening, but hoping this was not true and therefore would not side-track the lucrative deal he had with the Harkers.

"Calm down. Some odd stuff has been happening." He explained about the bomb at McAllistars and the attack on Nick. He also lied and said someone had tried to break into his house in the middle of the night a few days ago. Too dangerous to let Tazewell know that he was a target and he had been ordered to help or else.

"Who, what and why?" Tazewell was buying that a third party might be involved.

"I can only guess that they are still intent on cleaning up after Karlein and the Yank situation."

"So they are trying to find me?"

"Just a guess. You are a hard man to find; I have no idea where you are staying, so maybe trying to get information. I have doubled my security, until this blows over. Sammy is out trying to find the intruder, must be a professional." He gave a brief description of him.

He knew he needed to get hold of Fergus as soon as possible, so he sent Mad Mike to find him with a message. Complete the job and the girl must disappear quickly for good.

DI Samuels called in from a public phone box on Jimmy's private number. He updated Jimmy about Commander Allcock's demise and gave a description of the assassin. Jimmy was pleased, but did not let him off the hook; he still needed him to come through on the evidence against his brother. He did say he would send some cash for his information. Teddy Samuels felt a new kind of dirtiness inside. Would he never be free?

Jimmy called Jordy and handed him a note with the description. "Get this to Sammy right away and also everyone on the team you can reach. This is the guy we are looking for."

"Can I do it after lunch, boss?"

"Now! For fuck's sake, Jordy! Now — do you understand?"

Jordy ran out of the room.

Gina Jones was enjoying herself in Berlin. Good session this morning with the local team. New agents in Russia and Belarus. Still station chief for Europe with information she had kept that should see her promoted to at least Deputy Director of the CIA or maybe Director when the vacancy comes. She thought of the song from the film *South Pacific*, what was it? 'If you don't have a dream, how you going to make that dream come true?' She hummed it. She needed time on her own to think and call her best contacts in Langley to catch up on what was going on.

The Kaffee Bar on Stargarder Strasse was a top restaurant with five-star rating and she sat outside near the kerb in the sunshine. She was on her own; it was private before lunchtime, when it would be packed both inside and out. She loved German food and their strong coffee. She had her phone pressed to her ear, talking away, and a cigarette in the other hand. She did not notice a man with long hair on a pushbike come along the Strasse. He stopped at the kerb, got off the bike and calmly took out a semi-automatic Russian Tolkaren TT-33 handgun and fired one 7.62 x 33mm round into her head and five more into her chest. Death was instant. He then cycled away as if nothing had happened. No one came out of the café until they were sure the gunman had left. Later, he threw his wig, gun, jacket and bike into the River Spree.

"Logan."

"DI Williams." They nodded to each other. Denise took off her raincoat and sat opposite him.

"Denise, please."

"Drinks?" George appeared at the bar.

"Coffee, please," Denise answered, and Logan nodded in agreement.

"Coffee it is then." George went off grumbling to himself as he owned a pub and wanted to sell alcohol, not be a café.

McAllistar had gone back to the George & Dragon pub, where he, Eager, Gavin and Liberty had hidden out previously. It was safe and no one other than DI Williams knew about it. The rooms were cheap and the food okay. George, the landlord, was an ex-cop and friend of Eager's.

"So, you are bombproof as well as bulletproof." Denise was amazed that he was looking so good after the shooting. He was a tall, handsome man, normally of a few words. A man you automatically trusted and, being a good friend of Eager's, she knew that trust was solid. She was there during the rescue from the Hellfire Club and the stories others told of what happened inside and outside the club: this military hero who saved the day was like a hero out of the movies. A Brit Clint Eastwood at least.

When the coffee tray arrived and they had filled their mugs, they got down to business.

"Have you heard from John?" Logan asked.

"Yes, he called yesterday. He is running around California with Liberty and Gavin; they think they are being followed. He sounded very worried."

"Aye, he should be. When will they make public the videos and stop any reason to shut them up?"

She filled him in on the untimely death of Commander Allcock.

"The pie shop lady did it. I saw it in the paper on the way down."

"Not as far as I am concerned. The Kremlin wants a body to hang, draw and quarter. No one kills a top cop and gets away with it. She is a convenient fall lady."

"Kremlin?"

"Sorry, Met HQ internal nickname. I think they are close to getting the videos made public. My guess is the running and hiding slows them down. Why are you here?"

"The bomb. I need to put an end to it all."

"Logan, I am a police officer. Do not tell me you have come to kill Harker."

"If need be. How else can I live, knowing that they are still trying to put me down? What life is that?"

"We need to put them away one way or another," she agreed. "Did you ever meet or hear of Mad Mike Hegarty when you were in NI?"

"Heard of him. Is he involved?"

"He works for the Harkers now."

"That confirms it, then. The car bomb had the hallmarks of the IRA. One of his specialities, from memory."

"I am not sure. He has an iron-clad alibi on the night you were attacked. Midnight mass at St Martin's. Father Conor and several others of his congregation confirm it. So he couldn't have got to Derbyshire from London in time unless he flew. Left the church at one forty a.m. The assailant was on a motor-bike, we are told."

"You believe them? Mad Mike at mass?"

"Apparently, he is a devout catholic go figure. Father Conor has been at St Martin's for a long time. He is genuine and well-loved. I don't believe he would lie for him."

"Catholic priest, right? They lied in NI big time. Talked about peace and some encouraged and covered up for the terrorists."

"You seem bitter. That is not totally true, and you know it."

He held his head down, thinking and angry.

"There's more to this. I'm telling you this in confidence. Give me your word that this remains between me and you?"

He looked up and held her stare, looking right into her sparkling blue eyes.

"Aye."

"Harker was visited by someone who threatened him that if he didn't kill you and Tazewell Javelin then he and Nick would be toast."

"Again, that settles it, it was them. Who visited and how the hell do you know this?"

"No, not them, not just yet anyway. Special Branch have an undercover agent inside. Listen carefully to me now."

He looked like he was not believing this, a line maybe to put him off his mission.

"Listening? Nick Harker was almost smothered in prison hospital. You were almost killed by the bomb, Charlie Allcock was murdered, Jimmy Harker threatened. Makes you wonder? No such thing as a coincidence?"

"The Yanks have come back?"

"That's my belief," she nodded.

"But not the Kremlin's?"

"Not regarding Charlie. There is so much evidence connecting Molly, the café owner, that her prosecution will be a slam dunk. Only thing missing to me is an iron-clad motive."

"He put her away; prison is shit, I know — a good motive."

"Not in this case. Abused woman gave herself up, not really a big case of police detection and pressure; plus, why would she wait twenty years and…?"

She paused, thinking about it.

"And?"

"I think she loved him."

"Oh. What am I to do, stay here the rest of my life?"

"No." She looked around nervous and didn't want George to earwig. "When we find this hit man, I want you to have him and make him talk."

"Whatever are you suggesting, young lass?"

Denise explained over the second mug of coffee that this guy was pro. Nothing to connect him with Charlie's murder other than he may have been there. The only witness to that was the chief suspect. No prints in the café. If the police get him other than in the act of killing someone, which she doubted, he would probably walk away scot free. No doubt he would have a good brief; the evidence would have to be conclusive and overpowering, otherwise the prosecutors would not touch the case. Anyway, no way this guy would talk under any circumstances; they would get zero info.

What they needed was who hired him and any trail leading back so they could get to the mastermind. It had all been organised to look disconnected. Charlie poisoned by an ex-con with a grudge, Nick Harker killed in prison by a rival drug gang, Logan killed by the IRA who had seen his recent exploits in the UK and held a grudge regarding his hero status from his military work in NI, Javelin would then be killed by the Harkers because he had double-crossed them and ruined a lot of their street cred. Also, they are fighting for their territory back from his Yardies. What did they have in common? They were all involved with the Hellfire Club videos and had probably seen them.

"What if he doesn't talk? What do we do with him then?"

"Can we cross that bridge when we get to it?"

187

"Let's hope there's not a bridge too far."

"Are you in, Logan?"

He nodded and stared at her. She had a certain kind of beauty, for a woman that dresses like a butch police officer, certainly not to please. He could see her arm muscles and thighs were big. This was a strong lady with an angel face.

"Aye, I'm in, bread hooks an' all."

One thing left to do is put Sonia from the FBI on this Travis.

Chapter 44
Sit Reps

Travis sat in the Roman-style salt-water pool. He was naked. The other customers of the Post Hotel & Spa in the Rocky Mountains, Alberta, Canada, were kept away by his Secret Service protectors, who guarded every entrance. He had been hunting all day since five in the morning. The sun was going down and he hoped to go out later to get a glimpse of the Northern Lights. He was on his own, drinking the best champagne this hotel had, which was a Pol Roger Brut Champagne. He had been told this was a fruit-forward champagne and a favourite of Winston Churchill and British royalty. His H. Upmann Sir Winston cigar sat in an ash tray beside him. The pleasure of being able to smoke and enjoy Cuban cigars in Canada was a treat. Being illegal in the US, he had to hide them and only smoke in his den.

He was now the presumptive presidential candidate for the Republican Party and would be the leader of the free world soon. In his mind he was going to be the world's new Churchill or much better. Yes, he was flawed somewhat, but so was Churchill; you needed to be good and bad to know how to command and win. Only this annoying problem could prevent him from putting his marker down in the Oval Office.

He had shot an elk, a Big Horn sheep and a Shiras moose today. More trophies for his den. He enjoyed hunting, the chase, the great shot, not just wounding the beasts like amateurs, but always an instant killing shot. Painless for the beast. The Army in Nam was just a killing machine not half as much fun. Off to Ontario tomorrow — he wanted to shoot the biggest black bear he could, and find a place for it inside the Oval Office with the one he had already. He would get resistance, he was sure, though he always got his way. It would send a message to all that entered who they were dealing with.

"Where are you, guys?"

"I'm in Palm Springs," Amanda said.

"Langley," the general stated.

"Are we secure?"

"Yes." The general was confident.

"Well? Status?"

"I'm trying to clean up the mess Gerald's guys caused." Amanda sounded very angry. Gerald just coughed, awaiting his turn.

"Mess?"

"We found them and unfortunately I was at the other side of town. The goons decided to take them themselves and lost."

"What do you mean, lost?"

"One dead, one seriously wounded, who will have problems walking in the future. Targets drove off." Amanda sounded exasperated.

"Gerald, what the hell!"

"The status is as follows, Travis." He ignored Amanda's accusation. "Two targets have been taken out in Europe. The rest, there is a plan in process right now. Both terminations were clearly distanced from each other. A third was missed, but is back on our radar. We have two assets working in London right now."

"It's like fishing — we got some minnows, but the big ones got away." Travis was loud, but did not sound as angry as he usually did, dealing with failure.

"Amanda is right." No point fighting with his favourite lady; it would just infuriate Travis. He continued, "They were leaving the premises in Palm Springs when my guys arrived, one team of two. They had no idea the targets were armed. The briefing we got, it was clearly a newspaper editor and a visiting English cop, and we know they do not carry guns, and a young girl reporter. No weapons anticipated, plus we did not know that there was a fourth person who was armed and obviously weapon-trained with them. So to stop them and curtail the biggest threat, they made a call. As it happens, the wrong call, but that is always the case when we look in hindsight. The bottom line is, we are making progress."

"Not quick enough."

"Yes, sir. We have located her father, who flew into LA from Vegas and arrived back by air this afternoon."

"So we can guess they are in Vegas?" Amanda asked.

"I suppose so." The general sounded deflated.

"We need to pick him up and his wife as soon as possible." Travis was chomping on his cigar and stating the obvious.

"Already in progress, sir."

"I have heard from London that a detective there told the FBI about you, Travis, being a connection. She has put together the happenings in the UK and wanted the FBI to start looking deeper." Amanda put petrol on Travis's fire.

"We have got to stop this! Put her on the list." Now they could hear Travis was gulping his champagne and they knew his temper and blood pressure were rising fast.

"I have fixed it. It will not go to the FBI," Amanda announced with confidence.

How the hell did she do that? The general was confused.

Detective Brody, Diablo and Steve were in one of the LA FBI small conference rooms.

"How did you go?" the chief asked, not really expecting anything they could use. Brody reflected on how sweaty and crazy Diablo had looked during his 'dream-time' and he didn't really come up with much other than what he had told him. Yes, it was his punishment escorting him.

"It would seem to be a hit team. Two helicopters, at least four men and a woman, blonde. They were after something — a box is all I could see — and another woman, also short blonde hair, who came before and got the box. The dead were just in the way."

The chief pretended to be impressed. It was kind of what we knew, Steve thought, except for the other blonde woman, but he said nothing. Brody may have talked too much in the car. He was sceptical.

"So, not Chief Longbow then for sure?"

"No, they tried to copy and blame him. Longbow has good reason every time he kills." He saw their faces and corrected himself. "I mean, in his mind he is justified."

Brody thought he should suggest later to the FBI that Diablo fitted the profile of Chief Longbow. He reflected that this would be crazy; of course they knew he was okay, that's why they picked him. He would look stupid. He also thought he had been a little indiscreet in the car on the way back, saying too much he had picked up on this case; hopefully he would not mention anything specific.

"Steve, update us, please."

"Can I stay? I find it interesting and feel involved," Diablo asked.

"Sure, nothing you hear goes out of this room. Okay?"

Diablo nodded. "My oath."

Steve reported on the Palm Springs incident. Prints found all over the apartment; nothing, though, matched anyone on the database. They could only assume it was Bell and the Englishmen. The surprise was they were carrying weapons, if the neighbours were to be believed.

"We have now got to assume that Bell has got something very valuable. That her threat when she arrived is very valid and someone is very scared. These are very professional teams after her. There was a third man with them, driving the van they went off in. No one took the number plates. We have to find her, we must find her and take her in for her own sake. I do not understand why Eager, being a cop, has not brought us into his confidence. This, to me, means he does not trust the FBI, but why? Wouldn't it be better getting us involved and our protection?"

"I might be speaking out of turn here," Diablo started. "Could it mean they are scared of something bigger than the FBI?"

"Nothing is bigger than the FBI," Brody said, and then immediately regretted it.

"Or more to the point, what they have is very valuable and they do not want to lose control of it. By the way, Steve, you may not know that Eager's commander has died. He was poisoned by, it seems but not confirmed, a café owner's fish pie. She has been fingered for it," the chief said.

"Not a good way to go. Could it be connected?"

"Not according to Sonia."

"Is she coming back soon?"

"She wants a couple more days, which I thought, since she is there why not."

"She needs to nosy around a bit. Get the local office to intro her to police contacts, listen to the gossip and so forth. I would also get her to speak with the newspaper Bell and Hastings worked for, as I am guessing here," Steve ventured.

Yeah, enjoying her London junket, I bet.

"Guessing?" the chief asked. Steve was thinking in the time-line of the events.

"Okay, she makes allegations against a UK government minister. She upsets the local gangsters with her reporting on them. The paper then apologises and states there are no foundations to her claims. She loses her working visa, comes back and threatens on national TV that she will prove she is not a fantasist. The ex-editor of her paper and a senior detective come out here and as far as I can see are supporting her. The people who attacked them are heavy duty, if the neighbours are to be believed. Two teams, as one must have cleaned up pronto. So she has something on a major figure which she can prove. Being a reporter, she is going to sell it to the highest bidder."

"So why not trust the FBI?" Brody asked.

"If I may," Diablo interrupted, "whatever she has was done in the UK. It may be either she is scared her information will be taken off her like she claimed in the UK, or…"

"Or?" the chief asked. He had almost regretted leaving Diablo in the room, as this was far beyond his brief.

"Or it is a major US figure."

They were silent for a while, mulling over what he had said.

"There was a bombing in the UK by the IRA. Wasn't this McAllistar with Bell there?" Brody spoke up a little hesitant.

"What?"

"It was his car they put a bomb under. Army hero bombed by IRA."

"How do you know this?" Steve asked, surprised.

"Newspaper, just a few lines. I had a lot of time out in the desert and read it from cover to cover to help with the boredom."

"Chief, did Sonia mention this?"

"No, I get all my info from the press," he said sarcastically.

Good, the newbie missed this when in the UK. Steve was pleased that the chief was beginning to see her weaknesses.

"He was a high-profile figure in the UK due to Bell and the media, probably caught the eye of the IRA. So they wanted to make a statement.

No one is safe," Brody continued with more confidence since his news had interested the group.

"He previously worked for the Harkers, the bad guys. A lot of bad blood between them, according to Eager," Steve put in.

"So, did they have the wherewithal to wipe out three people in the Mojave using helicopters again, pros a week or so after Bell landed? Bomb another player in the UK? Now the same team attacks her in Palm Springs. How would they find her? We have so many resources at our disposal and even so it took us time to work out where she was, with a bit of luck." Steve was asking more questions but with few concrete answers.

Again silence; you could almost hear their brains ticking over.

"Not sure, so let's keep all our options open." The chief rose to go, signalling the end of the meeting. "Steve, a moment if you don't mind?" He stepped into the corridor.

The chief used his fingers to count the instructions he was giving Steve, even though he couldn't see what he was doing.

"Get her back here, I have sent a team to arrest her father, if he is not with his daughter. Bringing in his wife or girlfriend and any staff on the premises. We need to charge him with lying to the FBI; he knew where she was and maybe he is the driver, the third man. If he is not there, I will put out an APB. I am getting Claire to go to the studio he works at, check any other vehicles that might be missing or he has used; Bell's car was from there; she needs to ask around, pick up what is happening. I want to know everything about him, everything. We need also to find the owner of the house in Palm Springs. I doubt it was her father's; being an ex-cop, it would have been so easy to trace."

"On my way."

"Not finished yet. I will get Blobby tracing who from here in the last eighteen months of a high profile has been to London. Celebrities, military, politicians, the super-rich businessmen and anyone that catches his eye." Blobby was a desk agent now too big for active duty, he worked in research.

"The president's been there," Steve said jokingly.

"Everyone," the chief retorted, not impressed.

"We need Sonia to get more involved with the detectives in Eager's team. Something is going on and someone knows. On second thoughts, should we raise it to the London Bureau chief to pursue further? He and his team are more experienced and have the police contacts. Sonia can brief them." Steve wanted others to be involved, not trusting Sonia's skills.

The chief grimaced as he thought about it. He nodded, as he knew Steve was right. "I will call him personally and brief him this morning."

"Sonia?"

"I will get her to come back and help here. By the way, Steve, the CIA's European Director was just assassinated in Germany yesterday — not general news yet. She was based in London. Probably not connected; a bit out of the ball park."

"A lot of people dying in or around London," Steve said, and left in a hurry.

Chapter 45
Oh, What a Tangled Web We Weave

"This meeting is dangerous and out of my contract agreement," the man said in a low voice. Whispering as if someone was listening.

"We need to know how long until you fulfil your full contract?" the woman said.

"The terms of the contract are difficult."

"That's why we are paying so much," she said with sarcasm. He went quiet and ignored her barb. She broke the silence.

"Is Mr H following the plan?"

"He has had his warning; however…" He shifted in his seat, subtly looking around the cinema, which was dark and empty. *The Godfather Part II* movie was playing in the background. "I am not waiting on them. Not impressed with their professionalism."

"You need to focus on target number one again. This time you need to ensure he is no longer a problem," she said with force.

"Be careful," he replied with an underlying menace. No one questioned his professionalism.

"Can I help?"

"He has gone to ground. Telling me where I might find him would help."

"I'll see what I can do." She passed him a picture of a black lady with Tower Bridge behind her. "Meanwhile, she works at the Met HQ and I think may know where he is. She has just been added to the list, same terms, but we need her now as she can lead us to our number one target, I am sure. Okay?" On the back of the picture were a telephone number, name and title and the address of the HQ.

"I will send another message to Mr H."

She left one way and he the other, twenty minutes apart. He liked the movie.

Sammy was buying a newspaper from a street vendor. He noticed this small, slim guy dressed in black with a Beatles-type jacket with the trademark round top neck, no collar. A white turtle-neck shirt stuck out at the top. A slight Asian look to his face, the bit he could see.

Wearing a baseball cap, with a black moustache and goatee. Some things didn't look right to his discerning eye and high awareness. He checked the description he had been given, to be sure. Could the white showing around his neck look like a priest's collar in the dark? Was that a real moustache? He walked slowly for a man his age, and yet his physique looked so agile. More like a Bruce Lee, he thought. Some things seemed out of place for this guy — not sure why. Days of pounding around London wearing out his leather shoes; was he just hoping this was his man and making it fit. He followed at a short distance, excited.

Being discreet was one of his great skills. This man, though, seemed sensitive to his surroundings and stopped every few minutes to check around to see if he was being followed. He did it so well that a normal punter, Sammy thought, would not even notice. A foreign tourist in London looking around to catch all the sights and sounds. It felt more right, as he followed. He caught a taxi and Sammy hailed the one behind and kept on the tail of his quarry. The first taxi stopped in Regent's Park, the man got out and walked to a small hotel that looked like a house, Astor Park number eight. He looked around and then started towards the door, and for some reason changed his mind and walked on. It looked like he had the wrong address. Sammy knew he had feigned this; years of experience following people. He decided that this was his lucky day — wasn't number eight very lucky in China? Was this guy Chinese? Should he follow and risk this sensitive professional catching on?

The decision was made for him. A double-decker red London bus came along and the man jumped on it. No time for him to follow and jump on the bus without alerting him. No taxis around. He waited, as usually he believed in London you waited and waited on a bus and then two would come together. Not true this time, dashing his theory. He needed a public phone, but where? He remembered one was outside the Queen's Pub on Regent's Park; if he was quick, he could be back and watch the hotel before this man got back.

When Denise returned to her desk, there was an abundance of messages. One from Special Branch: 'Ring back urgently, Keith.' She had just lifted the telephone when DCS Sutherland walked in with two guests. He motioned to her to put the phone down.

"DI Williams, please meet Special Agents McVicker and Jameson from the FBI."

She stood up and shook hands. McVicker was a dapper fifty-year-old with greying hair and piercing brown eyes. Jameson was very pretty, and in her thirties, dressed in a blue designer suit, blonde hair, tight figure. He wore a dark suit, white shirt and red tie. The FBI kind of uniform, she thought.

"I'm sorry, boss, I just got an urgent message from Special Branch."

"It can wait, Denise. Our guests just need a few minutes of your time." It was an order. She showed them her cheap metal chairs opposite her desk and they sat down.

To her surprise, Sutherland excused himself, apologising that the commissioner had summoned him. "Denise knows everything we know," he told them as he left.

"We have been asked by our LA office to visit to see if we are missing something." He spoke in a cultured accent and she wasn't sure it was fully American. The lady had a pad and pen out.

"I told the agent from LA, Sonia, everything I know." It was obvious she wanted to move on and follow-up with Special Branch.

"We won't be long; we know you are very busy," Agent Jameson spoke up.

They went over the usual ground about Bell and the incidents during her time in the UK. It was taking longer than she wanted, even though she was rushing. They asked a lot of questions. Denise kept checking her watch. The phone rang again. She excused herself.

"Keith."

"What's taken you so long? We have a lead on the hit man." He then explained over the phone and she scribbled down the information. She asked if she could call back as soon as possible. He was not impressed.

"Sorry, just got some key information on a suspect and his whereabouts. We need to bring him in for questioning as soon as possible," she told the agents.

They seemed unperturbed.

"Well, if you think of anything, please let me know." He handed her his business card.

"Sonia said she would follow-up on this Preston guy; any news on that?"

"Preston who?" They now seemed fully alert all of a sudden.

"Travis Preston."

"*The* Travis Preston?"

"Yes, if he is the big politician." She thought she heard two whistles under their breaths. They both sat forward, almost in her face.

"Exactly what did you tell Agent Turner?"

"She didn't pass it on?" She was amazed. Covering, they said maybe she had held it back from them as a need-to-know due to Preston's position.

"You can tell us now."

"Just that if you connect some dots, he could be involved."

"You seriously suggesting that the Leader of the House, maybe the next president, is involved somehow?" He was a little indignant in his tone.

"Just saying that rumour has it he was at the Hellfire Club and may have been compromised. Then a US hit team invades us and kills the key witness and an MI5 agent and seriously wounds another potential witness."

"That all. Is there any proof to these ridiculous allegations?"

"That all? The proof, I am told, was handed over to the CIA by MI5 — a video. That is as much as I know."

"Why wasn't this communicated to the FBI earlier?"

"Not totally believed or supported by the higher yens here."

"So maybe not true. You need to be careful with wild allegations — they can impact the US elections. Strain UK and US relations. Yes, young lady, serious ramifications. You need to stop any of this talk!"

"Well, you are saying shut the fuck up. I'm another fantasist like Liberty Bell. Well, why are they chasing her in the US and killing more people?"

She stood up and walked out; interview over.

Steve turned up back at LA FBI HQ. He was summoned to the chief's office urgently. The chief stood up and closed the door behind him, looking very nervous and excited at the same time.

"McGill?" Steve asked.

"Not there; neither was his girlfriend. According to a neighbour, he thought they were filming at his house. Guys with masks and guns. So the team had reason to enter with Brody. A lot of blood all over the place — walls, curtains, tiles — and water, maybe pee. I have SOCO checking out the place. He had just arrived back from Vegas, according to the airline ticket."

"Anyone else see anything?"

"No, just this old guy doing his gardening. You know Beverly Hills." The chief rubbed his chin. Steve scratched his ass as usual.

"Yeah, I know. So they probably are in Vegas. What contacts does he have there? Can I get Blobby onto it as soon as we are finished?" Steve asked, finishing his scratching when the chief looked at him funny.

"Sure, looks like they have got the father and his girlfriend and the mother. A ticket from LaGuardia in her name and unpacked suitcases in the house. They will get the info they need one way or another and go to Vegas to complete the task."

"Right, I think I should go there." Steve was sure that would be their best bet.

"I have just got off communications with London. You will not believe what they were told by a Detective Inspector. She thinks that Travis Preston is involved."

Steve whistled and just sat up, open-mouthed.

"She is not supported by her seniors and London thinks she is some type of conspiracy theorist."

"You believe them?"

The chief thought about it for just a few seconds. "You tell me, Steve, how this fits with what we know." He was wanting some corroboration from the closest person to the case, as it is easy to jump to the wrong conclusions on such a potentially big case.

Steve thought about it for a minute. "It fits. This Javier Gonzalez, after boasting in a bar and a restaurant that he was going to get rich. He asked the barman about Travis Preston and how rich he was after watching the TV news on his presidential campaign. He visited Preston's new campaign office in Vegas that night and later he was killed in the Mojave. Some conspiracy theory," Steve said flatly.

"What if I was to tell you Blobby says he was in London two months ago, along with a few others, I must say, including the president?"

"Shit! This is too big and over both our pay grades added together." Steve started scratching again.

"I know, and it gets worse."

"How the hell?"

"The Brit detective told all this to Sonia."

"No report back?"

"Nothing. I cannot understand why she didn't tell me; she just asked for more time there."

"Maybe she thought it was utter rubbish."

"Even so, she should have mentioned it. We were looking for a potential US connection and this allegation is too big."

Steve thought about it. He did not want his distrust and dislike to taint his view of Sonia's actions. Then he thought, screw it.

"Ever thought, chief, why she was posted here so soon and made my partner, putting him on a desk job for a newbie? We were then working on the Bell case just after. Ever thought how these gunmen knew Bell, Eager and Hastings were in Palm Springs?"

"There's more."

"You are kidding me!"

"DI Williams is Eager's second in command. She has heard rumours that a video was handed to the London CIA of him by MI5."

"The CIA station commander that has just been killed in Germany, more like an execution?"

"Looks like it's connected."

"Get this. The CIA Director, General Gerald Hughes, served under Preston in the Army and is tipped to be in his cabinet when he gets elected."

"Oh, what a tangled web we weave when we first practice to deceive." Steve used a bad false Scottish accent.

"Walter Scott. I didn't know you had any Scottish blood in you?"

"Way back, my Great Seanair, grandfather. What are we going to do now?"

"Untangle the web without getting stuck in it and eaten alive. Not a word to anyone, understand? No one at all, not even your wife, Steve," the chief said, knowing Steve would know this was absolutely a secret he couldn't talk about, but emphasising.

Except me, thought Diablo, listening in on his bug under the chief's desk. A simple short-range bug you could buy at any security equipment store in the malls.

Chapter 46
Dirt on the Market

"Hello."

"This is Teddy here, a friend of your father. Is he there?"

"No, he left last night for LA, Mr Siegel."

"Oh, he mentioned me, good. I have tried his home and office and no one is picking up. I urgently need to see the merchandise. I have an important meeting in New York tomorrow and cannot put our proposal forward unless I am absolutely sure. Once committed, they can be very unforgiving if we do not follow through."

"Right, got it. Thanks for the accommodation and security. I have the, what you call merchandise hidden; however, if you fly via Vegas, I can meet you in between flights. Do you have a mini video player we could use?"

"No problem; we have a studio full of them. I take it that I cannot show our buyers?"

"I have gone through hell for this story and cannot risk anyone jumping the gun on me; unless, of course, they pay first, as you have suggested."

"Bring security with you, then. I will call Big Gary later with flight details and time."

"Can someone visit and check on dad? He has not called in. I have tried his home and it's worrying under these circumstances."

"Sure, I will pop round this afternoon; short distance from my office."

He rang off. Liberty turned to Gavin and Eager. It was time to tell them the deal her dad had struck. Afterwards, they had their mouths open wide and no one made a sound for a few minutes.

"Well, what do you think, Smalls?" she asked.

Eager looked perturbed. Gavin's eyes were almost dollar signs — he was obviously hoping to get a share.

"If they launch it just before the elections in November, right? That's over a month away. I can't stay and protect you that long. We are now playing with the Cosa Nostra. My life was so simple before I met you. Just murderers, gangs, thieves and rapists," Eager said with disappointment in his eyes and a lip he was biting.

She bent over, laughing. "Protect me! I think it was the other way around, Smalls, if I remember right!" She was trying to be funny, but it did not go over well.

"I am probably going to be sacked as it is, and they are going to try and take my pension off me. I bet the commissioner and his team are in a scrum right now. I need to get back and face the music, see if I can salvage anything of my career."

"Scrum?" Liberty was confused.

"Rugby term, you know, like your American football but the original. They get down and put their heads up each other's arses," Gavin explained.

The visual thought of that made Liberty smile and wince.

"Liberty." Eager sounded exhausted with the whole saga. "We need to end this now before we all get killed."

The phone rang again. Liberty picked up quickly and looked disappointed.

"Gavin, it's for you." Handing him the handset.

Gavin was going yes, yes, yes, and nodding. He finished with, "Great, I will let you know where and when."

"Who?"

"The Germans are very interested. Love sticking it to us Brits. That's the Australians, *National Enquirer* and *Washington Post* and *New York Times*. Should I call Sir Richard, the little bastard, and tell him it's all going to come out and he'd better ante up some dosh or he will be the only UK tabloid without this big story?"

Both turned on him. "Gavin, we can't trust him; it will get out before we publish. They will try anything to stop us!" Eager screamed at him.

"I was just trying to get my job back," Gavin said in a sad tone.

"Don't worry about your job with that maggot of a paper. We will share proceeds and you will be a sought-after editor and journalist.

Probably on all major TV shows. A celebrity — offers will flow in," Liberty said with her best sales hat on.

Gavin just smiled — that was the dream, if he lived to taste it.

"So we have an auction. Where should we hold it safely?" Eager asked.

"Not here, that could expose us. Not worth the risk," Liberty said, and was thinking hard. It had to be reasonably close, not a place that anyone would guess, busy with people. She looked in the hotel room's book and picked out local tourist pamphlets. They both crowded around, looking over her shoulder.

"Oh, the Grand Canyon. I would love to go there." Gavin was excited at the thought.

"It's not a vacation we are on, Gavin," Eager admonished him.

"They might find us and throw you both into it," Gavin responded with a laugh.

"Smalls, he's on the right track. Look at the Hoover Dam — it has a café with a big outside sitting area. I have been there." She passed the pamphlet to Eager.

"So how do we do this? The ones that lose the bidding war will run a spoiler pre-empting the winner," Eager suggested.

"Depends how much we tell or show them. The less, the lower the bids." Gavin was thinking he had been involved in buying dirt before, not selling it.

"What did you tell them?" Liberty was concerned.

"Just we have a dynamite story that will sell papers like hotcakes; a major expose that will rock Britain." Gavin was pleased he had dangled the bait without telling them anything.

"I will need a publisher for the book. It needs to hit the streets globally right after the media has wrung this story dry," Liberty stated, always one step ahead.

"You will need to complete it first." Eager, as always, the practical cop.

"I was doing okay until you came along and distracted me every night." She punched him in the chest.

"I have this business card from a literary agent who put it in my hand when I arrived at JFK. Kent Koll, literary agent. Smooth-looking customer."

"I have checked him out. Works with celebs' books with their usual stories of people they screwed. He also helps protect them when in trouble with the media. Makes money out of a lot of dirt." Gavin was pleased with his knowledge.

"Find his card and call him, as dirt is now our business?" Gavin asked.

"I called Denise this morning," Eager butted in.

"I know, I heard you. Not many men leave my bed at four in the morning. Is your girlfriend okay?" she teased, pretending to be jealous.

"London is in the middle of a war, I think. She is certain Charlie got poisoned by our friend Preston's people. Seems a hit man is in town." He caught them up on the latest.

"There's a second book in this," Gavin said, thinking of the dollars coming in.

"Maybe a film; your dad can pitch it to the studios. Better than all these shoot-'em-up action heroes. Do you know how false it is running and jumping out of the way of a thousand bullets? Do you know how long they would last in real life? About a minute, that's it," Eager added.

"How many times have you run from a gun in your thirty-five years as a Brit cop?" Liberty was making fun of Eager's favourite topic: unrealistic cop movies.

"Not counting the Hellfire Club firefight, well, I was almost killed in a riot in NI when Logan saved me. Paintball? I played it several times and these geezers brought automatic paintball guns."

"Oh, my poor baby, how did that work for you?"

"It is not funny — paintballs really hurt. I think I was on the field two minutes before I was sent off dead. The second time I didn't even make a minute."

"Oh, Smalls my hero, I am glad you are here to protect us." She laughed at him, very amused, which always irritated him. He showed it by turning his back to her. She came up from behind, linked her arms around his waist and whispered into his ear whilst chomping on the lobe.

"I have a plan that will save your job, not that you will need it when we sell our merchandise, so think about going back with something up your sleeve."

"Just what is your new plan? Me breaking into number ten and threatening the PM? Maybe I should tell the commissioner that you hypnotised me to follow you? Or I had a nervous breakdown and needed to go to a clinic in the US?"

"Don't be so testy. What if we held back one video, on condition they leave you alone and, get this, allow you to lead the investigation into the paedophiles on the tapes?" She held onto his lobe with her front teeth.

"Yes, and pigs will fly." He couldn't help but giggle; she was making him have goosebumps all over his body. He thought he heard Gavin say under his breath, "Go back to your room."

"Well, I did hypnotise you with love, yeah? No, if we can hold back Preston's tape, we can hold number seven and then they have a choice. Give up the rest and protect number seven."

"We won't get as much; number seven is the big hook after Preston," Gavin protested.

"You are…," Eager started.

"A genius!" Liberty finished, being her modest self.

An hour later, Teddy Siegel rang back.

"I have bad news. I have been to Pat's house. Police tape all around it. The cop on security said three people are suspected of being kidnapped."

"Shit! Dad, Cynthia and maybe mum. Shit, shit, shit! Dad said she was flying out when she read the Arturo murder. This is too much; I cannot risk them being killed. These people are for real."

"Slow down; logic it. What do they want? The tape, yeah, and you."

"I'll have to give it to them."

"No, you will lose your leverage and they will kill them anyway. Will Pat tell them where you are?"

"He is a tough Irish ex-New York cop — I doubt it."

"What if they threaten to kill your mother?"

Stunned. "Yes, I think he would, hoping I was well protected and could be smart enough to get away from them. These are nasty mother-fuckers!"

"We have some of those, too. You need proof of life and a trap — but how? Let me think about it and put the word on the street; also work our police contacts." He rung off. She fell onto the luxurious sofa next to Eager. Gavin had opened a beer for himself.

"Hey, big guy, pass me one."

"Me, too," said Eager.

She related the call. They sat there, shocked; suddenly this game was real, although they knew this already. This was, though, so close to home.

The chickens have come home to roost, Liberty reflected.

"I need to ring Steve from the FBI. I think he is a straight shooter. We need all the help we can get."

"Do not tell him where we are," Liberty demanded, too scared to argue.

"I am not an amateur. I will go down the street to another hotel and use a pay phone." He could see she had tears in her eyes; even so, she rolled them upwards when he said he wasn't an amateur. Yes, you wanted either to love her or kill her.

When Eager rang into LA FBI, he was immediately put through to the chief. A brief explanation and he had to ring back. Steve was already in Vegas. The chief wanted ten minutes to find him and then suggested a meet-up. He avoided berating or questioning Eager, as that could come later; he needed to carefully bring him into his net. Eager rang back from a street phone. He should meet Steve at the Hard Rock Café on the Strip in ten minutes. Eager had refused to go to the FBI office. They tried to trace the call, but he was too quick.

He had just put the phone down when the chief got a call from the director of the FBI in Washington.

"Just got a report from London office. Some loose talk about Travis Preston by a Brit inspector. Your agent was told, so you must know?"

"No, I wasn't told. Special Agent Turner is on her way back and I will debrief her then. She is new, as you know, although I cannot understand why she didn't tell me earlier. She said she wanted to tell me in person."

"So when did you find out?"

208

"I spoke with my counterpart in London this morning. He mentioned it, said the UK inspector was a bit of a conspiracy theorist and wasn't supported by her seniors, so he had disregarded the validity of it."

"So when were you going to tell me? Nothing in today's report."

"Well, I thought, rather than repeat this wild accusation and have it bantered around, I would debrief her first. I have asked Jerry to visit the Met at the highest level and have this DI shut up."

"So no validity to this; are you sure?"

No, I am not, he mused, thinking fast. Could the director be involved? Did he transfer her to LA as a mole? What if this was correct — would he and Steve be at risk? In the end, his training and dedication to the line of command, regardless, got the better of him.

"No, I am not sure. I am checking some activities that may be connected."

"Are you or are you not investigating Travis Preston, and if you are, why the hell wouldn't I know? Do you know how sensitive this is? It's an election year, for God's sake; even a whiff of this as a rumour could tilt the election, and the FBI would be the cause, right in the middle of the politics. I would be up before the Senate committee in minutes, and what would I say?" He was very angry.

"I am not in the business of sending in half-assed, not checked-out-thoroughly rumours on such a sensitive issue. And no, I am not investigating Travis Preston specifically, and yes, you would be the first to know if I do." He had his back up, and whilst he appreciated the director's concern, he had no right to speak to him like a rookie — this was not the FBI culture.

"You'd better come in today; nothing happens at all until I am involved, got it? And I mean nothing and now!"

"Right, sir."

Steve was waiting at a table in the café, easily spotted with his FBI dress code on; the rest of the clientele were holidaymakers, mostly drunk, in very casual clothes and some in costume. Eager did not notice any other agents around, outside or inside.

"Mr Eager, I presume?" Steve stood up to shake hands and thought the quote he used all the time would relax the situation.

"Special Agent Stanley." Eager shook hands and sat down. The waitress was upon them immediately and he ordered a banana milk shake. Steve had a black coffee sitting in front of him. The mood changed.

"Can you give me a good reason why I shouldn't drag your ass in for lying to the FBI and probably a host of other crimes I can think of?"

"Now, now, Steve. That is not the way to start. You need to listen to me carefully. I need your urgent help — three lives are at stake." Eager was calm and in his professional mode.

"Okay, spill it." Steve sat back and folded his arms across his chest. Body language, 'This better be good' obvious and he knew it.

"Where do I start?"

"Right at the beginning; leave nothing out and tell me why you didn't trust us."

"You'd better order dinner and supper, then. Let me give you a quick outline. This is not personal, as you will see; we do not know who to trust. Even now I am unsure about friend or foe." Eager looked him in the eyes to see any response. He was carrying the Colt inside his jacket pocket and hoped Steve would not see it. Another crime, he guessed.

Eager was very succinct, giving police reports following the events in the timeline they happened from London to Vegas, nothing missed out. Meanwhile, Steve was computing the information in his head, connecting the dots, working out whether Eager was telling the truth, the whole truth. Fucking hell, he thought, this is 'PrestonGate', and he was right in the middle of it, for good or bad. Then another agent walked in and came up, asking Steve to step outside.

"Message from LA for you."

"Yeah?"

"I quote: 'Back off everything, do not meet Eager. Nothing at all more, absolutely nothing. Do not call; I will see you in the office'."

"Read it to me one more time." He did. Steve stood outside the café, a bit mesmerised. Never in all his years as an agent had he had such a message. Too late with Eager, what was going on? Not even a 'Call me urgently'.

"Right, will do. Thanks for bringing this to my attention."

He tried to logic it out. The shit had hit the fan for sure, so he needed to ring Blobby to see if he knew anything. He turned it over and over in his mind. Now he had the full lowdown from Eager, he was being stopped in his tracks. The biggest case of his career. He asked Eager to wait and found a call phone in the café near the toilets. All Blobby could tell him was that the chief had been summoned urgently to Washington.

Eager was happy the other agent had not come to arrest him; not sure he would have pulled the gun on two FBI agents. He could see the headlines now, 'Rogue Brit cop kills two FBI agents', or even worse, 'Brit cop killed in shootout with FBI'. He shuddered and suddenly came back to real life as Steve returned alone.

"I have been told to back off this case," he told Eager, and at the same time ordered them both a beer.

"What?"

"Your DI Williams told our London agents and Sonia that she suspected Preston. The word must have gone back to HQ."

"Does that mean you cannot help us?"

"Not officially, it seems. I have a plan, though, to get the hostages back. It is as dangerous as hell. Especially after what you have told me."

"My knees have started knocking already, so tell me, please."

Chapter 47
Diablo's Mission

He said goodbye to the FBI office as he stood outside on his way back to his hotel to pack and fly home. There was no one he had worked with available: the chief, Sonia and Steve travelling and young Brody back to his LAPD office. He had called the leading agent on the Chief Longbow case (a name he hated) to tell him no dice, not connected. He was then able to recover the bug from the chief's office. He told the assistant he was leaving a small gift — a real home-made Apache arrow — which he showed her that got her attention and a moment's distraction.

He then made a detour to the local library and sat down to read about Preston's family history. It didn't take long to find the family ranch outside Lockhart, Texas, an area populated by the oil and gas industry. Preston's wealth came from this industry, with the addition of beef farming. The ranch was situated on the Southern Plains, once the home of the Comanche, Kiowa, Cheyenne and Arapaho. Today, the remnants of these once-proud tribes were split around reservations. Their way of life had been taken away from them by the white settlers and their land stolen. There were many wars between these Indians and the white man as they fought for existence and were gradually ground down.

He could trace Preston's ancestors back to Jedediah Preston, his great-great-grandfather, a young soldier who rode in 1846 with Colonel Christopher 'Kit' Carson, who persecuted and terrorised the Navajo Indians in Arizona. Carson then marched eight thousand of them, into captivity three hundred miles from their homeland. Jedediah was also with General Crook in 1873 as the leading scout with a rank of Major in the Apache Wars in Texas, Arizona and New Mexico. The Apaches were murdered; men, women and children in their camps by the white settlers and the cavalry.

The river running through Texas was called the Red River by the white man, but to the Indian it was red because it had carried their blood.

Tears rolled down his eyes as he read about the atrocities and government after government that simply had no time or political will to treat the indigenous people properly. He had known about this history; however, he had never read it in such detail and meaning for him.

Jedediah Preston was awarded a large swathe of land in Texas for his roles in the Indian Wars. This became the seat of the Preston family and the start of their incredible oil and gas wealth situated on those lands. Southern Plains Indian lands.

The urge came over him, the feeling that Preston could be punished for these crimes against humanity, regardless of when they occurred. This time he did not try to fight it — it felt so right. He was a bad man and maybe will be president, and Diablo knew he would be doing the country, nay the world, a big favour. He, as he always felt, would be on the right side of the killing. Preston had ordered his men not only to kill innocent people, but to blame it on him or Chief Longbow, as the FBI called him.

The papers carried stories about the presumptive presidential candidate who, having completed an exhaustive tour campaigning and won the right to contest November's elections, was resting on his ranch in Texas. The polls showed him so far ahead of the incumbent president, they were predicting a landslide victory.

Diablo told himself that this would be his last revenge, last serial killing, the murder to end it all. He was sure his urges would then disappear and he could go back to a normal life on the reservation knowing he had righted many wrongs and rid the world of a menace. He would go home and make his plans after serious dream-time.

This would be his mission.

Chapter 48
The Traps

In he walked at a leisurely pace. He had a smile on his face which exaggerated his Glasgow smile scar, literally ear to ear. Jimmy Harker looked up at him and nodded to sit opposite. Fergus sat there smug and waited on Jimmy to speak.

"Well?" Jimmy had eventually waited long enough.

"Done, boss." He leaned forward and put a piece of paper on his desk. The paper was a scrap piece of an envelope covered in blood. Jimmy handled it by thumb and finger, as if it was diseased.

"This his address?"

"Yes, boss."

"You sure?"

"Very sure. I went there and watched at the time I was told he normally leaves."

"You saw him?"

"Sure, the little fat wee bastard."

"Gone to the country then with my money."

"Nice little mansion for sure."

"He has already called blaming us. Described your bait, so she will not last long on the streets and that will lead back to us." Jimmy let his frustration come out a little.

"Aye, they will not find her whatever description they have. She was made up in a style to attract the Yardies. Cheap slut style. Look at her, an actress between gigs."

He showed a picture of a classy dark-haired lady, dressed immaculately, oozing class.

Jimmy nodded, impressed. "Well done. I'm sorry I doubted you. And the Yardie?"

"Trying to learn to swim on his motor-bike."

"So, no witnesses, then?"

"Nothing to connect us."

"Good. How do we get at Javelin?"

"You would need a small army. The building seems to have at least six guards, all well-armed. He leaves with several cars and again four to five guys armed to the teeth."

"The house is surrounded by fields. Only clean option is a sniper from a small wood about five hundred yards away. Can Mike do that distance?"

"I guess so. We will need to ask him. I was told once that a good sniper can shoot over a thousand yards, but it will depend on the quality of his equipment as well."

"Escape route?"

"Small mud road leading to the back of the woods. Not visible from his house. The main road does lead past the woods and it would only take the guards I guess thirty seconds to get there by bike, if they are not in shock or scared to move."

"We only get one crack at this, otherwise the roof will fall in on us. They are crazy and do not care how, when or who's there when they attack."

"Use Willy, then. He was very useful when we kidnapped this guy. Very quick."

"Ex-getaway driver for some big bank robbers. Age has not slowed him down."

"Yeah, he needs to wear bigger suits." Fergus laughed at the vision of Willy the Wanker in his suits two sizes too small for him.

"Where is Mike?" Fergus asked, as Jimmy was distracted, tapping his pen on the desk again as he thought.

"Mike?" Fergus repeated.

Jimmy wanted to tell him about the intruder.

"Oh, good news. Sammy thinks he has found our intruder in a boutique hotel in Regent's Park. Not sure one hundred percent he is our guy, but I trust Sammy's instincts. So he has joined Sammy with Willy watching the place for him to return. I told them to take him alive, if possible, then you can have him, see what he has to say."

"So if we get him, will we still need to do in McAllistar and Javelin?"

"Yes, Javelin certainly. McAllistar probably; the bomb near miss would have woken him and I am sure he blames us, so he will be on the warpath. We need first to know who this mystery hit man works for and how many more of them are out there."

"Busy time, boss."

"Think of it as a cleaning-up, paving the way for a new brighter future."

"Nick?"

"He is okay. The dick that attacked him was a lifer, says he was offered money by a woman who visited him. Needed it for his family. She knew his record and advanced a grubby hand of cash and promised another. He will not see the end of his term."

"Grubby hand?"

"Cockney for a grand."

"Aye. Description?"

"Black, attractive, well dressed and an American or Canadian accent."

"Sounds like someone I would enjoy playing with." The vision of Fergus torturing a woman in a sexual way, being a pervert on top of a ruthless killer, crossed Jimmy's mind. People like Fergus and Mad Mike are a necessary evil for his line of business; not his choice of colleagues, though, but the need justified his decision to bring them in.

Leslie De Silva, the LA Bureau chief, sat in FBI HQ in Washington outside the Director's office. He had ordered him in immediately and the Learjet had gone at top speed of over five hundred miles per hour from LA. He had ordered it to take-off almost vertically — quite an experience, like a rocket going up. He had not wasted a minute in getting there and now he was left sitting for almost an hour. A pissed-off boss punishing him for some reason (or none), or a power play or both. Put him on the defensive was the psychology, which was bullshit.

Gordon Shackleton was a political beast, a man who had risen not because of his detective skills or cases he had cracked. He was a charmer, a friend of the rich and powerful, a boss not a leader. He kept his nose very clean, played all sides, played safe. Threw people under the bus if it suited him and kept his hands from also being dirty. He was called 'The

Teflon Man'. De Silva met him often and his skin crawled when near him. He was sure his tenure would be short and then his life and many others in the FBI would be so much better. The FBI's culture was so strong that even a poor leader could not stop the organisation from achieving.

"You can go in now, Mr De Silva," his over-glamorous assistant told him after answering the intercom. She looked like she was entering a Miss World contest, not an FBI assistant to the top guy. Could he add womaniser to Shackleton's weaknesses? He hoped so.

"Leslie, sit down." Shackleton looked up from his desk. He was at least sixty years old. Kept all his own wavy brown hair, good looks, immaculately dressed, even though he was in his white shirt sleeves and blue braces. He was ploughing through De Silva's report, making it look like this was the first time he had been able to read it properly. De Silva just waited, legs crossed. He was a calm, calculating man who understood body language and the psychology of the games people play. It surprised him that Shackleton would be so obvious to an experienced old hand like him. Shackleton threw the report down on his desk like it was a hot potato.

"Leslie, do you understand how dangerous this all is? This is an election year, for God's sake. Innuendo, rumour and bull like this can cause a major problem for the FBI, me and you." He pointed right into his face to emphasise 'you'.

De Silva said nothing, preferring to listen and let the steam come out of this windbag. He continued. "This is a conspiracy theory aimed at the probable next president, and we are developing it into a full-blown enquiry! You can just imagine Capitol Hill and the press saying we are trying to sway the election; that is not our role and I have no need to remind you of that, I am sure."

"We have just put the facts that we know down in the report. There are areas that warrant further investigation, that is all. People have been killed and more are missing, presumed kidnapped."

"You have a woman that has been branded a fantasist by the UK media and government. The murders in the Mojave can be explained by other theories like drug wars and maybe this serial killer Cochise. If she has proof of anything, and I mean anything, she has had plenty of time to make it public or give it to us to protect her. Has she done that? No is the answer, and why is my question?"

"Not sure," was all De Silva could say. He did not mention that the nickname for the serial killer wasn't Cochise — not worth the wrath of correcting him. Too much time rubbing shoulders on Capitol Hill, planning his next move, to know the name of a dangerous serial killer; not interesting enough yet to be fully on his radar screen.

"Not sure? I'll say not sure. Last politician she attacked was in the UK and didn't she have to apologise, no proof? Just wild reporting. Do you think I can condone further use of resources and end up in front of a Senate committee asking me why on national TV the FBI is investigating a presumptive presidential candidate just before an election? How could I justify what you are doing?" Before he could answer, he continued, "No, I bloody well can't! I can't!"

"We have to do our job without fear or favour, and if the timing is bad, so be it." De Silva was trying to fight back.

"Fear or favour. That's not what this is. If we had hard evidence linking Preston to any of this, I would agree. What we have is tenuous circumstantial evidence, mixed in with conspiracy theories and rumours and surrounded by a crazy journalist trying to make her name. This does not do this great organisation justice by a hundred miles."

"Sir, there are enough coincidences and, as you say, circumstantial evidence to look into this further and before anyone else gets killed."

"Like in London? Yes, there are also people being killed. Could be the UK government, these gangsters the Harkers, powerful UK people being blackmailed and fighting back. If you want conspiracy theories, there are many more out there."

"Sure, all can be connected to Bell and DCI Eager's saga if we want to try and play that game." De Silva knew he was getting nowhere and no point in arguing with this guy.

Shackleton seemed to calm down. He lent back in his swivel chair with pen in mouth, thinking. Then he started again on a more conciliatory note.

"Look, Leslie, this is dynamite, you must see that? We need to put this case in cold storage until at least after the elections, when we can dust it off and start again. Hell, I will give you the best support you ever wanted to clear all this up if needed by then. You need to button this down tight. I mean tighter than a Jack Daniels barrel. Special Agents Turner and Stanley, in particular, need to keep their mouths shut. Got me?"

"What if he makes president and all this is true? How hard would it be to prosecute him?"

"I'd honestly say easier than now. Presidents get impeached and with iron-proof evidence we are not playing sides. If it proves to be true and comes out before then, let the media do the dirty work, not us. Got it?"

"Got it, sir — and if more get killed?" Leslie persisted.

"Unless there is a clear connection that gives us jurisdiction, then let the locals look after that side. So stand everyone down."

De Silva knew that to argue with a fool was pointless, and as he had been told on many occasions, those that did no one in the end knew the difference. He got up to go and then turned around.

"Sir, when you sent Special Agent Sonia Turner to me, who asked for that to happen?"

"My name is Liberty Bell. Let me spell that for you: L I B E R T Y B E L L." She picked up the phone on the desk, to the manager's amazement. She pointed the receiver at her.

"Call Travis Preston and tell him I am here."

"Sorry, ma'am. I can't do that. This is just a campaign co-ordination office and I would not get through directly to him. Can I help you?" Thinking this was another nut case and she had had plenty the last few weeks.

"Just tell your boss in Washington that Liberty Bell is here and demands to talk to Preston. Otherwise, I will hold a press conference right here. Do you have a video machine?"

The young lady manager was confused. Liberty pushed the phone in her face. Nervous, the manager said, "Did you say Liberty Bell? Give me a moment, please." Pointing to a seat just outside her cubicle. Liberty moved back there, but stood up, watching. The woman put her hand around the phone and was talking quietly.

"She said *what*?" A loud voice came out of the phone which Liberty could hear. She smiled to herself and looked at her watch. How long would it be? She guessed five minutes, assuming her boss passed this on quickly and didn't have her down as some crank. Eager was pacing up and down on the street, looking very nervous. Big Gary was stood by the entrance door, almost cutting out the light with his bulk and size. This made the manageress even more nervous.

She was wrong — it took four minutes and twenty-five seconds.

"I'm Mr Preston's personal assistant, Amanda's my name. Can I help you, er, Ms Bell?"

"Yes, tell him unless my family is on the streets here with me in Vegas in the next hour, I will hold a press conference in his own campaign office. He will understand."

"I am not sure what you are talking about. If you give me your number, I will talk to him and straighten this out and ring you right back. Is that okay?" She was using her sweet polite voice of an innocent assistant.

"No, it's not all right, Amanda. Do you really think I am dumb enough to give you my number? I am at his campaign office. Stop playing games. Have you ever seen the biggest video screen in Vegas on the Strip? Your boss is going to be playing there, prime time soon for the world to see. So, honey, get a fucking move on and get my parents back here to me pronto! One hour back at his campaign office."

Amanda lost it. "Okay, bitch, what do we get in return? Start thinking or I will kill one parent at a time. Want to hear that now? Which one is your mother, the glamorous one or the tired looking one?"

"You can have the tape back and we all move on. Nothing said, ever."

"Okay, now you are talking, bitch. If you have copied it, I will kill you all, slit that pretty throat of yours side to side."

"One hour and if you call me bitch again, I will pull your fucking tits off!"

The manageress looked amazed and even more scared. All Liberty could think was 'pull her tits off' — *was that the best I could do as a come-back?* She left and the team regrouped across and down street at the Starbucks café.

They had patched the call through to Amanda's radio phone. She stood there thinking quickly for a few seconds and then sprang into action. She called the general and told him what she wanted. He warned her it could be a trap. She said she had information that the FBI had stood down, so she was up against three, maybe four, but not the authorities. It had to be quick and clean.

She was in Vegas and the hostages were forty miles south, just off the highway in Primm's Resort and Casino car park, tied up in one of the Mercedes vans. *Pull my tits off? I can't wait until I get the annoying bitch and then we will see whose tits will become the biggest.*

"So what now?" Gavin asked, feeling the nervous excitement of the group. Big Gary had left to do his duties at the hotel and really did not want to play any further part in this. Being an ex-con, he had a lot to lose.

"So many questions just to get three coffees. Do I want this and that; so many options, it has taken me ten minutes. People behind me getting angry," Eager complained as he handed over three hot takeaway mugs.

"So what's the plan now?" Gavin asked again.

"The plan? Well, let's see…" She pretended to think. "We give them the video, keep the dupe, get my family back and then run as fast as we can."

"That's the plan?" Gavin was horrified.

"Worked last time," Eager laughed.

"That's not a plan. We are all going to be killed!"

"Well, that's the brilliance of our not a plan. They will expect us to have a plan and we will surprise them by not having a plan. It will work like magic." Eager was keeping a straight face, just. *Blackadder* humour and logic usually works for a laugh. Not this time, with Gavin sat stony-faced with his mouth open.

"So, this is the famous or infamous Ms Liberty Bell." Steve had entered the café with two big men in dark combat kit. They stood back just before the doors as Steve sat down beside them.

"Special Agent Stanley, welcome. Can I get you a drink?" Eager asked. He waved 'no'.

"Gavin Hastings." Gavin stuck out his hand.

"Yes, Mr Hastings, we've met. The three musketeers together — this is a treat." Steve was in a jovial mood. The kind you get before some real action. Gavin didn't get it.

"So, is the meet on?" Steve asked.

"Yes. I'm sure they will come within the hour."

"You do understand that I have been stood down on this case?"

"Which means?" Liberty asked.

"Which means I will have to stand back and watch until an offence is committed or lives are in danger."

"Lives are in danger," Gavin added hastily.

"My colleagues," Steve ignored him, "Are from a specialist arms team and old friends. I will have them on standby. But understand, I will do nothing if all goes to plan."

"Nothing, not even arrest them?"

"Nothing means nothing. Arrests may come later, but we need hard evidence."

"The kidnappers aren't hard evidence?" she pushed.

"Will not lead us to the big guy. I have been told by the highest authority to stand down. If I am going to lose my job, it is going to be for something worthwhile, something big."

"Slowly, slowly, catchee monkey," Eager added.

"I have some bulletproof vests outside. Suggest you try them on."

They left the café. Eager was able to put his vest under his jacket; he just looked a bit bulkier. Gavin was not to be part of the action, just an observer, so he declined. Liberty refused as it looked big and awkward; not her style, and it was too hot to put under a rain mac even if she had one. Steve briefed them and then disappeared with his small team.

They both stood outside the campaign office in the Strip, full of people, hard for anyone to do anything, they assumed. It was within the hour and Amanda turned up on her own. Gavin watched from across the street at what he thought was not obvious. His job was to take pictures and scream blue murder if it goes south. Steve was surprised to see a neat, small, very attractive blonde lady with a young girl's face and a great figure. Diablo was right: a blonde at the scene in the Mojave massacre. Pity Indian dreams were not admissible in court.

"Ms Bell?" Amanda was back in control, unemotional and all business.

"I'm going in," DI Williams told the two Special Branch detectives. "We have waited three hours, it's now" — looking at her watch — "seven p.m."

"We do not have a warrant," DS Keith Smith cautioned.

"Bugger the warrant! We have reasonable suspicion and we are talking about the potential murderer of Charlie Allcock."

"We just have our guy telling us what the crooks think. That's not reasonable cause," added DC Frank Cunnington.

"Well, it's a hotel. I'll make up a story to the manager and have a quick look around. And it's Sammy the Squirrel we are talking about finding this guy, he is the best at that around."

"Let's give it another hour. I need a piss anyway. I'll go to the Queen." Frank had a weak bladder, especially after lunchtime drinks.

"Okay, but a piss, not a piss-up," Denise cautioned.

"I'll keep that in mind," he said as he left hurriedly.

"Where is Sammy, then? He is supposed to be here." Keith was looking around.

"Oh, he is watching us for sure at a safe distance. We are probably muddying his water."

"If my guy is to be believed, they want him out of the way quick."

Denise waited until Frank got back and then went into the hotel. The manager was the receptionist as well. He was an Indian Sikh, well dressed in a suit with a green turban and sporting a big black beard.

"Namaste."

"Namaste ji," Denise responded. Indian was her favourite eat-out food. He was surprised and smiled broadly. He seemed very friendly to Denise and then nervous once she had shown her police warrant card.

"Is there trouble, some kind of hullabaloo? Not wanting trouble." His head nodded from side to side like it was wobbling.

"Your name?"

"Arun."

"No trouble, Arun, just want to check around the room of a Chinese-looking man."

"Why? Don't you need a warrant?"

"Not for potential terrorist activities. Just a tip-off. Probably nothing. His name he registered?" she lied.

"Raymond Fung from Hong Kong. Oh, my goodness. Room eight."

Street number eight and now room eight? Very Chinese good luck number, she thought.

He let her in and entered with her. She checked around, being careful not to move anything. Very tidy and nothing out of order. Small suitcase and backpack. Clothes packed inside were black for some reason. No ID or paperwork of any kind. The room safe was open, nothing inside. Under the bed, nothing; cupboards, wardrobe, all empty. She looked behind everything she could, again nothing out of the ordinary. They went back to the reception desk.

"Did he leave anything for you to hold?"

"Nothing. A nice quiet man. He told me he was here from Hong Kong as his uncle had expired."

"Expired?"

"Sorry, Indian for died."

Credit cards expire, people die.

She looked at the register: a simple signature.

"How did he book? Did he pay by credit card?"

"Oh no, he's a good customer; paid cash for five days when he arrived, just called from the airport and asked if we had space."

I bet that does not go into the books.

"Has he phoned anyone?"

"No outside lines in the rooms; he has to ask me, which he hasn't so far."

"Arun, it looks like a false alarm. We get forty a day and we have to immediately check them out. I would appreciate you not mentioning this to Mr Fung. It ruins tourism and upsets your customers…"

She noticed he was looking behind her as the door opened. It was Mr Fung and he walked past, just nodding to Arun. He was dressed in a black round-collared jacket and jeans with a white polo neck underneath. The baseball cap was there, but no pencil-thin moustache and goatee as per Molly's description. He carried a small brown attaché case.

"Not a word, Arun." Zipping her lips with her finger to demonstrate.

She went outside, crossed the road and got in the car.

"Bloody hell, that was close." She breathed out slowly.

"Yeah, you didn't have your radio with you. So we crossed our fingers," Frank offered.

"Well, thanks for that," she muttered.

"Looks like our guy. So do we pick him up?" Keith asked.

"You know when you go to a hotel and unpack, what the room looks like?" Denise was assessing the situation.

"A mess," Keith retorted.

"Some people are tidy and some messy, but this room was sanitised. Clothes still packed as if ready to leave in a moment. No documents at all; he must be carrying them, I guess. Yes, I think he's our guy. We have, though, little on him to warrant an arrest. Maybe Molly could recognise him from the café, but it proves nothing. He would say nothing and be out and gone in a day."

"I got a good shot of him." Frank was pleased with his camera work.

"I'll need it as soon as possible, okay? We need to watch him."

"My gaffer would not want the overtime and we would need several teams authorised for around-the-clock surveillance." Keith was sure it would not be supported for budget reasons.

"Mine neither; he believes Molly murdered Charlie and this guy would be a possible witness. Nothing more."

"Jimmy Harker believes he is a hired gun and threatened him unless he kills Javelin and McAllistar. Isn't that enough to get a warrant?" Frank asked.

"Unless you want to compromise your undercover guy? So, who is going to support the warrant? Jimmy Harker?" Denise sighed. Like chess, the next move was hers and always the hardest if you didn't look at every piece on the board and all the possible counter-moves. They sat there for a while, thinking.

"Sammy will be still around, right? Why not let him do the watching and dirty work?"

"Don't be stupid, Frank," Keith chastised him.

"No. He has a good point. I have an idea." Denise found her move.

"What?" they both said at once.

"You don't want to know." They understood her drift.

Sammy watched them drive off from his position down the street in a doorway of a house that looked deserted. Fergus had joined him, Willy parked around the corner.

They checked him out and left, why? How did they find him and most importantly, why? DI Williams he knew. It troubled him and his mind worked overtime. Not the time to make a move. He left Fergus to watch and jumped in with Willy and headed back to talk with Jimmy. He needed to be very careful; this did not seem right, they were missing something. He could even be working for the police. A trap?

Denise rang the George and Dragon pub. McAllistar was in his room and George went to fetch him.

"Logan, I want to pick you up as soon as possible."

"Best offer I've had this month, lass."

"There is an opportunity as we discussed. Be prepared like the Boy Scout you are."

She's very excited — something is happening; action at last.

"When you are ready then, lass."

Denise cringed. She hated the word 'lass' it was demeaning. She doubted she would change him, this Yorkshire man — should she say 'lad'? — but would try at the right time and occasion.

Chapter 49
Near-Death Experiences

Pat woke up in the back of their van. He was covered in blood. Arms tied in front of him by tape. He heard gasping and muted crying and sat up, leaning his back on the inside of the van wall. His vision cleared and he saw Cynthia and his ex-wife, Cherie, tied up and gagged, lying in two heaps on the floor. Their eyes were wide open in fear and they were watching him carefully. He was sure they thought he was dead. Surprise, not that easy to kill an Irishman.

It was coming back to him now. Cynthia had opened the door despite his warnings. She was expecting her yoga instructor and just did not think. Cherie was making some coffee in the kitchen. Where was he? Think! Yes, walking back from checking the front window when the first shot hit him in the back through the window. It didn't hurt: it was like a hot beam of air went through him. He didn't even hear the gun sound. Grunting, he got up quick, when a second shot knocked him down again. Adrenaline rushing through him, he made an effort to get up a third time.

"Stay the fuck down," was the instruction. Then a bang to his head and he was out. The blood was everywhere. The van looked like it was a blood bath. He knew from crime scenes, though, blood splatters everywhere does not mean he had been fatally shot. In films even the worst crime scenes do not do the bloody scenes justice. He heard someone outside the van on a radio.

"Roger that." How many, he wondered? God, his head hurt worse than the bullet wounds. How much blood he had lost he wasn't sure, he didn't know, just felt light headed. He also felt angry, very angry, as his mind cleared. Angry at Liberty for getting them into this mess, angry at Cynthia, who lived for her beauty salons, gyms and yoga, angry at himself, for not being more careful, and angry at these bastards who shot him.

They had been sloppy, a saving grace in his mind. They had frisked him, looking for his gun, which they found lying on the kitchen table. They had missed his 'Bollack' dagger taped to the side of his ankle. Their first mistake. He only did this when he felt he was going into a dangerous situation. The circumstances with Liberty's situation warranted it. Cynthia would laugh at him, the times he did this in the mornings as he sat on the bed, taping it. The 'Bollack' dagger was based on a medieval dagger that was shaped like a man's genitals. Two balls at the top of the steel blade before the handle. He had been given it by his comrades when he was promoted to Detective first grade. It was a gift and memento and a joke over the celebration drinks. They made out it was a replica of his personal parts. Cheap dirty jokes worked well with street cops. The good thing about the dagger was its razor-sharp edges on either side of the blade.

Their second mistake was assuming he was so hurt with two bullets in him that he did not need securing, as would normally be the case. So only his hands were taped at the wrists in front of him. This was a big mistake. Hoping he wouldn't faint or fall over, he reached down with both hands and after a bit of shuffling around loosened the dagger. It was then easy, with a bit of hand contortion, to cut himself free.

"We are ready to move and execute our orders. Over." The voice again.

"Wait, our friends want proof of life."

What were they waiting for and what were they doing and how many? He stood up and swayed a little. Putting his finger to his mouth to tell the ladies to be quiet, he cut them free. He held his hand up for them not to make a movement or sound. He looked forward and he could see the keys in the ignition. The back was blocked, so no access to the front seats. The blood was still dripping off his hair and he looked like a monster from a Hallowe'en party.

He frantically searched around the vehicle — he needed a bigger weapon. Under some cloths was a heavy wheel brace. Not the best, but better than nothing. He was certain once proof of life was given, they would be dead. Whispering to Cherie, he asked how many? Two: she put up her fingers to show him. Pulling her up, he showed her to stand by the sliding door with the brace. "Now," he whispered, "when the door slides open, hit the first person who sticks his head in with all your might, all your might; do not be afraid, or we will not get out of here alive." She looked very nervous and was trembling; this was her worst nightmare.

"Get one of them on the radio now." This was it! He felt like all the blood had drained from him, but thanks for adrenaline, a gift that kept giving, he was totally on his game. He told Cynthia to lie still on the floor and he pulled her mini skirt up to the top of her legs and dragged her closer to the door. The first thing they would see is these curvy long legs; a big distraction, he hoped.

The door slid open and a head with a black helmet and automatic weapon leaned in. Cynthia hesitated. Now, now, Pat was screaming in his head. The head started to look around and focussed on the legs for a split second, when Cynthia struck. She hit the helmet and it moved to the side of his head. The man was stunned but not knocked out. Pat jumped at him and slashed his throat. He did not aim for the main artery, but luck was with him. The man gave out an almighty scream and dropped backwards. The second man was on the radio and smoking, looking around, away from the van, on guard. He turned and froze for a moment. Pat went at him with a dive worthy of a baseball fielder. The man recovered his wits and moved sidewards, hitting him with the butt of his weapon. Pat passed out.

When he came round, he could hear Cynthia crying and Cherie was attending to him. "What happened?"

"Cynthia shot him," Cherie said, crying. He couldn't believe it; he had no idea she had it in her.

"Cynthia?"

She was sitting on the ground, head down and hyperventilating.

"Yeah."

Cynthia was off his angry list, he decided. Despite the drowsiness, he was thinking so fast it was like he was on some other planet or speed.

"Come in zero bravo. Over."

He saw the radio on the ground, rolled over and grabbed it.

"Zero bravo. We are here. Over."

"What's taken you so long? Over."

"Waking them up, particularly this Irish bastard. Over."

"Who is this?" Amanda had taken over, not recognising the voice.

"Your worst nightmare. You guys will join the dead. I am coming for you."

Liberty had heard her dad's voice and moved to leave quickly. Amanda hit her so hard on the side of her head with her fist that she fell to the ground. She was just disorientated for a few seconds and rubbed her temple, thinking it really hurts, and trying to work out what to do next. She was too groggy.

"The video, where is it? Where? Tell me now or I'll kill you!" Amanda yelled.

"Go fuck yourself." Another kick with her foot. Crowds of people were stopping to watch on the sidewalks.

"FBI. Stay where you are!"

Eager was running across the street towards them to help. He recognised Sonia. Great, he thought, help at last. Amanda just stood there, calm. A van was coming down the street. Liberty got up slowly.

"What is she after?" Sonia asked Liberty.

"This video." Liberty pulled a video out of the back of her skirt that had been hidden by her blouse.

"Hand it to me," Sonia commanded. She did as she was told. It was a dupe, she was not worried.

"Thank goodness she arrived like the US Cavalry." Eager was ecstatic. The van rolled to a halt at the side of them.

"Get in, everybody, now!" Sonia commanded, and then turned to the crowd. "Go away, this is an FBI bust," showing her badge.

Liberty took her chance and with her right foot kicked Amanda in the groin, bending her over.

"Get in the van!" Sonia ordered again, as one, armed man in black with a bulletproof vest, opened the door and held his gun towards Liberty.

This is not right. Eager shouted to Liberty, "Do not get in the van!"

Sonia shot Eager two times in the chest as he came around the van towards her. The crowd that had gathered actually cheered and clapped. They obviously thought this was an act, another tourist activity on the Strip.

Steve had appeared across the road with his support team, running towards them. Liberty was bundled into the van, Eager lay on the sidewalk. Sonia and Amanda boarded and it took off. Steve stopped his team from shooting as the chances of hitting Liberty and Sonia were too high. Instead, he took the licence plate number and called out for one of his team to ring 911 for the medics.

He then called into LVPD and asked for an all-points bulletin on the van. He told them not to approach as the occupants were extremely dangerous. Eager was trying to sit up. Gavin had appeared, camera in hand.

"Fuck, I am sore. Ruined my bloody jacket." Eager was trying to remove the Kevlar vest from under it.

"Here, let me help you." Steve knelt down and undid the vest. Holding and rubbing his chest, Eager tried to stand up, but couldn't. It was hard to breathe.

"Thank you, Steve, for saving my life." The vest had done its work. He would, though, be severely bruised and sore for a long time. He was alive, that was the good news.

The crowd clapped and cheered again as Steve helped Eager up. Eager bowed to them; he didn't know why, it just seemed the right thing to do.

"They have Liberty and Sonia." It had been hard watching from a small rooftop over the road. The van had blinded his view of the action.

"No, Sonia is with them," Gavin blurted out. "I have a pic of her shooting John."

Gavin had moved down the street, protected by the amount of people moving on the Strip. Steve was computing what had happened. He did not understand why Sonia was there. He had first thought when he saw her that she was sent to find him and had run across the situation by accident.

She shot John Eager! This was confusing and mystifying. Yes, he did not like her, but this was beyond belief. Eager had confirmed it was Sonia. Did she as a rookie fire by mistake, suspecting Eager as one of the bad guys? Was she taken as well or a willing participant? He needed to tell De Silva right away. He handed Eager's vest to one of his team. "Take this and we need the bullets to be secured as evidence."

231

"They're going to be pissed at Liberty when they find this dupe has only the first five minutes of Preston on it," Eager remarked.

Police cars were arriving, and an ambulance. The noise of the sirens was ear numbing. The crowd was still watching and beginning to realise that this was not a show, as fascinating as it was.

"Here, mister." A woman passer-by handed to Steve the radio phone that Amanda had dropped.

"Hello." He pressed the button.

"If you hurt her, I'll get you wherever and whoever you are." Blurted out.

"This is Special Agent Stanley of the FBI. Who is this?"

"My God, is she okay?"

Steve immediately grasped this was McGill.

"Ms Bell is alive but taken. Mr McGill, are you okay?"

"What do you mean, taken?"

"They grabbed her during the exchange. We have an all-points bulletin out, roadblocks will be put in place all directions; we will find her. Are you okay?"

"Yes, all three of us. Kidnappers dead. Where are you?"

Steve told him. Pat said they were twenty minutes away if they could get through the traffic. The paramedics were finished with Eager when they arrived. He had refused to go to hospital. They were packing up when Pat got out of the van he was driving.

"Oh, my God!" someone in the crowd shouted. This blood-covered body was a horrific sight and it was stood up and moving around like a zombie. The paramedics opened their mouths when they saw their new customer. They rushed over to him and made him lay on the ground, but he resisted until Steve and Eager stood by his side.

They told Pat what had happened and he managed part of his story when he just lost consciousness. The medics worked on him and then took him quickly to hospital in the ambulance. Cynthia went with him, while Cherie stayed, needing to know what was happening and being able to explain in full what had happened to them.

Gavin had been taking pictures. Not realising what he was saying, more focussed on the incredible story that was unfolding in front of him, he said, "This just gets better and better."

They all turned and looked at him with incredulity.

Steve was in discussion with local detectives that had arrived on the scene. He gave instructions to get the films from anyone in the crowd who had good shots of the incident, CCTV and the works. Cherie had told him where their incident happened and where the bodies were. Police and security from the casino, though, were already attending, a little baffled on what went down. Steve took down some notes on the incident, including a description of the blonde negotiator.

"I need to go to LVPD HQ and see if we can track down this vehicle. I will tell the locals that this is an FBI investigation. Mr Hastings, I need all the pictures you have; get them developed now. Where will you guys be?"

They told him the Sahara and the room number. The local police would secure both scenes and the second van. He would also ask for protection at the hospital for McGill. Steve then arranged for a patrol car to take them to the hotel and told them not to move at all. He would join them later.

When he got to the HQ, he found a conference room and called his chief, De Silva.

"Chief, you are not going to believe this."

"Oh, yes? I certainly will — I have been watching you all on TV. You have some explaining to do."

So have a few other people.

Chapter 51
Lockhart, Texas

They were sitting in the hotel room availing themselves of the free beer. Gavin had a whisky chaser. Eager had warned him they needed to stay clear-headed; however, he understood that what had happened today was highly stressful.

"So, what have we got?" Gavin began. "Two women having a nervous breakdown and I am no better; Liberty captured, probably dead by now; and you with bruised ribs. I'd say you got off lightly." He gave out a nervous laugh.

"Not a bad day, eh? Look, we managed to get back Liberty's family, granted not in good shape. We still have the videos. They are not going to kill her until they get the video they want, and then we are all targets."

"Well, that's reassuring."

"Look, the game's almost up for these guys. The FBI is involved, they have been compromised on the Strip."

"Wasn't that an FBI lady with the gun who went with them? Didn't Steve say he could not get involved?"

Eager ignored his negativity. "I have a game plan."

"You do? I pray it is better than our last two plans."

"Yes, you need to get the story sold and I need to find Liberty. So we split up. Get the buyers to meet you at Hoover Dam latest tomorrow lunch. We need big deposits and a contract before we hand over anything."

"To get deposits I need to whet their appetites big time. What more can I tell them or show them? Tell them too much and if they don't get the deal, as I have mentioned before, they will issue spoilers and ruin the whole deal. What about Pat's arrangement?"

"We need this bastard's video to hit the streets before he kills us for it. So we have to walk away from that deal." Eager was in command.

"From the Mafia?" Gavin was nervous.

"His friend has not pitched them yet. Was looking to see proof first on his way there. Today, I think."

"Isn't he Mafiosi and won't he be looking for his share?"

"Not sure, certainly connected. He may understand; if not, one more enemy we don't need at the moment."

"What if they do the deal with the incumbent Mitchell right now in return for the release of the video on national media?"

"Could work, Gavin; that way we get paid twice. They might not pay us until the pardon comes through, but that's okay."

"Might not pay us at all," Gavin said glumly.

"Well, at least they are not on our backs. Liberty is going to make a killing out of this." Eager was losing patience with his negativity.

"You mean all of us? We all went through hell with her to get to this stage and are still risking our necks. I am out of work after being at the top of my profession."

"Calm down, Gavin. She said she would share and she will. You will become a celebrity and everything you lost will be restored and more. We need her to beef up your part in the book, though. Ha."

Gavin didn't get the humour.

"Thinking about it, probably best if we get an intermediary. Who can get this deal or deals completed quickly and also the book sold to a big publisher? Who was this guy who gave Liberty his card at the airport?"

Eager rummaged around the desk Liberty had been working on and found it beneath her make-up bag. Strange place to put it, but that was Liberty.

"Kent Koll. Here is his card." Eager handed it over.

"I will need a lawyer. They will want the money put into escrow until we hand over the goods. Speaking of which, where are the videos?"

"Safe." That was all Eager was prepared to share in case they picked up Gavin.

"In a safe?"

"No. In a safe place. No need for you to know — safer that way, excuse the pun."

"You don't trust me?"

"They are in the casino vault. Liberty and I are the only people that can access them."

"What about me if you two, I mean, you know what I mean?"

"We both go toes up? Look, I will add you to the list downstairs, okay?"

"So do you think they can get the location out of her?"

"I guess, but they have to break into a casino vault which is highly secure. No one can do that in Vegas except in films."

"Will you give up the video of him to save her life?"

"No. Nothing will save her life. Once they have the video, we are all toast. You need to get this: we cannot negotiate."

"So what will we do?"

"Find her and get her away."

"So you are Charles Bronson now!" Gavin was becoming annoying to Eager.

"No, the FBI have got to help us, right?"

No answer. Gavin just shrugged.

"I will call London. I have a legal friend, international business; she is bound to have a contact I can trust either here or in LA for the contracts," Gavin came back alive. His part seemed easy to Eagers.

"Good, do that. Best you set up this Kent Koll at the dam before you see any others. Get the feel of him and what he can do. Use the limo service, but ensure the hotel name is not on the vehicle. Talk to Big Gary, he will organise it for you. Oh, and do not mention video number seven — we are keeping that as collateral for when we get back."

"If we get back." Gavin was like Eeyore at times.

"If we get back," Eager repeated.

Just then, the door-bell chimed. It opened straightaway and Big Gary let in Theodore Siegel, who he referred to as 'boss'. Eager and Gavin, highly nervous, almost dived to the floor when the door opened.

He introduced himself.

"So a bit of trouble? It is all over the news. I checked on Pat, he is doing okay. You simply cannot kill that Irishman, Big bones you see, he is bulletproof."

He seemed a reasonable man, so they explained the new plan and situation. He just listened, seemingly sympathetic. He needed to see the video of Preston and had brought a small portable video player with a screen with him. It took some time for Eager to access the vault and bring the video up. They played it to him. His eyebrows went up each time Preston hit the girl. When Eager stopped it, he just said, "Motherfucker!" and whistled. His mind, though, was working overtime.

It was agreed he would not approach his bosses with any deal until they got through the next few days. He left his card or told them to get Big Gary to call him, and he also loaned them the portable video player to use. They promised not to use the Preston video unless they really had to, and certainly not until Liberty was released. He agreed both plans could work and told them he could provide a second hideaway and protection if worse came to worst. He seemed very reasonable. No doubt in Eager's mind that there was more to this well-dressed, smooth, charming, handsome man. He left, as he had other business at the casino.

"What do you think?" Gavin asked.

"Seems a great guy."

"Taking the videos back now?"

"No, just a bag of empty beer cans."

"Oh, so you don't trust him?"

"Nope."

The door chimed again. Big Gary let Steve in after brandishing his FBI badge.

"Was that the Pope?" Steve asked, pointing his thumb towards the door.

"The Pope?" Gavin asked, confused.

"The honourable Theodore 'Teddy' Siegel, aka The Pope," Steve explained.

"He is a friend of Pat's, put us up here to help us."

"Be very careful. Never dance with the devil."

They nodded, trying to look innocent. Eager had hidden the plastic bag with the videos at the side of the sofa. Steve sat down; he looked tired and kept scratching himself, as was his habit, especially when he was nervous.

"I guess you know McGill's okay?" They nodded. "Well, they disappeared. The roadblocks went up very quickly as I reported a kidnapped FBI agent. Got their attention," he continued. "All major routes cut off between ten and twenty miles: that's the 95, 15, 613, 515 and 159. Helicopter brought in outside that ring found nothing, no black Mercedes van on the roads."

"Airports?" Eager asked.

"There are fifty-four airports in the Nevada Las Vegas area. If they did get out by air, the two I would guess within the roadblock circle, discounting the big airport McCarran, would be Nellie Air Force Base and North Las Vegas. Both are, say, a ten- to fifteen-minute drive with traffic."

"So where does that leave us?" Eager was now very concerned, his teeth grinding and moustache twitching.

"Guessing," was the reply.

"Yeah?"

"My best guess is that these guys are well-equipped and supported, so they had to have an escape route that was quick and effective. The blonde arrived what, within an hour? I'm betting she didn't drive, so a helicopter maybe. So I checked flights out of both airports fifteen minutes to two hours after they drove away. At Nellie, apart from fighter training aircraft, only one Learjet left, twenty-five minutes after. At North Las Vegas airport, apart from seven commercial flights, there were just a few light aircraft."

"Sounds like the private jet, then. Where was it headed?"

"The flight plan said Dallas International, but…"

"But?" Eager and Gavin, leaning forward.

"The big but is this. To fly from a military airport, it would have to be the president, vice-president or a black ops flight."

"CIA?"

"Precisely. It has not landed in Dallas airport yet, a maximum three-hour commercial flight. The Lear would do it in just over two, I would guess."

"So, say, thirty minutes to get to the airport and board, then two hours fifteen flight — that would make it five p.m. arrival Las Vegas time. It's now four forty-five." Eager was trying to work out the possibilities of intercepting it.

Steve used the room phone and called the local office. He spoke for some time; whilst he did so, Eager moved the videos.

"Not on the radar going to Dallas. Disappeared as they entered Texas air space."

"Got to be it!" Eager claimed.

"Well, not necessarily. A lot of black ops flights go off the radar. Hell, the CIA had had major commercial flights disappear around the world. It does, though, sound strange; and get this, Preston has a big ranch in Texas."

"Where?"

"I'm finding out now. Be patient." Steve was back on the phone and scribbling down the address. He handed his notes to Eager.

Eager read it out loud, "Blanco Canyon Bar, Lockhart, Texas. Where is that? Blanco Canyon?"

"The site where the Comanche's were finally beaten." Steve knew his Wild West history, being an avid cowboy fan.

"Why would he take her to his own place?" Gavin was bemused.

"Not sure. It would be virtually impossible to get a search warrant. No one would have the balls to ask without a fully signed confession from Travis himself. Plus, this ranch is big, at least fifteen thousand acres. She could be anywhere if she is there, and we are only guessing." Steve was stressing how hard this would be, tongue in cheek.

"So the plane would be CIA?"

"Not sure for certain; there are several covert organisations with the same access and clout, but it looks that way to me."

"So how do we find out?" Eager asked, concerned.

"I can't help further; my hands and legs are tied."

"You can't help?"

"Not officially. I have to go back to LA and get my ass kicked. I only got to stay saying an FBI agent was missing."

"So?" Eager was incredulous.

"So goodbye and good luck."

Chapter 51
Body on a Block

She threw the keys at McAllistar. He caught them with ease with his left hand, his quick reflexes coming back after his wounding.

"Keys?"

"Eager lives walking distance away. His car is in his garage."

"And?"

"And this would be a good place to take someone you might want to interrogate."

Logan looked around the pub. Screwing his face up and thinking hard.

"So, you know where this hit man is?"

"At the moment, yes."

"I'll get my kit." McAllistar ran upstairs and came back with an Army kitbag which looked full.

"You going to war?" she asked.

"Lunch, lass," was all he said, holding the bag up. Denise shuddered at the word 'lass' and didn't get his humour. She was getting in deep, like her mentor Eager, but what else could she do? Her superior would not take action without real proof that connected this guy to the killing. There was and would be none, as he is a professional.

"Shall we?" He followed her to her car. She drove him to Eager's house. He looked around the garage and then the house. The blinds and curtains were all drawn and there was access to the house via the garage. He could drive in with his quarry and no one would see.

Denise briefed him on the hotel location and warned him that Sammy and maybe others were there watching, or could have moved on him already. He left in Eager's Rover he had taken from the Russian assassins during the Hellfire Club saga. When he got there, he saw two police patrol cars and an ambulance outside the hotel. He watched and waited for a while. The paramedics came out wheeling a trolley with a person on board. The body was covered up with a white sheet. Three police officers eventually came out, placing police tape around the entrance. Several other vehicles arrived, and a white van. Detectives and scene-of-crime officers, he assumed.

Too late, they have done him in.

He made his way to a public phone outside the Queen pub on Regent's Park. He rang DI Williams. It took time as she was in a meeting. He used his code name she had given him so she knew it was urgent, 'Mr Quick'. He had asked her if this was the best she could come up with. She had ignored him.

"Logan, I know why you are calling — there has been an incident at the hotel: one dead, a lot of blood around; seems like a hell of a fight went on. Details are sketchy; our guys are on the scene, but as far as I can gather from the description, Sammy the Squirrel is the deceased and two other intruders took off with the guest."

"A bit of a fubar, then."

"Logan, where would they take him?"

"Not sure."

"Think."

"There's a cellar below the club, soundproofed and always swept for bugs. They use it for meetings and some dirty work. They call it the dungeon; a lot of dirty goes on there, I believe."

"Could be right. Although, Logan, they have just pulled a body out of the Thames in the dock area — a Yardie. He was attached to his small motor-bike by a big chain. Can you believe that? A barge was sweeping for rubbish and pulled him up. So a turf war has started. You need to be careful."

"Waste of a motor-bike."

"What are we going to do next?" Denise was worried they had lost their opportunity.

"I am ready. I'll go in and see."

"No, there are too many of them. I shouldn't tell you this, but we have an undercover guy on the inside. You might hurt him or compromise him if he has to help you. He could also be a witness you do not want around."

"So, I let them do our dirty work?"

241

"Not sure we will find out what he knows. They get what they can and then will kill him."

"Can this cop be pulled out of there?"

"Not sure; his handlers only speak to him daily. Let me check. Can you call back in thirty?"

"Yup." He looked around the pub: well time for a quick pint while he waited.

She talked with DS Smith at Special Branch. Yes, their guy had reported some activity going on, but he was not privy to what exactly it is. Jimmy Harker had left in a hurry with others. He was put in charge of the club security as they expected an attack by the Yardies. He had no idea where they had gone.

She relayed this to Logan when he called back.

"My other thought is Canary Wharf and the docklands area. Fits with the Yardie and bike being in the water. It is a huge wasteland as the docklands are dying off, much reduced need for workers since they started using pallets and containers. I am sure they have an empty warehouse there."

"You are brilliant, Logan, makes sense. I will need to pass it on as a tip, unfortunately."

"No. Give me an hour or so to see what I can do. They will have spotters out all around, and by the time the sirens and blue lights get there they will have scarpered. I can get past them as a worker."

"And?"

"You do not want to know."

Her stomach churned at the thought of being complicit in a minor war and killings if it came to that. "Logan, promise me: one, you will be careful; and two, you will never implicate me."

"Aye, and you promise no matter what happens you know nothing. I did nothing, right?"

"Right, Mr Quick."

He put his flat cap on and his old Army combat jacket which was worse for wear. He blended in with the dockworkers. Carrying his kitbag, he walked around slowly, which was the pace around the docks these days. The workers had seen most of their mates retrenched and there was no particular hurry as their time, they knew, was coming soon.

It was a messy area and lots of unused docks equipment lay around, remnants from a better time when these docks were nothing but hustle and bustle of working men. It took him some time to locate warehouses, more like big sheds, near the smaller ship-docking areas. There were no cars visible out the front. He walked around, looking and listening. As he passed one small warehouse, a door in the middle of a big sliding door opened. Fergus had come out to have a piss. Logan couldn't help staring at him and his scary face.

"Are you looking at me?" Fergus demanded when he zipped up.

"No, I'm looking for the foreman; got his parts he ordered." Logan lifted the kitbag up to show him. He did not recognise Fergus by sight, but had heard of him.

"No foreman around here. Fuck off back up there and ask, you moron," He pointed up the docks.

That's not nice, McAllistar thought. He played mild and scared. "Will do, mister, thanks."

He then walked away back towards the busy docks area. Satisfied, Fergus went back inside the warehouse. Finding an alleyway at the side of the next warehouse, McAllistar took out the shotgun and some shells, his Marine's knife and three jumping jack fireworks and matches. He put on a black balaclava, loaded the gun and left the bag in the alleyway. He was sure there would be a back entrance, so he followed this alleyway to the rear of the shed Fergus had come out of. A fire door was at the back, probably locked. He took out the jumping jacks and lit them. Then he ran to the front door. Each had six bangers tied together and when they went off it sounded like a war zone. He heard them open the back fire door. They would obviously be cautious, thinking maybe it was shots being fired. He opened the small door inset in the big sliding door at the front as quiet as he could and slipped inside. Fortunately, there were old boxes and a rusty forklift truck which was out of commission which he hid behind and which provided him good cover.

Sure enough, they were focussed on the back fire door. One man he also did not recognise had a hand gun at the right-hand side of the door, and Fergus, now looking out carefully, was unarmed. Jimmy was standing over a limp figure lying on what looked like a concrete table. Next to the table was a big oblong hole and he could hear water thrashing about. Fergus then stepped outside and had a look around. Returning, he closed the fire door, the other guy relaxed and they both walked back to the table.

"Fucking kids, fireworks," he cursed.

"Here on the docks?" Jimmy asked.

Fergus just shrugged. "Mary, go check around," he ordered the other thug, a big guy with long hair and tattoos all around his face and arms. He was muttering that his name was not Mary just low enough so the Glaswegian couldn't hear him. Fergus was a bully to the bullies and a girl's name was his sense of humour.

Jimmy scratched his head and looked around, nervous. He didn't ordinarily get his hands dirty or go anywhere near this type of work. His brother, Nick, supervised such activities and he missed him. This was, though, personal. This guy had invaded his home, threatened him, filled him with a tranquilliser, and probably had something to do with trying to murder his brother. Yes, this was very personal.

Logan stayed very still and watched. They settled back into what they were doing. The body was strapped naked to the concrete table by wires. His mouth was taped. They were cutting off his toes and fingers. Fergus was enjoying doing the cutting; he was like a kid playing in a kindergarten.

"This little piggy goes to market." He picked up the small toe and showed the man and then dropped it into a bucket at the side. The body wriggled and the head bobbed, a small muffled scream could be heard.

"This little piggy stayed at home." Another finger on his left hand was cut off. Plop, into the bucket after the show and tell. The body jumped a little in the air as much as it could and then dropped back and lay still.

"Hold it, Fergus. I want him to talk, not to die right now." Jimmy indicated to him to check their prey was still breathing. He laid his fingers on the man's throat and nodded that there was a pulse.

Jimmy ripped the tape off his mouth. Fergus threw some water from a bottle over his face. He started to come round.

"Tut, tut, 'Mr I will kill you, man'. Now how does it feel?" The guy was trying to focus on Jimmy's face. His own face was wracked with pain and blood was dripping down on the floor.

"So, who sent you?" Jimmy asked. He lifted his head as far as he could and then tried to spit at Jimmy. Fergus slapped him to the side of his head and he fell back.

"Naughty. This is a new suit from Savile Row. I do not want any blood on it. No, not at all."

He tried to say something, but it was a whisper.

"What did you say?" Jimmy asked. No answer.

"I think he said, go fuck yourself," Fergus translated.

He knows he is going to die anyway, McAllistar thought, so they will get nothing from him. McAllistar did not like torture unless absolutely necessary, nor unfair fights.

"Dear me, we only want to know who sent you and where is your lady friend? Then you can go, a few digits less, I admit, so you remember never to come back. Can I be fairer than that?"

Is Jimmy for real? He will never fall for that. Logan almost sniggered at this.

Logan was now wondering: should he go or should he stay. No way were they going to get any information out of him. He would have taken a different approach — less of the bloody torture and give him a believable opportunity that if he opened up he would have a chance for life. Maybe then he might get something. Now he would inherit a bloody mess. A guy that could be dying. He knew that he hated Jimmy Harker and always understood how dangerous he could be; even so, it was impossible for him to kill him in cold blood. The hit man on the table was no better: he took money to bloody murder people without a conscience. He deserved what he was getting, even though this was not how human beings should behave.

McAllistar took off his balaclava and stuffed it in his combat jacket pockets. It did its job in case there was CCTV outside. It would not fool Jimmy, and it was itchy.

The decision was taken out of his hands. The front door opened and behind him walked Willy the Wanker, who had been cleaning the getaway van at a garage down the road to remove all blood stains.

"Jesus Christ!" he shouted.

McAllistar turned and pointed the shotgun at him.

"Move here," he demanded. The others were looking down now where McAllistar was hiding, guns pointed towards his direction. No use using Willy as a hostage — they wouldn't give a flying fuck if he or they killed him. He had to work fast or he would be next in line for the slab.

"Logan? Is that you?"

"Jimmy, get your guys to put their guns down."

Jimmy motioned to them to lower their weapons. He knew McAllistar, and although he was capable of violence, he was unsure why he was here, unless it was to kill him. He thought it was worth a try to rationalise with him. Jimmy moved behind the stone table with his sacrifice on. Fergus and Mary spread slowly to each side, hoping the shotgun at this range would not be able to spread its pellets too wide.

"This is the man who tried to kill you. Have no pity. Go and let us complete the job for you. No need for any confrontation; we have all moved on." Jimmy was his calm self.

"What's left of him? He will tell you nothing, and these types probably do not know who hired them," McAllistar replied.

"He has an assistant here, a black woman paid to have Nick murdered."

"Do you at least know who he is?"

"Some sort of fucking Bruce Lee; killed Sammy with one chop to the throat. So go away and I will let you live, never mind him," Fergus said with confidence and then spat on the ground.

"Has he said anything at all?" Logan ignored Fergus's threats.

"We haven't cut off enough fingers and toes yet and I can't wait until we get to his genitals. That's the best part; he will talk soon enough then." Fergus had started to lead the conversation.

"He will die then, you moron!" McAllistar used Fergus's own insulting word to rile him up. He was no longer playing the mild worried guy.

"Enough of this malarkey," Fergus said, as he lifted his gun and started running towards McAllistar, who had both barrels of his shotgun pointed at him.

"STOP!" shouted Jimmy. The combination of Jimmy shouting and facing the shotgun meant that Fergus regained his control and stopped halfway.

"You." To Willy, indicating he wanted him to walk in front as he slowly walked towards Jimmy and the table. Fergus backed up slowly until they were all within two yards of each other.

"Let's all calm down. Logan, we are on the same side here. He was sent to kill you and Tazewell. He tranquillised me after getting into my bedroom and threatening my death if I didn't arrange your murder. I did nothing but tried to find him and stop him."

"The bomb under my car?"

"Not us. He meant it to look like the IRA and, before you ask, it wasn't Mike."

The body on the slab was listening.

"Commander Allcock?"

"Not sure. Is he connected somehow?" Jimmy was confused; he had heard it was the pie lady. McAllistar picked up on his furrowed brow.

"This piece of turd was seen at the café just before he keeled over."

"Let me finish this and we all move on. No more threats. Tazewell, as I have told you before, was the one who set you and us up, as it happens."

"The police are coming here."

"How do you know that?" Jimmy asked, concerned now.

"Well, if you dump a body with a motor-bike attached and it is dragged up two hundred yards from here, I'd guess they are going to search these warehouses soon." Logan was thinking quickly, not wanting them to make the connection he had with DI Williams.

Jimmy stared daggers at Fergus, who looked away. Just then, Willy made a grab for the shotgun and held it up, with Fergus coming to help. A swift kick in the balls for Willy and his tight trousers split. Fergus was upon Logan and they wrestled to the ground. Logan was an Army champion boxer, and boxers do not want to be on the ground with someone pinning their arms together. Logan rocked back and forth and after Fergus had given him the Glasgow kiss, breaking his nose, he went crazy. Logan grabbed him by the collar of his jacket; bad mistake, as he had lined razor blades all the way down. Blood rushed out of his hands and he let go with a grunt.

Somewhere in all of us there is a hidden strength that we can tap into in dangerous times.

No, this is not happening to me.

Logan managed to get the end of Fergus's nose into his mouth and bit hard. Fergus screamed and let go and rolled over. Logan was up in a moment. Fergus got up and came at him. Logan was angry and calm at the same time, and the boxer took over. Fergus was big and very strong, but a street fighter. The feet movements, timing and combination punching took its toll. He would not, though, go down, no matter what Logan hit him with. Jimmy was shouting for them to stop, as he had the gun on Logan. Neither would stop until they won. Fergus got an uppercut to Logan's chin, which stopped him in his tracks. He then went in for the kill, with a big punch to the side of the head. Logan was used to bobbing and weaving, and he moved enough to the side, helped by his groggy wobbling, so Fergus's fist just ran along the side of his face. With all the strength he could muster, Logan kicked him in the groin. Fergus was expecting more boxing and did not expect the kick. He went down this time, holding his groin and private parts.

"Enough," Jimmy shouted, and then pulled the trigger. He never did the physical work or trained on weapons, so the bullet missed Logan by an inch, the kickback of the big gun making him miss from point-blank range. Mary had his gun pointed at Logan and Willy had picked up the shotgun. They were hesitant to shoot. Not everyone, even thugs, can kill in the cold light of day with the prey looking them in the eyes. Logan had seen this in the Army and immediately understood that they weren't going to shoot if he didn't move. He was breathing heavily, turning his attention to Jimmy, who was also still hesitating himself, but telling the others to shoot. Jimmy ran for the back door and got out as quickly as he could. Logan was still facing the other two and so far out of breath that he could not have run after him. Fergus was getting up, and Logan had never seen such an ugly face. He was actually smiling, which, extended by the scars, looked like his mouth went all the way to both his ears. He looked into his eyes and saw pure evil. Both were tired and not in any condition to continue fighting. Fergus grabbed the gun off the other thug and pointed it at Logan. He had backed up to rest his back on the table while he shot.

"You fucking wee shite. Meet your devil!" Aiming from his waist. A hand missing fingers came off the table and grabbed his gun arm. The hold was not strong enough to hang on long, but it gave Logan the opportunity to grab the shotgun off Willy. Willy had been absorbed by the fighting and was not paying too much attention, his mistake. Logan didn't hesitate; he fired one barrel at Fergus. It was only several yards, so the pellets hit him right in the chest and had nowhere to spread after the discharge. Blood came out and Fergus flew backwards across and over the hostage on the table. Logan stared at him. Willy and Mary ran and Logan let them. Fergus was not dead, but seriously injured. Logan realised the farm cartridges were for game, not humans. He had never thought to check earlier.

So much for moving on.

Logan went over to the man on the table. "Well, you'd better tell me something or I will leave you here to die. If you help, I will get you to hospital."

He could see the man computing what he had said and working out if he meant what he said. He had faced extreme pain and his own mortality. He did not want to die and he knew the others would have killed him after he talked anyway. He came to a decision. This guy, he is my best bet.

Logan had to lean over to hear him. "I do not know much about who and why. In my trouser back pocket is a docket for Heathrow baggage storage; it's all I can give you."

Logan untied him from the wires and rolled him over to get the docket. Just then, he heard the sirens at a distance. "I'll get you an ambulance; lay still."

"Can you, can you get them to bring my toe, fingers and clothes?" The guy then lost consciousness as the pain of his torture overtook him. He had spoken calmly, like asking for a cup of tea, Logan thought. This guy is cool and tough as nails. Least he could do.

Logan picked up the shotgun and ran out the back, finding his kitbag, and after storing the shotgun, wiping his bleeding hands on his hanky, he made his way as quickly as he could via the little back road to the front area. He looked a mess and wondered why nobody seemed to notice. He mingled in with the workers when two police cars came into the docks area. One of the dockers pointed down to where the shots had sounded. He was telling them that was where lots of gunshots had come from. He was obviously counting the fireworks. The patrol was not armed and this was a dangerous situation, so he could see they were radioing for back-up before proceeding.

They will get the ambulance, he knew, so his conscience was clear. If the guy didn't die first.

Chapter 52
Hoover Dam

Gavin sat in the café outside area at the Hoover Dam on the concrete seats. The view was tremendous. He had walked around to take in various aspects. It was an amazing piece of engineering, a great human achievement. He read some of the signs and details in his travel brochure. 'Concrete arch-gravity', whatever that meant, but he was sure it was important. On the Colorado River in Black Canyon. Used to be called Boulder Dam. Built in the 1930s. He was amazed. It made his little auction of the videos feel small and he felt a little dirty doing this against the backdrop of what should be one of the Seven Wonders of the Modern World.

He had got there early and used a limo, as directed by John Eager. It was hot and he was thankful that the table umbrella kept him covered. He wanted to sit outside as he thought this would be more private. He had the video machine and one video Eager let him have of the now dead but honoured ACC of the Met Police. Eager's old boss, who committed suicide before justice could catch up with him. He was protecting the drug lords and the activities at the Hellfire Club; even so, the powers-that-be gave him a posthumous medal and covered up his misdemeanours. They thought this was the safest one to show, him being dead, if he needed to give proof showing the ACC with an under-aged girl having sex.

Gavin had his big, cold beer. He figured Budweiser, the so-called King of Beers, was lighter than the other lagers and ice cold it tasted great in this hot weather. He sipped it and looked around. It had been a long journey since they started investigating the Harkers and what was happening at the Hellfire Club. He was not sure it was all worth it. He'd lost his job as editor of the *Daily Crier*, he was one of the most powerful media execs in the UK, lost his credibility and seemed to be hunted with the rest, day and night. He could die for this, and what had he to show for it? So far zip, but he hoped that was about to change. Liberty was at risk, maybe even dead, which was a shame; the upside was they had the videos and her articles he had edited and half the book he could finish if need be.

His first appointment was late. He was coming from New York and said if he caught the early flight out, he could be at the dam by one p.m. It was now one thirty p.m. Still, he had his beer and had a vacation feel about being here and out of hiding. He now knew how it felt to be on the run or on the 'lam', as the Americans called it. Kent Koll, the literary agent who had handed his card to Liberty when she arrived at JFK, was his first guest. He wasn't that comfortable with meeting him as he was obviously an ambulance chaser to the stars. He liked that line and laughed at it. He may use it one day when he was back in charge of a tabloid, as Eager promised he would be.

"Hi! Gavin?" A small, thin man, bald, wearing blue jeans and a white tee-shirt held out his hand. Gavin stood up and shook it. He was just carrying a leather brown satchel, almost like a school kid's. It was obviously an antique. He had leather straps and one of beads around his left wrist and a Rolex watch on his right. He was New York Jewish for certain, Gavin summed him up, and one thing he did know is these guys are as sharp as tacks when it comes to business and making money.

"Sorry I'm late. The flight was delayed; not normally my way, I like to be punctual as a courtesy. Had to stay in town last night for a function. Celebration of one of my client's latest divorces. They will do anything to get in the media."

Gavin just nodded as he knew all too well about these 'celebrities', and asked if he wanted anything. Just bottled water was the answer. The waitress had noticed his arrival and was upon them for the order in seconds. Not like the UK, where you have to wait or wave to get attention. Low wages and big tips work well here for excellent service, he mused.

"So, where is Liberty Bell? I so wanted to meet her."

"Well, let's just say she is tied up at the moment and apologises sincerely. I am sure if we do business, you will spend a lot of time with her." Tied up: he hoped that was the worst she was.

"So, what do you have?" Kent getting right down to business, pleasantries over.

Gavin gave him an outline of the story, a synopsis he called it. He then showed him a portion of the video of the ACC and the girl. Kent's John Lennon-style retro round glasses he had put on to watch the video seemed to steam up.

"So, she is not a fantasist." He took his glasses off and said this quietly.

"Not at all. I have lived through this ordeal with her."

"I know all about you, Gavin. Checked you out as best I could. Lost your job through this — how does that feel?"

"Pretty bad." Gavin gulped; he was still embarrassed.

"The other videos, any US celebs on them?" he asked. Gavin hesitated for too long.

"There is?" Kent pushed. Gavin so wanted to tell him, but had been warned not to by Eager. He half nodded very slowly.

"I'm taking that as a yes. Why can't you tell me? All these Brits will be big news, but a major local would be mega. I mean, really big bucks."

"There may be someone really big, but it is under wraps for the next few days."

Gavin was a newsman, and it was almost impossible for him to hold back the latest breaking news.

"Look, tell me what you can do with the ten Brits high society paedophiles, government cover-up and the rest. People are dying." Gavin regretted saying that.

"Dying?"

"Some deaths seem connected, that's all, so best forget I said that. Let's concentrate on the videos we have in hand and the book. The book will tell all and will be dynamite."

"Any Royals?" Again, the hesitation let the cat out of the bag. Gavin shook his head again; his hands had been tied by Eager.

"Let me make some phone calls. I will give you two numbers: one for the ones you have mentioned and the second one if you have a big US name and or a big Royal. I am going to focus on the big credible newspapers and media companies, not the gutter press. Call me in one day. Thanks." This Kent was sharp. This suited Gavin, as with a bigger pay out for Preston and video number seven he could swing Eager and Liberty to just release and live happily ever after.

A quick shake of the hand and he was gone, back on his way to the city that never sleeps.

The next two appointments came at the same time. He briefed them enough with his synopsis to get them salivating without giving the game away. One was a German, Herr Heinze — "Call me Fritz." He represented German media giants Vogelsmann, a global entity. The other was an Australian, Robert, son of the founder of a global empire, Ozfax, who own all types of global media. Gavin showed a brief minute of the video and did not give away the name, just said he was a major UK player. They wanted more and plied him with drinks and promises. They ended up at five p.m. They shared the bill between them, which Gavin appreciated. The German was more detail-orientated and kept wanting more specific information. The Australian was more casual and easier going.

"If half of what you say can be substantiated, mate, this is the range of numbers we are talking about." He slipped Gavin a beer mat upside down. Gavin glanced at it and his eyes popped wide open. He tried to look cool, sticking it in his pocket and trying not to look at it again until they left.

The German wanted to talk to his CEO and was clear the contract would have clauses in it that would require everything they say to be true and supported, and he could not talk numbers until they saw all the information they had. He would sign a confidentiality agreement to give Gavin comfort.

The media giants then discussed sharing the deal and splitting the world between them.

On the way out, Gavin asked the Australian if he had quoted US or Australian dollars. The good old greenback was the reply.

Chapter 53
The Comeback

She was found in the van at Nellies Airport by the Military Police searching for the van at the request of the LVPD. Sonia's arms were tied up and legs at the knees. She was bruised on the forehead, otherwise she seemed okay. They took her to the base medical centre anyway to be checked out. She called Chief De Silva in LA. Her story was simple: she had heard Steve was in Vegas and wanted to team back up with him on her return from London. She had run across the incident in the street by accident and had tried to help. All she saw was the woman being kidnapped and she had shot one of them. When told that was Eager, she said this was her first shooting and under the strain of her very first live major incident she had made a mistake. She gave thanks that he was okay. She did not recognise any of her abductors. She denied she told them to get in the truck; her words were, 'Do not get in the truck.' Eager must have been mistaken, like she was, as she thought he had shouted, 'Get in the truck.'

"Do you believe her, chief?" Steve asked.

"I don't know what to believe any more. We need to watch her and for the moment cut her out of the loop on this one."

"And Ms Bell?"

"I told you, I have been told in no uncertain terms to stand down by the director. The LVPD can handle this kidnapping; we do not have jurisdiction. Unless we get a good lead and proof she is in danger, what can I do?"

"We need the video of him."

"Even if we had it and he was executing a person, we could not use it. Too political so near to the election. The FBI cannot be seen to be playing politics for any side."

"We can't just sit on our asses and let these people be killed. I took an oath and believe in the FBI motto: fidelity, bravery and integrity. Where's the fidelity, bravery and integrity in what we are doing?"

The chief just shrugged.

"Well?" Steve pushed. He knew De Silva was a good man. He was also a company man who followed the rules. Would he do that knowing what they were doing was wrong. If anything was influenced by politics, this was it. Steve got another coffee for both of them. De Silva was thinking hard and after a few minutes he said, "Steve, I am going to re-assign you."

Sonia stopped at the LVPD HQ to make her statement on the kidnapping and shooting, as requested. She spent a lot of time with the officers who attended the scene to get a full picture of what went down. They all told stories of the event. Lots of laughter at the sidewalk crowd cheering and clapping, thinking it was a show. The detectives in charge did not have a clue about the real background Steve had kept quiet, and so did she. She asked about Eager and Gavin, and one of the patrol officers said they were okay when he dropped them off at the Sahara. Mr McGill was still in hospital recovering under guard and will be okay. Nothing on the dead bodies to identify them. They showed pictures taken by the crowd they had confiscated. The blonde lady's pictures were mainly from the back and side of her body and face, so not enough to identify her fully.

She used their phone several times and then left for LA, as directed by De Silva.

"Blobby, can you research all the properties owned by Travis Preston and family in Texas?" Steve was leaning over him as Blobby very rarely left his desk and his multiple computer screens.

"Busy, will next week be okay?"

"No, it will not, a woman's life is at stake."

"Chief approved it?" Blobby was good, but he was a stickler for procedures and organised workflow.

"Well, not as such. It is better he doesn't know; for him, I mean."

"The trip to HQ?"

"Yes. Okay, let's trade then."

"Trade?"

"You take me out on one of the big busts. Promise?"

"You are not fit enough, you know that."

"I have a slight problem with the legs. Any other business, this would be abuse of a disabled person." Blobby used crutches as he was in a car accident after he joined the FBI. He was so good with research he was given a desk job and he never got to be a special agent — his dream. He put on weight as he couldn't exercise and gained the nickname Blobby.

"All right, I promise. Until then, I am off for the best coffee and doughnuts for you." Steve had no idea how he could deliver going out on a bust; however, the coffee and doughnuts were easy.

"Right, on it; give me an hour."

"Thanks."

Chapter 54
Fair Exchange

Liberty woke up feeling groggy with a big headache, and she needed water badly. She had no idea where she was. The room was dark; early morning, she guessed, just getting light. She heard noises, animal noises, and now she was coming around, her senses were on high alert. The sound was like growling. It was not too loud, more like someone grumbling to themselves. She sat up and saw she was lying on straw spread around a dirt floor. Shit, she thought, I am in an iron cage. There was a jug of water to her side. She didn't touch it, no matter how much she needed it, fearing it was drugged.

Then she saw them, two large black bears standing on their rear legs, looking through the bars at her. They were huge and at least seven foot tall, standing in a cage in front of hers. She could see, to get out she had to go past them. To her they seemed angry and hungry.

Holy cow, they are going to feed me to the bears!

"I see you have met Fred and Mabel. They are well fed, Ms Bell; you can stroke them if you want."

Fuck off, whoever you are!

She could not remember much after being dragged into the van. Yes, there was a needle and she was being held down, kicking and screaming. No point asking what they want, as she already knew. Her logic told her it would be impossible to visualise getting out of this alive now. She could save the others and these bastards would get what they deserved; Eager would see to that.

She did not want to die! She was too young and could have had the world at her feet if she had pulled this off correctly. She remembered how it felt in the UK when she was lauded for her undercover work on the drug lords and their activities. Everyone wanted a piece of her, she was famous. Yeah, her fifteen minutes of fame. Then, like all tall poppies, she was stitched up and fell from grace. Dubbed and branded 'ignoble', Gavin had called it.

They would expect her to cry and beg for mercy or tell all if they threatened to torture or disfigure her. Well, she wouldn't give them that satisfaction. She would deal with them in exchange for her life. Buy time, buy an opportunity to escape; even a crack in the wall was a chance. They had left her purse in the cage. Nice of them. So she started straightening her clothes, hair and putting her face on. Stay calm. Stay calm, she said inside her head.

"You look good. Thanks for taking the time for my benefit."

The voice came again and now she could see a shadow coming closer. A tall man stood in between the two black bears, looking with them through the bars at Liberty.

"Not for you; a girl has to always look good." Liberty was trying to sound and look calm.

"Pity," the man said.

Oh, my God, it's Travis Preston himself!

"A bit better accommodation with a shower would be nice." Trying to be cheeky.

"Well, this is no James Bond movie where you get a nice suite from which you can escape."

"I guess so. Don't I get any last request, then? What do you expect of me?" Keep him talking, make friends.

"As Goldfinger said to James Bond when he was being tortured and asked if he expected him to talk, he said, 'No, Mr Bond, I expect you to die!' Really, I am joking, I expect you to live. Just co-operate and be a good girl for once."

"You want the video?"

"Of course, and a signed confession that you made it all up, and you are free to go."

"The confession would be worth nothing, so you would kill me anyway."

"Not if you signed it after confession to a priest. He would witness it, plus other respected notables, and they would swear under oath that it was not gained under duress. Hell, lady, we would even video us having some champagne together after. Give you, say, a few million dollars for your trouble and silence — everyone wins."

"Sounds good if true."

"Look, little lady. I was drugged and set up for blackmail. She taunted me and spiked my whisky. I have worked hard all my life and I do not deserve to have my destiny taken away from me by some whore and a dirty lawyer. Surely you see that I am not at fault? How many men stray away from home?"

Liberty tried to look convinced. She had to keep telling herself that he had ordered people killed, like Arturo and his girlfriend. He was charming, but still a murderer.

"I will need to move fast if I am to stop them distributing the video."

He unlocked the cage. The bears just watched.

"That's more like it. Fair exchange, my daddy always said, is no robbery. Follow me. Do not worry about Fred and Mabel, they are friendly when I am around. Our breeding bears."

He breeds bears to shoot no doubt, she thought. How do I do this, as any phone call they will trace and then get the guys? Travis led her to a small ranch house, not what she had imagined. She saw a helicopter parked on a field to the side of the barn where she was imprisoned. There was a corral full of top-looking horses, a long row of stables and a bunkhouse to the back of it. It was surrounded by beautiful mountains and the sky was blue. The sign on the barn said 'Mustang Ranch'. On another day she would love to live in such a place, riding horses all day.

They stepped up to the porch. A big cowboy was sitting on a love seat swing. He was dressed in the classic checked cowboy shirt, jeans and felt cowboy hat. He stood up to his six foot plus as Travis and Liberty approached. He had a side arm in a cowboy holster, just like the movies.

"Travis, Ms Liberty." He tipped his hat to her with his greeting. This was not what she expected, so much respect and politeness. Maybe there was a way out.

"Wyatt, why don't you take Missy Liberty inside and get her some coffee and eats. She may want a shower."

He turned to Liberty. "By the way, any thought of running away, forget it. We are in what was called in the eighteen hundreds, the

Comancheria lands. It is an unforgiving land many miles from anywhere. The 4th Calvary found that out chasing the Comanches in their home territory. Best you could hope for is to die of thirst or be eaten by the mountain cats or bears."

I could steal the fucking helicopter if I could fly.

It seemed hopeless. Wyatt was helpful and she did take a shower. The clean clothes seemed small, but they smelt nice and were quality. The skirt showed more of her legs and she caught Wyatt several times looking. Poor boy probably lives up here on his own, frustrated. Is he an opportunity?

The blonde kicker was nowhere to be seen, nor was the FBI woman. Just good old Travis and Wyatt, it seemed. Liberty zeroed in on Wyatt; he was definitely very interested in her. She asked him a lot of questions. He was careful with his answers. He was proud, though, that he had served with Travis and he was the helicopter pilot for him now. This was a skill he had learnt in the Army. He was proud of working on the ranches and explained how Palo Blanco 3 was the biggest in this part of Texas and that the Mustang ranch had the best horses in the US and the best place to hunt and ride. She flirted with him, sitting on the swing seat. He was enjoying every second.

He was maybe in his late thirties and very handsome with his blond hair and clean look. He was a cowboy right out of the movies, a Randolph Scott lookalike.

His eyes often drifted to her legs and thighs. Could she take him to bed and get his gun somehow. It was worth a try, and a bit of fun with him would relieve her stress. She was just about to suggest an afternoon lay down to him when Travis came out. He was carrying a radio phone and a piece of paper. He noticed what she was up to.

"I wouldn't mind a piece of you myself."

Sick guy, a piece of me? She walked away.

He then whispered to Wyatt, "Don't worry, son, you can play with her before we get rid of her." He then handed her the radio phone.

"Here, ring your friends, tell them to get the video and be ready for our call where to meet us. No games; they are under surveillance, one wrong move and the worst will happen. Do you get it?"

"Yes, but you do not know where they are."

He handed her the piece of paper. "The Sahara's number is on there."

Chapter 55
Mr Quick

Logan left Denise a message before he left the airport. 'Meet Mr Quick at the house.' He had picked up the hit man's black metal backpack. A glance inside, he could see some paperwork, a large case which he assumed had a weapon inside, and enough plastic explosive to blow up a few houses. There were a lot of other items, including several brown envelopes, but this was not the place to pull everything out and examine it, so he set off back to Eager's house.

On the way, he bought some takeaway fish and chips because he was very hungry after today's happenings. He needed a good bath to soak his sore and bruised muscles. Eager had such a bath and he was sure he would not mind. He also bought three bottles of chardonnay which he felt he needed to relax and think. He smoked in the Rover with the windows open. Eager, a non-smoker, would be pissed when he got back.

He let himself in and then ensured that all windows and doors were locked. He kept the shotgun and knife close at all times. There was always a chance Jimmy and his guys would find him and come back, not to mention the hit man's lady friend Jimmy had mentioned. He was in the bath when the door-bell rang. He had to get out with a big towel, got the shotgun and looked through the upstairs window, carefully checking first before he let Denise in.

"I was in the bath. Can I finish? Help yourself to a wine," he told her, and struggled with keeping the big towel from falling down as he went back upstairs.

"Right, can I get you one?"

"Thanks, lass, a refill," he called back. She shuddered again at the word 'lass' and knew she would have to tackle it with him soon. If he called her that again, she swore she would punch him. She brought him the bottle and walked straight into the bathroom to deliver it. He immediately tried to hide his private parts with both hands.

"Got something I've not seen before, lad?" She got that message across and with one hand he took the now full wine glass. She sat on the toilet seat with hers.

"I didn't want to scare you," was the best retort he could find.

She laughed as if he couldn't. "You look like shit. Did you run into a truck?"

He recounted what had happened. She looked concerned and very impressed with him. She had been debriefed about the scene they found at the office.

"No one other than the man on the slab was found there."

"What? I shot him in the chest with the shotgun. Granted pellets were for game, but I doubt he could have run away."

Suddenly, she put her glass down and bent over him. He got nervous and thought she was going to kiss him. She took his nose between her fingers and with a violent jerk tweaked it back straight.

"That's better, it was ruining your good looks."

"Shit, that hurt, Florence bloody Nightingale!"

"Our first fight," she laughed again.

"You are in a good mood. Mind if I get some privacy to get out and come downstairs and show you some goodies?" He had not told her about the bag he had collected from Heathrow.

"Best offer I have had for months. Okay, champ, I will see you downstairs." Willy the Wanker was at least useful for his witty quips, as he said this, the last time she arrested him.

Logan slipped his clothes back on, nearly everything blood-stained. When he showed her the backpack, she told him to put it down.

"Prints, we need prints to connect him. You're going to mess it up, that is if he hasn't been so careful to use gloves." She searched the kitchen and brought out some disposable plastic cleaning gloves.

They took out the goodies and created an inventory. Explosives, timers, wires, detonators, foldaway sniper rifle in a box, ammo, small hammer, a glass cutter, reinforced security sealing tape, a special lock pick set, black balaclava, camera, rubber cups like you could use on your hands, and five brown paper envelopes.

They carefully opened the envelopes. Sure enough, there was one on Allcock, Jimmy and Nick Harker, Tazewell Javelin and McAllistar.

Bingo, scribbled in pencil on several envelopes were numbers. On one envelope the numbers started with a 1 followed by 307, the next 284 and the next 3260. One, they knew, was the international dialling code for the US.

"Sloppy." Denise found this break so good and unexpected.

"Our luck is getting better," Logan said, as he copied it down.

"Some things are missing?"

"Like?"

"Like a passport, wallet and money. There was nothing in his clothes unless the Harker gang had already pocketed them."

"Or there is another stash somewhere. He gave me enough to help him. He could have left himself an escape route."

"He is being protected twenty-four-seven, much to my boss's budget complaints."

"Not cuffed to the bed, I take it?"

"Not sure. I will check in the morning. He is out of it tonight with operations and the usual heavy drugs."

They completed the second bottle of wine, thinking about what to do next.

"They are cleaning up," Logan said solemnly.

"I have got to call this in."

"Think, how are you going to explain how I got this stuff?"

"You did nothing wrong — you saved this man."

"Why was I there and why did I leave? I will be roped in, questioned at length and maybe even charged."

"With what?"

"You're the detective. Leaving the scene of a crime, not reporting a crime, in cahoots with the Harkers, torturing this poor bastard he had me targeted."

"Okay, enough, you have a point."

"We can't leave it like this, though. This guy needs to go down big time. He is a menace to society. If he gets out, God knows who will be next."

"I'll say I found the left luggage ticket in his clothes or the room, checked it out and this is what I got. Continuity of evidence without you being involved."

"Stealing my glory, eh?" He was joking, of course.

"So what next for you?" Denise asked, interested in what he would do now.

"Jimmy made a plea for us all to move on and then tried to kill me."

"So you want to do that to him first?"

"Are you speaking as a copper or a friend?"

"So we are friends now; relationship is developing." She laughed again.

"What's wrong with you, you are always so serious. I had you down as a misery guts."

"I don't know, I guess you remind me of Eager. The office is not the same without him. Anyway, do not change the subject."

"To be honest, I would like to move on. No stomach for prison any more. If I was sure the Harkers would call a proper truce. They blame me for bringing their empire down by taking the videos from the Hellfire Club."

"Tazewell Javelin?"

"He set me up and I did twelve months of my life in prison, got Karlein killed and her friend Dusty, and I was nearly killed. He is a scheming piece of shit."

"So you will go after him."

"Friend or copper?"

"Friend."

"Yes."

"I have an idea. Why don't you let the Yardies or Harkers do it for you? Would that work? The turf war is starting and there will be casualties. Why not wait? Patience is a virtue."

"I'll think about it after another glass. You?"

"No, I have to drive now. I have had too many; I would lose my job if I get stopped." She waited and he was not totally sure why. Was it an invitation to stay?

The phone rang and broke the moment. She shook her head to tell him not to, but he picked it up. He mouthed quietly that he had told George at the pub he would be here if Eager contacted him.

"John, you're okay?"

She gathered around the phone with him. They needed to know what was happening. He brought them up to date. They also updated him fighting for the phone. When he had gone, they got another drink and sat down to discuss all the details. They were all in danger, no help from the FBI, Liberty might really be dead this time, and they were ready to release the videos to the press. Danger is electric and exciting, and they could sense it in his voice.

"I wish I was there to help," Logan moaned after the call.

"Why not? You can be there by afternoon tomorrow; they are behind us by about eight hours, according to John. You might make the difference. I wish I could come and give him one in the head for Charlie. The bastard." Denise was all for him to go and assist. He had the experience and training, even though he was not one hundred percent fit.

"Seriously, you are right. I could let things lay out here and be at their side. I do have some talents."

"You're not as fit as you were before your shooting."

"Not optimum, but I am the only one trained in combat and weapons. Eager would miss an elephant at ten paces."

"Well, we'll need to get to bed, then."

"We?"

"Yes, you have a choice — the kid's bed or behave yourself."

"Well, watch my wound and bruises."

"Come on then, you probably need a massage. And Mr Quick don't be."

And I thought she was gay.

Chapter 56
Supernatural Causality

Since he returned to the reservation, Diablo had been planning his final act as Chief Longbow. He had those urges again and often shuddered with excitement. He knew this time he needed to plan rather than act on instinct and passion. To take out a presidential candidate just before the election would be a major coup.

He read the newspaper on the election campaigns, where and when the rallies would take place. The movements of Travis Preston in particular. He went to the library and read up on his ranch, Blanco Canyon Bar. Even the ranch's name was an insult to the indigenous people. It was the battle with the Comanches which marked the beginning of the end of their freedom. He found maps of the surrounding area and learnt as much as possible about the properties and landscape around the ranch.

He had been involved in Vietnam and often the Army blundered about the war. American superiority in all areas of military equipment and training was thwarted by bad planning, emotional reactions and a cunning enemy. An enemy that was not afraid to sacrifice its troops and people. He knew he had to be prepared to pay the ultimate price if his mission was a success or a failure. One Indian with a bow and arrows plus a knife against many with automatic weapons providing unlimited firepower. He had considered getting some firearms to help him against the odds he would encounter. Indians had used rifles effectively in the wars. It didn't fit well, though, with previous Chief Longbow acts. It was an audacious action that will go down in the history of the Indian nations. Passed down from generation to generation, like Cochise, Geronimo, Crazy Horse, Joseph, Black Hawk and many others.

If, and that was a big if, he got away, how would they know it was him, Diablo, son of Eskiminzin the warrior chief? Should he then give himself up so the world can see who he is and why he did these deeds?

Make an anonymous claim for Chief Longbow? He could write a book bringing to light the often-forgotten plight of the indigenous peoples? Either way, he needed to write down some information before anything happened, otherwise it was all for nothing.

The FBI task force had run out of leads. Chief Longbow had not accelerated his killings and had gone into a stagnant period of inactivity. Pretty normal, they explained, as some try and fix their lives for a while and then later come back and they actually do more killings with shorter time periods between them. He was kept on a retainer to keep his 'ear to the ground', as the FBI agent in charge had said. This was an old white man's stereotyping of Indians. Who does he think I am? Tonto, the loyal slave to the Lone Ranger? Yes, Kemosabe, he did.

I am not a serial killer! I am an avenger of my people.

This Preston deserved to die for other reasons, not just the acts of his ancestors, not because he lived and prospered on Indian land while they lived a meagre existence on reservations even today. He was totally justified in his actions and the world would understand what and why he did what he was going to do.

Indians are superstitious and they believe in supernatural causality, that being several events are linked with no natural process. Diablo read in the newspapers three articles that made him think that there were good omens. The first was Preston was taking the second weekend off in October from his busy campaigning schedule at his ranch. The article made comment to the fact that he was so far ahead in the polls he could afford to do this. He, though, believed he deserved time to relax and prepare for the final push to Election Day in November. He stated he was going hunting and fishing.

The second article was a discussion on the fact he was not taking his Secret Service protection unit with him to his ranch. Congress changed the law after the assassination of Robert Kennedy in California in 1968 so that presidential candidates would have Secret Service security for a hundred and twenty days of the campaign. The hotel where he was killed had hired a security guard who was a part-time plumber for him. The person convicted had a gun that only held eight bullets, but thirteen were found at the scene, suggesting a second gunman. If the Secret Service had been there, he would probably have been president and still alive today. A candidate can refuse Secret Service protection. There was a media debate on the risk of Preston's cavalier decision on security. He had claimed his personal security was highly trained and were loyal soldiers that had served with him well in the past. He was okay.

The third was that the weekend in question was a national public holiday, Columbus Day. The arrival of Columbus on American soil was the historic start of the demise of the culture of the indigenous people. What better day to make this statement?

The three omens were good. The spirits of his ancestors would look after him.

Chapter 57
Back-Up

Liberty deliberately misdialled several times to get time to think. She saw their angry looks and got it right the third time. The phone in the room rang only two times. Gavin grabbed it; he was waiting on the LA lawyer calling him about his arrival or Kent Koll's proposal.

"Gavin, get me Eager!"

"Liberty, are you all right?"

"Gavin, get me Eager, now!"

He got the message. Eager had heard the phone ring and rushed in.

"Thank God you are alive."

"John, listen very carefully, very carefully, and do what I say. They have me and are willing to exchange for the video and a confession saying it never existed, good old fantasist me." She knew they were listening and was performing for them.

"Don't be stupid, they will..."

"John, listen carefully for once. We cannot make a mistake; they know where you are and you are being watched."

"But..." He got it and went quiet.

"John, you must not hang around. Get the videos from the three white bags in the hiding place. Get the video they want and be prepared to meet when they ring back with the location. Got it? The videos are in the white bags. Not a word to anyone; if you do, they will hunt you down. Let's get this done, give them what they want and move on."

She rang off, leaving Eager scratching his head. It was not like Liberty — no 'Smalls' and 'giving them what they want?' — of course, they were listening in. He wrote down verbatim what she had said. Gavin was looking over his shoulder. The door opened and Steve walked in, and they both jumped up almost out of their skins.

"Steve?"

"Come to help if I can, unofficially."

"Thanks. I thought you had been ordered to stand down?" Eager asked with a big smile.

"Well, my boss has re-assigned me to an old cold case here in Vegas," Steve said with a wink.

They understood what he meant. Some help, at least.

"I got Blobby to do some research on Preston's personal property. The plane definitely went to Texas." He produced a list of six places. Four houses: one in Houston, one in Dallas and two others, one in New York and one in Hawaii. There were two ranches: Palo Blanco 3, the main ranch and big house, and Mustang Ranch, a hunting lodge. "I have discounted the other houses and the big offices in Dallas as too risky for them, although I could be wrong."

"I agree, he would not take her to houses in big cities; offices might have private space. Ranches maybe, but would he take her to his own place?" Eager asked.

"I doubt that would bother him as he obviously does not plan on her surviving to tell the tale," Steve said solemnly.

"Steve, she just rang us. They are going to give us a time and place to hand over the video. She said they were watching us. I couldn't help but think she was trying to give us a message — we've played this game before." He laid out his notes of what she said on the call. They all pored over it.

"The videos aren't in white bags," Gavin's contribution before he poured coffee for all of them.

"Three white bags. There are two and they are black. Did she forget under pressure?" Eager zeroed in on this as maybe a clue.

"Blanco three, makes sense." Steve was quick at puzzles and codes.

"You're right! Blanco means white and three bags means three. Excellent!" Eager got excited and knew he was stating the bleeding obvious.

"Don't rush. Examine every word, there may be more," Steve counselled.

They looked at the notes and drank two cups of coffee each.

"Mustang Sally," Gavin started to sing the song.

"Gavin, we are trying to concentrate, shut up!" Eager was not in the mood for music.

"Must not hang around. Mustang." A hurt Gavin explained his song, talking slowly so they got it. His excitement at finding another clue was dampened by Eager's rudeness.

"By Jove, Watson, you have it! Sorry for my outburst."

"Apology not accepted." Gavin was moody and folded his arms together in a show of hurt pride.

"So both ranches mentioned, but which one?"

"Hunt you down. Hunting lodge. Makes sense. If she wasn't there she would not know the name."

Steve then pulled out a map Blobby had sourced for him of the ranches and property.

"The Mustang ranch is in the middle of nowhere. Bad roads to get there, if passable at all most of the year. My guess: this is so out of the way so she is there, but for how long?" Steve added.

"Great, let's get going." Eager being eager.

"We need to work out the logistics first. We have to get to Texas and then right out in the bush, for which we'll need a chopper. Then, I am guessing, we have professional armed guards to contend with, so we need weapons and a plan. Best we try and get her out without confrontation."

"No help from the FBI?" Gavin asked. Steve just shook his head.

"We need to call in some favours." Steve suggested, thinking of who would help under the radar.

Steve made some calls to small airfields and flight operators around Dallas. They would all fly them around by chopper or light airplane, but at a very high cost. Then there was the fact they were virtually heading to a possible war zone — what private pilot would stick around, and if they did, what would they say afterwards? Without a proper support structure and back-up, these operations were impossible.

To their utter surprise, Logan McAllistar arrived around four p.m. They all hugged, as it was so good to see him. Steve was introduced and their connection explained.

"What are you doing here?" Gavin asked.

"Come to help," was his short response.

They sat down and talked through their situation. It was not good, if not impossible.

"Harry the Hedgefrog," Logan suddenly said.

"Harry the what?" Steve was bemused.

"Chopper pilot in NI. Very good flyer. See, you had to hop over power lines and hedges in case you were shot at. They could hear your rotors, but the chopper would be over them and be gone, flying so low and fast, by the time they saw it they couldn't get a shot off," Logan explained.

"NI?" Steve asked for an explanation.

"Northern Ireland."

"Oh, and how does this Harry the Hedgefrog help us right now?" Steve wanted clear doable suggestions and was a little frustrated with so little progress all afternoon.

"Last I heard he was in Dallas trying to be a country and western singer. Right bloody Willie Nelson he was; we couldn't stop him singing. He was flying choppers somewhere near Dallas, I think."

"He would help?" Eager asked.

"Blood brother," was all Logan would say.

Steve gave him his phone as they could not now trust the hotel one. Logan had a little black book and after five phone calls to the UK he got a number for Harry. A call found Harry at home and they talked for some time. Logan left the room and walked around one of the bedrooms during the conversation. He came back twenty minutes later and handed the phone to Steve.

"He needs to know where we are going."

Steve then got on the phone and after some explanation handed it back to Logan.

"Thanks, Harry, balls to wall, mate."

They waited for feedback. "He will help us, has access to a chopper, an old civilian Bell Jet Ranger, but it will more than do. We need to let him know where he can pick us up. Get this, he has some weapons we could use."

"How much?" Eager asked, worried about their escalating costs in the US.

"Beer tokens."

"Beer tokens?" Steve asked.

"Yes, buckshee, maybe a bit of fuel and a beer afterwards; and beware, we will have to watch him perform!"

If there is an afterwards. Eager's body shook at the thought.

Eager could feel his bad knee starting to ache just thinking about action, running, hiding and jumping.

They agreed they had to get to Dallas as soon as possible. Eager asked Gavin to stay at the hotel and handle the phone when they called. He was visibly relieved. He needed to meet the lawyer and get the sale moving. They would take the Preston tape, however; they just had to dupe it. Steve said he could do that at the local FBI office. There was silence for a moment as they made their minds up they could trust him. Gavin would hide the dupe and if anything happened to them, blast it out to the media.

The plan was simple. Steve would leave and book flights to Dallas and return with the dupe. They would then sneak out down the service elevator and leave via the staff entrance. They had to take a risk; if someone was watching, they could elude them. When they called, Gavin was to find another phone that was safer to call them on.

There was another knock on the door and Gavin opened it, expecting to see Big Gary. In walked Pat McGill, complete with chest bandages.

"What are the gob shites doing with my girl?"

One more for the team.

Chapter 58
Snipe and Slash

"Good police work, Denise, finding the gear; an absolute godsend to the investigation. I have no idea how SOCO and our guys missed that ticket in the room." Bill Sutherland seemed to be searching her eyes as if he was not convinced, they missed it.

"Just good old woman's intuition, sir," Denise lied, looking straight back at him without blinking.

"I rang you last night to catch up."

"Sorry, sir, I stayed at a friend's and forgot to leave my number."

"You are an important part of this team, Denise. I need to get hold of you."

"Right, sir, it won't happen again."

Is that a toupee on his head?

"SOCO said there was another type of blood on the floor at the docks, so he must have put up a hell of a fight."

"Really?" So they had time to come back and move the big Scotsman while the police waited on back-up.

"You found him, Denise, you should interview him. See what he will tell us, if anything. Apart from two left-hand small fingers and a small toe missing, he will be okay to talk to us."

"Molly?"

"We can't ask her to identify him just yet. We need a line-up when he is ready for that."

"It does look like he was the one at the café and he is a hired killer."

"Just her word for it. It does stink, though; but what was the motive? These guys are expensive."

"Did we trace the US telephone number?"

He stepped closer to almost whisper. "Well, yes and no. One is the US country code and 307 the area code for Wyoming, a sparsely populated state, but the phone number didn't work when I called. I was also not sure this would be the place of his support. Also, it was too easy and too much of a sloppy way to save the numbers, so I got the guys to play around with the numbers." He hesitated, milking his moment of brilliance.

"And?"

"Reverse them and it is the main switchboard number of, you will never guess."

"CIA HQ Langley main switchboard," Denise said without hesitation.

Sutherland looked at her and his mouth was slightly open. She could see him thinking, *How the hell could she guess that?*

"The plot thickens," she announced, seeing all the connections in her mind.

"What connects Charlie to the Harkers, Tazewell Javelin, Logan McAllistar and DCI Eager?"

She just shrugged.

He wasn't around when the Hellfire Club saga was going down and the commissioner had not chosen to tell him about the videos. It was not her place right now.

"Eager, any news?"

"Can't contact him, sir. I am sure he will be on his way back soon."

"Well, let me know if you get anywhere with our man." He walked out.

Sure, you would interview him, but you know he will say zip all, so I get to be the fall detective. She reflected on her evening with Logan McAllistar — quite a surprise for both of them. He is a man's man, for sure, but can be very tender. She was day-dreaming a bit, not like her. Back to business to the hospital. When she got there, she was directed to a private room on the second floor. No police guarding. Then a young constable came along with a tea in his hand from the vending machine.

She put her arms on her hips. "Where have you been?"

"Pee and tea. No one relieved me. I've been here four hours on my own, ma'am." Spilling the hot tea as he spoke due to nerves.

"Do you know what we have in there?" Angry.

"Yes, ma'am."

She went into the room. The curtains had been drawn so you could not see in. She came back quickly. "Where the fuck is he?" The young constable looked terrified.

"He's gone! How long were you away?"

"Just a few minutes," he lied. He was chatting up the young nurses in casualty.

The handcuffs were hanging on the metal closure for the bed. There were no clothes in the small mobile cupboard at the side of the bed. She told the constable to call up operations and sound the alarm. Everyone needed to be looking for him and be told he was extremely dangerous.

She called Sutherland straightaway. She thought he would explode and imagined his toupee flying in the air. She got the constable and hospital security to start a search of all parts of the hospital. She knew he would be well gone. Tough guy, just recovered from having three of his digits cut off and operations to put them back, and he manages to get out of handcuffs and escape. He would know that if the micro-stitching doesn't take and he doesn't get drugs and treatment, they will rot and come off. He is more scared of failing his bosses than what happens to himself.

He's gone for his second stash and escape route.

Mad Mike was in the copse opposite the country home Tazewell Javelin was staying in. He had a Lee Enfield Number 4 sniper rifle and telescopic sight. It was a 7.6mm and good at the range from the copse to the house. It was widely used by the British Army and he had known about this weapon in NI. He was, though, not totally comfortable as he had not had time to practice to hone his skills and get used to it. Jordy had been instructed to be his spotter support, as Fergus was out of action and the hit man was in custody. He had binoculars and stood to the right of him.

They had been there from six a.m., and it was now eight thirty a.m. It was bitterly cold and Mike kept blowing his fingers to keep his trigger finger warm. Jordy had gloves on. Willy was in the van fifty metres away, hidden behind the thickest trees on the dirt lane, awaiting the getaway. Tazewell came out slowly with his John Wayne crab-like walk due to his bad hip. He was slow and his minders were behind him and to the side of him. A perfect shot for Mike. Jordy watched Javelin nervously and kept turning to Mike. As he was going to shoot, Jordy leaned in towards him. The loud bang got everybody down on the ground and it was difficult to see if Javelin had been killed. Mike thought he had hit him by the way he fell, although he was certain it wasn't a kill. Soon, bullets were coming their way from his Yardie protection men. They ran for the van and jumped in, taking off like a bat out of hell. Shots followed them down the street. They could see the Yardies jumping on motor-bikes to chase. Willy also saw through his side mirrors and he knew what to do.

Inside, Mike screamed at Jordy, "You dumb fuck! You made me miss! Why did you move like that? You have started a war when it could have been all over."

Jordy said, "I didn't move." Then, to appease Mike, he just shrugged an apology.

Two motor-bikes, each carrying two guys, easily caught up on both sides, their goal to shoot the driver. Willy suddenly swerved the vehicle side to side dramatically. He caught one bike, which went off the road and hit a barbed-wire fence. The other was shooting through the side window. Willy ducked the best he could. Mike opened the back doors and pointed the Lee Enfield out.

"Stop and turn the vehicle around quickly," he yelled at Willy.

"Hold on!" Willy did a handbrake turn, spinning the vehicle around and facing the other way. The motor-bike had shot past, skidded and then did a turn-around, facing the back doors of the van. Mike fired several times at them, mostly trying to disable the bike. The two guys jumped off and ran for cover to the side of the road.

"Go!" Mike screamed, and Willy drove forward and spun the van around again. Then they were off. The Yardies had dropped their weapons on the road. The bike was leaking petrol and both tyres were blown. They ran back to get the weapons, but it was too late — the van was too far away.

In the van, they were sweating and trying to get their breath back. They knew they had been very close to death. Finally, Mike said, "You are better than that Jackie Stewart, Willy, some yoke you are."

"Yoke?" Jordy asked.

"Means awesome."

279

"Well, they were no Evel Knievels for sure," was Willy's modest reply.

The hit man picked up two scalpels as he limped out of the hospital as fast as he could. His left foot was bandaged and he carried his shoe. A hand was also bandaged, but it was again his left, which was lucky for him as his best fighting and shooting hand was his right. He saw taxis across the street and jumped into the front one.

"Where to, mate? That looks nasty; they let you out like that?"

"Heathrow airport terminal number two." He then nodded as if agreeing the hospital should not have let him go.

"Typical, they are so short of beds that people like you are not treated right. I blame the pensioners; nothing better to do than block up the system cos it's free…"

He tuned the cabby out. He had to get his stuff, find somewhere for the night and make a new plan. No way can he send back that he failed. Not going to do that for certain. Thank God for the morphine. He had grabbed the bag from over his bed and stuck it under his jacket, and it was still connected to his wrist.

When they arrived, the cabby turned around. "That will be fifteen pounds, thanks. I hope you feel better."

He got out and walked around to the taxi driver's window. He pretended it was difficult to search his pockets. "Can you help me?" Pointing with his bandaged hand to his inside jacket pocket. The cabby leaned his head out of the window, stretching to put his hand inside the pocket. The man struck with the scalpel in his right hand, slashing the cabbie's throat all the way across. Blood spewed out and he jumped back. It took only seconds for the cabbie to slump down dead. He then leaned in and removed the cabbie's wallet and moved off and limped to terminal three, not two, as if nothing had happened.

He felt everyone was looking at him with the bandages and the limp. When the balloon goes up, he would be easily identified. Two heavily armed policemen walked by him and gave him the once over and then, after a tense moment, walked on. The other baggage ticket was hidden in the heel of the shoe he carried. He recovered a brown parcel package and went to the toilet. He went into a stall and opened it. He took out a wad of British cash. There were several passports in the briefcase, US dollars and UK pounds, a return air ticket to Hong Kong and a Walther PPK pistol and some spare rounds. He placed the Walther in his trouser belt, one of the scalpels in the jacket side pocket and the other in the package box, and closed it. Before he left, he took the cash out of the cabbie's wallet, cleaned it to get rid of prints and shoved it in the toilet tank. It could look like a robbery, he thought.

He decided to go to Wimbledon, which was further out of London to the North West. He was a tennis fan and had heard so much about the area. He took the underground train to Waterloo Station and then a train to Wimbledon. He needed several days to recover and implement a new plan. He knew vengeance was bad for his business, a bad trait for his line of work. It didn't matter; they were going to pay and suffer badly before they died.

DCS Sutherland had the whole team in the big meeting room. He brought in DI Teddy Samuels from being literally out in the cold. Well, cold cases. Thirty detectives, all looking at their watches; it was five p.m. and almost time to go home, except for the afternoon shift.

"I have just come from the commissioner's office and I have no need to tell you that he is absolutely furious. We had Commander Allcock's killer in our custody and we let him walk away. Yes, I did get my ass kicked, if you're asking. We are the laughing stock of the force, and wait for this to get out to other constabularies."

"Sir, the uniforms let him go," one officer objected.

Sutherland held his hand up. "Stop! We should have checked. They put a probationer on security; I mean, right out of college with no relief. They obviously didn't get the memo on how dangerous this guy was."

"Or didn't read it, the bongos," someone said at the back of the room.

"Enough! It's on us. We should have visited earlier after he came out of the theatre. Yes, the buck stops with me, but I cannot think and act for everybody on my team. We also lost a cabbie, his throat slit ear to ear, because this guy was able to walk away. I can't speak for everyone, but I personally will not sleep until this bastard is back in custody."

281

Denise looked down. She was with Logan and had not cared to follow through. She felt guilty, and by the look of the heads down around the table, she wasn't the only one.

"Right, enough flagellation. Let's catch this bastard." He went to the whiteboard and started allocating duties. DI Samuels caught the worst duty, checking all the flight passenger lists out of Heathrow today and all the other ones scheduled for the next three days. Fortunately, SOCO had taken pictures of him and they had been circulated to all ports. Detectives were allocated areas of London for hotels, B&Bs, cafés, restaurants, takeaways and anywhere he might be able to stay or get sustenance. Other hospitals, chemists and doctors' surgeries were included. The list of follow-ups was exhaustive; however, the normal moans and groans and questions about overtime never came up. Denise was not allocated any specific duties, so she waited till the various teams rushed out to be on the streets or to the phones.

"Denise, what do you think?"

Just then, she was called to the phone in her office. She excused herself and said she would be straight back. When she did, she told him about the shootings and the attempt to kill Tazewell Javelin.

"How come it has taken to now?"

"Their guy inside has just been able to get to a phone. He is in the doghouse with Harker."

"Neighbours?"

"Country location in Kent. No idea why so many shots were not reported. Get this, there was a shoot-out with some Yardies on motorbikes, apparently."

"Was anyone hurt?"

"They are not sure; our guy says they are hunkering down for reprisals."

"Get on to the locals and see what they know. Before you do, tell me, what would you do in our runaway's situation?"

She thought about it. "I guess he has a few options; one is to get out, two is to hide and get better before he moves, and three, finish his contracts."

"And your best guess?"

"This guy is tough and resilient. I would say his pride has been hurt and he fears failure. So he will lick his wounds and complete the contracts. He must be pissed at the torture they put him through, so he will target Harker and Javelin first."

"This Sammy the Squirrel worked for Harker, so they got him when Sammy was murdered and took him and tortured him; but why were they after him in the first place? Did they know they were targets?"

"Yes, sir. The inside man said he had visited Jimmy Harker at night and threatened that if he did not kill McAllistar and Javelin, he would kill him and his brother."

"I am missing a lot of information. Has anyone put this in a report?"

"I assume Special Branch would have. I heard this when talking to them."

"I think, Denise, you need to download all you know tonight on a report so I can find out what I do not know. Start with connecting the dots for me; how are all these targets connected?" He was getting angry.

She was looking at his hair. *He must have a toupee on.*

"Yes, sir, will do. Sorry so much has happened. I don't know what you don't know."

"Well, try hard. Cover everything you know and we will be sure. What about McAllistar? Should we give him protective custody until we catch this blighter?"

"I think he is out of the country, so he is okay."

"You think, or you know?"

She had to be careful about it before answering.

"I know. He is a friend of DCI Eager and called to see if I knew where he was in the US. I told him 'no', and he said he was leaving anyway."

"You didn't think to tell me this?"

"I didn't think it was relevant, as it was before we found the info from our hit man friend."

"A word to the wise, Denise. They say Eager was a great team player and detective and that recently, since getting embroiled with this reporter, he is out of control. He will probably not have a job when he eventually comes back. The commissioner goes red at the mention of his name. You do not want to go down the same path, okay? So let me be the arbiter of what I need to know and we will get on just fine. Right?"

"Right, sir."

"Get me that report and you focus with Special Branch and your team on his targets. Surveillance until we find him."

"Yes."

He definitely has a toupee on.

Chapter 59
Harry the Hedgefrog

"So, Ms Liberty, here is proof of payment of the one million I offered you. It is an offshore account; I obviously cannot send it direct to you. These papers include the passwords and how you can get the funds to your bank, but only after we have the video and the signed statement. So all in good faith, as I promised. I have to go to the Columbus Day celebrations and church tomorrow. Good photo opportunity. All goes well, you can join me for that glass of champagne."

She looked at the bank transfer and said, "Thanks, we're good."

"Phone them and tell them to meet my guys at eleven a.m. at this address tomorrow. Once I get the video, I will send Wyatt for you to join us. They can come, too, if they like; we hold one hell of a hoedown in Texas."

He left for the ranch house and Wyatt stood with her when she phoned. Gavin answered and she gave him the address and time.

"Where is Eager?"

"Just stepped out for a smoke."

She thought that was a clue that he wasn't there, as he doesn't smoke. She told him about the money and the invite to the hoedown as if she had bought it hook, line and sinker.

"We must not hang around there as we have to get a ride back to London." Gavin hoped she would understand her own clue given back to her meaning they had got it.

"Pass on the address, eleven a.m. sharp, so they need to fly tonight, I guess."

"Thanks, Liberty, see you soon. Stay safe and sleep well tonight."

She handed the radio phone back to Wyatt.

"So, you are leaving?"

"Yes, well, someone has to fly Travis. By the way…" He whistled and out from the barn came four Indians armed to the teeth with automatic rifles. They were big, fierce men with warpaint on their faces. She thought this was done for her benefit to scare her; if it was, it was working. They walked slowly towards them, examining Liberty with what she thought were evil stares.

"These are Tonkawa Indians and they are fiercely loyal to Travis. Their ancestors fought with the 4th Cavalry against their biggest enemy, the Comanches. They will look after you until the morning. You need to stay inside, as they also release the bears at night to feed. Do not let that feed be you!" he laughed. "I will pick you up around lunch, if everything goes okay."

"Okay."

She watched the helicopter take off and went inside the ranch house and locked the door. Those Indians never took their eyes off her and then the door, which made her skin crawl. She watched them set up a fire outside the bunkhouse and sit with blankets around their shoulders, smoking pipes and cigars. Still looking towards the ranch house door.

She was sure that Gavin was trying to tell her they had her location. He had emphasised 'tonight' when he said 'sleep well'. Was she going to be rescued or was that wishful thinking? How could they, unless the FBI was on board? This was such a remote place.

The fridge had a lock on it and she worked with a kitchen knife to open it, bending the knife and scratching the enamel of the fridge. No luck, but when looking around she saw the key hanging with the others on the back of the kitchen door.

So why put a bloody lock on the fridge?

There was plenty of cold beer in the fridge. Mad Pecker lager — she had never heard of it. Beer was beer to her. The food was not enticing at all, so she settled down to think what she could do if they were really coming. Put all the lights on and do not switch them off until dawn so they could see where she was. Five Mad Peckers later, she had not added anything, only one action to her list.

Fuck, the bears will be out there tonight!

The cowboy bar was packed. The music all country and western. Everyone was dressed in Western gear. Twenty guys and gals were line dancing, thumbs stuck down their belts. It was a dynamic happening place full of laughter, drinking and smoke. It was known to be a pick-up joint.

The taxi driver had laughed, knowing this watering hole. "You gents enjoy yourself, mind," were his parting words.

This is where Harry had asked them to meet. He had a turn on stage as this was open-mike night. Eager, Steve, Logan and Pat made their way to the bar, which was also packed three deep. A bar that stretched about thirty metres, Eager reckoned. You didn't need to smoke, just breath in, cigarettes, cigars and weed.

They were in the 'Last Drop Tavern' in south Houston. The last place before going out of town to the country areas. They got there just in time as Harry took to the stage. He had a cowboy hat on, long dangling hair tied at the back in a ponytail, complete with a grey beard, green shirt covered in badges, blue jeans and black cowboy high boots. Logan hardly recognised him from the smart Army Air Corps Staff Sergeant. Soon, he was singing a Kenny Rogers song, *Lucille*, and they heard him sing like Willie Nelson through his nose: 'You picked a fine time to leave me, Lucille.' The song went down well and then he finished his small set with *Flower of Scotland* in homage to his country. This did not go over well at all. It was hardly C&W. Logan thought he should not give up his day job, but would never tell him that to his face and destroy his dream.

Harry saw Logan and came over with guitar in hand. They were all drinking Budweiser out of the bottles. It was very noisy.

"Need a beer?" Logan asked.

"What?"

"Need a beer?" Logan cuffed his hands around his mouth as he shouted.

"Don't touch the stuff," Harry shouted back, still nasal like Willie Nelson. He then indicated with his hands they should go outside. They followed and managed to squeeze through the crowd to the car park. That was also busy, full of trucks and people smoking, drinking and talking. A few couples were busy big time on bonnets and by the fences. Kissing was the mildest form of their sexual acts, and they went about their business with not a care.

Eager noticed a big motel next door, lights flashing 'Vacancies' and other signs like 'Rooms to Let'. *By the hour*, Eager assumed.

Introductions out of the way, Harry led them to his red Dodge wagon. It was something none of them had ever seen before, a very distinctive vehicle. Harry called it his 'legacy classic power wagon'. There was only one passenger seat, so they gave that to Pat due to his injuries. The rest got in the back with their carry-on luggage. It was a cold night and by the time they got to the little airfield they were freezing. Luckily, it was not that far from the Tavern. Harry unlocked the security gate and Logan jumped out to close it after they drove through.

It was a small airfield with three big hangars and several wind socks, plus a narrow, tall building which they assumed was the flight tower. Only one runway. Several field lights around the perimeter fence. Harry stopped at the smallest hangar and slid open the big door. The Bell Jet helicopter was inside. They were happy to go inside to escape the cold. There was a small office which Harry opened and they crowded inside. On a desk was a flight map on which he had circled their destination. Upon gathering around, he showed them where he suggested they land.

"Open land about three miles away behind a lot of forest. If we circle around and come in from the North, I doubt if they will hear us. Always a chance, though, as there are no flight routes passing over the area; noise travels far in the bush at night, could warn them."

Eager wasn't looking forward to a hike in the dark over rough terrain with his dodgy knees.

"You're right, at night in the countryside sound travels well; they will probably hear the chopper," Steve suggested.

"Yeah, right. I will go in autorotation."

"What is that?" Pat asked.

"I will turn off the engine to the main rotor on approach to landing and aerodynamics will work it."

"So let me get this right" — Pat was not a good flier — "you are landing in the dark, in an unknown terrain, without using your engine?"

"Right."

"Jesus, Mary and Joseph." Pat made the sign of the cross.

Logan couldn't help saying as he did so, "Spectacles, testicles, wallet and watch."

Harry was not fazed by this due to his extensive flying experience.

"He is the best," Logan added.

"Weapons?" Steve asked. He had brought two pistols on the plane with his FBI badge; that is all they had.

"Right, I've got these." Harry dug into a big metal filing cabinet and brought out an M70 Winchester hunting rifle, a 9mm Browning and a Buck folding hunting knife used for skinning prey.

"We are probably up against professionals with high-powered automatic weapons. God knows how many. We have these plus my two pistols." Steve was disappointed. He was used to sophisticated back-up with the best equipment money could buy in the FBI.

"I'll take the rifle and the knife," Logan said. Harry was showing him the four magazines, each loaded with five cartridges. Eager took the 9mm and Pat one of Steve's pistols.

"What about you, Harry?"

"I'll stay with the chopper, not my gig."

"Right, we all need to be blacked-out. For God's sake, John, put that bloody safety on. I am going to lead, but not with you behind me cocked and ready to shoot me in the arse!" Logan lectured.

In the Marines, Logan was used to and experienced with such expeditions. He handed out his black-out warpaint and checked their clothing. All had dressed in as much black as possible. Pat had bought a black bomber jacket to cover his white shirt and bandages before they left Vegas.

They talked about their plan, standing around the office table. Logan would lead the march and when they were within one thousand yards he would go and recce the ranch. They would wait on his return, no smoking, no lights. It was a full moon tonight and would give them enough light to find their way. Harry had given Pat a two-way radio; he needed warning when they were coming back, especially if they were chased.

"If you get split up and you can't make it back to the chopper, I will go without you, if they are close behind," Harry stated, then he pointed to a location half a mile from the landing zone.

"If this happens, go there and lay low until tomorrow night, same time, same place. Do not try and walk out of here, it's impossible, you will never be able to do it. Best I can do, but only if they think we all got away."

"What if they do think one of us is here?" Eager asked.

Harry just shrugged.

"Do you think they will be expecting us? I mean, a full-on FBI raiding team?" Pat asked.

"No. We have been stood down and I guess they know that as someone was instrumental in making this happen. So they are expecting a couple of lost Brits turning up tomorrow at the rendezvous time. This location is so far out, I doubt they think we know about it," Steve replied with the optimism they needed.

"So maybe some farmhands?" Eager asked.

"No, John, we go into this as if they are expecting us. Ready for us. Otherwise we could get sloppy. Even with the autorotation, they might hear us before," Logan admonished him.

"Got it."

It was now two in the morning. Flight time was going to be around forty minutes. They left their hand luggage and all personal effects, including wallets, in the office, which Harry locked up. He dragged the chopper with his truck out of the hangar and then warmed it up, ready to go. They all piled in, with Logan in the front seat with Harry. Nerves were at the highest and they all had second thoughts on their adventure. Harry was drinking from a hip flask.

When they were in the air, he handed it to Logan.

"Want some?" he said over the headphones.

"What is it?"

"Good old Johnnie Walker," was the reply.

"I thought you didn't drink now?"

"Beer, I don't drink beer."

Logan took a swallow. He was tapped on the shoulder by Eager to share. They were all cold and had been listening on the tourist headsets in the back.

Harry the Hedgefrog was true to his name. He went in a big circle north and then approached the LZ, jumping over trees, flying as low as he could get. Then, all of a sudden, he went horizontal and when high enough switched off the rotors.

"Here we go. Hang on to your seats!" Harry sent the warning. It went eerily quiet and it felt like a bit of a rollercoaster as they started to free-fall at an angle, gliding down. The LZ he had chosen was in a wide opening and was grassed and fairly smooth; even so, they bumped down hard. All of them had their hearts in their mouths. Pat was having the worst time: he was holding a cross from his neck in his fingers and part of the chain in his mouth, praying. His wounds were aching.

"Thank the fuck for that. I didn't think we would make it in one piece," Harry said out loud. There were gasps as they all let out the breath they were holding in and started to breathe again with deep intakes of air.

Did Harry just say what I thought I heard? Pat trembled.

Once out, they started to march in a line, with Logan leading. He took his time as the terrain got more difficult and he did not need one of them to have a twisted ankle and need to be helped or slowing them down. The moonlight was good enough to see well and bad enough for them to be spotted if they weren't careful. When he could see smoke at a distance which he knew located the ranch for them, he put his hand on his head to signal to the others to come to him.

"I will go and recce. If I am not back in, say, thirty minutes, you have a choice; come and find me or go back and get out. If you hear gunshots, I would advise you to get out." They all nodded.

He went ahead carefully, but soon disappeared from their sight. There were some large rocks and they sat on them, looking around nervously. The rocks were cold, but better than standing. No one spoke.

Logan finally got close enough to be able to see the ranch. The big open fire in front of the ranch house surprised him and he saw the four Tonkawas squatting around it. They had warpaint on and were passing a bottle around, drinking; they looked the worse for wear. The lights were full on in the main ranch house and some smoke was coming out of the chimney. He waited and watched for movement in the house. After ten minutes, he moved to the back of the ranch house. Several bedroom windows and what he thought was a small toilet window. He was not sure if she was held prisoner inside and who would be with her guarding, and how many. The top little window had a beer bottle on a walking stick hanging out of it. He moved closer and listened. There was movement in the house and some kind of noise. Why hang out a beer bottle? Maybe Liberty sending a message — this is where I am — or a warning.

He made his way back to the team.

"Four drunken Indians outside around a fire. All have warpaint on and rifles. The ranch house has movement inside and a beer bottle sticking out of the toilet window at the back. I do not know how many guards are inside, if any."

"That's Liberty, the beer bottle flag," Eager stated with certainty.

Pat was allocated the Indians due to his wounds and he now had the rifle. Eager was to provide back-up for him and to be available if it went wrong inside. Steve and Logan were experienced with entering rooms with suspected bad guys in and both had courses in counter-terrorism training.

The Indians were sleeping. Pat and Eager slowly took their rifles away, except one, who had it on his lap. Logan and Steve stood to each side of the entrance door.

"Ready?" Logan nodded. "Go!" Logan used his army boots to kick the door open and they both rushed in, taking each side of the doorway. The lights were on and Liberty sat on the sofa, looking startled. Then she recovered.

"What kept you guys?" There were six beer bottles on the floor in front of the sofa. Steve put his finger to his mouth.

"No one here but little old me and my Indian friends out there." She wasn't drunk, but a little tipsy.

"Come on, we need to go," Logan ordered her.

"Let me just get my purse."

"Come, damn it."

The Indians woke up with the kicking in of the door. The one with the rifle stood up; however, Pat was fast and hit him full on the head with the butt of his rifle and he fell over. The rest stayed still.

"There's an iron cage in that barn; lock them in there." Liberty pointed and then showed the way. They were all made to follow, helping their friend. When they were put in the locked cage, there were looks of hate and unbelievable anger on their faces. They had failed, and this was not the way of their tribe.

"Shit, where are the bears?" Liberty had realised that the bears were missing; maybe Wyatt wasn't joking and they were out there somewhere.

"Bears?" Eager asked.

"Big fucking black bears. I thought he was joking when he said they let them out at night to eat."

"Come on," Logan commanded again, and they all started to move back to the helicopter as fast as their legs could carry them. They heard cries and whistles coming from the barn.

"Move! We need to move; we have three miles to walk," Eager shouted as he helped Liberty walk in her fashion shoes with a slight high heel and a state of alcohol-infused happiness. He could not stop her talking and expressing her gratefulness to them.

"And, Steve, thanks for coming; wow, you are great. And you, dad, and you, Logan. Logan, what are you doing here?"

"What about me?" Eager wanted her gratefulness to him.

"You?" She wobbled as her foot struck a rock and her shoe came off. She sat down, trying to get it back on. He bent down to help her, while the others were moving on, not noticing.

There was a loud whistle from the ranch and Eager jumped up. Facing him twenty yards away were two big black bears standing on their hind legs and growling fiercely. Liberty looked up. "Bastard lied to me. He said they were well fed. Hey, Fred and Mabel, we are friends, okay?" She stood up and kicked off both shoes and picked them up.

"Fred and Mabel? Really?"

"Let's run!" She meant it.

"We can't out-run bears."

"I just have to out-run you, old man." She started laughing at that old joke.

"Come on, start walking slowly backwards with your head held down." Eager had watched many wildlife shows on TV.

"Why?"

"Shows them respect and that we are no threat."

"Fuck we are! They are hungry, shoot them."

"No, walk backwards."

"No, shoot them, Smalls."

Three loud bangs came from behind them and the bears ran away. Logan had come back.

"Stop messing around and get your asses in gear."

They started running after him. After several hundred yards, Eager was exhausted and his knees hurt badly, so he stopped and bent over, panting.

"You go on. I will catch you up."

"No, we go together." She seemed a lot more sober now. She pulled him up. The whooping and hollering was getting closer. The Indians had got out and were following.

They just made it to the chopper in time. The rotors were going and Harry was ready to take off. Several shots came close to them. Logan put his gun out the window and fired six rounds in all directions. Harry took off as the Indians cautiously moved forward. They lifted their rifles and started to aim at them. Up quickly, down just as quick, and over the trees went the chopper, an amazing bit of flying which he kept up until they were out of range. The passengers all felt a little sick.

"I would not like to be in those Indian moccasins when Preston finds out," Pat offered.

"Or that handsome cowboy, Wyatt," Liberty added.

"That was easier than we thought, though." Logan was relieved.

"Not out of the woods yet by a long chalk." Steve toned down the merriment.

Oh, for the sake of sanity, please let this all finish, Eager prayed.

Chapter 60
Storm Brewing

"So you missed! I thought this was your, let me say, expertise." Things just seemed to get worse for Jimmy. God, he wished brother Nick was out of prison and by his side. He needed his violence, temper and impatience, which he had previously thought were his problems.

"Boss, wait a minute. How did you find Jordy?"

"What the hell has that got to do with anything?"

"He definitely leaned in on me just as I squeezed the trigger. I think he did it on purpose."

"Excuses, Mike. Excuses."

"No, listen. How did they know where our Chinese was? Sammy had it all sussed out and then the cops turn up, check it out and go away. Then how did they know about him anyway? How come they dragged up the Yardie and bike a few days after he was dumped? That doesn't happen, right?"

"A grass in our midst?"

"You're dead on, boss. Where did you get him?"

"A contact in Newcastle said he had just come out of clink and needed to get away from there. He was recommended as mean, useful muscle."

"Why did he have to get away?"

"Pigs all over him all the time."

"I'll watch him. Can he be checked out?"

'I will try. I am more worried about Tazewell. His Yardies are already moving in on our street vendors. Some knifed, some beaten up, and a lot of runaways or changed allegiance. They will be here next."

"So what do you think, a frontal attack on the club?"

"Not sure. Tazewell wants the club and would not risk getting it closed down after a shoot-out. No, he wants me out of the way now we have shown our hand."

"Fergus out of action?"

"Two broken ribs and a lot of chest bruising. He was finding it hard to breathe for a while. I need him back on board. I have stripped our members from Manchester to help here."

"So we attack or sit here on our thumbs?"

"I am not sure. I guess awaiting his next move."

"I wouldn't, so I would; his next move maybe our last."

Jordy broke into the room without knocking, which was forbidden. Before anyone said anything, he showed them the evening paper.

'LONDON TAXI DRIVER'S THROAT SLASHED BY ESCAPED PRISONER.'

Jimmy grabbed the paper and read the article out loud. He felt he was in a negative whirlpool, being sucked down, because now things just got worse.

If it wasn't for bad luck, I wouldn't have any luck at all.

They developed a defensive plan only after Jordy had left the room. Mike was charged with getting the team ready to defend or attack when the time comes. The paper carried a picture of the Chinese hit man and every member had to look at it, remember it and carry it. Weapons were issued, from knives to pistols. Jordy was kept on protection duty for Jimmy and now was not privy to the meeting and plans. He didn't seem to notice — either dumb or just playing it cool. Jimmy thought about the situations around him, the morass he was in, and it brought to mind his butchered Shakespeare: *'Will no one rid me of these turbulent people?'*

Denise drank coffee in her car with the two Special Branch detectives, Keith and Frank. They were known unkindly as 'Bill and Ben the Flower Pot Men' from the ancient kids' TV show. Their biggest terrorist bust was when they inserted a bug into a flower pot in the home of a suspect. The bug picked nothing up for weeks; in fact, you could hardly hear it at all, only the odd watering of the plant, which didn't help. Their break came when this suspect heard that talking to plants made them happy and decided to test this theory. So he started telling the plant the awful activities he was going to do to see if it withered; the plant was a cactus. It didn't, of course, and by sheer luck became a fountain of information on a forthcoming bomb attack.

"Our guy is getting nervous. Thinks things are getting scary. Maybe time to pull him out," Keith said.

"That would be stupid at this point," Denise countered.

"If these bastards start killing each other and he gets his, we will be in big trouble. We are not supposed to put our undercover people at unnecessary risk," added Frank.

"Goes with the territory. We have an opportunity to bring them all down or let them do it to themselves." Denise wanted them to understand the many years they have been frustrated trying to get the Harkers. They have been protected by the police and high-level influential society people.

She continued, "If he comes out, we lose our intelligence and are outsiders once more, unless Jimmy Harker talks to plants."

They both suddenly looked at each other.

"No, tell me you didn't?" She started to laugh.

They were quiet until Frank said, "No, he doesn't talk to them."

Glad we go that sorted, she thought, still giggling a bit.

"Javelin?" they asked.

"Good subject. I asked the Kent police to check out his place. You know, say they had complaints of gunshots in the area. He was gone, lock, stock and barrel."

"Bugger." Keith always liked to know where the bad guys were.

"He's back in London then, organising his troops for revenge." Frank liked the thought of lots of action.

"Organising the Yardies is like trying to be King Canute and holding back the sea. He seems to have a lot of influence over them, though. Lots of activity on the streets; they are moving into Harker territory big time. Jimmy seems to be sitting on his hands." She had taken the bull by the horns and visited Jimmy Harker at the club.

"What did he say?"

"It's what he didn't say that interests me. Oh, he was polite in his normal charming way. Asked me where DCI Eager was, gave me his condolences for Commander Allcock. Never mentioned Javelin, the Yardies or our hit man. I said it was a PR visit and he offered me drinks and food. I refused, of course. I just wanted to see if he volunteered anything. Okay, foolish, but I did get to test his temperature."

"And?"

"Underneath that calm exterior I sensed fear. You know, like a swan gliding along whilst underneath the water its webbed feet are going like crazy. He didn't look me in the eye at any time; not like him, quite the ladies' man."

"Does Sutherland know you visited him?" Keith was concerned.

"Not yet. He did tell me to keep surveillance on him."

"Denise, it could look bad on you if your senior doesn't know. You know if it goes to the rubber-heel squad they will make a case out of it, you being on his payroll."

"That may well be. I will tell him later and get another bollocking. So we are sharing surveillance tonight? I have my guys who will work to four a.m. Can you take over from then until he leaves for the club in the morning?"

"At least we get time for a drink." Frank was missing his evenings in the local pub.

He had found a B&B in the back streets of Wimbledon. Just to his liking: an old house, a bit run-down and cheap. The best thing was that the owner was an old lady who appeared to live on her own. She seemed to be Russian, or certainly Eastern European. Her English was not the best. His room was a granny flat in the back yard in a converted garage. She was glad to have him and he sensed she needed the money. He paid her for three days in advance; this way she would be satisfied and he wouldn't need to see her again, as he planned to move on as soon as he had recovered enough. He told her he would not be taking breakfasts as he was on a strict diet. That seemed to please her, another saving. He explained away his bandages as a car accident that had delayed his departure back to the States. She bought it all hook, line and sinker.

He had purchased some more bandages, antiseptic cream and painkillers from a local chemist. The morphine bag was almost empty and pain was coming back. He did his best to clean his wounds. The toe and fingers did not look good, but were not green yet. He then slept for a long time, waking up mid-morning the next day. During a painful walk down the alleyway between the house and the granny flat he could see the landlady sitting watching television with her cat on her lap. He went out for some bottled water and fruit. A local convenience shop was just down the street, and it also sold newspapers. Once inside, he noticed all the newspapers had the taxi driver murder on the front page and, to his dismay, also a picture of him. Police wanted to talk to this man as he is a suspect. He is extremely dangerous — do not approach. Since then he had added his false goatee and wore the baseball cap low. The picture was not very flattering; obviously taken when he was in hospital under anaesthetic. It was not perfect, as he looked very rough, though it was unmistakeably him. He purchased the water and some apples, not looking the young man serving in the eyes. The boy seemed oblivious to him; he just wanted to serve him and let him go. The shop would be empty then and he could go back to his computer games. He guessed he was not the one who displayed the newspapers as well.

On his way back, he looked through the house window again. She was not there; however, the television was still on and it was the news, and up comes his picture. She had missed it this time, but her only entertainment, it seemed, was watching the box. Her house phone sat on a small table at the side of her seat. If she sees his picture and picks up the phone, he is done for. He had checked out an escape route after he had arrived; there was only one way out, through the front yard. The rest of the garden and sides of the building were blocked with high walls. In his condition, he didn't fancy climbing and jumping.

Then a car stopped on the road out front. He rushed back to his room and watched. He saw it was a middle-aged woman, probably her daughter visiting. She brought in shopping bags and didn't stay long; when she left, he heard her say she was working all week and would come back on the weekend. That would give him his four days, unless other friends visited. He had to make a decision. It was too risky; the odds were bad at her not seeing the news, as she was glued to the TV. He figured the murder would stay featured for the next few days unless there was a tsunami or something. Like all people who let strangers stay in their homes, she had really looked him up and down when he arrived. So no chance she would not recognise him. This gig was already messy enough. The choice was to silence her for good or cut off the TV and phone or lock her up. He really needed time to plan and recover.

Denise checked in with her team watching the street outside Jimmy Harker's residence; it was two a.m. It was located in the Camden area of London. A six-bedroom, terraced home, three storeys high. This was a beautiful, quiet street where the upper middle class and rich lived. She knocked on the steamed-up car window and heard them jump.

"Sleeping?"

"No, ma'am, just taking turns at resting our eyes. Very quiet." She was straightening her hair and it looked like her make-up needed some adjusting.

I hope they are not playing touchy feely on duty.

He opened the back door for her and she slid into the old Ford Cortina.

"Here, two coffees and a couple of muffins." She passed them forward with extra sugars and milk in sachets. They were very much appreciated.

"These should keep you awake. Report?"

"Not much. He came out of the club at three a.m. They used the back entrance where the old Hellfire Club was, like bats out of hell. I almost thought to stop them for speeding. Joking. Two vehicles and at least five men with him. They went to the back of this house and must have parked inside his garages. Lights all out and we have not seen hair nor hide of them since," Tommy, the senior detective, reported.

"Who says, crime doesn't pay? That house has to be three million plus," Rhonda, his partner, added.

"Looks like he is expecting guests. Keep your eyes open, both of you; do not get caught" — she paused for a few seconds — "napping. I am on the radio phone; if you see anything suspicious at all, call me. The guests will probably be armed, so you will need armed back-up. Do not try and interfere yourselves. No heroism."

"Will do."

"Oh, and Rhonda, do you believe in Karma?"

"Ma'am?"

"They all get what they deserve in the end, and that, for Mr Harker, is looming."

"And they say only the good die young."

Her second visit was at four thirty a.m. to see Frank and Keith, or the Flower Pot Men as she now called them, who were parked a further distance away down the street from where her team had been. Keith was more experienced with surveillance and had positioned the car so they had a better view of the house and street without being so obvious. It was still dark; the street lights helped, although there were many dark corners around the area.

She again was let in the back door, this time a Mini Cooper S. It was tight in the back and 'Bill and Ben' filled the front seats, obscuring a view from the back out of the front windscreen. *One bullet into this vehicle would kill us all*, she thought.

"Where's the coffee and muffins?" Keith asked, miffed she had not brought them. Her team had obviously told them. She ignored him.

"Nothing. All very quiet, wasting our time," Frank complained. Just as he spoke, four off-road motor-bikes came down the street. The Yardies. They went directly in front of Harker's house and started honking their horns, shouting and brandishing weapons. They were wild and noisy and some neighbours ventured out and then quickly ducked back inside.

"Call armed response?" Keith asked.

"No, it's a warning. Sent to upset and scare Harker. They will be gone before our guys get here." Denise was certain. Several of the bikes back-fired, which seemed like shots. They were not certain. As she had forecasted, the bikes soon took off with a roar down the street and split in different directions. No movement from the house.

"Trying to interrupt his beauty sleep," Frank suggested.

"I think that's the show for tonight. Give it another thirty minutes and then go get some rest. I will come back at seven thirty and watch him go to the club. He is well protected — they would be fools to try something here."

"On your own?" Keith asked.

"Most of the time I have a parrot," she laughed.

"I meant you coming back on your own?" He was not used to her being funny. Something had changed and he couldn't quite put his finger on it. Keith did not like that he made a note to return after dropping Frank off and getting that coffee she forgot.

Tazewell was meeting the Yardies' boss man, Jumaane, on the roof of his new location, his country life brought to an abrupt end by the attempted assassination. He had rented a roof-top penthouse apartment of a twenty-four-storey building in one of his old clients' name, in Bloomfield. Access was secure, with security in the foyer and CCTV everywhere. The lift to his apartment needed a special key and even so it had a video camera and he would be immediately alerted if anyone got in and pressed the penthouse button. Money was rolling in, so he could afford the very best of everything. He believed no one in their right mind would try and get in, with limited access and a difficult exit. Privacy was his protection; no one knew where he was except Jumaane. The Yardies were also just a phone call away.

Jumaane spoke little English, but he did understand when Tazewell spoke slowly.

He, though, broke into Yardie/Jamaican language mixed in with his English. Tazewell was getting better at it. He had to be careful: they were easily upset, very sensitive people. He needed them and they needed him. He often thought he had to walk on egg shells around them, same as when he worked for the Harkers — he had swopped one grovelling job for another, although better paid for sure. That would all change when he had taken over the Harker empire fully. Part of him was happy Jimmy had broken the truce and shown his true colours.

Tazewell handed him a box. He opened it like a child with a rush. It was a big, solid gold Rolex watch. There were better watches and other brands, but he doubted Jumaane would know the brands. He put it on his left wrist as he had his other gold-bling-no-name watch on the other.

"Jeezum Pees, Tanks, thenk yuh." This was good gift worthy of him.

Tazewell explained slowly the strategy he needed them to follow. He wanted them to keep taking territory whilst embarrassing Harker by their night visits. He would not like his neighbours to know what he did for a living, so the bikes and noise would be more than he could take. He cautioned to choose two different times and different days and after which discontinue, as a trap by the police could be set by then.

He would not want his street cred also completely ruined as they moved his people off the streets and replaced them. To be seen as weak and non-responsive would be his end. The police were watching him and his gang, and when he responded that would be his mistake, one way or another. So have patience and keep pushing him.

"It will be dangerous; the Harkers did not get where they are by being nice people."

"Mi Nuh Biznizz."

Tazewell knew this was 'I don't care' and nodded his support for his confidence. "More money will come to you, a lot more." Tazewell incentivised them by holding out big carrots.

"Big Tings!" He agreed good times. Money and success were growing.

"Tell your guys well done and keep going."

"I will tell them to Tun up de ting." Step up their game.

They shook hands.

"Inna di morrows." See you later.

Chapter 61
Columbus Day

The Tonkawas had a radio phone and they had called in the escape to Wyatt. *Boss is not going to like this*. Rather than be shot as the messenger, he told Amanda, who was sleeping in a guest room in the main house. Preston's family had returned and would accompany him to church, one big happy family. Preston was asleep, although he soon would be getting up and after some exercise be ready for the big day. Amanda chose not to bother him straightaway. Damage control was needed, and that required a cool head and a calculating brain. There was no need for upsetting him on this day of all days when she can fix it. She made her first phone call to General Gerald, then to her contact in the FBI. They had a frog helicopter, the Tonkawa had said. She had asked Wyatt what a frog helicopter was and he shrugged, saying he did not know. The Tonkawas said it was not flying but hopping over the trees.

Using a helicopter was vital in this area as it was impossible to navigate by vehicle, and who would be stupid enough to do that? Wyatt had said it would have been fifteen to twenty minutes ago by the time the Indians had got back and reported in. He didn't mention he had turned the radio phone off several times before answering. If they are headed for a major city to get out of Texas, they had to be still in the air. They can all still be caught. She had told Preston to let her have the girl; oh, but no, he had said, you catch more flies with honey. Bullshit.

Today, starting at the church, as this was a big photo opportunity as a 'wake' of vultures — as the media were known when they were feeding — surrounded the ranch and his church a mile down the road. Then there was the big hoedown celebration back at his ranch. Everyone would be there, from the state governor, senators, big money businessmen who supported him, celebrities, as they called themselves, singers and actors. He was also going to announce his running mate at the event. Yes, it was going to be a big day. Preston exercised, had a sauna and then a shave and shower. He was in a good mood. Today they would also snare those little bastards who had caused him so much trouble.

The general rang back after a few minutes. The team had been despatched to both Houston and Dallas airports. Air traffic control had reported no flight plans in that area, nor had any illegal flights been picked up on the radar. They flew too low, was his best guess. They had to be heading for Houston. She told the general for the team to meet her there and then got Wyatt up to fly her.

"Why don't you guys kip down at my place? It's not flash, but I can make you comfortable until this calms down." Harry passed out of his fridge the celebratory victory beers and held onto his hip flask. His customers always needed a drink after he had flown them.

"Thanks for the invite, Harry, but you have done enough already. We need to get back to Vegas and Gavin." Liberty was keen to complete the sale and stick it to this arrogant Preston.

"We need to go. Gavin has got all the videos and if they get him the whole deal is lost and, to be honest, I couldn't live with that at this stage." Eager looked and sounded exhausted.

"Me? If I was them, I would watch the airports, especially the closest to Houston. My two pennies' worth," Harry advised.

"Steve?" Eager turned to him.

He thought about it. "If they don't know Liberty has escaped, we have until this Wyatt returns at midday, in which case we can get out to Houston by then, but…"

"Yes?' Logan pushed. They all looked at Steve, waiting on his 'but' to be explained.

"Well, it doesn't make sense they leave these four Indians up there without some form of communication. I mean, even day-to-day up there in that region they may need help if one is sick or hurt, instructions, orders for groceries and so forth. I've gotta believe they have a radio phone and Preston's lot have been alerted."

"Unless it is only smoke signals they have." Liberty was joking.

"Which means they will be on the lookout for us." Logan was agreeing and ignoring Liberty's attempt at humour.

"They have no idea I'm here and part of this, so I can fly out, get back and move Gavin to safety," Steve suggested. He needed to get back on the FBI radar screen anyway.

"I have an idea," Pat said, face beaming. "If Harry can drop Steve and me off at the airport, I will hire a car."

"What, we are going to drive back? It will take twenty-four hours just driving," Liberty objected.

"No, you don't get it. I will hire the car with your credit card for two days, say I'm dropping it off at Vegas and come back to Harry's place. We wait and then go back to Houston and catch a flight for cash. They will pick up the card and be waiting for us to drop off the car at Vegas."

"Dad, I think you are a genius." Liberty was impressed.

"Or a very devious person," Eager muttered.

It was logical, Amanda thought, that they would hire a helicopter somewhere close. Who would do an illegal flight under the radar like a frog? Who would fly them into a dangerous area and be part of the rescue plans? The FBI had stood down — she had confirmed that with her contact — and if they had been involved a few arrests would have been made. It had to be a small operator paid good cash. Tourist flights? She found the Yellow Pages phone directories for all major cities in Preston's secretary's office. She found Houston's and looked for helicopters to hire, training schools and tourist flights. There were quite a few in the Houston area. She nailed it down to three that worked from small airports outside the city. It was early, she knew, but worth a chance to call and see what she got, if anything. Two of them had professional recorded messages, the third had a casual Scottish accent saying, 'This is Harry here; leave a message if you want a thrilling tour of the city and beyond.' Eager is English — there could be a connection.

She relooked at his advert. 'Harry Beattie, FAI World Aerodynamics Champion 1969.' Maybe he flies like a leaping frog? He would be worth checking out first and the other two after. She went with Wyatt to go to the small airfield by chopper to get there quicker. They also took one of Preston's security men; all were well armed. It was now four twenty in the morning, and if her hunch and calculations were right, they could be still flying and they would make it just after they had landed. Wyatt took the chopper under the radar as well, with no flight plan.

These people have become more difficult to tie down than I imagined; hopefully this is the end of them.

The omens had been good and his luck continued. Diablo had hitch-hiked from San Carlos to El Paso. It was taking too much time, so he caught a bus to San Antonio and then a train to Houston. Then back to hitch-hiking to Preston's ranch area. It would have been a fourteen-hour car drive; so far it had taken him already twenty-six hours in all. No car — he had decided nothing to track or find. He carried his golf bag with his weapons and a small backpack with water bottles and food supplies. His plan was simple: he would execute Preston when the opportunity arose and disappear into the Comancheria, where even the 4th Cavalry found it impossible to follow the Comanches. He was an expert tracker and had the best training in fieldcraft and survival from a young age. No one would be able to follow him, even if they knew he had gone into the wilderness. He would not take any risks with the killing; getting caught would be an embarrassment.

The good luck continued: as he hitch-hiked out of Houston, a big Ford truck pulled up, the back full of Indians. It seemed to be leading a convoy of small trucks and cars. He climbed in the back; there were at least twenty Indians sitting down, all squashed in together. They were in full Indian regalia and carried placards. 'Columbus Day No!' 'Make it Indigenous Day!' 'Destruction of Our Culture & Peoples Started on Columbus Day' and more.

"Welcome to our team." A pretty young lady dressed as a squaw, hair in plaits, bright blue eyes.

"Thanks, what are you doing?"

"You're not going to the demonstration at Preston's ranch?" He had to think quickly; staying with these people was the best cover he could get.

"Oh, didn't realise there was an organised demo. I was going to make a point to that Preston myself."

"So the Apaches didn't get the memo where you live?" She laughed. The rest were listening and nodding. He thought some may think he was a planted spy, as they looked at him so suspiciously. He did not want to give his details of any kind, so he made up a name and location.

"My name is Mangas and I live on the reservation in Oklahoma. Very slow there and my tribe are lazy, too lazy to come with me."

There was more laughter. She continued, "Well, we are glad to have you, Mangas. We have representatives from most major tribes. Kiowa, Caddo, Cherokee, Wichita, Comanches and Apaches — the ones not too lazy to come."

He laughed and the tone of the others changed to be friendlier. A young brave in his late teens spoke up. "We are tired of the Anglos celebrating the start of the demise as cultures, destroying what was spiritual and caring for mother earth. Then we have Thanksgiving, where they came, were given hospitality and then brought disease and death to us. Both need to be changed and seen for what they were."

He nodded in total agreement. "So why here, why Preston's ranch and not the capital?"

"The world's media will be here today, watching the man who would be the new president. His family stole Indian land and he enjoys riches that should be ours. What better place? So why did you come here?" she explained and asked.

"His family stole our lands many years ago."

The truck banged and bumped around and she fell on him. He gently helped her to sit up straight. Their eyes met and he felt a shiver going through his body. He knew she would feel the same: it was like electricity passed between them. The young man stared at them, obviously jealous. She sat up and ignored him the rest of the journey. He wasn't sure what he had done wrong; however, he didn't want any complications on this trip. Women!

They arrived at St Mary's Catholic Church. It was all wooden and white, with a tower and a cross on the top of it. Outside, at the entrance, was a big white cross, also wooden. The church was surrounded at the sides and back by gravestones. Many were Preston's family dating back centuries. Two priests stood at the door, one a young man and the other an elderly man. They had several women and men dressed up in their Sunday best on each side of them. They were expecting Preston, and this was the reception committee. The media had set up and it seemed that there were hundreds of them with their outside broadcast vans. They had been positioned directly across the road from the church, with an excellent view of Preston entering and exiting. His sound bites would make international headlines and prime time.

The place was surrounded by various Texas police organisations. The State Troopers were there organising the roadblocks and the crowd. The Texas Rangers were positioned around the perimeter on all sides. City police were parked on the road both sides. Diablo wondered if the Texas Rangers would live up to their prestigious reputation if they followed him into the Comancheria. The Indian convoy was shuffled through, past the church and isolated down the road. The media had little to do as they waited for Preston, so they focussed on the Indian demonstration, many following the convoy, asking questions and taking film and pictures of the placards.

When they got off the bus, the Indian girl went to them and started giving interviews. Diablo tried to disappear into the background and slowly sneaked away. He knew the FBI and Secret Service would review all the media's pictures and videos with a fine-tooth comb. He would be recognised by the Chief Longbow team, game over.

She was very much aware of him and out of the corner of her eye watched him sneaking away to become invisible, while continuing her interviews.

He distanced himself from the front of the demo and hid behind the last truck right at the back. He sat down and took out a map. This was no place to make the killing. He would not get close enough because of the media, the Indian demo and the police. His chance of living after the arrow hit would be, he estimated, twenty seconds max. They would just fire and fire, even if he held his arms up, giving up with no weapon. The ranch was not very far. He could cross the fields behind him and enter via cutting the cattle fence and finding his way to a safe place near the ranch. Then it was all up to luck again. He could see Preston's entourage coming down the road towards the church. Now was the time all the security was focussed on Preston and the church. He doubted many were left at the ranch. Now was the time to move.

"Who are you and what are you doing hiding?"

"What do you mean?"

"I saw you slipping off out of the way."

"I did not want my family to see me on TV. They did not want me to come." He made up the best story he could on the spot.

"Liar!"

"Okay, calm down. I want to see Preston personally to get my point across, so I was going to sneak across the fields to the ranch. This place is a real zoo."

"What are you up to? I do not believe you."

"Believe me or not, that's the truth." It was just a different point he was going to get across.

"What's in the golf bag?"

"Just personal possessions."

She looked like she did not believe him. Behind the truck, listening, was the young brave.

"Do not do anything that makes this other than a peaceful demonstration or you will answer to me."

"I am not a terrorist. I am a man of peace, a healer and teacher. What is your name?"

"Chimalis."

"The blue bird; suits you with those eyes."

"You know Cheyenne, big deal; do not change the subject."

"I promise that I am doing nothing wrong." He looked to the sky and put his right hand on his chest. "On my ancestors' good names." What he was about to do, he knew in his heart was not wrong, and his forefathers would approve.

"Will I see you again?" she asked in a softer tone, which sounded to him like a wish.

"If the spirits are willing."

She left abruptly. He could see her turning around to check on him several times as she walked away.

I will meet her again, if not in this life then the next, I am sure.

310

Chapter 62
Death Hath No Friends

Harry left with Steve, Pat and Logan for the William P. Hobby Airport. Logan had decided to keep Pat company on the way back. Eager and Liberty waited in the office of the hangar. This suited Liberty and Eager, as they had not spent much time alone since their reunion.

"It is good to have you back," Eager told her.

"Smalls, you are my hero, rescuing me again."

"Yes, it is becoming a bit of a bad habit."

She laughed and started to clean Harry's scruffy desk down and put his paperwork on the shelf behind.

"What are you doing?"

"Time for a bit of Gladiator sex. Come here."

She grabbed him by the neck and pulled him on top of her on the desk.

She was undoing his belt. He was fumbling with her blouse and bra when the lights went out in his head.

Harry returned to an empty office one hour later. Where were they? He had no idea where they might have gone. His telephone rang.

"Harry, what's going on?" It was a call from the control tower and owner of the little airport.

"What do you mean, what's going on?"

"A chopper came in without any approval or flight plan. I saw them go to your hangar and they left with a woman and a man. Three of them all had weapons. I thought it was a terrorist attack. A black one. Harry, what are you up to?"

Yeah, right, they would pick the smallest, deserted airport in the world to make a statement.

"Me? Nothing. My customers have been picked up for a hunting trip."

"What about some notification and proper procedures? I was just opening up and they came in like they owned the place. Houston traffic control have no record of their flight plans."

"I'm sure it is a mistake, an oversight. I will talk to them and it will not happen again."

"Yeah, you do that." He then put the phone down.

Useless git.

Harry couldn't work out how they had got onto him and the airport. Smart as foxes, he thought. So all the drama was for nothing; they now have two of them. He opened his hip flask and took a swallow and waited on Pat and Logan to get back. What then? With apologies to Robert Burns, he thought:

'The best laid plans of mice and men. Gang aft agley.'

Diablo encountered the first fence. It was just over the hill, away from the road and the church. It was a cattle fence, just metal poles and square mesh thin wire. Texans from history hated fences and this was not meant to keep people out. It was for control of cattle and not, from a distance, to spoil the view across the plains. His pliers easily cut it. Then he headed due north towards the ranch across the field. The beasts didn't seem to notice or be bothered with him. He came up over a large mound in the ground to see the ranch house, smaller workers' accommodation, barns and sheds, garages. Workers were working furiously to set up a big tent and a dance floor. Caterers were rushing in with the food for the day and setting up tables, chairs, serving areas and a line of big barbeque grills and smokers. A big stage area was just being completed and the sign read, 'Texas Wanderers', as big a band that only a millionaire could afford for a private event. Roadies moved back and forth, and a technical sound and lighting control centre was being set up to test the lights and sound when the equipment was in place. This was going to be some hoedown.

The fence surrounding the ranch was seven or almost eight foot high, he guessed. It was a steel palisade with triple spike points at the top. It was a showstopper, and he had hoped for something less. He looked around at the rear of the ranch; down the hill was a tradesman's gate. So many trucks were parked just outside as the staff unloaded and carried their equipment into the ranch's main area. He made his way down and got in between several big trucks. There was so much activity and so many suppliers, the two guards on the gate were just overwhelmed. There was what must have been the organiser just inside the gate, shouting.

"Come on, people! We need to be ready in thirty minutes. Do you hear me! In one hour, Mr Preston will be back to open the event," she repeated herself to everyone walking in and out. She was going to have a heart attack, Diablo thought. It was easy for him to go to the back of a truck and pick up a trestle table and walk with it right into the ranch. As he got past the gate, the organiser, a tall Texan woman, called him.

"Hey, you!"

He kept going.

"You, Indian, chief whatever."

He turned slowly, thinking the worst.

"Yes, you, Hiawatha. Get a move on."

Phew! He did move faster, thinking if I get a chance with a second arrow, I know who gets it. Dumping the trestle table with the others, he looked around to establish where his prey would stand long enough for him to nail him. He knew that being a politician he would be centre stage, making speeches and introducing dignitaries. How could he strike and get away? It seemed impossible, unless chaos happened. He so wanted the arrow striking to be on every channel in the world, so he had to hit him on the stage. The hoedown was due to start at two o'clock and go on till late. He decided he needed the darkness if he had any chance of getting away. He slipped away to look around the ranch area and see what he could use to cause a diversion.

He noticed a black helicopter landing on a small airstrip at the back of the ranch house. The strip had quite a few helicopters and private jets parked at the side and a line of more in the sky coming in. When it landed, what caught his eye was that two people were being bundled into the back door of an outbuilding just behind the main house. They looked distressed. It didn't take long for him to work out that these could be the people Preston was accused of chasing.

He decided to sneak across and have a closer look. He had left his golf bag inside a barn at the back of some animal feed sacks. There were windows down each side of the building. He peered in carefully; yes, there were two people on the ground, sitting up against wooden climbing bars against the far wall. A man and a woman. It was a fully kitted-out gym with all types of weights, a boxing ring, punch bags, running and stepping machines, everything you would find in a top-of-the-line gym. A blonde woman was bent over, shouting at them and waving her arms. No one was looking in his direction, so he watched as he waited.

Amanda was telling them that playing games was over. The extra security guard had been dismissed. Wyatt stood watching, revolver holstered.

"I told Travis you were unreliable bastards, so the game stops now. I am going to tell you what we are going to do. Lover boy here is going to take a big jump from the helicopter into no man's land. The animals will eat his carcass and he will never be found. So say goodbye now." She indicated to Wyatt to take him by a nod of the head. Wyatt kicked him and then pulled him up by the collar. Eager's hands were tied at the back by plastic cuffs. Wyatt was carrying a big Bowie knife in a leather cradle on his belt, which he took out.

"No blood in the chopper, or clean it thoroughly," Amanda warned him.

"You will not get the tapes, then." Liberty tried to get her attention to get Eager off his fate.

"Oh, no? Well, one team is at this moment on the way to pick up the other scumbag at the Sahara. He knows where they are and believe me, when he sees your body, he will talk."

"They are in the hotel strong room; only I can access them."

"Really, well you will not be in a fair state to get them when I am finished with you. I am going to give you a chance, what was it, to rip my tits off, and then I am going to beat you so badly your own mother wouldn't recognise you."

"I'd like to see you try it. I guess a little girl like you will keep my hands tied and get help."

She ignored her attempt at riling her. "Then, with a little make-up and a wig — by the way, your hair looks shit — some crappy clothes and your ID, I will get the tapes no problem."

Liberty almost laughed as she agreed her hair did look like shit. It was a strange thought under the circumstances. *Take a note: if I get out of this I'll go straight to the hairdressers.*

Amanda, surprised at her grin, took it as confidence — a big mistake when facing her. It will soon be wiped off her face.

Wyatt had cut Liberty's plastic cuffs off on Amanda's orders and now was dragging Eager out of the gym by his cuffs.

Diablo was debating what to do. This was not his problem. He wasn't law enforcement; in fact, far from it. He decided to let it go and just watch. Eager was being walked out of the building towards the chopper. His last walk. Dead man walking. He had his head down, knowing he was fucked. It came to Diablo that this could work in his favour. If they escaped, could that be the distraction for the security guards he needed? Take them away from the main event. He was not sure that he was justifying intervening or it would really work for his task.

Wyatt was loading Eager into the back of the chopper. He pushed him down on the rubber floor. He then lifted his Bowie knife and hit him on the head with the big butt. Lights out again, and this time no plan for him to have a headache or for him to wake up. Just to be sure he would not cause trouble while he was flying, he decided to stab him in the stomach. He lifted the knife and was about to stab him through his clothes when Diablo struck. He had found a brick at the side of the runway. Wyatt fell on top of Eager. Quickly, Diablo pushed him off and turned Eager over, who was moaning with pain. He cut his handcuffs off with Wyatt's knife. Eager looked up and their eyes met. The relief on his face was thanks enough. He thought he was certainly going to die.

"I need you to escape and give me a big diversion. An explosion or fire or anything to take the attention away from Preston, who will be on the stage at the hoedown soon. It's the only way we will all get out of here alive. Do you understand?"

He shook Eager, who was taking in what he was saying but had no idea what he was doing here. His guardian angel was all he could think, but he looked like Tonto?

"I have helped you, now you need to help me. Your friend in the gym over there also needs help; go get her, stay there until you hear announcements and then come out. Once you have caused a diversion,

315

head for the tradesmen's entrance and go across the fields to the road. I have cut the fence."

Diablo left. Other jets were coming in and security in vehicles were picking up the VIPs. Wyatt started to come around. Eager found the brick and hit him again, twice, with an anger he had never felt before. Seeing the blood seep out of his head, Eager was shocked and concerned about his own brutality — he had never been a physical, abusive cop. Human beings were not built to be this way.

This bastard was going to kill me!

Amanda told Liberty to stand up, which she did.

"Get in the ring," she ordered her.

"No. Come and get me." Liberty lifted her fists up in a boxing pose.

Amanda laughed. She had no idea who she was dealing with: a highly trained martial arts expert, slayer of men.

Amanda walked towards her and side-stepped and hit her three times in the chest. Liberty never even saw it coming, she was so fast. She fell down, trying to breathe, holding her chest. Amanda picked her up like a rag doll and threw her into the boxing ring and jumped in over the ropes.

"Did that hurt your tits? I bet it did. Come on and take your punishment like, er, the tart you are." She then kicked her at the side of her legs to get her to stand up.

If Pat, Liberty's dad, gave her anything, it was his Irish blood and the temper to go with it. She was very angry. Eager, her friend, was being taken to be executed and this asshole was trying to kill her bit by bit. She had had enough and jumped up with an amazing renewal of energy her adrenaline was providing her. Amanda had been walking around her.

"That's good, come on then."

Liberty threw a haymaker punch that Amanda simply knocked aside and then pummelled her chest again. Down she went for the second time.

"Hurts, doesn't it? You can do better I am betting; this is too easy for me."

Liberty got up and pretended to come towards her. Then she ran and skidded under the ropes, out of the ring.

"Door's locked, little girl." Amanda had the key around her neck. "No way to escape your punishment." She obviously got a kick out of hurting people and was enjoying the fact that she could take Liberty and beat her to death.

Liberty looked around and made a run for the row of dumbbells. She picked up two which said 'seven pounds' and held them, one in each fist.

"Come on, then," she shouted at Amanda, who laughed, jumped out of the ring and walked slowly to her. She knew that the weights would slow her punches down and it would be like fighting a tortoise. *This is no fun. I should finish her now.*

Eager had reached the door and found it locked from the inside. Through the little windows in each entrance door, he could see what was going on. He ran at it with his shoulder and bounced off. The surprise noise made Amanda turn, but Liberty, who was fighting for her life, was not distracted. She jumped forward and hit Amanda to the side of the head with one of the seven-pound dumbbells. She dropped like a brick.

Eager charged again and the door gave way. He ran in with Wyatt's gun held in the right-hand stance, ready for trouble. He saw Liberty hitting Amanda's body with a dumbbell and rushed across to stop her. She was beyond mad, crying and shouting, "Fuck you, fuck you," hitting her in the ribs with all her might.

He dropped the pistol and shouted, "You'll kill her." He then grabbed her around the waist and pulled her off. She dropped the dumbbell, but was still kicking and screaming. "Kill Smalls would you!" She was temporarily insane and wildly out of control and had no clue Eager was holding her.

He managed to calm her down until she recognised him, and then she hugged him and cried.

"What were you doing? You could have killed her."

"Making it a fair fight." She went from crying to laughing, still a bit crazy.

"What happened with Wyatt?" She had come to her senses.

"An angel came down and rescued me."

"An angel? Are you crazy?"

"Well, I had a little help; let's say he is not so good looking now."

"Is he dead?"

"Not sure. You will not believe this, but I was saved by an Indian. My bloody head hurts, next time you go underneath, that's twice I have been knocked out today," he complained.

"So what is our plan?"

"The Indian told me to wait until the speeches started and then create a diversion, a fire, an explosion or something."

"Seriously, you were saved by an Indian? Maybe you had an illusion or brain damage?"

Amanda started to move, moaning loudly. Liberty turned her over on her back and grabbed both her nipples between her thumbs and fingers. Then she started to twist and twist. Amanda screamed in pain. Eager pulled her away.

"What do you think you are doing? She will have security running in here."

"I told her I would twist her tits off, the bitch."

The sound system had come on and the whole ranch was filled with loud country and western music. Then someone was on the microphone, testing it, "One, two, one, and two."

They grabbed Amanda and moved her to a cupboard full of mats. They pulled out the mats and shoved her inside. They needed to gag her and tie her up, but nothing that would help was around. She had been badly hurt and was bleeding from the mouth. When they moved her, she screamed and screamed. The music was back playing, drowning out the sound.

"I figure she is so hurt she will not even try to escape." Eager was confident.

"So you are serious about creating a diversion?"

Does Gladys Knight have the Pips? Eager thought, using her saying, as he was so sure he would help the angel that saved his life.

Pat and Logan returned with the hire car and found Harry drinking his Johnnie Walker from his flask and looking despondent.

"I have no idea how they found us." He told them what had happened.

"I'm going to drive there; they have my daughter again," said Pat.

"How you going to get in?" Logan asked, gobsmacked at what had happened.

"Through the front door. I don't care. On the news they said he was having a big Columbus Day party. I am going to crash it!"

"Aye, they will get you as well," Logan counselled.

"I'll take you. He has an airfield there," Harry suggested.

"You okay to fly?"

"I'm a bloody Scotsman; I can take my Johnnie." Harry was indignant.

"The three musketeers ride again," Logan said, indicating he was up for the trip as well.

If at first you don't succeed, try again. Harry felt his brave Celtic blood rise.

The small landing strip had been very busy. It was deserted now until the VIP guests started to leave later. Security traffic control had left to be at the hoedown to protect Preston. Harry did his autorotation landing trick as they approached as low as they could to perform this aerodynamically. They needn't have worried — the band was playing and the noise level high. Pat took the pistol and Logan carried the knife. Harry stayed with the helicopter and promised to be there unless something he could not control happened. He parked amongst the other flying machines that were lined up at the verge of the airstrip. They walked casually, looking around, working out the layout and looking for places Eager and Liberty could be held.

The hoedown was in full swing, and all types of cowboy dancing were going on. The band was a big success and people were cheering and yippie yi yaying.

They searched away from the party. The big house did not seem to make sense. Several outhouses were looked into as they made their way forward. Luck has a way of swinging backwards and forwards; so far in the last two days it had them euphoric and then down on their knees again. Luck was about to change as the gym doors opened and Liberty and Eager literally bounced out. Pat whistled like he had done when Liberty was a schoolgirl. She looked up, saw him and ran like crazy several hundred yards into his arms.

"Come on, quick." Logan indicated they needed to go.

Eager resisted. "I promised to create a diversion for the Indian. He saved my life, so I need to do that. You all go."

Logan and Pat were mystified. Liberty used her fingers to make the sign of madness at the side of her head.

"John, come on, you are putting us all at risk!"

"No, let me set fire to the shed there."

"That building would be better if you are training to be an arsonist." Pat knew his wood — what would burn quicker and better — as he pointed at the gym.

"He's been hit on the head twice today, sees Indians and angels." Liberty was still convinced he was not all there.

"Liberty, you are not helping. We cannot torch the gym. Has anyone got a match or a lighter?" Eager asked. Logan, being a smoker, had.

"Why not?" Pat asked.

"There's a body locked in a cupboard in there."

It was getting stranger, Pat and Logan thought. Pat took Liberty by the hand to Harry and his chopper. Logan and Eager went into the closest shed. It was a barn with storage of straw for the horse stables.

"Perfect. All we need now is some kindling," Eager noted.

The band had stopped and over the loudspeakers they heard, "Governor, senators and ladies and gentlemen, may I ask the next President of this here United States to come to the stage." Huge cheering and clapping and the band started to play the US national anthem, 'Star-Spangled Banner'.

"The tractor." Logan pointed to a tractor which was sitting to one side of the barn. Eager had not even noticed it. Logan grabbed some sacking, opened the diesel tank and dipped it in as far as he could. It came out with diesel dripping from it. He took his lighter out and set fire to the rag and stuck it back in the diesel tank.

"Go!" They ran as fast as they could, Eager coming a distant second with his bad knees.

"I am proud to welcome all my friends to this special occasion. I want you all to have lots of fun tonight. When I put my hat in the ring..." The explosion went up with a great big bang. "Fuck! What was that!"

Security rushed in that direction like they were on fire as well. The ranch foreman went for their old manual fire-watering machine.

Diablo had hidden on the top section of the barn with doors that opened to let storage be hauled up. It was fifty yards from the stage. He was not sure that the man he saved would follow through on his promise and was surprised when the explosion went off. It was his cue and he opened the doors wide enough to shoot through, pulled back his bow and shot one arrow into Preston's femoral artery in his thigh. He sent another quickly into his chest as he started to keel over. No one seemed to notice Preston as they were all looking towards a major blaze now reaching into the sky. The omens continued to be good for Diablo, so he packed up quickly, slid down a rope and made for the shadows. He walked towards the tradesmen's gate.

A security guard had spotted them headed for the chopper. He fired several shots at them. He was not a good shot and they were now at a distance, climbing into the chopper. Someone in the crowd shouted, "Terrorists!" Mayhem followed as they tried to either run away or take cover. Panic and fear can create a wave effect that you can actually feel as it encompasses everyone in its path. This played into Diablo's hands as the gate guards were running like chickens with their heads cut off. The media was blocking the front gate and the police were trying to get through. Diablo took the same route back to the road. Once he got to the top of the mound, he could see the young brave showing the cut he had made in the fence to a Texas Ranger. Chimalis was with them. *Time to put some distance between me and this ranch.* He turned north and started to run over the fields; he had the ability to run a marathon. It was now getting dark and he would be hard to follow. He did, though, need to put as much distance as he could between him and the ranch and then find a hiding place, as they would bring helicopters soon with big lights and the dogs.

The first person to notice and get to Preston was a stagehand. He was not in good shape. The crowd now had also noticed and the screaming continued. His wife came to his side, crying and holding his hand.

"Pull them out," Travis Preston ordered. The stagehand started to do it.

"No!" shouted a first aid officer who had just arrived, as he had been assigned with others to the hoedown, as was mandatory for such events.

"Pull them out and he will bleed to death. Get an ambulance." He started to apply bandages to stop the bleeding. He knew you keep the arrow head in as it also prevents some of the bleeding; take it out and the blood will flow copiously.

The media allowed into the event to hear Preston's speech were at the fire when they heard he had been shot. They rushed back, vying to be closest, trying to get the best shots until security and the police got control.

The news came through to the FBI and a team was assembled and sent from Houston. The Chief Longbow serial killer team also heard and were dispatched from Washington with the Director of the FBI. The senior special agent of the team said, "Get Diablo, we might need him on site."

General Gerald Broad arrived at the ranch in his Learjet. He surveyed the situation. Travis seriously wounded, one guy dead in a helicopter, Amanda found in a cupboard during the search, with possible brain damage. His guy in London missing and the contracts only half completed. Travis felled by two arrows, for God's sake. It was the biggest cluster-fuck of all time. The assailant on Preston, they were saying, was an Indian serial killer. How does that fit in with everything else going on? Others were escaping by chopper, which the FBI believed to be part of the attack, but he knew better.

Even if Travis survives, there was no way he would be well enough to stand for election this time. So, with his dreams in tatters, he assessed the way forward. Should he pull the plug on the operation and let the cards fall where they may? Or make one last attempt to clean up as quickly as possible? His team in Vegas couldn't find the third person, this Gavin Hastings, and the videos. Due to Travis's insistence that there was a cleansing due to his big ego and pride, this situation had got out of control big time. It could have been handled better and these people were like slippery eels. You had them cornered and then not. Bloody amateurs giving us the run-around.

If the FBI get the two Brits and this Bell woman, their defence will come out and questions will be asked as to who else was involved. There will be a Congressional enquiry, wild conspiracy theories, and the FBI that — now the election is probably off — will be unleased to find the truth. The media will lap up the video of Travis. He came down on the side of no choice: he had to tidy up. He avoided the word 'cleanse', which now gave him a nasty taste in his mouth. It was damage control time.

He met with the FBI director Shackleton to feel the pulse. The FBI and local police had rounded up all of the Indian demonstrators. They had been demonstrating outside the ranch's main entrance after the church service. Two had shown a Texas Ranger, just after the attack, the cut fence where he had got in. They were also assisting with drawings and identity kits on the one called Mangas, an Apache who had joined them on the road. He had a golf bag which now they believed contained his bow and arrows. A team had been despatched to his reservation in Oklahoma. They were working on him trekking in the surrounding plains and maybe headed for the hill country to escape. The blue helicopter that took off after the explosion was being traced. No flight plan, nothing on the radar. Could an Indian serial killer have such at his disposal? Did he miss it? Or was it a guest who panicked and got out of there? Would it pick him up at a predetermined location? No one had claimed responsibility as yet, although it always took Chief Longbow several days to send in his note. It looked like a co-ordinated attack by an Indian terrorist group. Longbow now had a tribe of followers.

The general thought all this was good. They are headed in the wrong direction on the main event.

This all has to end now.

Chapter 63
Liberty's Revenge

They had taken a big risk and flown from Hobby airport to Vegas, being the fastest way. Bus and car would have taken nearly two days. They needed to complete the media deals and get those videos and articles out. They felt that the driving force behind their attacks was now negated, although they could not be sure. Security at the airport was tight and the police and plainclothes detectives were checking and questioning everyone. They had no reason to suspect them. Liberty's body had been bruised, but the bruising was hidden by her clothes. Eager's head, with a big gash bandaged, was explained as a car accident. His British accent put them off the scent. They were basically looking for people that were indigenous.

The hire car credit card payment had been tracked, however; after a check, they knew the car was back at the Houston airport depot. While Pat and Eager used false IDs and McAllistar was not on their radar, Liberty was.

McCarran airport Vegas to the Sahara, everything went well. Pat saw several characters hanging around when they arrived and got the feeling they were not alone.

Big Gary had a note for them from Steve: *Gavin has moved, call me*, and his telephone number. Steve gave them the address he was at. Gavin, he said, was with a lawyer and a group of businessmen and was busy finalising the media deals. They packed quickly and were ready to go.

"I'm not sure we have not been followed," Pat said.

"Oh, no." Eager felt his head hurt and his legs feel heavy. "I thought it was over."

"Not over till the fat lady sings, isn't that what you always say, Babes."

"Babes?" Both Pat and Eager repeated this at the same time and looked at each other.

"Logan, you all need to leave in different directions. I will watch and see who follows. I guess they will follow Liberty if given a choice."

"If we do not get this right, we will lead them to Gavin and the videos," Pat added.

"They will not know what Gavin looks like, right?" Eager suggested.

"Right," Liberty responded.

"Then why don't we set up Logan with a bag that would look like he is carrying the videos and take him to the main entrance. Say goodbye and good luck. They will follow him, don't you think?"

"Oh, aye, and follow me where and do what to me?" Logan asked.

"A sightseeing tour of Vegas. Round the block for enough time for us to leave."

"If they have a second team?" Pat asked.

"They will follow Liberty for sure," Eager put in.

"Right, Smalls. I am not letting Gavin complete my deals. I shiver thinking what he might be doing. So you go after Logan, as they don't know dad."

It was agreed that they would keep the hotel room at the Sahara. Logan would leave as planned. Liberty would say goodbye to him while Pat and Eager watched. Liberty would then go inside and five minutes later Eager would leave in a taxi. Pat would watch both and see if he could identify anyone following. Then, if all was clear, he would leave with Liberty. They all had to put the address in their memory — no pieces of paper. Eager and Logan would meet back at the Sahara and await a call.

Steve had rung his boss in LA. It was decided that De Silva would fly to Vegas and meet him there at the office. It was time for some straight talking. The assassination attempt on Preston, a dead body and a brutally beaten woman meant the situation was out of control. His boss had given him a nod to help, but probably did not realise to what extent he had. Their only way out was to clean up the mess and bring light on the devious activities of Preston and his helpers. This would not be a popular move, especially in light of all the praise and sympathy Preston was getting. The pressure would be to sweep this all under the carpet. The Indian would get the blame for the murder and two attempted murders, if Preston made it, which was touch and go.

The video of Preston was their ace card if things went bad.

Sure enough, a car followed Logan's taxi and again another when Eager left with his plastic shopping bag full of empty beer cans. Big Gary had ordered a limo to the delivery back entrance. Liberty and Pat left ten minutes later. It was a gamble they thought worth taking. The address was an office on Patrick Street, well off the Strip. It was a legal office of a firm that only had one lawyer. He was a friend of Gavin's LA lawyer and had agreed to let them use it.

When Pat and Liberty entered the small meeting room, it was packed. Kent Koll was there and the Australian Robert Richards. There were four other lawyers in the room and they had been watching the videos. They all stood up to say hello and shake hands.

"Ms Liberty, it is good to meet you again." Kent Koll shook her hand.

"JFK, right?" Liberty remembered.

"What you have here is dynamite," Robert said with excitement. The Aussies loved sticking it to the Poms.

"I saved the best to last," Gavin said with pride.

"Who?" Kent asked, curious.

"None other than — don't worry, Liberty, we have signed and sealed contracts — da dah… Travis Preston."

"Travis Preston? Wow! He has just survived an attempted assassination." Kent was surprised. You could have heard a pin drop for a minute, as all had their mouths wide open.

"I know, we were there."

They were amazed. "You were there?" Robert asked, incredulous.

"Well, you might say not as willing guests. You will have to read it in my second book." Liberty was firing on all cylinders.

Gavin played the video. It was clear this was Travis Preston, no doubt about it. The lawyers were leaning forward and it stopped. They had to play it several more times.

"I think that we need to hold this until he recovers or not and pick the best time to launch it," Kent said, and Robert nodded his head in agreement.

"I'm sorry." Liberty stood up. "You guys do not know what we have been through and how many attempts on our lives have been orchestrated by Preston's people. I have been kidnapped twice and chased around the world. I have been beaten." She lifted her blouse to show the big bruising, disregarding the view she was giving them. "DCI Eager has been hit over the head twice yesterday; many people have been killed, including my old school boyfriend and his girlfriend. My dad's been shot, mother kidnapped, Logan shot. We must get this out or we are all at risk, and there is no doubt we have been followed here by a hit team."

They were even more incredulous. She could almost hear them saying she was a fantasist again. Eventually, Robert spoke up. "This British cop, Eager, is he here to verify?"

"Yes, he should be back at the Sahara by now. We sent out two decoys around Vegas when dad spotted us being followed."

She could sense they were all feeling uncomfortable now, being in this small room with her and the possibilities of another attack. So they ploughed through the contracts and articles. Robert was organising the world release and Kent had sold the book rights dependent on the verification and final draft. Advances were being made to the lawyers' escrow account. So big, Liberty's eyes opened wide. Gavin had done a great job.

"The videos need protection. Anyone who has had them is either dead or being chased to be killed," Liberty added on a sombre note.

"I have taken and hidden copies whilst you guys were flying around." Gavin knew he had done a good and thorough job.

"Do not worry; these videos will be locked up in Oz tomorrow and I will also take extra ones for security." Robert was confident.

"Where will you all be?" Kent asked.

"They are still witnesses at risk. We will call you on a regular basis from a public phone until we are sure the danger has evaporated," Pat said, taking control without a clue where their next stop was.

Paperwork exchanged and handshakes all round. The meeting broke up and the lawyers left. Robert stayed behind and had a coffee with them. He had called for security to come and protect him and the videos.

"We have a secret location we take high profile people with big stories. It is better to isolate them as competition is high and other freelance or media firms will try and speak to them and then run spoilers or entice them with a better deal. Gavin knows how this works. You can hang out there."

Having no better options, they agreed, and he would organise a corporate jet to take them there.

When his security turned up, it was an armoured car. He was not messing with this deal. He had spent a few millions now and these videos and the stories behind them would make hundreds of millions with all the rights he had negotiated. It was like dropping atom bombs on the UK and US.

Pat would not go. He would go to his home in LA where his girlfriend and ex-wife were. Not having the videos and not knowing where Liberty was headed, he figured he was safe. He certainly would not be caught off-guard again.

Logan and Eager were picked up with the luggage and taken to the private jet facilities at McCarran airport. Eager was hesitant when Liberty ran to him with dramatic excitement and said they were rich.

"What's wrong, Smalls?"

"I killed a man today, for God's sake. I am a policeman. This adventure has cost us all too much." He was definitely on a big downer.

She shook him by his drooping shoulders. "Eager, wake up. We have always being doing the right thing. It is not our fault these heartless bastards wanted to kill us and make it all go away."

"I have to go back; my old life is waiting."

"You'll go back into a big storm that will envelop you and destroy you. Stay with me; don't be silly," she appealed.

"No, I can't. There is unfinished business there."

"Like what? They don't give a damn about you. They will throw you out with the garbage like they did me. Stay with me!"

"Like all those kids that have been abused, someone needs to do something about it. Like Charlie being murdered because of me. Like the Harkers need bringing down. Like this fucking government going to get a kick up the bum and I want to be there when that happens."

"We are rich; we can be together."

"Really, you are rich and will be a celebrity again, and you want to be with this old man? What's our age difference? Twenty-five years? I will be in an old people's home while you are still young and enjoying life," he laughed sadly.

"You are a fucking idiot!" She was getting mad. He was inconsolable now that it was over.

"I will come back if you disappear again." His attempt at a joke was not received well.

"Okay, let me say what's good for the gander is good for the goose. I'll get through all this and come to you. To your cold, wet country, on one condition."

"What's that?" he asked, still trying to work out who was the gander and who was the goose.

"With the money I send, you get a decent house." There were tears in her eyes.

"Will do." They hugged and hugged and he didn't expect she would be true to her word, but it was a nice gesture. Logan looked away, as did Gavin.

Robert got the jet to drop them all except for Gavin and Liberty at LAX on the way to Arizona.

Gavin came up to Eager and handed him a package. "I held back number seven as requested. You may need it." He hugged Gavin as well.

"Look after her, Gavin, and make the books great."

"Sure. You will be a hero in them and I won't mention the growing pot belly and bad knees." Sometimes his humour after the few beers he had on the jet was not the best.

Logan was booked on British Airways, the same as Eager. It took some juggling at the desk to get them together and on their way home. Squashed in cattle class together, they sat quietly. Eager took out his notebook and started scribbling his checklist and plan.

Chapter 64
The PM's Retreat

Eager had made his way with Logan to his house. They called Denise and she agreed to meet them there. It was mid-morning when she arrived. Coffees all round and all had so much to catch up with. Eager noticed glances between Logan and Denise. *Something going on there?* was his thought.

The hit man had not been caught yet. The Yardies and Harkers' people have had some skirmishes fighting for territory. No one killed yet. DCS Sutherland was a creepy asshole with a toupee, she was certain. Eager was in deep trouble with the commissioner screaming about him not being back.

She noticed her old boss was very calm and confident; she had expected a nervous Eager who was in for a tough time.

The news from the US was that Preston would recover; however, he was out of the presidential race for the time being. It would be delayed. An Indian serial killer was being hunted for the murder and two attempted murders at the ranch. He was suspected of being in an area the Comanches used to live and hide in. The articles had not been released yet. So the bomb was about to go off any day. Eager knew he needed to act first.

A good night's sleep, shower and clean clothes, and he was ready to meet the day. Logan said he had nothing better to do, so he would tag along.

"Excuse me." Eager stopped the man on a bicycle just down the street from number ten.

"Mr McClements, right?"

"Who are you?" McClements was wary of strangers accosting him, being the Prime Minister's communications guru.

"Detective Chief Inspector Eager, sir."

"You! You should be in prison the trouble you have caused."

"Mmm, perverting the course of justice, I'd say you will get twelve years with people who are better than you. They do not help paedophiles and perverts — they beat them up. I'd say you are going to have a rough time of it."

"Are you threatening me? I will call the police."

"I am the police."

The Bulldog looked around nervously and put on some bravado.

"Well, not for long," he said with menace and delight in his voice.

Eager didn't take the bait.

"I've actually come here to help you and the PM." He looked at his watch. This troubled McClements that he was so calm and cool.

"You see, about this time tomorrow a lot of shit is going to hit the fan and it is headed your way. Elephant shit the size of footballs. There were extra dupes of the tapes and the great British public is going to be wondering why this government covered the originals up and let these perverts get away with abuse of little children. Including Lords, major party contributors and even a Minister. He is back in the cabinet, I hear."

McClements tried to look calm, but you could see him swallowing a lot and sweating at his brow.

"So why tell me? Are you going to gloat?"

"There is a way out of this mess; and by the way, I have held tape number seven, and do you know who that is?"

He was quiet and Eager went through his demands.

The next stop was at the Met HQ. When he walked in the building the jungle drums started like a tsunami wave going up and through the building and encompassing all the offices. When he called by his old team's offices there was a big cheer and clapping, a standing ovation. DCS Sutherland came rushing out of his office. He saw Eager saying hello to the team.

"DCI Eager, I need to see you right now in my office, if you please!"

"Sorry, I am off to see the commissioner."

"I will add insubordination to your charges."

"Do what you want." He walked away to go to the fifth floor.

"Sir, it's do what you want, sir!"

"Whatever," Eager shouted back. Denise and the team were laughing until Sutherland turned around on them. "Get back to work."

His toupee has moved, she was sure.

Eager walked past the commissioner's assistant and went straight into his office. He heard, "You can't go in there…"

The commissioner looked up. "What the… Eager, how dare you! You've decided to come back and join the unemployment queue, have you?"

He was dressed in full uniform and was again on the way to the palace.

"We will be there together then, or I will visit you in prison," Eager replied.

"What are you talking about? Have you been drinking?"

"I've come to help you and the force."

"Okay, you've got my attention and I am listening, before I get you thrown out of here."

"I wouldn't do that, sir, as I will just go to my friends in the fourth estate and hold an impromptu press conference. This is the deal."

The commissioner was turning red in the face.

Eager told him about the video dupes and the wave of terrible press that was about to hit the Met and the government. Put him in charge of the investigation reporting directly to himself. Send DCS Sutherland back to wherever he came from and Charlie's old team to report to him. He would take the press conferences and say that he had been working on these cases and they would soon be charging individuals. The commissioner was very quiet; the worst could happen before his retirement at the end of the year and his Lordship disappearing. God, he had earned that reward for all those years of hard work and great service.

"This is tantamount to blackmail."

"If you say so, sir. Better than allowing a paedophile ring to operate and all those kids get no justice, and how many more of them have been abused since? No, call it what you will, I want to get justice and stop this abuse."

Sir Michael looked him directly in the eyes. He was searching to see how confident he was. This was not the Eager he had known. In fact, he was impressed: he was senior officer material now for sure.

"I will have to see the PM."

"I think you will find her amenable."

"How can you be so sure? The unions can't bully her — she won't let you."

"I have tape number seven and you know who that is."

He gulped. "You will bring down Royalty?"

"No, I won't; she will if she doesn't play ball."

"I suppose you want a promotion as well." The commissioner was being sarcastic.

"No, just the opportunity to clean all this up. Plus get Charlie's killer. Then I want to retire and get out."

"I will see what I can do. In the meantime, wait on my call."

"Oh, by the way, I met McClements and the deal is no one gets punished, so your Lordship is safe."

All's well that ends well.

Chapter 65
Epilogue

Eager was right. The wave of negative press hit the UK day after day. They held back names and fed the news media piecemeal one pervert at a time to wring the most out of the deal with Liberty. The Preston video was held back awaiting his recovery. Timing was going to be vital for maximum impact.

John Eager himself was a new man, reinvigorated by his boldness, leading a team that was very loyal and determined. They would get results and then he would retire, maybe write the book on all the goings on and he even considered joining Logan in the countryside. He held no hope that Liberty would come back to the UK and accepted that their unusual friendship was a thing of the past.

Sir Richard Carlton, the Chairman of the *Daily Crier* tabloid, was the man who had allowed the government and his board of directors to hide the facts on Minister Stephens' paedophilia in exchange for government and party advertising that hardly happened. The retraction he had printed front page allowed McClements to brand Liberty Bell a fantasist and then had her work visa revoked without a fight from the paper. The public distrust in the *Daily Crier* then impacted Gavin Hastings, the then editor: he was sacked due to falling readership and revenues.

Sir Richard now turned on them. '*DAILY CRIER* VINDICATED! GOVERNMENT FAILURE TO HOLD PAEDOPHILES ACCOUNTABLE!' The article focussed on the Minister Stephens video and had video picture off-takes over six pages. He also named McClements as the man who branded top investigative reporter Liberty Bell as a fantasist and drove her out of the country. The article simply stated that McClements needed to be investigated and sacked. Sir Richard had bought the stories at great cost in his gamble to get the newspaper back in the people's hands as having reliable reporting. He wished he had Gavin and Liberty back.

Minister Stephens resigned and left for an undisclosed overseas location. The long arm of the law would catch up to him, as Eager was determined that the abused children would get justice.

Eager was true to his word, handling the press conference like a top public relations expert. The original videos had been returned and he immediately had his team working out a strategy to start bringing these people to justice. There were more, and they had to research how, where and who else was involved. The commissioner supported him as requested and a team of lawyers from the prosecuting authority were added to his team. This was total focus and the drug lords could keep. They would find that these culprits were the tip of the 'iceberg' as the paedophile ring circled the earth.

The commissioner got his lordship and was set to retire at the end of the year.

Logan McAllistar went back to Aunt Bessie's farm, which he had inherited. It had not been worked for years as she was too old and her husband deceased. He decided to start to revitalise it and live a quiet and comfortable life. Denise Williams and he started an on-off relationship. She spent as much time on weekends out of London in Derbyshire with him. Both were unsure where it would lead. McAllistar, though, still had revenge on Tazewell Javelin in his mind. If the drug turf war did not kill him, he would consider it.

Liberty and Gavin worked away in the Arizona desert on two books. She also gave interviews for TV at secret venues. She had again become a sought-after reporter and her career was well and truly back on track, and set to rocket when the Preston video was released, as well as the books. There was even talk of a film.

She was too busy to think about Eager day to day, but had her moments in the evenings when she thought about her promises to him. Would she be able to keep them and would he want her to?

Gavin awaited his time to get back to the UK and hopefully a major editor's position and be also back in the limelight. Like Eager promised, he had several new options available to him, including TV work, and Sir Richard was keen to talk to him.

Tazewell Javelin continued to work with the Yardies, expanding their territory. He continued to scheme on new ways to develop his empire once the Harkers were out of the way. He even got back in contact with the Russian mafia, encouraging them to get their drug money from the Harkers that he had stolen and revenge for their people that had been killed in the process. One more way of exacting big pressure.

The FBI concluded that the Indian serial killer had orchestrated the events at Palo Blanco 3, as the case was known. Wyatt was dead and Amanda had been induced into a coma. They were afraid of serious brain damage. She would not tell the true story when and if she recovered. She would, though, if capable, seek revenge for sure. The Indians who had travelled with Diablo that day were all interviewed and sketches of Diablo made. It was confusing, as they concluded some were helping him and deliberately getting the artist to draw wrong features so none of them matched. They therefore zeroed in on the young brave and Chimalis, the bluebird, who had spent more time with him and had pointed out the cut fence so onside with the investigation. The young brave's sketch was close to how Diablo looked, but Chimalis's one varied quite a bit. They released both to the baying media.

Diablo had not been found. Did he come in the blue helicopter and run away into the Comancheria? They found his old golf bag up a tree, soaking wet. He had lost the dogs, the trackers and the Texas Rangers, who all gave up ten miles into the bush. Diablo kept moving and using his living-off-the-land skills. He did, though, have to consider what he did next. His identity would be known, so there was no way back to the reservation unless he wanted to give up. He needed a new plan.

The Apache reservations were swamped with FBI and State trooper raids, but they only found one Mangas, who was ninety years old.

When LAPD Detective Brody read the newspapers and the wanted pictures sent to all police on a national alert, he recognised one of the artist's impressions. Reading the articles of the Indian statements that the serial killer had travelled with, they said he carried a golf bag. That definitely rang a bell, following his earlier thoughts that Diablo fitted the FBI profile. He called Special Agent Steve Stanley with his theory. Interested, he said, "I'll check it out. Thanks." Steve laughed as he knew this would be a major embarrassment for the serial killer task force. Still, his friend there needed to know and he would keep it quiet maybe, or until Steve writes his memoirs, he guessed. They had been searching for Chief Longbow and there he was all the time under their noses and on their payroll. Steve couldn't help seeing the irony in it all.

His friend, though, when he got his call, didn't; he went deathly silent and he could hear his brain ticking over and Steve thought he could even hear his heart thumping, thinking of the damage this would do to his career. He had to catch him now, but did he really want to, as it would all come out.

Brody's application to join the FBI had been rejected and no reason given.

Steve's unofficial role of helping was never common knowledge and he remained in the LA office. He kept Gavin's oversized cowboy hat with the intention of returning it one day when he accepted Eager's offer to have a vacation in the UK. It seemed only fair, as Eager had given him a bobby's tit helmet.

Sonia was transferred back to FBI HQ and a desk job. No action had so far been taken against her, although she was watched and not trusted. Blobby never got into action; just a regular supply of doughnuts for his help. De Silva remained the chief in LA with a strained relationship with his boss. Still, he knew all things must pass; it was just a matter of time to bridge to better days.

The drug lords of London were still at war and gradually ruining both businesses for each other. One would win eventually and one would lose. It would be up to DCI Eager and DI Williams to put them both out of business for good, a major task on top of the ever-expanding international paedophile ring.

Nick Harker's attempted murder case was coming up soon and vital evidence had been stolen from the police, as planned. They were sure a mis-trial would be called, thanks to their now enemy Tazewell Javelin's idea. Nick was recovering fast and anxious to get out and help his brother Jimmy fight for their businesses and territory. He also had to even things up with Eager and McAllistar when the opportunity arose.

Jordy disappeared and his body was never found. He had been nailed as the inside informer. Special Branch's 'Bill and Ben' knew the truth of the matter — he was collateral damage and their inside man remained in place.

Preston was recovering slowly. The election had been delayed to early the next year. He, though, thought he still had a chance, not knowing fully what was going to hit him in the next few weeks. The general had to come through for him or he was done and dusted.

The hit man had called in for help, his last resort to escape. His toe and fingers had fallen off and he was in serious need of medical assistance. He had murdered his landlady. Unfortunately for him, his employer's people decided to meet and terminate him, body dumped in the ocean. The Met police are still looking for him.

General Gerald Broad still had some cleaning up to do to ensure the trail never came back to him. They could nail Preston, if worse came to worst, but not him. Covering up and surviving was now his main priority.

The PM had to introduce the situation with the subject of video number seven to the Crown legal team. No action had been taken, only a quiet chat with one of the senior aides, so with arrogance the subject is still free to continue his activities with his rich friends overseas. No one was game to show this video to HRH.

Harry the Hedgefrog gave up on his dream of being a country and western singer and returned to the UK and got a job as a helicopter pilot instructor in Edinburgh. He wrote to Logan saying he was taking up the bagpipes and traditional Scottish music.

Eager and Liberty are destined to meet again in the future.